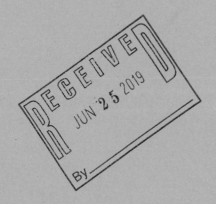

Rouge

Rouge

RICHARD KIRSHENBAUM

St. Martin's Press 🜺 New York

ROUGE. Copyright © 2019 by Richard Kirshenbaum. All rights reserved. Printed in the United States of America. For information, address St. Martin's Press, 175 Fifth Avenue, New York, N.Y. 10010.

www.stmartins.com

Library of Congress Cataloging-in-Publication Data

Names: Kirshenbaum, Richard, 1961- author.
Title: Rouge : a novel of beauty and rivalry / Richard Kirshenbaum.
Description: First edition. | New York : St. Martin's Press, 2019.
Identifiers: LCCN 2018057651 | ISBN 9781250150950 (hardcover) |
    ISBN 9781250150967 (ebook)
Subjects: LCSH: Cosmetics industry—Fiction. | Beauty, Personal—Fiction. |
    GSAFD: Suspense fiction
Classification: LCC PS3611.I775 R68 2019 | DDC 813/.6—dc23
LC record available at https://lccn.loc.gov/2018057651

Our books may be purchased in bulk for promotional, educational, or business use. Please contact your local bookseller or the Macmillan Corporate and Premium Sales Department at 1-800-221-7945, extension 5442, or by email at MacmillanSpecialMarkets@macmillan.com.

First Edition: June 2019

10 9 8 7 6 5 4 3 2 1

For Dana, my Zelda

Rouge was different, an entity unto itself. A substance far more fraught than the pastes and powders and creams of the time. Rouge was imbued with a deeper meaning, a natural state of a woman inviting approach. Rouge was the color of invitation, arousal just before, during, and after sex. And for this reason, the amplification of rouge — the high-flushed, pink, or even red sheen of a woman's cheeks — was considered, at first, the realm of a disreputable woman.

Rouge

PROLOGUE

New York City, 1983

The morning was overcast, a dead shade of grey. And this was horribly fitting. It was as though god knew that the bright spot of my world was gone and, without her critical eye, the sky could let its guard down and bore us with its dullest shade.

Madame always detested the color grey; as she often said, "It's neither here nor there and I cannot abide indecision." She would utter the word "indecision" with her usual verve and a raised penciled eyebrow. She most definitely would not have approved. I assumed the weather would comport itself in time for the burial.

I decided to take a Xanax with my mimosa before the funeral, not because of an outpouring of grief, but rather due to the sheer fact that Madame had actually died. It was inconceivable that the life force had left her or, as she would exclaim, "Kaput!" when she read the obituary of a friend or an acquaintance in the newspaper, the sound of her large cabochon emerald slamming into her marble-topped gueridon.

From the moment I met her, a mere lad of twenty-seven, she was invincible to me. Indestructible, immortal, and outsize. She appeared as a giant in my eyes, even though she stood only five feet tall, her tight black chignon setting off stormy eyes and a strong, aquiline nose.

Her beauty was striking even when she was in her eighties. Strangely, I always see her in profile, dramatic even in silhouette. I could not picture life without her—the rants, the demands, the to-do lists, the details large and small, and, occasionally, the endearing gifts that she dispensed just when I thought I couldn't *bear her another second*. Her caresses were almost always gruff, yet her endearments, when offered, were surprisingly generous. They were often embarrassing—from lavish David Webb animal-print enameled cuff links to Calvin Klein briefs when she knew a new man was on the horizon.

"*Babisiu,*" she would say in her native Polish. "Baby, bring me a cup of tea, *The Times,* and the magazines." When she was melancholy, she would stroke my face. "You remind me of my first husband," she would say, "may he roast in hell." And she would read the papers to see if she had been profiled in the party pictures and to cluck at her own glossy advertisements.

My name is Bobby De Vries. It wasn't always. I was born Joe Bob Devereaux. I'm a southern boy, backwater trash from Louisiana. However, thanks to my abundant charm, boyish good looks, hidden assets, and a few, shall we say, "favors" along the way, I was propelled from the bayou to New York, where I answered an ad for a domestic service agency and was dispensed to Josephine's *maison*. I was told she hired only "good-looking young people who had no family and no life." I certainly fit the bill.

Once ensconced in *chez Josephine,* I had the great fortune to attend the University of Madame Josephine Herz. It was a master's degree in business and in life, and she prepared me for all of the tasks at hand. She was, at once, a tough general and rancorous professor, and she tore me up and made me over a million times. One night, when I was collecting her legendary Van Cleef "zipper necklace" and depositing it in the wall safe, she lay on the bed on her aqua satin pillows in her

Mainbocher, her dark eyes pitched skyward, and she rechristened me Bobby De Vries.

"Tell them you're from the Charleston De Vrieses," she said. "You'll get more respect."

"Who are the Charleston De Vrieses?" I asked.

"How the hell should I know," she quipped.

She loved saying my new name, the "De" being the punctuation point. "Bobby De Vries, get me a glass of tea—with a sugar cube," or, "Bobby De Vries, my *babisiu,* get me my jewel box. I want the emeralds." I was totally entranced from the moment I started as her junior butler and finally, after many years, once I had proven my unflagging loyalty, as her personal assistant.

The day before, I had provided the funeral home with her black Chanel bouclé suit and her favorite diamond star pin. I sat with the family in the drawing room. Jonny Blake-Herz, her grandson, always seemed to detest me, but his newest wife, Charlene, was smart enough to know I held many of Josephine's deepest secrets, the most valuable possessions in the vault. Charlene made sure I had proper seating in the limousines and a front-row seat at Temple Emanu-El. There was the will to consider, of course, and my twenty years of servitude had accrued to my being named as a trustee. Many of Madame's orders and wishes were already known to me, and I had made these my own. As Madame used to say somewhat sardonically, "Where there's a will, there is a relative!"

The long black limousine pulled up to the temple's imposing carved limestone façade, revealing a ring of omnipresent photographers, all there to record the comings and goings of the rich and famous. After all, Madame Josephine Herz, née Josiah Herzenstein, and much later Princess Orlove (when she remarried in her forties), had cut a wide swath through international society. At eighty-three, she was more powerful than ever. Her death sent shock waves through the business and social press. THE DEATH OF BEAUTY, they wrote. AN ICON JOINS

THE FIRMAMENT. Josephine was credited with inventing the beauty business and, in turn, becoming the wealthiest self-made woman in the known world. This, Josephine would not hesitate to remind me, was back when "Vomen could not get a loan!" When she was animated or angry, her true accent emerged and the *w*'s always became *v*'s. She would, of course, bang the table with her emerald cabochon or Burmese ruby when retelling this story.

Chanel sunglasses and flowers were in abundance in the soaring synagogue—as were furs of every species—chinchilla, mink, sable. A throng gathered for the first wave of important guests: Barbara, Frank, Lauren, and Pamela. These people needed no introduction to the press or to one another. The vast ceiling height was perhaps the one thing that could overpower all of these egos. The rest of the synagogue was filled with what I call the "professional mourners," the climbers who wanted to be seen at *her* funeral. It was arguably the most important event on the New York social calendar for the season and, of course, a once-in-a-lifetime opportunity for networking.

"There's nothing like a good funeral," the great comedian Alice Stark had often said. She often relayed to her good friend Josephine the business connections she had made when someone famous passed away. Today would be no different. They would all come. Friends, colleagues, relatives distant and near, and, of course, rivals and enemies. Many of these people had had a front-row seat to Madame's century. Madame's close-knit group approached me personally to offer condolences. Many overlooked the family, who by all accounts had always been a bit distant. The privilege of the offspring and the grandchildren was on grand display. These children, now grown, rich, confident, well educated, and diffident, were the end result of great wealth. This subtle and lingering arrogance as potent as one of her signature fragrances. I made a few introductions to Charlene, who, as third wife and social climber, wanted to *know* Nan or Pat, the only other social doyennes who mattered. And then, concluding this catalog of impressive guests, this growing armada of naval jewels, the other cosmetic pioneers arrived to pay their respects: Mickey Heron from Heron Cosmetics and his long-rumored mistress, CeeCee Lopez, the founder of Queen CeeCee's Hair Relaxer, who was, in addition to being Mickey's girl, the world's richest African American entrepreneur.

The funeral had all the bearings of a state funeral. After all, Madame had gone over all the details with me for years. Her favorite, Senator Lautenberg, delivering the eulogy: the sheer drama of her incredible life and her unassailable will to succeed. The daughter of Jewish Polish apothecaries who had braved new continents and built the largest beauty company in the world. Six thousand global employees, billions in revenue, homes and art and foundations. Buying and selling and buying it back for pennies on the dollar during wars and depressions. Her story read like a novel or a fable. Her son, Miles, now in his fifties, dabbed his eyes for effect as he recalled how his mother had braved the Nazis and English and French society. Only Picasso had not succumbed to her charms, deigning only to draw her and not paint her, the only artist of the twentieth century who had held out against her dollars and her will. And then there was her beautiful grandniece Jennifer, who pulled the iconic pink-and-green Lashmatic mascara out of the bottom of her bag and said to laughter that if her grandmother had invented the contact lens, it would not have had the same impact on women's eyes—and lives.

Finally, at the tail end of the service, after remarks by the three rabbis, a visiting archbishop, and the wife of the vice president of the United States, all of whom had their own rhapsodic eulogies, there was an audible gasp.

She had arrived.

As we all knew she would. Swathed in sable and diamonds. Looking resplendent and confident and haughty. Acting the part of the victor, her icy blond hauteur more at home in Locust Valley than this citadel of Jewish prayer.

She took a discreet yet visible spot, exactly the row Josephine said she would, which sent audible shock waves rippling through the crowd. Constance Gardiner was in attendance and enjoying her triumph over Josephine's demise, if nothing else. Constance, the society matron, the horsewoman, the belle of New York society. The *other* beauty industry pioneer. Their rivalry had been legendary and even scandalous. Constance had outlived Josephine! And in this way, Constance . . . had won; even their longevity, competitive.

I personally had always found Constance a bit masculine for my taste and also a bit *scary*. I knew she was going to approach me and deliver her final chess move. The Xanax had not dulled the anxiety and anticipation of that moment entirely. I tapped my English brogues and looked at my rose-gold Patek, which Madame had given me for my fortieth birthday, knowing that for a man like me, age was not something cosmetics could solve.

The rabbi intoned the prayers and let the crowd know that the family was receiving, after the cemetery, at Josephine's grand and fabled Fifth Avenue duplex. People always gaped at the gargantuan rooms, ceiling heights, and Dubuffet murals. They also repeated the story that after being turned down by the building's white-shoe board in the 1930s, Josephine had simply bought the building lock, stock, and barrel under a corporate name. After divorcing her first husband, she lived with her younger Russian prince, taking New York society by storm. Some said it was a marketing ploy when she married him and launched her Princess Orlove line of lipsticks, rouge, and perfume, but she outlived him, too! The funeral was perhaps the one time Constance would ever even think of being in the same room as Josephine, and she appeared to relish the chance to inventory the riches of Josephine's life and, more important, the ruins.

After the service, I stood, pulling on my navy cashmere overcoat, comforted by the buttery feeling of the material, and saw her making her way through the crowd. Constance was always so very sure of herself. Suddenly she was before me, her South Sea pearls worn in defiance, each one the size of a large marble. Her face was still beautiful, pulled yet handsome. And she still had that Kate Hepburn style, wearing defiance as casually as her slacks. It was as though Constance had chosen to maintain 1930s-film style forever.

She took a moment to nod to the notables and to greet those people offering her condolences, as if the two beauty industry pioneers had been comrades-in-arms, despite their half-century-long battle. Finally, she spoke stridently.

"I'm so very sorry, Robert," she said, using my formal name, "I know how dedicated you were to her. It must be very hard to know she is gone." She paused. "And isn't coming back." She spoke in a clipped mid-Atlantic accent.

"Yes, we all admired her so," I said. "The woman who invented the beauty business." I had rehearsed the line over and over with Madame. I promised her I would say it as a parting gift, and I had delivered on my promise.

"That is debatable, depending on who you talk to and who signs your paycheck," she said. "So, are you going to come work for me now? I will double your salary, of course."

"Madame made me independently wealthy," I said, "and I would only work for a prestige house." I said this somewhat more meekly than intended.

"My, my . . ." She laughed. "You really learned from the old goat."

"Come now, Constance. This is, after all, her funeral." I had regained my confidence.

"Fine." She dug into her black crocodile Hermès purse. "Let's not make this any more uncomfortable than it has to be. I thought you should see this. Now that the old dragon has gone to her reward, I am suing for patent infringement." She shoved papers into my hand. The old case. Perhaps the most acrimonious battle that had raged between the two women.

"There is no way you can overturn the patent," I said.

"She stole Lashmatic from me all those years ago and I'm prepared to fight again," she said.

Miles, incensed at her mere presence, strode over with Jonny and joined the conversation. Soon, Charlene joined the ever-growing crowd. "Constance," said Miles, "don't you think you could have waited till the body was cold before you started hovering like a vulture?"

"I thought, perhaps, the private schools and family privilege would have given you a bit of polish, but you're as direct and blunt as your mother, may she rest in peace. I'm just here to claim what is rightfully mine."

"I think it's time you left," Charlene said, drawing herself into a regal posture.

"I just needed the opportunity to serve you the papers, given you people have *layers of protection*. I would have preferred not to have done it at a funeral, but . . . I had no choice." She looked at me as if that were apology enough.

"Constance, don't you think that Josephine anticipated you would come?" I said, withdrawing another crisp envelope from my pocket. "We are countersuing you, your company and also personally. You do know now if we win, you have to also pay all our legal fees."

"Well, we shall see who pays whom." She was caught off guard by the counterattack, so well planned and perfectly executed.

"Constance, if you pursue this action, we will have to call CeeCee to the stand," I said, delivering my final chess move. Checkmate.

She reddened. "What do you know about CeeCee?"

"Everything," I said. This was the final hand that Josephine had dealt for me. The rip cord, if you will. I had pulled it.

"Leave it to Josephine to play dirty, even in *death*."

"You're wrong. Her business is very much clean and her family is very much alive."

"Miles." Constance eyed Josephine's son and her handsome grand-son, Jonny.

"Yes," Miles said.

"I may have hated your mother, but she was indeed a worthy op-ponent." Her voice cracked before she turned on her Chanel sling-backs and disappeared into the throng of mourners and hangers-on.

"Bobby, you did very well." Miles patted me on my back. Even Jonny smiled at the exchange. We glanced at one another, our strange little tribe, and turned to attend to the long line of friends and business associates waiting to be received.

Later, as I walked outside past the flashbulbs toward the waiting cars, I looked up to a parting sky. The sun had broken through the film of grey clouds, casting a lovely and unique pink glow. Pink, of course! The exact hue of the Lashmatic package. I smiled, knowing that Madame had found a way, as she always did, to break through.

And, better yet, to get her way.

1

HOLLYWOOD DREAMS

New York City, 1933

A Technicolor sky hung over the city even though it was only early May. At times, even New York City seemed to have caught the bug. The pear trees that bloomed like white fireworks every April may as well have sprouted palm trees. Everyone, it seemed, had just stepped out of a Garbo movie, and Josephine Herz (née Josiah Herzenstein) would be damned if she would not capitalize on this craze.

A young, well-kept woman was the first to grace her newly opened, eponymous salon on Fifth Avenue. With bleached-blond "marcelled" hair, a substantial bust, and a mouth that looked as though it had been carved from a pound of chopped meat, her new client had all the ammunition to entrap any man in the city, to keep him on the dole, and her cosmetic hygienist, in this case Herz Beauty, on the payroll. She lowered herself onto the padded leather salon chair like a descending butterfly and batted her eyes as though they too might flutter from her face.

"I want *thickah,*" she whined. She said this in a Brooklyn accent that would have killed her chances had she been an actress transitioning from silent to talkies.

Josephine nodded and reached into her arsenal, procuring the favored Herz moisturizer for a dewy complexion. She removed and unscrewed the glass jar, leaned over her client, and began to apply it to her cheekbones in soft, round swirls.

"No!" The client swatted her hand away as though to scold and dispose of a landed bug. "Not my skin," she said. "My lashes."

"Oh." Josephine withdrew her hand and held it, poised high above her client's face, as though hovering a spoon over a boiling pot.

"I want thicker lashes," said the blonde. "Like Gloria."

"Gloria?" Josephine was perplexed.

"Swanson!" the client said, shaking her head, miffed that she was not understood.

"I see." Josephine replaced the glass jar in her holster bag and procured a separate, zippered case. "For the thick-eyelash look, you have two options: tinting or application." She removed both a small black cake and a moistened brush to apply the pigment and a plastic box of spidery lashes and displayed them as though they were a cache of jewels. The tube of adhesive gum came next.

The blonde's eyes widened. She shook her head and sat bolt upright on her chair. A convalescent, revived from the dead. "Ya don't mean you want to glue them on?"

Josephine took a long, deep breath. "How else do you think women get them?" she said. "If there were a drink ve could drink to grow them, I assure you I'd let you know," she said in her Polish-tinged English.

"I just assumed . . . ," said the blonde. Miffed, she reached into her pocketbook and produced a magazine clipping from a crumpled stash. She unfurled a luminous, if wrinkled, image of Gloria Swanson, the Hollywood glamour girl, from the latest issue of *Motion Picture*. All lips, pouting like a put-out princess. She had the brow of an Egyptian goddess, the same distinctive beauty mark, and the eyelashes of a jungle cat. "Like that," she said, pointing at her eyes. "I want to look like that for a party tonight."

Josephine's perfectly lacquered blood-red nails grazed the wrinkled page. She studied Gloria's fabulous face, the brow, the lash, the pout.

"Application," Josephine said, returning the image.

"Geez," said the client. "You'd think by now you people would come up with something better than that."

It was her duty, Josephine had come to feel, to tolerate stings and slights like this. But a new thought occurred to her as she prepped the lashes for application, as she meticulously heated and applied the adhesive gum. Her client was right. She often worked the floor to do just that: to listen to her patrons, her clients. And now that she was in New York, she knew enough never to be too far away from what real American women wanted. And so she took in the woman's request with deep reverence, as she knew nothing was more important to her future sales than her clients' needs. Blanche or Betty—or whatever the tacky blonde's name was—was right. It was high time someone came up with something better. Josephine was certainly up to this task. The only problem was that across town, a woman named Constance Gardiner was doing the very same thing.

Josephine Herz was not, of course, the first to invent mascara. But she would be the first to invent one devoid of mess and fuss and to make it available to the masses. As early as ancient Egypt, women found their facial fix. Considered to be a necessary accoutrement in every woman's and man's daily regime, kohl, a combination of galena, lead sulfide, or copper and wax, was applied to the eyes, the eyebrows and lashes, to ward off evil spirits and to protect from sun damage. Most any image of Egyptian gods or goddesses will reveal hieroglyphs, not only on pyramid walls but on the Egyptians' faces. The bold, black lines on the female face lost fashion over the centuries, especially in more recent times when Victorian ladies eschewed color of all kind on the face. But it was not long before women craved—and chemists created—a new brand of adornment for the eye. Coal, honey, beeswax—all the traditional ingredients had to be tested and tried. Josephine could smell a market maker from a mile away, and in this, she sensed a new moment for the eye. From Los Angeles to Larchmont, women were craving new ways to look like the stars of the silver screen, new ways to dress, look, and behave in a modern woman's ever-changing role. These women needed a product that would make them look and feel like Garbo or Swanson, something simpler, cleaner, and quicker than the application of false eyelashes every six to eight weeks. These women needed a product that was cheap, fuss-free, and less mess than the old option made from charcoal, which, in the very worst cases, caused blindness.

2

A NEW FRONTIER

Sydney, Australia, 1922

The heat was unbearable, constant, itchy, and apparently determined to do battle with her skin. It was ironic how brutal the journey had been given that the point of it was to flee a brutal adversary at home. Her mother's favorite phrase came to mind as she grasped the railing of the ship: "Wherever you go, there you are." Were her dear mother here right now, she would also be telling Josiah to protect her skin by putting on her hat. Instead, in a flash of rebellion, she stared head-on into the sun as though the sun itself were her enemy and she would win the face-off so long as she did not betray fear.

Oy vey ist mir. She could not keep this lament far from her mind as she thought of the distance between her loving mother and herself. The distance increased with every second, along with the ache in her heart. She could practically smell her mother's distinct scent: sweet, earthy, like the kasha and sweet white onions simmering on the stove. The warm, instant relief of being in her soft arms and her lilting voice. She did not need to close her eyes to see the outlines of her home: a medieval town surrounded by water on all but one side, stacked with red brick that fortified it from intervention and escape. Josiah had been held here during her childhood, safe, if confined. Home was not perfect by any means, but the comfort of the familiar is a strong incentive for any incumbent, and she struggled to remember why she had left in the first place.

Of course, she knew why.

They had heard the terrifying stories, and her mother and father were not willing to live with this risk. Tales of the pogroms, of drunken soldiers arriving at night, soldiers looting homes, tearing through hidden drawers; watches and jewels, belongings and books. Soldiers terrorizing fathers and sons, beating them, and, in the worst accounts, locking their daughters into the bedrooms and forcing them to do unspeakable things, the soldiers' laughter and moaning audible through the door—and the daughters' screams. Her mother and father had heard these accounts from reliable sources, first from women gossiping at the market, a crowd gathered by the butcher, obstructing the line for milk. And then from their beloved rabbi, who had heard it from the men themselves.

And while these atrocities had taken place in Lwów, not too near, not too far, from home, the threat was too much to bear. It began to pervade daily life. A sense of palpable anxiety as the drunken Polish peasants leered and the sense of unease grew like a boiling pot until it accompanied her at all times—while she was walking into town, writing a letter to her aunt, even bathing at night. There was always an invisible guest trailing noiselessly behind. So it was decided, after many family meals and meetings, that she and those sisters old enough to relocate would move to a place free of threat. Australia, a distant continent, seemed as good a choice as any. It may as well have been a disparate planet, so intrinsically different was it to everything she knew from her native Poland.

Others had left before her, of course, and her uncle Solomon and aunt Masha had written back with good news about the pioneer life. Still, it was hard to imagine Australia as the next obvious stop. This enormous, distant island, covered with hills and grass and sheep. And the vast, unfathomable ocean, an incomprehensible force, a planet unto itself. Josiah had been swimming only a handful of times in her life—

in a country lake near her home. Nonetheless, the plan was made: her uncle and aunt would house and employ her. She would work at the counter of her uncle and aunt's five-and-ten-cent store, live in their home, and help out with the brood of nieces and nephews in the evenings until she could afford a place of her own. She would learn the English she had dreamed of studying one day, starting with the handful of words she had read in the papers stacked in her father's office. A new life awaited on this bright, hot planet, a better life to be made and found. She believed her mother. She wanted this life. But at the moment, she could not see this bright future because the sunlight was making her blind.

An unusual beauty, petite but imposing, Josiah had a powerful presence. Pale skin and black hair, large oval onyx eyes, and a strong, elegant, and beak-like nose gave her a regal, if withering, look. Her eyes were her greatest weapon, perceiving others' motives even while obscuring the impression she made. This appearance had proven both an asset and a weakness, inviting sisters and friends to confide in her while putting off boys her age, who were somehow convinced of her critique. But intuition and intelligence prevailed, earning her the adoration of sisters, friends, and, in recent years, a handful of older boys. Unfortunately, at the moment her intuition was telling her one thing: Go back.

But it was too late for this. She had been brought here on a wave, the first wave of Polish immigrants, the first of what would soon be a tidal force. A wave of women seeking safety, families seeking freedom to express their beliefs, people seeking resources, a new life, people fleeing a profound and terrifying threat. The rewards were enticing enough to intrigue. But the threat made this urgent. The threat was what pushed people out of their homes, made the rewards even worth considering. The threat was what compelled a twenty-two-year-old girl to leave behind all she knew and loved to venture into the unknown alone on this strange massive and rusted ship. This threat was what brought her to this foreign place, two oceans and three continents away from home, in cramped bunks shared with two other girls, the salt air barely masking the scent of so much proximate sweat.

Daunted, Josiah glanced across the deck at a large cloudy hill. The hill was lush and white. And then it was green, peppered with white dots. Why the sudden transformation? Soon enough, she understood: the dots were not clouds, but sheep.

"What have I done?" she muttered.

Another passenger answered, a girl her age, Sonjya, whom she had taken meals with during the trip. "If all else fails, we can knit," she said.

Josiah smiled, comforted by the camaraderie. But just as quickly, a swell of yelling and footsteps rolled toward her, and she felt herself being pushed to the front of the ship. She gripped her meager case and the cream straw hat with the blue-and-white ribbon—it seemed so cosmopolitan at the time—and, squinting into the sun, allowed the swell to push her forward toward the dock.

3

A NEW WORLD

Greenwich Village, 1922

Constance Gardner trudged up the stairs of a dusty hallway. Peeling brown paint lent it a certain charm, like an arm with a bad sunburn. But she didn't mind. It looked exactly as she had hoped. Far from the gilded prison of the Martha Washington Hotel and other appropriate ladies' residences, this was the true New York. So what if she would now *reside* on the sofa of her brother's alcove studio? Actually, Jimmy was technically her stepbrother, her mother marrying James's father, McCalister, once her own had run off with a rich, older widow, leaving her and her mother to fend for themselves. While James and she grew up with different last names, they grew up under the same roof and never noticed the difference. James, the sensitive one, always looked after his younger, bolder sister and, despite the age difference, vice versa.

His secondhand couch was also brown—nubby and itchy mohair that had receded in spots. Yet, she could fall asleep to the sounds of Washington Square Park, the music of Greenwich Village on a Friday night—shouts, laughter, a saxophone, where crickets had been the night before. The harmonious din of artists dreaming up their art. And she would wake up, a member of a new workforce, walk to work with men and women doing their part, their tight tailored suits and skirts flaring as they marched, an army of productivity. This was what she came for. The sound of New Yorkers living in New York. It was all music to her.

Within minutes, she had transformed the room. A woman can transform a room if need be with simple things: a silk scarf tacked to the wall as a tapestry, hers a classic Poiret floral tableau in a bouquet of lavender, baby blue; a pink vase of fresh flowers; and a pretty scent—a few sticks of incense or, in a pinch, a spray of her favorite Jean Patou perfume. In the same way, she would also transform her name with the addition of an *i*. Gardener with an *e*, she thought, sounded subservient, conjuring images of lawn care. Gardiner with an *i* depicted a gold-coast life of debutante balls and garden parties, an association with the regal gentry who controlled Gardiner's Island, of all things, which had been granted to the family in 1639 by royal patent. The Gardiner, not Gardener, life was what she aspired to. In this fashion, she transformed herself and the room. Even before her brother could heat the watery cabbage soup he had saved for her, she had turned a single man's alcove into a chic two-bedroom boudoir. She would spend the weekend settling in, wandering around her new neighborhood, picking up the "accoutrements" she would need to begin her life as a professional woman in New York.

Accoutrements! The word alone made her feel giddy.

An androgynous, statuesque beauty with strawberry-blond hair and a rebellious smirk, Constance was a chameleon. She was an English girl raised in Canada and, now, a Canadian in New York. A natural blonde (as a child, at least), she had grown into a handsome woman, attractive enough to land an appropriate Ivy League college man and forgo a life of work. But the lazy life held little appeal. She was a member of a growing group of young flappers who had attended college and, some by design, others by necessity, they were women who wanted more for themselves than nuptial bliss. She had applied and been hired for a respectable job in New York: as a secretary for a health and pharmaceutical company on lower Fifth Avenue, Dr. Osborne's

Health and Vitality, Inc. Its gleaming offices were as inviting as the company name.

Her new look was perfect for the new job: a coiffed flapper bob, freshly golden, in the style of Marilyn Miller, her favorite vaudeville star. Yes, it required a little extra time to heat and deploy the curling iron, to twist and set the waves, to place the pin just so to frame her heart-shaped face. But this was time well spent. Especially when paired with the new lip tint she had "borrowed" from her older friend Lisette and the dark, strong arc she had learned to draw above her eyes after hours studying Marilyn's brow in a pictorial from *Photoplay* magazine. So what if this cost her an hour of sleep. An hour of sleep paled in comparison with the rewards of a well-honed face. Luckily, her physique was genetic and healthy, even if perfecting her look took a little extra time.

She thought now of the stark contrast between her past and present life. Constance had left behind Canada, a country she loved, after spending her childhood running through lush fields under puffy skies. From there, she moved to the protected grassy knolls of a Seven Sisters campus. A lithe, athletic kid, a "tomboy," they called her, she had tumbled and sprinted through her formative years, happy as the clouds were white. But she left it behind without regret. Canada was merely a backwater camping ground for Constance's true quest and ambition. She had known, from as early as five or six, that she wanted an urban life, a momentous life. She wanted to be like the people she saw when her parents took her to Montreal, striding over the sidewalks like modern statuettes. She knew as soon as she saw them. She wanted that life. A childhood in the grass and sunshine was a perfect training ground, not only because it instilled an unflappable can-do grit, but because it formed the foundation of her comfort with nature, the study of which would consume her adult life.

Nursing school and a life of pearls and cashmere was not to be. But not for lack of interest. She had too much interest, in some ways, to be good at the job. She was determined to work with the blood and cadavers, as opposed to standing at a doctor's side with a ready tool and pleasant smile. A year spent working in an army hospital during the war had taught her all she needed to know. There were people who needed help, and she was equipped to give it. Of course, her parents wished for a more traditional vocation for their little girl, but Constance was equal parts stubborn and persuasive. Despite their wishes, she applied for the job and dropped out of nursing school the day she heard back. If she had to spend years training in a lab, she would rather end up a chemist than somebody's cook.

And so she happily indulged this interest in mixology in a much-needed drink. After gulping down the soup her brother had heated, she insisted they celebrate. She dragged him back down the peeling, rickety stairs to the speakeasy she had been told about just down the street.

"You're the perfect flapper," James praised and scolded her at the same time, observing her cranberry velvet cloche hat. "How did you find out about this place?"

"Just because there's Prohibition doesn't mean we can't have a drink. If you must know, I also like to dance and I happen to love jazz. Let's not get into what you like, brother dear," she teased him, but as soon as it came tumbling out of her tinted mouth, she saw the forlorn look on his face. She had gone too far, hinting at his proclivity to meeting older and sometimes younger men late in the evening hours. "No worries," she said, patting his hand, "we both like what we like." After that, they kept a tacit agreement to avoid discussion about serious personal topics. It was the Canadian way.

She glanced around the bar as her brother took the first sip of the illegal gin. Its sour smell, the afternoon light, the heated conversations in their midst. It was as though they had all inhaled the same intoxicating drug simply by walking in the door.

"Is it always this wonderful?" she whispered.

He looked around and shrugged.

She raised her glass and toasted her brother. "To life." She giggled. "My new life."

He smiled. Her excitement was contagious. And then, with a brotherly pat, he whispered, "You're going to need some new clothes."

"What?" she said.

"The professional girls dress up for work," he said.

She inhaled, looked down, appraising her long skirt, its belted waist, fitted bodice, and the buttons nearest her neck. It was appropriate but hardly daring. "Guess I'm going to have to go shopping."

"I'll help you," he said. "I heard there are some darling things at Lord and Taylor."

4

THE ART OF LISTENING

Melbourne, 1923

Being a counter girl was not the worst fate, given that it combined two of Josiah's favorite pastimes: watching people and talking to them. And best of all, listening. She could work on her English while distracting herself from the home in Poland she dearly missed. That it gave her a break from the back of the store where her cousins and uncle spent most of the day, stacking and stocking the overstuffed shelves, was also a perk. She could pass the hours advising customers on the thing they claimed to have come in for, while, in fact, talking to them about the thing they really wanted to talk about. *Themselves.* She made a game of it, predicting what was weighing on their minds while upholding a semblance of small talk. Intuition availed her with special insight into their worries and woes.

Josiah's uncle and aunt were no substitute for the warmth of her own family. Her uncle Solomon was stern and anxious, and his wife, Masha, was critical and small-minded. Somehow, in spite of her uncle's demeanor, the store was a cheerful place, two places really: in front, a de facto community center for Melbourne's hardworking men; in back, a stockroom for medicines and salves. Each had their own healing power. Talking was perhaps the best cure of all.

The Australian summers and winters were basically indistinguishable, and both required a certain set of provisions to deal with the harsh climate. This year, there were floods of biblical proportions and then, after the water receded, a sweltering and lengthy heat wave that put everyone on edge and gave women a bit more permission to wear less restrictive clothing and strip to their lace undergarments. Extreme conditions were the norm in Melbourne, and they created a cycle of their own.

A steady influx of foreigners and a thriving farming community made Melbourne a busy city, causing many of its residents to refer to it fondly as "the Paris of the Southeast." The store offered Josiah two disparate habitats: one, a busy workplace with a constant stream of tasks that needed her attention at all hours; and the other, at the counter, an endless stream of customers and their diversions. Other people's problems. Both were surprisingly intriguing, with the back room sating the curiosity of her probing mind and the counter offering a more mindless pastime. She learned the basics of retail in the back—stocking, pricing, ordering inventory—while honing and flexing her knack for soothing people's woes out front. It was here that she learned the art of customer service, understanding how to decipher her customers' actual needs, as opposed to their professed ones.

The lady customers all had a version of the same gripe: their husbands had wandering eyes, and too many women to wander to, many of them clad scantily in the latest bathing fashions and permitted to dress in much less clothing because of the oppressive heat. The wives were thus doubly embattled, their skin slowly blistering under the Australian sun—and their souls withering because of the atrophy and the competition. Working at the counter of her uncle's store afforded Josiah a bird's-eye view. She was privy to the ways of this new world and, in her small way, able to make her mark. She learned to both soothe and sell.

A lady entered the store, sighing heavily, her greying hair pulled into a messy nest of a bun. She approached the counter and busied herself at a console for eyewear. Within moments, it was clear to Josiah that the lady was not staring at the eyewear, but rather staring at Josiah's bare arms and flushed face.

"You're very lucky," the lady said. "Your skin glows naturally. And it's so perfect and pale."

"Nonsense," said Josiah, fanning herself. "This damned heat is what's making me glow." She tried to smile.

The lady sighed and nodded her head in agreement.

"Truly, though," said Josiah, "nothing good comes without hard work."

The lady studied Josiah and set her bags down.

"I have something for you," said Josiah.

She reached into a lower drawer where she kept one jar of the cream she had brought from home, almost as a souvenir, a token that sparked memories of her mother. Its milky-white fluid glistened like a pearl. She filled an empty sky-blue glass medicine jar with a few dollops. "Apply this after the bath. Make tiny, gentle circles." She demonstrated the motion. "Not too hard. You don't want to stress the skin. It's important to moisturize and stimulate."

The lady looked on, mouth agape.

Josiah might as well have been selling opium, so precious was the promise her potion offered.

"Don't worry," she said. "Give it a week or two."

The lady smiled and took Josiah's gift with a somber look. A look of profound gratitude.

She was back for a refill in less than a week, at which time Josiah accepted a small fee at the lady's insistence.

"You must let me pay you," said the lady. "This cream could save my marriage." She stuffed a pound into Josiah's hand.

Josiah smiled, warmed by the woman's relief. She put the money into her pocket and resolved to mention the transaction to her uncle. When the time was right.

5

LESSONS IN BUSINESS

New York City, 1923

The office was not quite the center of commerce Constance envisioned when she applied for the job. Her first day of work she was given a seat on a spindly wooden chair in a small back office, equidistant from the lobby and the lab. She shared this office with a dowdy and weathered receptionist who wheezed when she spoke and a typewriter that rattled with every letter she pressed. The defects were hard to ignore. But she forced herself to think of all the perks. This job offered the most important things: a steady paycheck and a stronghold in New York. Perhaps she could make headway at the company once she gained Dr. Osborne's trust.

At lunch, she conducted a subtle interrogation of her office-mate.

"Do they ever let the secretaries into the lab?" Constance asked.

"Oh, no, we're not allowed back there." She did not look up from her reading material, *Ladies' Home Journal*.

"Why not?" Constance asked.

Her office-mate shrugged.

"Who gets to go in there?" asked Constance.

"Strictly approved personnel."

Constance nodded. The laboratory door opened briefly and she caught a tantalizing glimpse. She resolved in that moment to obtain a tour by whatever means necessary. It would take her only a month.

The lab may as well have been a candy shop. It was crammed with a colorful spectrum of tubes and jars, each bubbling with a different concoction. On one wall, a set of connecting tubes conveyed a river of red. Nearby, a vat of brown liquid simmered under a lid. In the next room, a potent smell accosted her at the door. And along the back wall, jars of powders, stacked floor to ceiling, brought her back to a Persian spice store she had wandered into as a child in Montreal. Fine powder—red, white, and black—teetered from the floor to the ceiling in jars, jars packed so tightly as to make the wall a checkerboard.

There are moments in life when dreams crystallize, when disparate ideas—hopes and plans—merge into one. This was that moment for Constance. Her senses flooded with possibility.

"This is the aspirin. Biggest seller." Dr. Osborne gestured carelessly at one wall. "This is the cold remedy. Very popular. Does well for us." He stopped at a vat of bubbling lard, brownish with a golden tint. "This is the beauty cream."

"Beauty cream?" Constance repeated, trying to dim her excitement.

She leaned over and inhaled the putrid smell of lemon and lard. This was the fount of beauty for Dr. Osborne's dutiful customers? "And these?" She pointed at the powders.

"Oh, those," he said. "We're not exactly sure what to do with those."

"Why not?" asked Constance.

"We're experimenting with different scents for the Ladies' Beauty Cream, but, at the moment, I'm a little stumped."

"Why's that?" Constance asked.

"I don't know," said Dr. Osborne. "Maybe because I don't know any beautiful women."

"I see," said Constance. She was leaning against a counter and realized that Dr. Osborne was getting closer.

"Maybe you could teach me something about that."

"About what?" asked Constance.

"Beauty."

"Oh, I don't know," she said, instinctively taking a step back.

"You're awfully beautiful," he said, taking a step closer.

She took another step back, but he reached for her and gripped her by the arm.

"Are you willing to teach me about beauty?" he asked.

"Hmm," said Constance. She looked him in the eye. "That depends. On what you're willing to teach me about business."

Just like that, Constance completed her first business transaction, trading time in the lab for input on Dr. Osborne's Ladies' Beauty Cream and other sundry favors. It was not the first time she had used her looks to advance her career. At twenty-two, Constance was no stranger to the unwanted advances of young men. But she had learned to tune out the effects. Certain sacrifices were necessary to achieve one's goals. Even for a buffoon like this. Not least of all, a man.

6

WORKING THE COUNTER

Melbourne, 1923

Josiah stared down the mirror, focusing on her eyes. A woman instinctively knows certain universal truths. Draw attention to the good. Downplay the defects. Josiah had long employed this strategy in regard to her own looks. She was not the type of woman who would be called a natural beauty, but she had the commanding presence of an empress. In truth, she didn't have time for the beauty regimen she extolled. She was petite but strangely imposing. Her eyes were large, oval, black, Slavic, and penetrating, consuming much of her pale, round face. Yet over time she proved the axiom that beauty comes from the inside, that beauty begins with confidence. Her greatest challenge was the fatigue of long hours and too little sleep. Even with Josiah's creams and potions, this was hard to conceal.

The girls she grew up with in Poland fell into two distinct categories: Raphaelite beauties with long, mournful faces, light eyes, and pink skin like the angels on Italian church ceilings; and darker, more angular women with black hair and eyebrows who looked like the old Russian czars as they aged. Josiah fell into the latter category. All of them were Jewish. Within her tribe, some were overly inbred, with the palest skin and a slight overbite, looking as if they could disappear at a moment's notice or succumb to a slight case of influenza. Yet a few were truly beautiful due to a unique alchemy of their Sephardic past and Eastern European highlights. Even so, Josiah did not always love the face she saw in the mirror. She saw the extremes, the very large eyes, the absurdly high cheekbones with a near razor's edge. She saw the excessively pale skin that caused her mother to call her Zwłoki, Polish for "corpse." She saw the way, over the years, her looks afforded her power—how her face changed, from unique as a child, to striking as a teenager, and eventually to beautiful as a woman. Her face drew others to look. In an era of silent movies, her face was that of an engaging vamp, a Theda Bara type. The actress was already a favorite of Josiah's, and even more so when she found out she was born Theodosia Goodman and that she was also the daughter of a Polish-born Jewish tailor.

Now, as she stood alone at the mirror, she struggled to understand why: what was it about this unusual face that drew others' attention? She worked hard. That was true. And she cared about people. She was genuinely interested in the ladies who stopped by her uncle's store, who stood at the counter like grazing cows, pretending to search for products while actually probing her for advice. She cared about these people and they cared about her. She knew what they were really asking and what they wanted to hear. And it cost her nothing to offer this. And her interpretation turned a nice profit.

"Do you have anything for an upset stomach?" meant "Do you think my husband is cheating on me?"

"Do you have anything for chapped skin?" meant "Am I still beautiful?"

"Do you have anything for the nerves?" was code for "My husband has left me."

"What can I do for dry hands?" meant "I'm worried sick."

She had a special knack, not only for decoding the clues of her customers, but also for soothing their nerves, for saying just the thing to send them off with a brighter outlook. She knew that her words were enhanced by her image, so she began to provide two things, a product and a service, face cream for their skin and advice for their souls. She had come to think of the face cream as something more than a beauty salve, as a talisman for the comfort and counsel she offered.

And so it seemed a natural progression to offer these women a product that was both a promise and a good-luck charm. She had secreted a small cache of precious items on her voyage across the Pacific Ocean from Poland: the agate cameo from her sister, the twenty marks her father gave her the night before she left, and a couple of rubles collected over the years, all tied in her mother's faded cotton handkerchief like a scented potpourri. Beside this pouch was another small stash of precious cargo, eighteen pots of face cream, sequestered under her two pairs of silk stockings and her trusty woolen bras. It was this cream that her mother had insisted she apply every night, after her bath and before dressing for bed, the bathroom still hot and moist from her cleanse. The cream must be applied in tight, gentle circles while the skin was very clean and the pores were open.

That first winter in Melbourne, Josiah began to share this cream in tiny glass jars "borrowed" from her uncle's stockroom. Though their needs were not as urgent as those of the girls who had fled Poland on her ship, the good ladies of Melbourne had their own concerns. They needed encouragement, affirmation, and friendship. Josiah could provide all of the above from her post at the counter of her uncle's dry goods store. And best of all, she could do so for ten pence a pop.

7

THE GARDINER GIRLS

New York City, 1925

It was a novel idea, if not a new one, and Constance was determined to prove the concept. Put simply: Women would buy cosmetics—and buy in abundance—when the product was recommended by a friend. What better way to stimulate sales than by re-creating the most intimate exchange, a conversation between neighbors at the door of a woman's home. The trick was for the salesman to seem inviting as opposed to menacing, alluring as opposed to demanding. The trick was for the salesman to seem like the homeowner's friend. But not just any friend—like that friend or neighbor in her own community whom that homeowner admired most. The trick was for the salesman to be a woman, not a man. These saleswomen needed to be pretty, polished, and poised. "The three *P*s." And after two years of developing a basic product line of color cosmetics with a local lab and creating a simple botanical label she affixed that proclaimed "Constance Gardiner Beauty," Constance was ready. Her brother would sell the line from pharmacy to pharmacy, and she would invent the first female army of door-to-door saleswomen, known simply as the "Gardiner Girls."

Constance stood at the door of an ample colonial home in Bronxville at eleven o'clock on a Monday morning. The house, all yellow clapboard and white trim, was one of the most impressive on the block.

It looked, in early May, with cherry blossom petals fluttering, as though it were offering a personal invitation. Constance smoothed her dress, with its tidy collar, fitted bodice, and playful but still serious skirt, rang the doorbell, and cleared her throat as the woman of the house opened her door. The size of the house was somewhat intimidating, but today Constance was abiding by her father's advice: "Start at the top."

"May I help you?" said the woman. She was a handsome woman, clearly proud of her sizable manse.

"My name is Constance Gardiner," Constance said, launching into her presentation and placing her foot in a position that would block a closing door. "I'm happy to share the most wonderful news for every woman in this community. Such a glorious day today, isn't it?"

The woman nodded.

"I couldn't help but notice that the cherry blossoms, such a delicate pink, would make the most gorgeous shade of lipstick. And the pink of this orchid." She handed the woman a small stem that matched the one affixed to her lapel.

"Why, thank you." The woman relaxed, realizing no criminal would come bearing flowers. Constance had discovered this trick one day after too many slammed doors.

The homeowner looked Constance up and down, assessing her lovely clothes unapologetically and her shoes. She caressed her orchid and smiled.

"I happen to be selling cosmetics from the Constance Gardiner Beauty Collection and I'd be happy to tell you more about our products if you have a moment this morning." Constance shook her head, highlighting her blond locks, and straightened her knee, blocking the door. "You have the most gorgeous complexion," she said. "Like peaches and cream in a bowl." Constance smiled. Compliments always worked. Compliments and flowers. Women were such easy targets.

"That's very kind of you." The woman blushed and smiled in spite of herself.

"This shade of lipstick I'm wearing," Constance went on, "would look absolutely magnificent on you. It's true that because of your naturally luscious complexion, you barely need makeup at all."

The woman blushed again.

"But if I were to recommend a shade, it would be this one." She opened her bag and a display case. "This luscious shade of peach is called 'Sunday Picnic.' And then, just maybe a touch of 'Turquoise Sky' on the eyes to balance out the glow."

The woman tilted her head and leaned forward as though to peer inside Constance's bag.

"Would you like to hear more about our products?" Constance asked.

"I don't really have time this morning. I'm just finishing setting the table and I need to get dinner going because my husband is bring-ing some of his colleagues over tonight. But thank you." She tapped the door again.

This time, Constance moved quickly and squeezed her entire body in the door. "All the more reason," she said. "If he's bringing his colleagues home tonight, you may want a couple of tricks up your sleeve. He'll be so proud to show you off."

The matron giggled. "Perhaps he wouldn't mind if I make a little extra effort on his behalf."

"Of course he wouldn't mind. He'll appreciate it! And I'm sure he'll thank you in spades." She grinned in a suggestive way. For a split second, Constance worried that the smile had been too suggestive, but the matron seemed convinced. "He'll think you look like you did on your honeymoon!"

"Is that a fact?" The woman's eyes twinkled at the thought.

"You don't mind if I come in for a few minutes? It's easier to show you these products indoors without all this glorious sunshine."

The woman looked right, then left, as though ensuring there were no lurking spies; then, giving in to Constance's—and her own—temptation, she giddily let Constance in.

Inside, Constance availed herself of the ample space on the matron's highly polished dining room table, spreading out her wares like an Istanbul trader. She fanned out each color in a rainbow like an equatorial bug trying to attract a mate. Each shade of lipstick, eye shadow, and blush was different: blushes from rose to magenta, eye shadows from powder blue to sky blue to lavender to emerald green, and lipsticks in every shade of pink and red from coral to tomato.

So was born the concept of the Gardiner Girls, a special kind of workforce—part salesgirl, part sister, part den mother, part movie star—all in the comfort of a woman's own home. Constance Gardiner was the perfect salesgirl for her own product, not only because she was the ultimate proponent of her brand—lithe, well-appointed, immaculately put together—but because she was the ultimate ambassador. The challenge for Constance, with her blond patrician looks and bearing, was how to appeal to women from every echelon—not only the matrons with the mansions and mahogany dining room tables, but the women making do in small sculleries in tiny homes and apartments. For these were the women who most needed the promises the Gardiner Girls held in store. These were the women who, Constance was certain, harbored their own glorious dreams, women who would buy her products in droves.

8

THE COTTON

Harlem, 1927

"You're gorgeous and high yeller. Girl, you gotta see my friend at the Cotton!"

CeeCee had heard this endorsement time and time again, ever since she had blossomed into a beautiful young woman from a gangly teen. And while she had no desire to be a dancer or a singer, spangles and feathers holding little allure, she decided to listen to her successful and sophisticated cousin and give it a try. She would high kick the hell out of the chorus line if it meant getting her "high-yellow ass" up to New York's famed Cotton Club. "High yellow" was the term for light-skinned, mixed-race blacks. High yellow supposedly meant she was considered the elite of the African American community, but in reality it meant living in a kind of limbo, excluded by blacks for being too light yet considered by the whites to still be too black. Nevertheless, CeeCee Jones knew she didn't have much of a choice. The standard options were clear. It was either a life as a "domestic," living with a man, a man who might have a steady job as a train porter, if they were lucky. With this man, she would raise a large family. Her other option was perhaps the stage and dancing at the Cotton Club. Lord knew her mind worked differently and New York City would at least provide a different form of stimulation than bucolic Virginia. She consumed the discarded newspapers as if she were eating an ice-cream cone, having picked up the habit of reading the local papers at the Hewitts'. She told herself her time and higher education would come—this was her consolation to herself. She would take her cousin up on his offer and try out at the Cotton Club.

It was not lost on her that the first song she heard backstage was called "Creole Love Call," performed by Adelaide Hall and Duke Ellington's orchestra. Nor did she complain when she was given a costume for the Brazilian number that featured a ruffled skirt hemmed to her underwear in the front, floor length in the back, with a hat that was made to look as though she were balancing a bowl of fruit on her head. The fabric banana seemed to have come loose. She would have to sew it on. CeeCee's late mother had been the daughter of a slave, a sharecropper who had a baby with a white man she never knew. The irony was not lost on her.

"What you doin' sitting there, girl?" Gladys Potter, another inge-nue, saw CeeCee sewing quietly in the corner between sets. "We're on in ten." Gladys slipped on her own fruit hat.

"Sewing bananas," said CeeCee.

"Girl, this joint is bananas!" Gladys took her place in the line of the other girls as they prepared to rhumba onstage for their number, "Riot in Rio."

CeeCee's journey to the Cotton Club had been facilitated by her older cousin Rudy, who now lived in New York City. Rudy was a talented jazz trumpeter in Duke Ellington's orchestra. Ellington was a pioneer in "jungle music" for the white audiences slumming it in Harlem, seeking exotic flavor and high style. The Cotton Club, which broke all the Prohibition rules, was overrun by mobsters and socialites, giving it an air of urbane sophistication and subtle rebellion. CeeCee's cousin Rudy was at the center of it all. He was now playing for the dapper Ellington, who had seen him play at another venue and offered him a five-dollar-a-week raise, snagging him away from his former band position.

"I'd rather play 'Someone to Watch Over Me' than hits from *Shuffle Along*." He shrugged and grimaced at some of the overt canards of the lyrics and blackface projected onstage, but musicians could give little input on the material they were forced to play. And he knew he was lucky to have a steady-paying job in a popular orchestra.

"Cee, you're gorgeous," he had said. He had taken her aside at a family funeral in Virginia in his aunt's shanty. He looked her over, amazed that this once gangly teen was now an incredibly beautiful woman. "You gotta see my friend at the Cotton Club."

"I have no desire to be a dancer. Or a singer," she said.

"Girl, it's better than being a housemaid at the Hewitts'. You're way too pretty to be polishing silver."

"I'm running the house and they're paying for secretarial classes for me. To study."

"Yeah, but you're still in Virginia and wait till you get to"—he blew a pretend trumpet with his elegant tapered hands—"New York!" He laughed, flashing a row of brilliant white, oversize teeth. "Harlem is happening and you don't get called uppity dressing this way. Only here." He pulled at his starched French cuffs and gold cuff links. "I can't wait to get back north."

And though CeeCee was content, she was also smart enough to know when opportunity knocked. Within days, she had given notice to the Hewitts, a lovely and progressive family who were sad to see her go but supportive of her move. They drove her to the train station, where she had to sit in the colored car, and gave her forty dollars as a bonus for working the four years. She hugged each of the Hewitt girls and promised to write as she boarded the train. Then she sat, gazing out the window, clutching her tattered suitcase, watching the South chug by. She held firm to her belongings and the address of the boardinghouse that Rudy had given her. She was on her way.

———————

"So your cousin is really as pretty as you said, Jonesy." Herman Stark, the portly stage manager of the Cotton Club, surveyed CeeCee like a ripe apple and then flashed a smile at his talent manager, Lou Savarese. Lou had the best nose in the business for new talent. He could smell star quality. They both gave each other knowing glances as they saw her beautiful features and lithe, toned figure.

"They usually look like sacks of potatoes when they show up, but not this one." Lou raised a bushy eyebrow.

"I told you." Rudy nodded proudly.

"She ain't high yellow," said Lou. "More like high white." Only her light brown complexion suggested a biracial history. The Cotton Club was noted for its strict rules; the showgirls all had to be "tall, tan, and terrific"—light-skinned, over five foot six, and under twenty-one years of age.

"Heck, she even has long straight hair. Never seen that before." Lou reached out and grabbed a handful of hair as if she were an inanimate object and yanked it to see if it was real.

"It's a secret formula," CeeCee said. She pulled away in a ladylike fashion and raised herself erect.

"Yeah, who was your daddy?" Lou laughed. "That's the secret formula!" He guffawed.

"Can you dance?" Herman asked.

"She can do everything. She's like me. She sings, she dances, and she polishes silver. Heck, she may even play the trombone. The Jones family is very musical," Rudy said, beaming.

"So you're saying she knows how to blow . . . ?" Lou laughed.

"Enough, Lou, this one seems to be more ladylike and right off the farm. No need to corrupt her on day one." Herman shook his head. "You're sure you want to be in this gin joint, girl? You seem a bit finer than the usual stock-in-trade."

"Oh, yes." CeeCee gave her brightest, high-wattage smile. "I've always dreamed of dancing at the Cotton Club." She was glad Rudy had prepped her on what to say.

"Sure. Okay. Well, you're certainly good-looking enough and, being that you're Rudy's cousin, we'll try you out."

"You'll still need to show the choreographer your routine in five."

"With her looks I'll take her if she has two left feet." Stark exhaled.

"Gotcha." Lou nodded his head in agreement.

"You get thirteen dollars a week and free meals and shoes. You'll take them in the dressing room with the other girls. You have to do your own makeup and hair and you have to be on time. No ifs, ands, or buts. We don't tolerate lateness. If you're the Queen of Sheba and you're late—you're o-u-t!"

"Of course, I understand. Thank you. That sounds perfect," CeeCee said.

"Now you know the Cotton Club plays to an all-white audience. No mixing with the crowds unless a stage-door Johnny wants to see one of the ladies. But that's up to you, sister."

"She'll be doing no such thing. I'll break legs," Rudy said.

"Yeah, wait until the wolves see this one." Herman flashed his diamond pinky ring in her direction. "Honey, if your cousin weren't attached to you like glue, you'd be rolling in it. Like the other girls."

CeeCee smiled. "I'm not like the other girls."

"That's what they all say," Lou said. "Until week two and a ten-dollar bill. Now go to wardrobe and get fitted. This week's theme is 'That Night in Rio.'"

"Everyone wants Latin now, and she can easily pass." Herman said this without any irony, as though he actually meant it as a compliment. He yawned and flicked the ashes of his cigar.

Week two finally came and went. So did the constant passes and pinches of the musicians who sweet-talked her, the management who intimidated her, and one drummer who pushed her up against the dressing room door. She managed to escape several attempts and was soon enough considered uppity by the other girls who had invited her on double dates with the hordes of well-brought-up white men who showed up backstage for a date. CeeCee declined all offers and went home to read. Soon she was given the name Queen CeeCee, but she knew it was derisive.

"Oh, here she comes, with her books and her nose in the air . . . Queen CeeCee," they said. She tried her best in the chorus line but knew she had two left feet. Two weeks came and went, and she was reading the *New York Times* "Help Wanted" section. She was not cut out for this line of work. She knew she needed a different type of job. And quick.

9

STAFFING UP

New York City, 1927

Despite the fact that she was a veritable mutt—part English, part French, part Canadian—Constance easily conveyed an image that she was "to the manor born." She did not fight the assumptions that followed her into a room. Her bobbed blond hair, supple body, and classic oval face made her a perfect piece of casting for the *Mayflower* girl in New York. With looks like this and a good name, a woman was afforded certain luxuries, including an excellent array of options for mates, the respected and glamorous friends who came with entrée into this world, and all the opportunities that followed—party invitations, club invitations, summer spots, winter ski holidays, and the various pastimes of the rich that cemented these bonds: horses, tennis, beach clubs, skiing, dinner parties, and, in later years, cards. Constance's circuit from the East Side of Manhattan to the best parts of the Hamptons, Southampton, of course, to favored spots in Palm Beach and the various ski destinations ensured that she had a built-in community for life. She understood that this community and rotation would form the foundation and contours of her social life. Yet she never expected this community to be the back on which her business was built.

Without ever selling directly to her friends, Constance used her social network to help build her business. They were her first consumers and her first cheerleaders. They were the ambassadors of her brand in drawing rooms and the press, as some even owned the magazines and news outlets. Constance knew that the richer they were, the more they wanted everything for *free*. And she was smart enough to gift the heiress she met at the Breakers or a Park Avenue dinner party a few moisturizers and the press agents covering the social events she crashed—and was eventually invited to—lipstick samples for their wives and girlfriends. It became clear to Constance that these women, this echelon, would not be her core business. The women who wanted, who needed, who aspired, to use Constance's cosmetics tended to be women without privilege, women who could not afford the houses, the horses, the homes, the holidays. The women who wanted—and, Constance felt, in some altruistic sense most needed—her cosmetics were those who did not have access to the daydreams of luxury. Her products provided not only an arena for these daydreams, but a means by which these women might achieve them. While the prestige came from her social network . . . the sales came from the average, everyday women who lived a humdrum life and wanted or needed a small yet important affordable pick-me-up.

The old boys' club was, of course, a function of Constance's world. What she did not realize, nor could have predicted, was that she would form a new club, but not one for the upper-crust girls; they were settled into their memberships, ladies' clubs, and the seasonal perks that came with that lifestyle. Instead, Constance inadvertently formed a club to which she might not have deigned to belong. The customers of the Constance Gardiner Beauty Collection, now legally Gardiner Cosmetics, had far less than Constance's friends and those she aspired to be friends with. Still, Constance instinctively knew that these basic women would become her core customers and community. These plain and good women would form the financial base she needed to succeed. Slowly and quietly, she set out to reach these women. To do it without losing her original club would be the most perilous and important challenge for her business. She knew she needed staff who could relate to them. She hired Molly Simpson, a young blond girl fresh off the farm from Minnesota, to shadow her and become the first official Gardiner Girl. Molly had pretty, non-intimidating looks, and to Constance's delight she was down-to-earth and perky. Constance struck up a conversation with her one evening when she was a cigarette girl at a nightclub and found her personable and vivacious. At the end of the evening, she excused herself for a moment from her society friends and offered her a job on the spot. Molly was perfect; she was pretty without being threatening, and naturally chatty without being overly loquacious. Constance knew that someone like Molly could talk herself into more homes than she could, since she was one of these women. Her short bobbed blond pageboy haircut and cute upturned nose gave her a friendly, non-menacing look. She could have talked and walked her way into and out of the safe at Tiffany's without attracting notice. She was perfect for the job.

Constance's first office was a modest affair. She had steady sales, steady enough that James was able to leave his job as a bookkeeper and work for her full-time. Now, she needed a real office. She was a firm believer in the idea that a company should never grow bigger than its bottom-line expenses and she chose an office accordingly. She rented a room on the fifteenth floor of a respectable building on Fifth Avenue, as she knew the address would convey prestige. A building with a doorman and fine solid marble tiles on the entry floor, handsome bronze elevator doors, and a respectable location. Though the building was only a few blocks from Central Park on Fifty-seventh and Fifth, she chose an office without a view, or rather a view of the interior courtyard where the building's trash was kept. In actuality it was little more than a utility closet with an attached stockroom. It boasted a wooden desk, a chair, and a black typewriter. But she was proud when she put her sign up and she and James painted the inside walls mauve.

There was no need for a view to impress clients. She did not have clients. She had customers. At least, she did not have clients yet. What she needed was a clean, quiet space where she could make phone calls to the various stores that stocked her product, or soon would, and a room in which to test and stock the products when they came back from the lab. Molly was hardly ever there, as she was out most of the time selling products door-to-door and training future Gardiner Girls in the field. All Constance needed was a bookkeeper and assistant to tally the orders from the stores and to help with the endless trips to the post office for shipping and fetching deliveries. Her first purchase was an official-looking metal file cabinet to store the purchase orders from the myriad small pharmacies she and James would canvas each day. He was in charge of selling to the local pharmacies and eventually to the department stores; Molly was in charge of door-to-door sales; and Constance focused on new product development. Gradually, as the business began to grow, she saw the need for an excellent assistant.

She posted an advertisement in *The New York Times* and the *Daily News* classifieds: "Seeking Hard-working Assistant for Growing Cosmetics Company. Must type and be amenable to late nights." Forty-nine women answered the ad, each one sending a thoughtful letter and submitting a carefully penned résumé. As she pored over the résumés and thoughtful notes, the nurses and stenographers and assistants and hygienists eager to be considered for the job, Constance could not ignore the louder message embedded in these typewritten notes: I Want to Work. These women were eager, desperate, for employment. It was as though a revolution were at hand: other women like herself who wanted and needed to put in a hard day's work. Each one of these rosy-cheeked women was wild with the possibility introduced by need and desire, each one of them was determined to do something new.

The first applicant was an older lady with a round figure. She seemed nice enough, but perhaps not the most powerful ambassador for the brand. The second was petite, recently divorced, and supporting a family of four. The third, fourth, and fifth were all women who had worked in family stores or had done nursing during the war and did not want to say goodbye to that taste of freedom—and the pocket money it would afford. Most of the rest were combinations of the above; older widows supporting families, younger women seeking income before finding a mate, and women who had experienced the freedom afforded by their experience during the First World War and the power that extra cash could provide.

But none of the applicants seemed to Constance to encompass all of these virtues as much as one, CeeCee Jones, a twenty-one-year-old single girl who had moved to New York after working as a maid for a wealthy family in Virginia. CeeCee had not been to college but had taken courses and hoped to go one day. She mentioned that she had read cast-off medical texts she found in a thrift store in preparation for her eventual goal, medical school. The moment she walked in the door, Constance simply knew this young lady was a winner and that she could not succeed without her at her side. She was also a dusky, exotic beauty who appeared to share her drive and inner strength. It was as if two like-minded moths were dancing around the same flame.

CeeCee Jones was, in fact, a light-skinned biracial woman. Her résumé said she had been working as a housekeeper for the Hewitt family. Over the years, first as the granddaughter of an emancipated slave and a white man she never knew, CeeCee had learned many things about business and domestic life. She knew how to run a kitchen and how to turn a staff of ten into an impeccable regime. She knew how to care for and discern good china, place settings, and silver for every type of affair. She knew how to clean and press and iron and fold while strengthening the fabrics in her care. She had taken a stenographers' course paid for by Mr. Hewitt to help him with his office billing. The Hewitts were a kind and liberal family who believed everyone should and could achieve their destiny through education and hard work, and CeeCee took advantage of the opportunities and their largesse, as she knew higher education was a necessity for every woman to thrive.

Through her own ingenuity and interest, CeeCee had long invested herself in the study of hair, not only because she gravitated to self-improvement, but because she had learned firsthand the perils of poor self-care. African American women, privileged and burdened with the most luscious and distinct black hair, understood the lengths to which a black woman must go to present her hair as she wished. Long captive to notions that a black woman must "tame" and straighten her hair, she had sampled and studied those materials available to her community.

Lye, a toxic substance used in the preparation of soap, was applied to straighten or "relax" hair. The method, though effective, was time-consuming and harsh, causing irritation to a woman's scalp. Like so many black women, CeeCee had watched her hair begin to weaken and fray, had even watched in horror as large patches of her hair fell out. Lye and the other chemicals caused dandruff, itching, and baldness. Never a woman to complain, CeeCee endeavored to find a better solution herself.

The women of the Hewitt family had long black hair as well, and CeeCee had aided many of them with their washing and daily upkeep. So she began to consider and eventually to concoct her own homemade straightener and pomade, borrowing from the methods she watched the Hewitt girls employ. She knew the value of lanolin and moisturizing the scalp with shea butter. CeeCee began to use her secret formula on herself. Finding it so effective, she cautiously began to share it with other women she knew.

The response was resounding. The black women she knew needed a good product; they were committed to using that product every eight to twelve weeks, and they welcomed one that would be more forgiving than those available to them at the time. With the modest revenue from her first batch of pomade that worked without the harsh effect and with the help of her cousin Rudy, she set out for New York, securing a room in a boardinghouse in Harlem.

She mentioned to Constance that she was working in the chorus line at the Cotton Club on 142nd Street and Lenox Avenue but that life in the theater was not for her. Constance smiled, knowing that most young women would want the opposite: a life on the stage rather than an office job. This greatly appealed to her core values. Constance could immediately see that CeeCee was a different sort.

When CeeCee saw the advertisement for Gardiner Cosmetics, she did not delay. She answered the ad promptly, writing her response with great care, and began planning the appropriate attire even before she received a reply. She arrived for the interview before the appointed time and waited fifteen minutes to be seen. From the warm orange cast of light coming into the office through the window, she could tell it was nearing seven in the evening, but from the activity in the office, it may as well have been nine in the morning.

Constance preferred to begin her interviews with a minimum of small talk. "It says on your résumé that you ran the housekeepers in a large home."

"Yes," said CeeCee. "I have managed a staff as large as ten. I started as a maid and worked my way up."

Constance nodded and noted the young woman's big, bright eyes. "It also says on your résumé that you worked in the kitchen of this home. Are you aware that, in addition to clerical duties, this job calls for time in the lab? The temperatures in the lab can be quite high."

"I was not aware of that," said CeeCee, "but it sounds fascinating. I'm very interested in the art of cosmetic production and have some experience in the field."

"I see," said Constance. "How so?" She looked closer now at the young woman's well-defined lips, her large oval eyes.

"My hair. It requires time and a process to tame and straighten it. The hair of most colored women I know requires a fair amount of care."

Constance nodded, looked at CeeCee's hair. It was straight and sleek and pulled into a dramatic and tidy bun. It gave her the appearance of a white or Latin woman.

"Products for us are scarce," CeeCee went on. "So I've had to devise alternatives."

Constance smiled, refreshed by the woman's candor and ingenuity. She leaned in, focusing intently. "Oh, I see. . . ."

Constance was thoroughly taken aback by CeeCee's claims. Even more surprising, she had not expected to be immediately charmed by a young African American girl so new to the city. Constance saw two things: CeeCee's inner fire and, more important, that CeeCee was light-skinned enough to "pass." She felt something else: the heat of attraction that she had tried to banish many times before. It spread through her chest and down between her knees. Constance was tantalized by the idea of sharing office space in such proximity with this young, caramel-colored beauty. She offered CeeCee the job "in the room," hiring her right then and there.

"Thank you, Mrs. Gardiner. You won't regret it." CeeCee smiled her best high-wattage smile.

"Miss. Miss Gardiner. Although it might be Mrs. one day. It all depends on whether I accept a certain gentleman's proposal, but that is for another time entirely." Constance offered up a public white lie. While she had been pursued by a number of young suitable men, she was not attracted to any man who would keep her under his thumb, i.e., making her stay at home without embracing her career. No matter how rich or handsome these men were, she had eschewed all offers, yet did not want to publicly appear as an old maid. Or worse.

"Of course," CeeCee said.

"You will report to work at eight thirty on Monday, and I give approximately one half hour for lunch. Evening and weekend work is required. I pay higher than most; eight dollars and fifty cents a week."

"That's very generous." CeeCee nodded. She thought of the delicious steak sandwich at the Cotton Club that was $1.25. This was the only thing she would miss. They shook hands to cement the deal, and CeeCee rose and smoothed her belted skirt.

"Oh, and one other thing . . ." Constance looked her over.

"Yes?" CeeCee looked up.

"Let's not mention to anyone else you are colored. We'll just tell people you're Spanish or something like that. Brazilian or something exotic. Deal?" The idea had come to Constance when CeeCee mentioned she was in the line for the Brazilian show at the club.

"Deal," CeeCee said. She was accustomed to this. Not fully accepted by either the blacks or the whites.

"We'll just call you something like CeeCee . . . Lopez." Constance smiled at her creativity. "That should do the trick."

"Yes, it should." CeeCee looked down but knew better than to say anything further. She was now CeeCee Lopez. And she had a real job.

10

THE YANK

Melbourne, 1924-1929

Running up against the mounting demand for her creams, Josiah racked her brain for a solution. Her time with her aunt and uncle caused more than a bit of unspoken stress at home. Her passionate opinions and strong personality had her at odds with her aunt Masha within weeks of her arrival. When they had an explosive argument about how the table should be set, everyone agreed that a boarding-house might be the best option. Her new attic bedroom faced the hills and endless pastures, not to mention the ungodly sheep population. Sheep for miles and miles. As she gazed out the window, a new thought occurred to her. This would be her eureka moment. Sheep produce lanolin, a necessary ingredient for her creams since she was running low on her stock from Poland. Necessity and boredom were the mothers of invention. She realized she could mask lanolin's unbecoming scent with other local staples such as lilies and lavender, which were cheap, available, and abundant.

It was not long before Josiah's business created another sort of tension with her uncle. When he caught her selling her products out of the store, he fired her from the position on the spot. She was distraught but immediately rebounded by renting counter space at the store across the street. Of course, now she and her uncle were not speaking; he accused her of being ungrateful, failing to appreciate all that he and Aunt Masha had done for her. Josiah was too strong, too opinionated, too uppity. No man would ever want her. She was a bad example for her nieces, who were developing her habits of being argumentative and contrary. Josiah laughed to herself at the hypocrisy. Nevertheless, she had no leverage: she needed money to manufacture the orders she received, but she had none left over after paying for rent and food at the boardinghouse.

Within weeks, Josiah was working overtime as a waitress in a local teahouse. She was a hard worker but terrible at taking orders. She was nearly fired, but the teahouse owner saw an uptick in male clientele with Josiah there, as she was not shy about putting her ample cleavage on display on a sweltering day. So he bit his tongue and started serving beer at her suggestion. Within days, Josiah and her saucy personality had turned a money-losing teahouse into a profitable tea and beer hall. She was well aware of her value. One day, while lamenting her poverty to another waitress, a handsome, sandy-haired young man strolled in and took a seat at one of her tables. He spoke with an unusual accent, and someone called him a Yank.

"Miss, can I have a refill of some coffee and a doughnut?" Jon Blake was mesmerized by the animated waitress and her deliberate movements. She even poured coffee in a seductive, European manner. He marveled at her long elegant arms, lovely hands, and lily-white satin complexion, not to mention her shimmering nails.

"Yes to the coffee. No to the doughnut. I'll bring you a Danish," Josiah said without looking up from her pad.

"But I want a doughnut, not a Danish," he said. He looked somewhat perplexed and found himself staring at her velvet décolletage.

"I was saving the doughnut for myself after my shift. Vhat?" She looked at him in a stern manner. "You don't believe in vomen first?" She put her hand on her soft, round hip.

"Of course I do. I didn't know. I would love a Danish," he acquiesced immediately, which she liked.

"Here, you'll love vhat I give you." She nearly slammed down the plate with the Danish, almost daring him to disagree. As he ate, he marveled at the strong-willed young woman and was intrigued by her alluring accent that he couldn't quite place.

"How vas it?" she teased him.

"I liked it very much." He grinned at her, his soft blond hair falling over his high forehead.

"You see, I am always right." She smiled for the first time. "Where are you from? London?"

"No, New York City."

"America? Really?" She suddenly turned on the charm. A real Yankee in front of her. "Vhat else would you like?" she said sweetly.

"I would like to take you out." His eyes wandered back down from her eyes to her chest.

"When?" Josiah thrust her wares forward in a suggestive yet feminine manner.

"Tomorrow night for dinner?" He combed his hair with his fingers.

"Tonight, Yankee. I vant to go tonight."

Within days, Jon Blake and Josiah Herzenstein were inseparable. She avoided the glares of her disapproving uncle and aunt as they strolled down the street.

"A *shaygets* no less." Her aunt Masha sniffed loudly. "You'll have to write your sister and tell her of your niece's downfall."

Josiah turned her back and laughed. "Those are my backwater relatives. You'll see, one day they'll come running." She hooked her arm through his.

Jon was a journalist at the Australian outpost of the *New Amsterdam Times* and he understood the power of the press—as well as the power of the newspapermen. Within minutes of their heated kisses, he offered to deploy the paper to help promote Josiah's new business. He devised an alluring ad featuring Josiah, looking glamorous, in which she told women why they needed her cosmetics and touted a combination of romantic advice and science. Slowly but surely, the journalist grew from suitor, to collaborator, to kindred spirit, and eventually to husband.

Intrigued by the quarter-page ad, which Jon bought Josiah as a present, a local newspaper editor wrote about Josiah's product. It was Josiah's first lesson in advertising and publishing: while publications touted a separation of church and state, if you advertised you were more likely than not to get a story, an editorial, or a mention. Josiah would make use of this her entire career. She received twenty-five orders within a week of the ad's appearance. The photo they had included of her smoldering eyes and lily-white skin seemed to be the magic ingredient. The orders increased to one hundred and then two hundred. Then, when she placed a half-page ad with a photo featuring her décolletage, the orders rose to five hundred and then seven hundred and fifty. She quit her job as a waitress and worked eighteen hours a day to fill the orders, breaking only to see Jon for dinner, where they talked further about her business. From the rented counter, word spread about Josiah's first product made from lanolin and local herbs. She was the first to mix in local lavender and scent and proudly called it her "Miracle Moisturizer." Her sister Shayna, whom she had brought over from Poland, was a talented artist. She created her first label: "Herzenstein's Miracle Cream and Moisturizer." It was black and white and featured a garland of flowers and two doves over the words "European Secret."

"What's the secret?" lady clients clustered around Josiah to ask.

"If I told you, it wouldn't be a secret. Vould it?" Josiah laughed. "All you need to know is it's a European secret. Look at Theda Bara." She would show her clients an ancient crumpled pictorial in *Photoplay* magazine. "Her father and my father were born in the same village in Poland. Theodosia Goodman. Theda Bara. The same. We both have the Polish skin secret. Also Anna Held. Another Jewish girl from Varsaw. She became the most famous Ziegfeld girl. I am telling you we all had the same secret stuff." The women would marvel at the stories and their pocketbooks would be open before she was finished. The sound of the cash register was music to Josiah's ears. Jon's reporter salary, in American dollars, meant meals and luxuries he bestowed upon her generously. Meanwhile, she was able to plow more of her profits into her burgeoning business.

Before a year had passed, Josiah opened her first store on Melbourne's Collins Street. She was a natural saleswoman, expertly tapping into the current climate, diagnosing women's skin, and prescribing the creams they "needed" to be beautiful again. Placebo or miracle drug—no matter. Converting one woman at a time, Josiah quickly became Melbourne's pied piper. And when she found out that Jon was actually Jonathan and that his mother was Jewish, Josiah decided marriage to him was in the cards. He was handsome, generous, and happy to take orders from her complacently. The combination was alluring.

A frantic letter from her mother about her "downfall" and the importance of Jewish progeny may have compounded the decision. Josiah answered her dear mother with a businesslike missive. She had met a handsome American Jew (partially true, as he was Jewish only on his mother's side); she would have an American passport soon enough; and one day, she promised a Jewish child named after her father, Menachim. She wouldn't tell her mother that it would be named Miles or Morton, but she had her plan. She organized a courthouse wedding with the efficiency worthy of a fund-raising CEO. Jon was bemused and delighted as Josiah arranged for the attending rabbi, even though Jon's father was Presbyterian, and organized a wedding dinner at the teahouse, inviting a few of the distant relatives with whom she was still on speaking terms. Their honeymoon was the tiny apartment she found on Elizabeth Street, and she flaunted the address whenever she could since their combined salaries allowed them to take up residence in the better part of town. She would commandeer his check every two weeks, and he was quite willing to hand it over for some sweet entreaties. After all, she was proud of her handsome husband and his regular, guaranteed paycheck.

"Here's how it vorks in my house," Josiah said as she pleasured him in bed. "Your money is my money and my money is my money. Deal?" She stopped right before he climaxed.

"Yes, yes, it's a deal." He laughed. "You drive a hard bargain."

"At times like this, it's easy." She reapplied her lipstick and smoothed her lingerie. Although he had needs, Josiah had little time for romance, as they both worked different shifts. He was lazier and often went to the men's club to play squash and cricket, whereas Josiah was working across town. They did enjoy each other's company, though, and he tried hard to please her.

She stopped in front of Katz's Jewelers one day. "I vant that ruby ring. I spoke to Katz and you can put it on layaway."

Jon smiled and made a note to come back on his own and buy the ring for Josiah as a surprise.

With constant work and continued success in Melbourne, she decided it was the right time to expand the business. To add new products to her first shop and possibly open a second one in Sydney. It seemed to everyone, including her jealous uncle, that Josiah Herzenstein, now a married woman, was on her way.

11

FAMILY SECRETS

New York City, 1929

West Fifty-eighth Street.

The Stork Club. Constance took a deep breath and silently took in the tony and well-publicized new club in slow motion. She couldn't believe she was actually going to be dining at the high-profile hotspot and in the VIP section, no less. Feeling slightly intimidated, she pushed away any fears and assumed the posture of a regular.

Think it, be it. Her motto had always proven successful, so why not now? She bent down and allowed her date, Van Wyke, the privilege of kissing her quickly on the lips in a patent exchange for the invitation. He hailed from one of the oldest and most venerable families in New York and she gladly allowed him to lead her from the coatroom to the table and to navigate the evening. She had read about the club and its habitués like most mere mortals in the newspaper gossip columns and could smell the rarefied air virtually wafting from the newsprint. It was the gathering place for café society—socialites, celebrities, and sports stars, all of whom went to see and be seen. At the Stork Club, glamour was finally in her grasp. And now her satin-gloved hand was being kissed by none other than the owner, Sherman Billingsley. She knew last season's satin Poiret gown was still light-years ahead of what women were wearing in New York and she was happy she had made the investment when she was in Paris.

The Stork Club was designed in the vein of a traditional men's club; a long, wooden bar, seemingly lit from within, with green and amber bottles glowing like Christmas lights. Deep burgundy velvet curtains sealed the front windows, creating an air of secrecy inside. The tables were set with crisp white linens and sparkling crystal, no doubt wiped down by exhausted servers reprimanded for the slightest smudge. In the center of every table, a bouquet of peonies and gardenias drew the eye like constellation stars, casting a gentle floral scent into the darker notes of cigarette smoke and perfectly cooked steak. The most beautiful adornment arrived at the Stork Club every night: an array of gorgeous female guests who glittered more than a Hollywood film set and perched around the tables, with the gardenias at the center, like exotic rare birds.

It was a known fact that Sherman favored society people over show people, and it was said that the Wyke family was so blue-blooded as to appear purple. Billingsley, a noted snob, treated Van Wyke like royalty as he knew his father's pedigree. They were led to one of the best, central tables to meet friends who were already seated, having started on their bootleg martinis. With fanfare, Van introduced Constance to his best friend, Topper Stanton, and his fiancée, Lally Seward. A perfectly matched set, they both had a disaffected look bordering on boredom that came only with being very rich, very social, or entirely superior. Constance saw Lally surveying her from head to foot to see if she was worthy. Constance's social intelligence was such that she could read facial cues and was chilled to detect an ever-so-faint hint of a smirk, which suggested that her surfeit fashion choice was a bit too bold for a first dinner. By contrast, Lally's simple black velvet, sweetheart-necked evening dress and strand of discreet pearls suggested a much older matron or a debutante born to the purple. The latter she was. Lally was chic yet understated, and her appropriate and somewhat bland fashion choice proclaimed, "I'm too rich to have to try so hard." Dinner, she knew, was a test, and it wasn't going to be an easy one to pass. During the first course, which was pleasant but stressful, Constance decided to take a different tack. She would be the one to leave early. She knew this would throw them off and level the playing field. She had done it in business meetings and it was anything if not strategic.

"Darling," Constance said with her most winning smile, "I have to leave right after dinner. James, my brother, is ill," she explained to the table. "No worries, it's not influenza. He's prone to migraines." She nervously remembered to place her soup spoon under the dish and on the plate as she had just seen Lally do it. She had always just left it in the bowl. Constance was glad she was keen enough to observe and made a mental note not to make the same mistake twice. No one seemed to notice her faux pas. The spoon had lingered for only a few moments before she put observation into action. She had been wise enough to consult an etiquette book as preparation, but if she was going to be part of this crowd, she needed to know and do more. She was still a bit unsure of all the knives and forks. "Just work your way *in*," the book had said. It didn't offer specific soup spoon etiquette, however. Next time, perhaps she would not order soup.

"That's marvelous that you are so maternal. Isn't it, Topper? Isn't she just the cat's pajamas?" Van Wyke, heir to the banking fortune Wyke and Co., nodded to his childhood friend Topper Stanton, of the Stanton Munitions family. He shook his balding pate as he slapped Topper on the back in a hail-fellow-well-met tradition. Van and Topper. Topper and Van. More brothers than friends, they had both been sent at six years old to Milton and then Groton in the upper grades, growing up together in the elite WASP enclave of boarding schools, squash matches at the clubs, polo, sailing, and weekends in Old Westbury. Van was eager for Topper's approval of his choice of companion. Constance was beautiful, yes, but she was a working girl from Canada and not exactly from their set.

"If she's so pretty, why is she not engaged yet?" Topper had asked before the dinner, somewhat suspiciously.

"She's a flapper who works. Went to Smith, I believe for a year. Has a career. Very different from all the debs we know," Van had explained. Topper was a bit surprised when she entered the Stork. She was a full head taller than Van and quite striking. A natural blonde and arguably beautiful. What was this blond Amazon doing with sweet yet meek Van? Something didn't quite add up.

"Well, I won't ask for a kiss, then, Connie. Are migraines catching?"

Van laughed nervously and nudged Topper and Lally, the Seward Oil heiress, to do the same. Constance knew her invitation to dinner at the Stork Club was a significant advancement in the state of their courtship. Their dates had become a weekly event in less than a year. While Constance was hardly attracted to Van, to either his bland humor or his doughy build, she knew exactly who Van Wyke was on the social pecking order, and best of all he did not seem to object to her having a career. She was also savvy enough to know that while she herself was wildly independent, single women didn't just "go" to the Stork by themselves, and here she was and in the very best company at one of the club's prime tables, treated to the best of everything. It only solidified why she was with him. They had met a year earlier at the captain's table on an ocean liner from France, where Van had traveled to meet his father in Paris for business and summer vacation and Constance had gone to learn French beauty secrets for Gardiner Cosmetics. On the boat, they struck up a convenient, if platonic, friendship, which he seemed to want to overturn. He was fascinated by her business and her unique style.

"No worries, I am quite healthy," Constance said, and gave him a peck on his cheek.

"Well, it must be very exciting to be in the beauty business. You really develop all your own products?" Topper was intrigued.

"Yes, that's my favorite part of the job. The ideas, the formulas, the invention." Constance spoke softly. She knew enough not to talk about herself unless she was asked and to compliment the other women at the table who might be threatened by her successes.

"Van, you found yourself a beautiful version of Madame Curie. How fascinating." His blue eyes sparkled and he leered. Was he flirting? Constance blushed. He was the handsome one, but taken. She would have preferred Topper, of course, but had little use for men, so it was less vexing.

"Thank you. And Lally," Constance said, offering her a small white-and-pink bag, "I put some of my lipsticks and powders in this bag for you. I do hope you will use them. You have such a lovely complexion. Peaches and cream. Topper, I would say you chose very well." They all laughed at the compliments, and the gift seemed to warm the glacial divide between Constance and Lally a bit. She had succeeded in downgrading from frozen to defrosted. They made more idle conversation until dessert.

"It really has been divine. Topper, Lally. I hope to see you both soon, and so sorry I have to skedaddle." She rose after a scrumptious chocolate soufflé and tea.

"Lovely to meet you as well, Constance. So sorry you have to play Florence Nightingale tonight, but that bodes well for our Van here. I do hope your brother will be on the mend. Van, I really don't know how you landed such a pretty one. And smart too. If you're lucky, she'll tell us all what to do."

"Lovely to meet you, too, Constance," said Lally. The pretty pug-nosed strawberry blonde offered Constance a cool hand. "And thank you for the cosmetics. While I usually wear nothing, I will try. I suppose it's time I used a bit of color." She shrugged in a dismissive way.

"You don't need a thing on your skin. Only if you prefer. Lovely to meet you as well. I do hope to see you both again." Constance punctuated the "do" and the "hope" as she had heard it done in the new talking pictures and radio shows. Van walked her to the coatroom, leaving Lally and Topper at the table.

"I do hope to see you both again," Lally said, mimicking her affectation as she left the table. "She's quite attractive, but a bit common, don't you think, Tops?" Lally held up a ciggie as Topper lit it for her with his gold monogrammed lighter.

"I rather quite like her gumption. I think she is good for old Van. He's going to need someone to tell him what to do. Never had a mother, poor chap. She died in an auto accident when we were at Groton. He needs a pushy sort to motivate him. Better a blond beauty like her than Alexander Lefcourt's Jewish gal, what's her name . . . Guggenheim something or other. Poor chap. His father lost everything in the crash and now has to marry out."

"Well, that's understandable, since she's rich as Croesus." Lally idly wondered what she would do if her own father had been wiped out and she were forced to marry outside their set.

"We all have to make choices."

"Well, clearly . . ." Lally blew a smoke ring in the air to punctuate the thought.

"And I choose you." He kissed her. She pulled away and offered her cheek.

"And what about you, Lally? Do you want to be a thoroughly modern flapper and work?" Topper put his arm around her creamy shoulders, their pallor offset by her velvet gown.

"Yes. I rather think I want to work hard . . . at play," she said. "I think Father and Mummy would disown me if I had a *job*."

"Clearly." Topper nodded, thinking about the Sewards and their lovely and eligible daughter. Lally was pretty enough and had the right name and breeding. Why was he now thinking about Constance? She was a different sort, yes, but refreshing. He felt a bit guilty about not disclosing to Lally that his own father had lost much of their fortune in the crash, but he had been sworn to secrecy.

"Well, I rather liked her," Topper said. "I think she's smart and fun and perfect for Van. I think I will encourage it."

"I'm not so sure."

"Yes, but you're not exactly running after Van Wyke and neither are your girlfriends. The only girl who would pay him any attention in school was Patricia Porter Pringle. We used to call her 'Three Ps.' The old joke was, 'Here comes Three Ps. She has three Ps and five chins.' How can you compare someone like that to someone like her?"

"To her? A common social climber in last season's garish couture? At least Three Ps has breeding. She will make someone a very fine wife, I can assure you." Lally shook her blond pageboy in dissent. She was not about to break ranks with her group for a backwater Canadian!

"Perhaps. . . . The way I see it . . . he has the name and she has the looks. It's a story as old as time. Dance, shall we?" He offered a hand to his fiancée, and as she rose to the strains of the orchestra, he took in her ample behind. Lally, for all their protestations, wasn't exactly tall and thin. And so he fixated on the Seward Oil stock as he led her to the dance floor.

Way uptown, on West 100th Street, Constance wrapped herself in a sensible, blue-black woolen coat to hide her evening gown. She exited a filthy yellow cab and stepped into the police precinct. She was not happy about having to come, but she had little choice in the matter, having received a message before dinner. She knew exactly what she needed to do. After speaking softly to a number of officers, they all were quite respectful, but each shook his head after her as she went. "Poor girl," they said to one another. They had seen the familiar scene too many times before. Her brother, James, had been arrested for lewd behavior, and the poor, confused wife or girlfriend had come to bail him out.

"I'm here to see my fiancé, James McCalister. He was wrongfully arrested." Constance was grateful they had different last names. She knew that calling him fiancé instead of brother would help in this situation. Each one of the Irish or Italian cops had silently pointed her in a different direction. She was finally led to a holding pen on the third floor that was filled with derelicts, prostitutes, and seemingly homosexual men, a few of whom were pale, slight, and shivering and some of whom looked strangely quite masculine. All sat quietly behind bars, awaiting their fate. Each of the officers shook his head at the sight of her. Such a pretty girl, without a clue. The protestations were all too familiar. The "not my husband," "not my fiancé." "There must be some mistake. . . ."

The sheer terror and embarrassment at having to pick up a loved one who had been arrested for being a "pervert," a menace to society, a queer . . . would have been truly heartbreaking and devastating for one who did not know. Constance overheard one woman who was so disgusted she yelled obscenities at her husband in the cell, stormed out, and just left him there. But Constance knew perfectly well and thought the whole episode was a waste of time, not to mention highly annoying.

Police raids had become more commonplace among bars and bathhouses that catered to homosexual men, and James had simply been in the wrong place at the wrong time. He wouldn't tell Constance he was caught in the bathroom with his pants around his ankles. That would be too much information.

Constance explained to the officers that her beloved fiancé was only meeting a college friend for a drink. Of course, he had no idea it was a bar catering to perverts. The officers took pity on her and released him when she posted bail.

One cop, an older man named Kelly, said, "I wish I had my turn with that piece to show her what a real man could do. Poor, stupid girl engaged to a pansy."

Constance heard his crass comment but knew enough not to make a scene. She just wanted her brother released, so she bit her tongue. A police warden went to fetch James after her papers had been stamped, and she closed her eyes to replace the precinct with images of the Stork Club, to visually drown it out. James arrived and appeared visibly shaken.

"Darling," Constance said for effect in front of the warden. She hugged him and drew him close. "Follow my lead," she whispered.

"This is my fiancé." Constance kissed him lightly on the lips. "He was drawn into this whole episode unwittingly," she said loudly enough for all to hear. "They should all know what a real man you are and that you made love to me right before you met your friend for a drink." The officers nudged each other and snickered. Constance had given quite the performance.

They walked out of the holding area to whistles and catcalls.

"I think you're the next Sarah Bernhardt."

"As long as you're out of that place." She patted his hand in the taxi. "James, I will have our lawyer handle getting this dismissed, but can we agree you will be more discreet moving forward? I am dating Van Wyke now, you know. I can't imagine what he and his set would say if they knew."

"I'm sorry, Connie, I'll try to be better. I never thought I would be arrested for being me." He looked forlorn.

"Perhaps it would be best if you can find a nice young man like yourself and have him visit our apartment after dark. That might be safer," she advised.

"Yes, I agree. I'm sorry."

"No need to say you are sorry." Constance looked directly ahead at the traffic and held her brother's hand. And she thought about what would happen if she herself were arrested for her own proclivities.

12

A WILL AND A WAY

Melbourne, 1929

Josiah wasn't satisfied with domesticity or abundant profits. It all got plowed back into inventory anyway. She had no desire to be barefoot and pregnant so soon after getting married, and she had made it very clear to Jon Blake she was not going to be a stay-at-home wife and mother. He certainly did not want that for her either. After several years in business and an impressive track record, Josiah made an appointment at the local bank, seeking a loan to expand her operation. While she was making money hand over fist, selling her miracle creams and her new array of moisturizing lipsticks, she wanted a line of credit to open her second store. Unfortunately, she was summarily denied, as women rarely received bank loans at this time; it was uncommon enough that they owned their own property. Jon tried to calm her down by explaining that it was most likely due to news of the stock market crash in the United States. He assuaged her with a eulogy read from the column of the famous newspaperman Will Rogers.

"Rogers was in New York on Black Thursday," Jon said, smoking his cigar. "He writes, 'You had to stand in line to get a window to jump out of. . . .' I am telling you, Josie. It's not because you are a woman. No banks are lending now. I told you, I'll give you the money." His generous tone belied his lack of real funds.

"No. I vill not take any money from a man. This is my business." She sliced the air with a dramatic hand motion.

"And I'm your husband." He gathered her in her arms.

"You're still a man and the answer is no."

"Fine. Then don't complain."

"I don't explain and I don't complain." She stood, looking at him forcefully. "I vill find a way." She demurred his advances.

Jon was right: the news of the Wall Street crash, which followed the London crash in September, had reverberated around the globe and made even the bravest businessmen fearful. So Josiah did what any self-respecting businesswoman would have done: she pawned her engagement ring and sold the ruby ring from Katz's and added it to Jon's allowance. She had skimmed money each month from the food budget to create capital for her business—and this ended up a boon to her, as she had slowly achieved her financial goals and would always be the sole owner of her company.

Using her profits from Melbourne and the proceeds from her jewelry, Josiah set her sights on greener pastures. She opened the Sydney shop in just three months, and upon her return to Melbourne, after just one weekend of sleep, she agreed to accompany Jon on a business trip to London. That night, in a dream, she had an epiphany. In it, she stayed in London and achieved great success. English pounds were the leaves on trees. Josiah was not one to disregard the unconscious. She had welcomed and believed in signs her entire life. And so she decided she would accompany Jon to London, but she would not tell him she would not be returning to Australia. London, she now knew, was where money grew on trees. It was as simple as that. She devised a simple plan to install her younger sister Shayna, now called Sybil, whom she had brought over from Poland the previous spring, to oversee the Melbourne and Sydney stores. She would bring over her middle sister, Raisel, a year later. Their youngest sister, Chana, who was only six years old, would be too young to travel. Sybil, who had neither Josiah's sensuality nor her sauciness, had a photographic memory and an accountant's head for business. She had helped Josiah pack her trunks with astute efficiency. Everything to Sybil was numbers and Josiah knew her ledgers were in safe and capable hands.

"You have eight brassieres, five dresses, five pairs of shoes, fifteen pairs of underwear," she said, and they shared the unspoken knowledge that she would be changing her life forever.

Yet the sisters were not nostalgic or emotional. They had the genetic makeup of the ambitious and practical and were willing to do what it took to succeed.

The trip to London was very different from her first trip from Poland. First class versus steerage. Afternoon tea versus rationed water and biscuits. It was less a voyage than a well-deserved honeymoon with the luxury of sleep. The boat was a glorious ocean liner with seventy cabins and two dining rooms, one for the more well-heeled guests and another for everyone else. Within days, Jon was enjoying smoking cigars in the men's lounge and Josiah found herself bored and anxious on the ship. But everything changed in London.

"This has been divine," Jon said, stretching out on the bed, reading the *Times* in their hotel suite. Their three weeks had been a merry-go-round, some sightseeing and much time spent with Josiah visiting factories and storefronts, taking in the London competition, or lack thereof, while Jon met with the editorial staff and his American publishers, who had come for a global summit.

"I have to get back to Melbourne for the big conference next month. I'll book passage for us next week." He gazed at her lovingly. "But let me take you to see the Elgin Marbles at the British Museum before we depart."

"Jon, I want to talk." She turned down the gramophone in their suite.

"Talk?" he said. He slipped his arm out of his suspender.

"I am not going back, *liebchen*," Josiah said. "I am staying in London. I found a manufacturer."

"A manufacturer is more important than us?"

"I am pregnant," she said. "I want to have the baby here. Better medical care. Best to have English passport." She shrugged.

"This is how you tell me?" He looked at her with wild eyes.

"You married Josie. Don't be surprised. I just signed a lease in Mayfair. Best area. I will have the best store in London. And I had a new idea, Jon. It won't be just a store but . . . How can I explain it . . ."

She struggled to find the words, as she often did. "Not a *maison*, sounds like a brothel. But a salon, that is it. A salon with treatments for vomen's beauty." She laid out her case. "Not just lotions and potions but hairstyling and treatments."

"But what about me? It's my baby too. And you signed a lease without telling me?" He stared at her, in shock.

"You go back and oversee the operation with Sybil until baby is born. Ask for a transfer to London. You tell them your family is here now. London is the key to Europe and then America. We will make a fortune. The vomen are so ugly here. Bad skin and teeth."

"You're kidding me," he said.

"You think I kid. Ever?" The mad look on her face made her look more alluring. And worst of all, her plan made sense. He liked the salon idea.

"No," he said, looking down.

"Listen." She approached him and caressed his cheek. "I am not like the other vomen. You married for better or worse. Better is money. Worse is we spend a few months apart." She softened only about 1 percent as she saw how downcast he was at the news. It only made her more determined.

"You are cold-blooded, you know." He shook his head. "I really don't matter to you."

"Yes. You are the father. You give them the looks. I give them the money. Lucky kid. Pfssht." Josiah blew air out of the side of her mouth and put her hands on her hips. "Now I make love with you and you book your ticket and all is good." As usual, Jon Blake obeyed orders.

The next day Josiah gave Jon $1,000 in cash to mollify him. All in

$50 bills for effect, so it was a big stack. Once he left for Australia, she spent her days and nights opening her first salon in London. She had rented a floor in a town house in elite Mayfair and began to cultivate London society for handpicked clients and friendships. She decorated the salons in vivid colors, inspired by her travels. She extolled the virtues of her new idea: makeup that made you more beautiful, without looking as if you were wearing makeup! It was the ultimate magic trick, selling something invisible to make you look visibly better.

While in London, she had some difficulty getting reservations in the best restaurants and clubs. She noticed that if she shortened her last name to "Herz," she had better results. She tried to make a reservation at the Savoy as Josiah Herzenstein and they were full. Ten minutes later, she requested a reservation under Madame Josephine Herz and was given a table. Unfair? Yes. Stubborn and inflexible? No. Thus she became Josephine Herz. Whatever it took to get it done. Nothing and no one stood in the way of the newly christened Josephine Herz.

Josephine Herz Beauty was the world's first global cosmetic company, with its unforgettable slogan: Yours for beauty, Herz for Beauty. Years later, when asked why she didn't take her husband's name, she tartly replied, "No one would believe I looked like a Mrs. Blake. But when Madame Herz showed up, they knew I meant business."

Not only did she sell an excellent product, her newly christened salon would teach women how to be beautiful and confident, educating them about the application of her products and selling a variety of creams, powders, lipsticks, and, most important, dreams. London was a test drive, of course, for Paris and then for New York. Her salon idea was a new retail concept. Her temple of beauty would woo customers. The products were jewels to be displayed, discovered as though they had been buried within an Egyptian tomb and carted away like booty. Throughout, they displayed and "taught," "preached" the necessity of their products, presented like candies and chocolates in appealing clear bottles and jars.

Josephine brilliantly merged the basic allure of gloss and color with marketing designed to create a craving, then sell the fix du jour. Within the year her London salon would be profitable and she would open in Paris, in a limestone former embassy on the fashionable avenue Montaigne. Les Salons de Josephine were impressive, yet clean and clinical beyond the ornate façade. Not unlike the laboratories of Constance's pharmaceutical company, they were modern enough to exude an atmosphere of "health" and "science." But most of all, Josephine captured women's exploding interest in their place in society, both as objects to be admired and as forces in their own lives. It was a global phenomenon that would eventually become the new American workforce. And while Jon Blake returned to Australia without his wife, Herz Beauty was born.

13

MICKEY

Across the sea and much farther downtown, an unlikely competitor was honing his game, a vendor-cum-boxer from a long line of Jewish fruit sellers and lotharios. He liked them in every shape and color, Mickey Heronsky liked to say, "and not just the fruit!" A tough, exceptionally handsome Jew from the Lower East Side, he was often compared to the actor John Garfield later in life. Mickey was indiscriminate in his love for women. He was discriminatory only about their beauty.

His critical eye was honed first on the mean streets of the Lower East Side, where his father and his grandfather sold produce, first out of carts and then at a freestanding and well-known fruit stand and store. Fruit vendors went back two generations in Mickey's family, his grandfather founding the best of the crop on Norfolk Street. Carefully stacked rows of dewy, plump fruit had long provided the staples for the wives and babushkas of the Lower East Side. Mickey had worked for his grandfather and later his father and had learned the ropes of the business. But he had learned a more valuable skill than sales: the art of picking perfectly ripe, fresh fruit and selling it to women of all shapes and sizes.

Over the years, he had learned how to pick the cream of the crop, drawing on his naturally handsome face—square jaw, thick black hair, wide-set sleepy eyes, and rippling biceps. He enjoyed a similarly burgeoning cadre of women. Though he grew up with the traditional Jewish accent—mouths that formed *aws* to sound more like *ew* and struggled to make a perfect *r*—he had done his best to polish the accent over time, although ill-pronounced words would come tumbling out to produce a somewhat comic effect. Yet he perfected the clothes. And the hair. And the physique, with frequent trips to a boxing club. The success of the family business and a keen eye for the fashions and styles of the times had helped to amass a peerless image and the wardrobe to match. He was known as the Valentino of Norfolk Street.

Though he was reared on the fruit trade, this was not to be his life's work. He preferred a more glamorous clientele than old women in scarfs doing their daily shopping rounds. Two things would influence Mickey more than anything else: the Depression and the silver screen. The recent stock market crash had created fear, causing his business to drop off dramatically. Cinema had introduced him to something more tantalizing than any customer, more valuable than the stacks of coins his family amassed over the last forty years, more perfect and delicious than any ripe tomato or plum. Mickey, like many of his customers, could escape the drudgery and cruelty of the Lower East Side and revel in the platinum blondes and dinner parties of the Park Avenue set he could only dream about. The smell of rotting fruit and herring from the fish store across the street was masked by the madcap Clara Bow and the soon-to-be-famous platinum-blond Jean Harlow. This style and glamour would influence every move and every decision over the course of his life. And he, like others, was entranced by the celluloid: silk-sheathed blondes answering glittering telephones in the bubble bath or descending a curved Park Avenue staircase with élan. Not the cold-water walk-ups of his youth.

Later, when Mickey founded his own cosmetics company, Heron Cosmetics, he would embrace the ways and fashions of the English, like many of his successful friends in Hollywood. Suits from Savile Row. Huntsman & Sons and English brogues. He favored an English secretary to answer his phone. He said it "classed up the joint." And he was most often found in a double-breasted pin-striped suit. His gold monogrammed lighter was Asprey. He smoked a Cuban cigar, and when he grew successful enough to have a car, his chauffeur drove a Rolls because "Bentleys are for queers and broads." If it ever felt odd or arbitrary to Mickey that he had more of an affinity to the British culture than his own, he reminded himself of the common ground. The Brits, like Mickey, understood the importance of a caste system, and the Brits also understood the concept of projecting a royal image. He would often joke to his employees and lackeys, "Dress British and think Yiddish." And much later, he would wisely make the long, elegant white-blue heron the symbol of his company.

When Mickey was sixteen and his father passed away, he dutifully took over his family's fruit business, borrowing the tricks he had learned from years in sales: the importance of a beautiful display, the magnetic power of charm, the value of loyalty, and, of course, the actual names and numbers of his customers—and their daughters. Each of these women was, first and foremost, a customer. Second, she was a guide to the needs of the younger, changing generation. Third, when treated right, she was an electric force of marketing, waiting with implicit potential to sing his praises to her friends. Finally, and most important, she was a product herself, an object of beauty and desire for him to covet, consume, enjoy, and, when the stars aligned, share a drink and, ideally, his bed.

The affair between Mickey and CeeCee started as most affairs do— with ardent glances and unspoken tension simmering for weeks before reaching the boiling point. Appraising glances roamed from mouth to blouse to hips. Appreciative smiles turned to flattering comments. Flattering comments turned to the occasional brush of the hand. And then, in the usual fashion, the request of a phone number and then the inevitable.

Despite a lifetime of appreciation of women, Mickey was most beguiled by Miss CeeCee Lopez. He had always considered himself a card-carrying member of the Women's Party, and his devotion to CeeCee was no different. But his infatuation with CeeCee grew quickly from admiration to obsession. Never before had Mickey found so many virtues in one woman: a beautiful supple body, a perfect face, and the most incredibly delicious smooth skin. She was intelligent, quick, and funny to boot. It was safe to say that Mickey, an experienced boxer, was down for the count.

Mickey's interest in CeeCee started as it did with most women, as simple curiosity. He surveyed her as he did every other woman who stopped to peruse his fruit at the stand. He observed how she handled the plump peaches, checking for blemishes on the surface and their firmness. As she did, Mickey assessed CeeCee's own curves. She looked perfectly irresistible to him in a fitted short-sleeved cotton blouse and an A-line cotton skirt that hugged a robust rear. He noticed the craving, the coveting, the must-have desire that accosted him every time he faced an intriguing prospect. But in CeeCee, Mickey found a quality that he had not known he prized, a sense of humor.

"May I help you?" he asked.

She did not look up. She did not, in fact, need his help. "I'm fine." She didn't take the bait.

"Those peaches are perfect right now," he said. "Freshest I've ever had."

"They're not quite ripe," she said, more to herself than to Mickey. She was familiar with the tricks of the salesman and had no need for enticements. As a housekeeper in a bustling home, she had long been tasked with the shopping and management of the home's weekly inventory. She knew what she needed and preferred not to dally.

"I have another box in the back," he said. "Would you like me to bring them out?"

"No, thank you," she said.

"I have some beautiful plums. Some strawberries, fresh from up-state." He tried his best to turn on the charm.

CeeCee finally turned from the fruit to Mickey. It was clear she would have to make a quick refusal to fend off further advances. But she was surprised, when she looked up at Mickey, to find such a handsome face. His rectangular jaw, his thick lips, and his gnarled forehead conjured a strong, inviting tree. His jet-black curls were untamed, lustrous, and inviting. He didn't look Jewish, more Italian, even with a bit of Irish, the short, upturned pug nose and his lips reflected the majesty of some of the black jazz stars she had met. She knew he too couldn't place her background. It was a common theme.

Mickey stared at CeeCee, taken by her lovely face. The symmetry, the almond-shaped eyes, the luscious smile, the smooth complexion, the brilliant white row of perfectly arranged teeth. Was she Spanish, French? Clearly somewhere the sun shone.

"What are you making?" he asked her, smiling now with the knowledge of her interest.

"A peach pie," she said. "For my boss's client who is in from the South and loves peach pie."

"Are you a cook?"

"No," she said, "I do everything."

"Everything?" He smiled.

"Everything."

"Not fair," he said.

"And why is that," she said.

"Because I want everything too. Especially a girl who can do every-thing."

"I think . . . you deserve everything you get." She eyed him, render-ing him speechless.

The exchange of money and the backroom peaches were not only a chance to secure her number, but an opportunity that Mickey did not waste to grasp CeeCee's hand and give her a bag of free ripe plums in addition to the peaches.

"Come back tomorrow?" he said. It had the inflection of a question, but it was, in fact, a statement. "I'll have something even better for you."

CeeCee smiled, accepting the gift and the invitation. She turned and headed back to her apartment to make the pie for Constance's meeting, nursing her smile as she walked, not unaware of the delight she felt in Mickey's enticements. She felt the heat of his eyes on her back as she walked away. She returned the next week, curious to see his next offering. He invited her to join him for dinner that night and, for the next three years, the two hardly spent a night apart.

14

SOMETHING BORROWED

New York City, 1930

Harald Forrester-Smith, the venerable Park Avenue lawyer, sat in his sun-faded leather chair in his oak-paneled office. With ramrod-straight posture, he shook his large, defined head. In profile, with the sun pouring in on another day in the gritty city, he looked like a marble bust of a disdainful Roman emperor. He had seen many things in his career as a lawyer, but this request was entirely unfamiliar. He scratched his impressive thatch of white hair and slipped the thick gold pocket watch out of his vest pocket. "Clearly not responsible." He flipped through the papers he had received on his desk. This was a new, vexing generation indeed, impulsive, demanding, and frivolous. One would have thought the stock market crash the year before would have brought these two young men to their senses, but no—it seemed to have had the opposite effect. He looked with dismay at his watch again, which he held in the palm of his hand.

One half hour late, the sheepish Van Wyke and his wingman, the dashing, degenerate Topper Stanton, arrived looking as though they were recovering from a bachelor party; at least, this would have offered some explanation as to why they were hungover on a Monday morning and not coming directly from work. Harald had seen the look before and shook his head once again. Decadent. Dissolute and drunk, no less!

Apologies for their tardiness were extended, with Van stumbling into the leather high-backed wing chair and Topper tucking his wrinkled and stained white shirt into his pants. Van squirmed in the chair like an errant fifth grader. Strong black coffee and tomato juice were immediately summoned and produced on a highly polished silver tray by an efficient and stern grey-haired secretary. Her pernicious glare as she handed the young men their beverages set Harald Forrester-Smith's legendary ire into action as they both surveyed the general wreckage. Silent, withering looks were exchanged, at which point his secretary shook her head and sniffed, turning away on her capable and sturdy heels, making a clucking sound as she left. The sound only damned them further.

"I am so, so sorry, Harald. Father would never approve of our tardiness and my current state. It is unconscionable. I am truly sorry." At least Van had good manners, as opposed to the unrepentant playboy Topper Stanton.

"And what say you, Mr. Stanton?" he asked. "I don't assume in your condition either of you is coming from the office?"

"We were actually with a mutual out-of-town client last night," Van offered. "He was eager to see the sights."

"And I am sure you were both marvelous tour guides."

"Well, let's just say the Statue of Liberty wasn't the only woman we showed him," Topper joked. "You know what they say . . . 'When in Rome.'" They both cracked up laughing.

"Mr. Stanton, please do me a favor." Harald peered at him through his wire-frame eyeglasses.

"Of course, Mr. Forrester-Smith."

"Tell me a joke?"

"A joke? Are you serious?"

"Yes, tell me a joke."

He and Van looked at each other quizzically but he shook his head and did as he was told.

"Well, let's see. I just flew in from Chicago. Boy, are my arms tired." He and Van dissolved into peals of laughter.

"So that is your joke?"

"Yes, sir."

"Well, Mr. Stanton. It is clear to me that you will never earn a living as a comedian. You don't possess the talent of Mr. Chaplin or Buster Keaton. So I would advise you to become more serious. And for the record, Van, I was young once, but please have some coffee and come to your senses. Life decisions are at hand for you both, and you need to be alert." He shook his head so hard they saw spittle fly from the corner of his mouth.

'Yes, of course. I am sorry. We both are. Aren't we, Topper?" Van shot Topper a look. Topper nodded.

"Apology accepted. As you know, I have been a trusted adviser to both sets of your parents and your late mother's estate, Van. I know what close friends you are, so while this may appear a bit unorthodox, may I speak freely to both of you together since your parents urged me to and I serve as trustee for you both individually?"

"Yes, of course. Nothing is between us."

"Good. First, I want to congratulate you both on your recent engagements. It is quite respectable you both have found love, and hopefully you will both settle down to responsibility through the institution of marriage. I understand it is a different world today with you young people. However, I want you to know that marriage is not something to be taken lightly. It's the most important decision one makes in life, and it has far-reaching effects on family and children. What is the moral character of the young lady, et cetera, et cetera. I personally do not believe in prenuptial agreements for first-time marriages. I know your parents have told me you will not have one with Lally, Topper. However, Van, in all my years this is the first time

I have ever been confronted with a situation like the one I am presented with today. And I must say . . . I am at a loss." He grasped the air with his wizened, veined hand.

"And what would that be?" said Van.

"Now, I have had young men and their families demand a prenuptial agreement before their son marries someone unsuitable such as a showgirl, but I have not seen a case where a young woman . . . namely one"—he peered down at a sheaf of papers for confirmation—"Constance Gardiner and her lawyer, are actually asking for us to furnish her with a prenuptial agreement excluding all your rights and claims to her business, Gardiner Cosmetics, in the event of a divorce. Is that correct?"

"Yes, sir."

"Van, this raises so many important questions. Namely, are you aware that you are marrying a businesswoman? There are no businesswomen. Are you aware that your wife intends to be working when she gets married and that if you divorce, you have no legal rights or claims to her business? Van, have you read what you are getting into?"

Van's face turned a beet purple. "I am very well aware. Constance is a brilliant young businesswoman and that's one of the reasons I find her so . . . interesting. Her company is already doing hundreds of thousands of dollars in turnover."

"That may be so, but as your trustee, I have to ask: Does one want to be married to a woman who works? Lally, as an example, has a small income off a trust. She comes from a fine, notable, and respected family and will not be working. Are you sure about this woman, Van?"

"Yes, entirely, Harald."

"He understands," Topper offered. "Van is the one who doesn't want to work. It's a match made in heaven." They both guffawed.

"I don't think this is very funny at all. What will happen when there are children? Don't you think they would find the situation very confusing?"

"I assume we will have nannies. My mother was hardly available."
Van shrugged.

"Your mother was a noted hostess and a bridge player."

"Yes, she went to and hosted a great many parties and played cards.
She was hardly around. What is the difference between a woman never
being around because of card parties or cosmetic meetings?"

"There is a big difference."

"Such as?"

"Your mother didn't work. She was admired in her circle for her
many talents."

"Harald, with all due respect, I admire Constance for her intelligence, not her bridge or golf score. And she is beautiful and, if you
must know, I never had anyone of her caliber pay attention to me."

"You are aware of the Wyke name and legacy and the prestige it
brings to the table?"

"Yes, but my looks haven't brought many women to my table," Van
said, looking down.

"I see." Harald Forrester-Smith at last understood as he studied the
two young men: the handsome Topper and the prematurely balding
and lumpy Van. Still, he had to press on. "Van, are you sure?"

"More than anything. It's her business and if she wants to protect
it, so be it."

"Well, I do hope she appreciates how forward-thinking you are. I
do insist, however, that if you sign her prenuptial agreement, she has
to sign one for you as well, that your trust is yours if the marriage
dissolves. What is good for the goose . . ."

"I think that is fair. Thank you, Harald. That is very good advice.
However, anything after the marriage and children should be considered fifty-fifty."

"Fine. And you, young man." He gazed at Topper. "Sit up straight
and stop slouching."

"Yes, sir."

"Can we discuss your situation in front of Van?"

"Yes, Van knows of everything."

"Well," he sighed. "You are aware, Topper, that your father called me and your trust is no more since the crash?"

"Yes, of course."

"Does Lally know?"

"I'm not sure." He looked away, now serious.

"Well, I suggest you tell her before you walk down the aisle. The poor girl needs to know the truth before you marry, Topper. It would be unfair." He paused for dramatic effect. "I have known you since you were a small boy. I will tell you how I see it. You have it all: looks, personality, good breeding. But you, young man, are lazy. And if you are both not up front about your realities, your expectations, you are actually doing a great disservice to these young ladies. Have I made myself clear?"

"Yes, thank you, sir." They both nodded.

"And when will the weddings take place?"

"Topper and Lally will have a big wedding in Locust Valley at Christmas. Constance doesn't want a fuss, so we are planning on getting married at City Hall and going to the Breakers for a few days for our honeymoon. Topper will of course be my best man."

"And vice versa," Topper said.

"It's nice to see such close friends. I want to be clear that I had no intention of raining on anyone's parade. That said, I do hope you will both give some serious thought to what I said. I have seen good marriages fail for less."

"Thank you, sir. It's been a pleasure and an honor to have your guidance." Van looked Harald in the eye. "And thank you for the coffee. I am feeling much better. We greatly appreciate your advice."

"I always try to do the right thing for the families," he said.

"You have more than executed your duties." They stood and shook his hand before walking out of the office past his secretary, who "harrumphed" at them as they passed.

As the chauffeur opened the door to Van's father's Packard, Van and Topper fell into the back seat and burst into hysterical laughter, pulling out their hidden flasks of gin.

"Hair o' the dog." They toasted each other.

They took turns mimicking certain phrases of Harald's, which prompted more toasting, laughter, and swigs of gin.

"Old fool. Here's how I see it . . ." Topper grinned, his bright white teeth and tan rosy cheeks suggesting eternal youth, protection from the vicissitudes of life.

"We are both marrying women for their looks and money, et cetera, et cetera." They both broke into sidesplitting laughter. "And they are marrying us for our venerable names as they were raised to do."

"Here, here. To the girls."

"To the girls!" At that moment, Van asked his driver to pull over. The car pulled up to the curb just in time for Van to vomit. Topper followed suit.

15

LONDON CALLING

London, 1930

Josephine paced her elegantly furnished and newly rented Belgravia study and read her sister Sybil's letter with careful deference. After reading it a second time, she laid it calmly on her antique French writing desk, her Vionnet dress catching on the bronze ormolu and creating a run in the skirt that she tried to smooth, despite the news. The entire town house, which she had rented from an impoverished lord who had gone bust in the crash, was so ornate it seemed the type of place that would immediately stifle feelings, with its plush carpets and ornate boiserie. The house conveyed true grandeur except for three or four "holes on the walls" featuring faded empty spaces where a Reynolds or two had been recently plucked and sold. She poured a small glass of schnapps and steadied herself, her stormy eyes convulsing as she digested the contents of the note—and the liquid. When she had downed the last burning drop, she took the small, clear glass and threw it into the fireplace, watching it explode into razor-like shards. Not even a passing affair! In less than a year, Jonathan had a pregnant mistress in Melbourne. And with her money to boot!

While she knew she had banished Jon to Australia, and essentially had cut herself off from him physically, it made little difference to her.

Jon Blake was a *khamer*, a cheater, and a donkey. She was working night and day for her, for him, for them, and for their soon-to-be-born child, and he had betrayed her. He had dashed her simple dreams. All because he was lazy; a *shikker*, a drunk. A good-looking good-for-nothing! And she had been a fool as well, never questioning his ever-increasing requests for money. The shame was deafening, as she knew her uncle and aunt were relishing the news.

Jonathan's own letter arrived days later with a profuse apology. He had physical needs and she had created the situation. She was cruel and not a wife to him. That said, he wrote, he was stupid, horrified, and contrite. A low-class girl who worked in a saloon and meant nothing to him had seduced him, entrapped him. He would do anything, he pleaded, to save the marriage. He loved his wife, feared her, had never met anyone quite like her, and was desperate to one day see his only true child, the son or daughter she was carrying. He had paid the girl to go far away and would never see her or the baby again. It was nothing; he had been a fool, a drunk, and would change his ways. Josephine chose the one thing she knew would hurt the most: silence. She wouldn't write him or speak to him by telephone or send his allowance. She would wait until her own baby was born to see if she had any feelings left.

Sybil would come for the birth. She would take Jon's place, and he would have to stay and help oversee the operation if he wanted any chance of reconciling with her. She had just brought over her middle sister, Raisel—now called Rachel—and Sybil had trained her to look after the Melbourne store. Josephine's father had once told her that the original Mayer Rothschild had five sons whom he dispersed through-out Europe to create an international banking family. Josephine never forgot this tidbit. Only Chana, too young to travel, remained behind with her mother.

While Jonathan's son was born prematurely, Josephine's was born late, as if he didn't want to be pried free of such a powerful life force. In typical fashion, Josephine worked up to the very last minute in the shop in Mayfair and, when she felt the labor pains, called Sybil to take over her duties at the shop. She checked herself into the hospital for the delivery with the same efficiency as going into the stockroom to handle reorders.

Eight days later, she had a small bris with Sybil and a few new friends who were "sympathetic" to her religion and the shop. She knew deep down that while business was strong, it had been a bit hard going cracking the fashionable London set, as she had not entirely penetrated the inner core of London's carriage trade. Yet she was making major inroads with a few fashionable women of her kind: Lady de Rothschild, a formidable new client who had sent many of her friends for skin treatments; and Madame Marks, whose husband, Michael Marks, co-founder of the Marks & Spencer department store, was a Polish Jew and had kindly recommended the mohel who would perform the ritual circumcision. During the ceremony Sybil cried for their father, who had died years earlier in the influenza epidemic as the rabbi gave the boy his Jewish name, Menachim Ephraim, honoring both her father, Menachim, and Jonathan's grandfather Frank. At the last minute, touched as she was by the infant's crystal-clear blue eyes and recalling her original promise, Josephine had decided to honor Jonathan's side of the family.

"I never break my word," she said when Sybil complimented her on the lovely gesture. In polite English society, however, the boy would be called Miles Frank Blake-Herz.

Two days later she was back at work, and one month later she had slimmed down to her original figure. With a vast array of capable British nannies on hand, Josephine found that her fury and passion for work had only just kicked in.

The door chime gave the subtle and lovely hint of entering customers. It was Josephine's favorite sound, next to that of the cash register drawer opening and closing and the sound of her staff making change. The door chimed twice, and a slight, fair-haired gentleman of about twenty-seven entered.

"Madame Herz, please," he said.

"I can help you, sir," said the front store manager as Josephine sat quietly tallying the day's receipts. She surveyed the man's expensive suit of clothes.

"No, only Madame Herz will do, if you please." He seemed to be somewhat uncomfortable in a woman's environment. "I can return if she is not here," he said, playing with his gold signet pinky ring.

"No, she's here. I'll get her for you, Mister . . . ?"

"Cavendish. Thank you."

"Yes, sir." She smiled faintly, somewhat disappointed at losing the chance to wait on him.

After a few moments, Josephine smoothed her skirt and entered the front of the store.

"Yes, Mr. Cavendish, how can I help you?" She saw he was somewhat startled by her youthful appearance. She was equally taken aback by his. Josephine's lips and face seemed fuller and her figure more voluptuous since the birth and she knew it.

"I . . . well, this is somewhat impolite . . . ," he stammered.

"Go on, I am not a proper English lady," Josephine said. She had an inkling why he was here. It had happened before.

"My friend, who is a client of yours, Mrs. de Lorraine, once told me of a special cream you gave her for . . ." He paused. "Indiscreet . . . moments." He looked down.

"Oh, that." Josephine saw his reddened cheeks and decided to have some fun with the well-brought-up young man.

"Yes, I only give it to my best clients. To ease the pain of intercourse." She shocked him with her straightforward language about the sexual act. No society woman would ever discuss sex with a man she didn't know without using a euphemism.

"Would you . . . I mean . . . is there . . . um . . . some of that special cream I can buy directly?" he asked.

"Why not get it from Mrs. de Lorraine?" Josephine smirked, knowing that Lianne de Lorraine was a well-paid courtesan, popular among the city's elite young nobles.

"Well, that's just it. Mrs. de Lorraine and I . . . are no longer acquainted and I would like to give the gift of that cream to another lady. A friend who seems to be . . . experiencing pain," he whispered, and then blushed, sensing a comrade-in-arms.

"I usually don't do this." Josephine abruptly went back to the stockroom and took out two slim, dark blue vials of a special lubricant she had invented using mineral oil with a secret dash of olive oil. She kept her special stock stashed away and gave it out as a special gift to those of her clients who were experiencing marital problems or the inconvenience of menopause. She returned with the vials and placed them in a small shopping bag, arranged with tissue paper.

"Mr. Cavendish, I want you to know I don't sell this. I just give it to my clients when I hear they have problems." Josephine wanted to be clear she was not in the sexual-aid business.

"Thank you so much." He looked around at the impressive shop, lined and stocked with an array of high-end beauty creams and cosmetics, as well as the newly built treatment room for European massage and facials and an area with a hairstylist.

"My pleasure," she said, handing him the small mauve bag with ribbon handles.

"How much do I owe you, Madame Herz?" The young man wiped the perspiration from his upper lip, to Josephine's delight.

"Nothing at all."

"Are you quite sure?" he said, not knowing what was appropriate.

"Quite. Just send your new friend to me. I put my card in the bag and tell her to ask for me, Mr. Cavendish, and I will take care of all her needs." She paused. "And yours. Since you seem to have a bigger problem on your hands," she said in a saucy manner that made him blink twice as she looked down at his trousers.

"Why, thank you, Madame Herz." He seemed relieved and kissed her hand in the European style. "May I ask you an impertinent question?" He adjusted his silk cravat before leaving, staring at her ample bosom.

"Of course. There are no impertinent questions in my book."

"Is there a Mr. Herz?" he asked.

"No, not technically anymore."

"Meaning?"

"Meaning, I am still deciding."

"I see." He nodded. "I do hope to see you again, Madame Herz." He looked at her firmly before opening the door and leaving the salon. "I didn't realize how beautiful the woman behind the beauty business was." He bowed slightly, leaving Josephine in a flushed state as the door closed behind him.

"Well, that was interesting." Josephine seemed slightly overcome by the encounter. "I wonder who he is?"

"Madame Herz, you don't know? That's Viscount Cavendish. He is the Duke of Cambridge. He is in all the papers. . . . You know he is fourth in line for the throne."

"Really? Well, he was first in line for lubricant at Herz Beauty." They both laughed out loud.

The next day, Josephine received a personal note and invitation to dine with the duke at his private apartments. And while she would never have accepted a month earlier, she decided she was still a woman and, more important, that it would be good for business. Within weeks Josephine was whispered to be the mistress of the Duke of Cambridge, and better yet, every fashionable lady in London was suddenly her client.

16

EMPRESS

London, 1932

In an opulent yet discreet Edwardian room in a grand town house off Mayfair, Josephine was on top. Literally. She rode Cavendish like a stallion as he whinnied and brayed.

"I have to turn off the damned radio. It's ruining my mood." The duke got up and walked, stark naked, to the wooden art deco radio cabinet and snapped off the BBC with disdain. "That's all I need to hear about during lovemaking . . . crazy Churchill talking about the dangers of German rearmament. Kills the mood." He groaned as Josephine admired his tall, lean body, all white, pink, and blond. She thought his uncircumcised penis to be odd but overlooked the extra flap of skin for the betterment of her business and social goals.

So what if he has an extra flap of skin, she told herself; I have an extra flap of brain. She enjoyed this joke alone, reminding herself to tell it to Sybil, who would be mortified.

"But you, my dear. I can't get enough of my brilliant Jewess." He surveyed Josephine, spread out on the bed, her ample figure and high, lush breasts arranged so sensually, he thought she was built for sex. But it was Josephine who took control, unlike the well-raised English ladies he knew who were all so passive. And this was the secret ingredient to his passion. It ignited his lust when she called out positions and made simple yet strict demands.

"On your back, boy."

He immediately lowered himself on top of her, to a small smack of her hand.

"You don't listen, you von't get anything," she said. "On your back. . . ." Josephine smiled and watched as he obeyed her wishes and desires, as did most men. Josephine was a commanding presence in her store and in the bedroom. She raised herself on top of him and worked away to his delight, the small of her back slightly damp with perspiration.

"You know, darling," he said afterward, "I can't get enough of you. You're simply not like the other girls. You won't even let me buy you a trinket."

"I buy you, Duke," she said bluntly.

He laughed. "You know, you have the bearing of an empress." He tossed his blond hair. "And if I could bottle your scent, I would."

"Thank you, darling. And you would be better not to eat salmon before you see me," she observed.

It was in this moment that Josephine had an epiphany, a eureka moment of sorts. A scent. This was what was missing from her brand. The star missing in the Herz firmament. A fragrance for the store. Cavendish had given her her next idea. He may as well have paid her in gold.

"Listen, darling." Josephine stood from the bed and slipped into her black lace brassiere. "I think the time has come when we must say goodbye." There was no emotion in her voice.

"Goodbye? I was just saying *hello*." Cavendish sat up in the bed. He would not let go so easily. He had never met a woman like Josephine Herz. Smart, sharp, and magnetic. Sexy and original. Of course, he couldn't marry her. She was already married, and not Church of England. But that didn't stop him from wanting her. On the contrary, he had never wanted anyone quite so badly.

"Listen, darling." She had him help her with the clasp of her deco diamond Cartier bracelet, the baguettes arranged in a stunning geometric pattern dotted with cabochon emeralds. It had been a gift to herself from herself. "My husband is coming to London. Miles needs a father and I have decided to forgive him."

"When does the old chap arrive?" Cavendish confronted the slow realization that his favorite liaisons were about to end.

Josephine looked at him and marveled at his perfect features. His lovely peaches-and-cream complexion, more akin to that of a milk-maid than a man. His perfectly formed muscular chest, his defined abdominal pack. "On Friday."

"I see." He moved toward her and gathered her in his arms. "I have never met nor will I ever meet another woman like you."

"Yes, you will. There are plenty of us now." She was touched but somewhat aghast at his romantic side.

"No, you, my dear, are an original."

"Well, yes, that is true." Josephine started applying her very own lipstick in the round deco mirror.

"Can I still see you? After he arrives—for an assignation?" He took his white shirt off the wooden hanger and put it on slowly.

"Once he is here I am back to being a sadie. . . ." She smiled slowly.

"Sadie?" He looked perplexed.

"Sadie, the married lady." She rolled her eyes and he laughed. "Don't vorry, though, I can fulfill one of your requests." She kissed him.

"What's that?"

"You shall see," she said cryptically. She walked to the door, turned as he followed her like a puppy, and bestowed a final, impossibly romantic kiss.

Six months later, despite his stopping by the store to beg her to rendezvous, Josephine spurned all invitations. Jon Blake was now ensconced in the town house with Miles. Their reconciliation had been civil and tidy and in her son's best interest since she was working constantly. Josephine spent the next several months immersed in research and development, creating a signature fragrance. Once it was done and she approved the scent and the packaging, she sent a sample bottle, wrapped in tissue paper, with a note to the duke. Cavendish saw the small distinctive bag with the Herz Beauty logo when his footman delivered the package. He opened the present and note with haste. It was classic Josephine, he thought, as he sat at his campaign desk and read her curved yet strong script.

"Dear Duke, you said you wanted to bottle my scent. Here it is." He unwrapped the frosted bottle of her new fragrance and gazed at it, shaking his head. Only Josephine could pull this off. He smiled and spritzed the *parfum* on his wrist. It was so potent and feminine he almost swooned at the distinctive scent.

Not to mention the name of her new fragrance.

Empress Josephine.

17

STAR EMPLOYEE

New York City, 1934

Four years had passed, slowly and quickly at the same time. It seemed like yesterday and yet, a lifetime away. Constance's marriage four years earlier to Van was a functional, businesslike affair. She worked seven days a week, he spent a few hours each day at the family office on Park Avenue and most of his time playing polo or golf or sailing at his clubs in the company of men. They met up for a dinner party or a night on the town on Saturday evenings. Once a month Constance would submit and allow him the privilege of fumbling atop her supine and immobile body as he grunted and pumped away. She steeled herself with gin, and while he was atop, she ran the monthly numbers in her head. She would often recall her bawdy American grandmother, who once counseled her about marriage and sex. "Constance," she said, "when you get married if you want to keep a man, just lay back and *spread 'em for Old Glory*." She had that goal in mind and was achieving it. It was fair to say that Constance Gardiner, the ever-so-focused Mrs. Van Wyke, had reached her goal and in doing so had become formidable.

The business had grown as well, with five offices and fifty employees. Some full- and some part-time, but fifty nonetheless.

It was not long into her tenure at Gardiner Cosmetics before CeeCee Lopez made herself indispensable. Her organizational skills were impeccable and her natural flair for management brought calm where there had been chaos before. Though she began her post at the front desk, answering the phone and ushering guests into the expanding office with offers of cold and hot beverages, it was not long before she had advanced to a full-fledged administrative position once there was more staff. CeeCee was a natural leader. She liked people and she understood them. She knew how to put them at ease, how to make them feel cared for, and how to play on their weaknesses and strengths. It wasn't that CeeCee set out to identify a person's Achilles' heel, but she had a highly attuned intuitive sense of what people yearned for most, and she employed this, consciously or not, to excellent effect.

Though Constance hated to lose CeeCee's presence as the first face of Gardiner Cosmetics when clients, vendors, and customers entered the office, she quickly saw that CeeCee's strengths were best utilized in a role with more responsibility. Within months of her employment and the growth of the brand, CeeCee was promoted to office manager, and six months later, she was promoted to director of new products. CeeCee was blessed with the same intuitive understanding of business that she had with people. She was able to assess a marketing plan with a similarly searing eye, sussing out the weaknesses and the strengths—and communicating both in a few words. She quickly became Constance's secret weapon in almost every arena, from long-term planning for the brand to tweaks on specific products. Her best and strongest asset was being able to root out and train the ever-expanding army of Gardiner Girls with Molly; understanding who would be a leader in her local area; who possessed the ambition, social skills, and confidence to become a best-selling door-to-door saleswoman. Constance's dependence on her added a certain heft to the relationship.

CeeCee also had practical knowledge that Constance found invaluable. As the inventor of her own pomade for African American girls, CeeCee had a strong perspective and vast knowledge of hair. CeeCee intimately understood the importance of hair in a black woman's life, the cultural weight placed on managing, cleaning, straightening, and "taming" her hair. She knew the hours and dollars black women spent in salon chairs. And she understood the importance, the necessity, of these hours to conform to white people's—and potential employers'—expectations of a black woman in this society. The chain of community, as one woman would do another woman's hair, was a crucial lesson she brought to the training of the Gardiner Girls. And she stressed the camaraderie, the sense of sisterhood and community. While her focus was on her job at Gardiner, she hoped one day to empower other black women with better solutions for the care of their hair. Not all women had enjoyed the mobility that CeeCee had, advancing from a youthful environment of oppression to one of opportunity. She hoped to have her own company one day. But for now, her position at Gardiner Cosmetics was the perfect way to learn the trade, to bolster her understanding for a future business. It also made CeeCee the ultimate resource for Constance; CeeCee was not just an assistant but a fellow inventor. Appreciation quickly grew into affection, and dependence gradually grew into need.

It was not long into her employment that Constance began to harbor feelings for CeeCee. The difference CeeCee made to everyday life could not be overstated. The order she brought to necessary tasks, the sense of calm that she brought to the office, the feeling of relief Constance felt in her presence, was hard to deny. Molly and the other women in the office all enjoyed and respected her input and company. When CeeCee took over as office manager, things just felt better. The concurrent surge in revenue could not be written off to coincidence, and Constance rewarded her with a small raise and then a bonus.

The Gardiner Cosmetics business began a rapid expansion. Pharmacies and department stores all vied for the best-selling face creams and cosmetics. The next frontier, her Gardiner Girl door-to-door model, was gaining strength and attention in the local press. Now everyday women could earn money, help their husbands, their children, and themselves with much-needed funds. CeeCee had helped Constance develop a simple product kit. Most Gardiner Girls who could not afford the kit and wanted to be in business would commit to a simple and affordable down payment and pay for the kit over time through profits from the products. And once they did they were able to earn money and work part-time, which allowed the average wife and mother to drop off their children at school, pick them up, and make dinner while being able to work a few hours a day for the needed extra income. It was hailed as liberating, innovative, and a breakthrough, even a movement. And it meant hiring women and educating them from products to sales. . . . Navigating this transition was crucial, and Constance could not have faced these challenges without CeeCee Lopez. Though her title and duties had changed, CeeCee was more truthfully a partner in the Gardiner business and it was not long before Constance seemed to require CeeCee's input on every important decision.

That this dependence might be more emotional than professional occasionally occurred to Constance, but she was loath to admit this to anyone, most of all herself. It had not escaped her that she might harbor an attraction to strong and independent women. Indeed, she ran in a circle that embraced the value and modernity of such an arrangement. But the world was far from wholeheartedly embracing such a lifestyle. Rather, hers was a sort of secret society, inhabited by a special few who considered such inclinations acceptable.

The patrician, modern society girl emerged on the silver screen at the same time, from the liberated Claudette Colbert in the hit movie *It Happened One Night* to the modern woman wearing the smart androgynous trousers and the stately square-shouldered blouses of their patron saint, Katharine Hepburn. Women like Constance and Katharine cultivated an attitude of intellectual confidence, professional ambition, subtle androgyny, and sexual openness. But just because this new brand of woman was embraced in certain circles did not mean the general population was ready for it. The world was decades away from embracing same-sex couples as mainstream, much less as

well-known society fixtures, and businesswomen, which was controversial enough, and the country was arguably almost a century away
from embracing a relationship between a Caucasian and an African
American or mulatto woman.

As she looked back, Constance could not pinpoint the moment she
knew she was "open to" openness. As a girl, she had always favored
activities more typical to the other sex. Growing up in the Canadian
countryside, she ran; she played rugby; she climbed trees. But it was
not until she was admitted to a Seven Sisters school that she began to
meet like-minded girls and to find in those like-minded girls a culture
that favored exploration. At Smith, Constance learned not only that
her penchant for boys' activities was acceptable, but that the ten-
dency to call sports a "boys' activity" was a fallacy in the first place, a
fallacy that must be righted over time.

It was still decades before this notion would grow into a movement.
She could attend for only one year and left as the First World War
called upon her. The war had done its part to melt the glacier of public
perception. In college, Constance studied the history of the women's
rights movements, starting with those first brave millworkers, then
moving on to the long-suffering temperance groups and from there
into the sewing circles that would spawn those first feisty, unstoppable
suffragettes. (For later: Rosie the Riveter barely needed to pump her
fist to a generation already emboldened by freedom, a generation of
women who had earned income while their husbands were at war.) But
it was not just wartime necessity and postwar exuberance that fueled
Constance; something else was lighting her interest.

She could not deny, if only to herself, that her attraction to other
women was more personal than political.

So did Constance find herself in a sort of sorority at school, a ladies'
group that did everything from studying, to socializing, to sleeping
together. These pastimes were accepted among them within the ivied
walls of their Seven Sisters enclave, but it was well known that such
activities were not to be discussed or flaunted outside them. If anything,

the tacit secrecy of their pact added to the experience, lending the fun of the forbidden to an already pleasurable act. It did occur to Constance that there was some irony in forming a business that promoted a cult of femininity even as she embraced a version of femininity that resisted being the focus of the male gaze. But the two were not mutually exclusive, being a modern heterosexual woman, eventually a wife and a mother, even a professional, and being Constance. Would she call herself a lesbian? Certainly not. A modern woman? Yes. That Katharine Hepburn and her acolytes wore a different shade of lipstick from those of the more old-fashioned glamour girls only meant there were more shades to produce and sell.

All of this combined to create explosive energy between Constance and CeeCee: the openness, the secrecy, the shared professional goals, the common ambition, and, of course—Constance, the very respected, rising socialite Mrs. Van Wyke, would be lying to deny it—the added intrigue of loving a woman with a different-color skin.

18

NEW YORK, NEW YORK

New York City, 1935

Josephine sat in her capacious drawing room, gazing at her collection of art. Sometimes, she marveled at the simple fact that she had a collection of art, let alone that she owned an apartment with a drawing room. She would not have even thought to imagine this life as a child, growing up in a Polish shtetl, nor would she have believed it had someone told her at that time. And yet here she was, sitting in a lavish apartment in one of the best buildings in Manhattan, not only the owner of the drawing room and apartment in which she was lounging, but the owner of the building itself. The art—her Matisses and Picassos—collected during trips to Paris, Vienna, and Berlin, was a reward she had bought for herself at landmark moments in the formation of her business. The paintings gave her as much pleasure as the jewels on her hands, which were conciliatory gifts from Jon over the years . . . and, most important, the famed emeralds to herself from herself.

The purchase of the apartment would always be a point of pride for Josephine after the London years. London had eventually made her rich and famous. Richer than she could have ever imagined. And everything was going according to plan, if not sooner. Once she had conquered London society, although she knew the royals sniffed a bit

at her, with the revenue from Australia, London, Paris, and her fragrance, she set her sights on New York. While she still did not trust
Jon, they played off each other as a formidable team. Not that she had
any patience or much respect for him, but he had worked hard to get
back in her good graces and little Miles loved spending time with his
father when he was not playing cards or inebriated. He had agreed to
leave his job in journalism to oversee Miles and the vast group of nannies while Josephine worked. While this new job entailed very little,
Jon did bring him to school by limousine each morning and was there
at pickup.

After expanding into fragrance, Josephine decided they would move
lock, stock, and barrel to the New World, to conquer the biggest market of all, America. The launch of her Parfum Empress Josephine,
with its trademark scent of tuberose, jasmine, and gardenia, was as
intoxicating as it was successful; women in the know in Europe dab-
bing it on their wrists and necks made a lasting impression on the
men they desired and who desired them. With its distinctive frosted-
glass packaging and clever atomizer, Parfum Empress Josephine was a
sensation. She had cleverly added the French spelling of *parfum* rather
than "perfume" to the package to give it a more European and luxurious feel. Not to mention the nod to the original empress Josephine and the positive association with royalty. While the lingering
scent proved a bit too cloying for Josephine personally, it not only
made her famous but printed money—and she could now do whatever she pleased whenever she pleased to do it.

And the first thing she did after disembarking onto American soil
was to plant her flag on Fifth Avenue, creating a state-of-the-art store
and treatment salon. After taking over two contiguous Mayfair
shops and combining them, and her Paris salon, she decided that the
Fifth Avenue location would be her biggest and best yet. And when she
opened the store to lines around the corner, it was instantly profitable.
Spending most days and nights at the store, she soon realized that
she needed a residence that was within walking distance to work so she

could see little Miles and, most important, oversee Jon, who was overseeing the army of nannies who were overseeing him and keeping him on a tight schedule.

"Why are you feeding him hamburger?" she would grouse. "I vant him to have a sirloin. Cut it up into small pieces. Give him green beans and liver. I vant him to have spinach. It puts hair on the chest." She would decry every decision, give Miles a quick peck, and go back to the office. Nothing was ever good enough or right when it came to the care and feeding of her son. And yet she spent so much time in the New York store, she even kept a few additional outfits in her office. After all, she had to ensure the consistent quality of the products, perfect the presentation, and greet her important clients. Everyone joked, even in the press, that she hardly left her eponymous shop. Due to the success of the store and her bold-faced fragrance, which had become so fashionable she could barely keep it in stock, she set out to find her new home. She was certainly at a point where she could command an apartment on Park or even Fifth. She hired the leading broker Frank Morgan Jr., who found her ideal home in the storied 635 Fifth Avenue, a duplex comprising two classic-six apartments stacked one above the other, with an elevator that opened directly onto the apartment into a majestic black-and-white checkerboard marble entrance hall. An opulent spiral staircase would draw her guests' eyes to the second floor when Josephine descended from above. She rushed to make an offer minutes after viewing the listing.

But the treatment she received by the co-op board defied her expectations, even though Frank had secretly anticipated such a reaction. A long review of her board package ended in their rejection of her application. Outraged and certain of the reason—the anti-Semitic sentiment in New York was hardly a surprise—she debated the appropriate response. She could have Jon, her former journalist husband, write a nasty letter to the editors of *The New York Times,* she could tell all the art houses and clubs, or she could do something that would bring her much more satisfaction. Without delay, Josephine made a second offer through a corporate shell, this time not for the apartment itself, but for the entire building. The price was almost two times greater than the value of the building and land, and this time the board had no choice but to accept. When the board found out that the buyer of the building was not a Delaware-based corporation headed by a Mr. Sheridan Sloane, Josephine's corporate lawyer, but in fact Madame Josephine Herz, they were forced to accept her, which they did politely, though through clenched greetings of "Good morning" when they passed her in the lobby.

The sentiment toward Jews in New York was no surprise to Josephine. Of course, she had fled her own childhood home due to the same sentiment. But here, in New York, Josephine found a more subtle opposition toward Jews. At first she thought that she would be accepted by the New York elite if she could match or surpass them on their terms, such as through the accumulation of wealth, homes, art, memberships at important clubs, and affiliations with politicians or other powerful friends. She knew she would not be accepted in all the same places as a gentile with lesser assets, but she had expected to be tolerated by these people. What she had not expected was a more subtle form of discrimination from a small group of prosperous old-money German and Swiss Jews, who referred to themselves as "our crowd." They were the Lehmans and the Guggenheims, the bankers and financiers who had immigrated to the United States in the 1800s, amassed a fortune, and had become socially prominent. They were already ensconced uptown in their mansions and many in their group turned up their noses at the new wave of Eastern European Jews flocking to their shores, viewing the new group as crass and loud. So Josephine would find a need to embrace and be embraced by other outsiders: famous musicians, artists, show people, or more liberal-minded successful members of the old guard.

This was all true, but it was still unsatisfactory to Josephine. Unacceptable. She had come too far and achieved too much to settle for mere acceptance in a club. Rather, she strove to create her own group of like-minded, forward-thinking artists, intellectuals, and titans of business. And so, rather than aspire to membership in clubs where she was not welcome, she simply formed her own. A different sort of salon.

In a sense, the Herz Beauty salons were a product of this idea. Josephine loved a salon in the traditional sense: a regular, informal gathering of like-minded people, the purpose of which was to socialize, to educate, and also to elevate one another through community. She and Jon would become part of the fabric of New York life by hosting these weekly events, inviting the best and the brightest into their glamorous home. Artists, poets, singers, painters, socialites, visiting foreign royalty, actors, actresses, directors, politicians. Society people soon followed. That was the trick . . . and no luminary was too bright.

The salons proved to be not only great fun, but one of Josephine's best inventions, because the salons soon earned a central spot in New York City social life. Over time, to be invited to a salon at the home of Josephine Herz, the Mr. and Mrs. Jon Blakes, was a great honor and a coveted prize. And for Josephine, these weekly events increased her social circle and social currency exponentially.

Notable guests came from every realm. Salvador Dalí was often present, chatting with a new muse. Robert Benchley was often telling an amusing story to a starlet. Gloria Swanson stopped by once—with her rumored boyfriend Joseph Kennedy—as did the playwright George S. Kaufman and the novelist Dashiell Hammett. And when Mrs. Vanderbilt came, Josephine knew she had done the impossible.

"Everybody vants a good party. A good drink, a good view, and some caviar," she would say, shrugging. But she knew better. The rich, she would later say, were "bored and boring." When she cleverly provided interesting people, the rich and bored became interested. Because she viewed this as a new business tool and the business paid for it, no expense was spared for these fetes. Guests buzzed about with bubbling drinks. Waiters roamed with crowded silver trays, passing blinis heaped with caviar and crème fraîche. A jazz band from the

Cotton Club played the latest Broadway musical hits. Vaunted conversation usually devolved by nine or ten o'clock. Debauchery followed. The drunken dalliances—and ill-advised jaunts to Josephine's roof and sometimes to nearby Central Park—were always kept very discreet, with the guests abiding by a tacit rule: What happened at Josephine's stayed at Josephine's. But Josephine meanwhile accumulated a vault of secrets that she guarded fiercely should she ever need to extort an enemy or prove a point.

But the best thing about these salons was the most obvious: they inspired her. They inspired her with respect to the most important thing in her life. For no sooner had she established herself at the highest level of New York society and perfected her best-selling skin salve and signature fragrance than it dawned on her that the next move for her business was a concept she had already invented. The products she made were excellent, yes, and they did seem to sell at ever faster rates thanks to the advertising and latent marketing power of her own customers—which is to say word of mouth and their own need for refills. But these social events, which Josephine loved so well, and which enriched her mind, her marriage, and her social status, would be the key to her success in business as well.

Yes, her salon had yielded the beauty and fitness salon. Then came the next big idea. It came to her like many other eureka moments: in the bath. And she laughed at the absurdity of its obviousness before she emerged, wrapped in a towel, to tell the news to Jon.

"What is it?" he asked, as he knew that look she had when she had an idea.

"I know what to do next," she exclaimed, laughing with delight.

"What to do next with what?" he asked nonchalantly.

"A salon . . . in the salon," she said.

"We just had one last night," he said.

"Not here," she explained. "At the store as well. We vill not only have a gym, a sauna, and massage rooms. But a real salon for our customers. Once a week we vill host a guest lecturer and invite our best clients. . . ." She drummed her perfectly lacquered nails on the marble-topped table. "I vill replicate our own social events for our everyday clients!" she declared.

Josephine's Fifth Avenue salon, a four-story palace of beauty that spanned an entire city block, invited a woman to come for a day of beauty, to clean, to exfoliate, to massage, to steam, to refresh and renew. Here she could attend lessons in how to apply Herz products, she could learn the techniques of a true Herz woman, she could view the shiny lacquered color of every single Herz product lined up like sugary tarts in a Parisian patisserie, she could purchase every one of the products she used in this salon, she could return for monthly, even weekly, treatments to maintain this level of beauty—and she could become reliant on a product she did not even know she needed before she walked in the door. Like a high priestess in a vaulted church, Josephine built herself a temple in which she could preach the gospel of beauty and then sell indulgences one product at a time.

Despite the obvious ironies, it was not a stretch to compare Josephine's salon with a house of worship. In many ways, the salons—and the industry she formed—had much in common with a temple or church. Not to be compared with missionaries, who defined certain religions as a disease and then offered the cure, Josephine saw herself as an educator rather than an instrument of salvation.

"If you vant to be pretty, it takes *vork*," Josie commanded.

Any woman could have, could attain, beauty if she put in the effort and time. And paid the price. Yes, there was a small price. But nothing good came for free.

The salon was an experience. A day trip. A trip in a day. A woman would come into the Herz salon and book appointments from nine to five. She might begin with a facial, continue to a massage, take a class in technique, and, of course, enjoy a tour of the products. She could indulge in a lavish and healthy lunch, share the camaraderie of other women, and soak in the gentle tutelage of Herz Beauty technicians.

These beauty technicians, dressed in neat beige uniforms with white collars, their hair pulled back tightly, had the cool proficiency of Red Cross nurses, the welcoming smiles of sorority girls, and the firm tones of English governesses. They came; they cleaned; they conquered. They tweezed; they plucked; they pruned. They steamed; they squeezed; they moisturized; they patted dry; they scrubbed; they toned; they tweaked; they trimmed; they tugged. They analyzed the imperfections and told their clients how to minimize them and maximize the positive: the motto of their fearless leader, Madame Herz. And then, once a woman was buffed and preened, they sold her every single one of the products she'd used. A woman left the Herz salon refreshed, looking ten years younger and feeling ten pounds lighter, not only because of the day of reprieve, but because she had shed so many dollars from her pocketbook. And then once they were stripped of their blemishes, blackheads, and cash, they were offered a gift. Her new and innovative gift to them, her clients. A Thursday evening to meet a great artist, hear a great violinist, and munch on seductive and exotic Russian blinis and frigid vodka. And meet other like-minded clients in a cosseted atmosphere. It was ingenious and over time became an empire, and the Herz empire was best understood in phases. The education phase. The evaluation phase. The cleansing phase. The lotion phase. The foundation phase. The rouge phase. The lipstick phase. The powder phase. The eye phase (which the great cosmetic scholars might separate into the era of eye shadow and the era of mascara). The product-selling phase. The fragrance and finish phase. The evening salon phase. It was this progression that would define the evolution of both Josephine's beauty empire and the American beauty industry. While Constance bristled at the Polish Jewish upstart, she had to hand it to her. While she was an insider and Josephine was an outsider, Josephine had cleverly found a way into her world, and as with the best competitors, it was driving her to be better, more innovative . . . and, also, insane.

19

PALM BEACHES

Palm Beach, 1935

The pink coquina-stone Mizner mansion stood at attention, the palms waving. And it was for sale. Constance's heart raced as she entered the monumental foyer with the glamorous curved staircase and pecky cypress beams leading the way up to the formidable bell tower that could be seen in the distance over the bridges. She immediately knew she had to have it but kept her frozen business smile in place so as not to betray her excitement.

"Interesting," she said as Topper's wife, Lally Stanton, the strawberry-blond heiress and part-time real estate broker, took her through the massive property. Topper and Lally had moved to Palm Beach after they had married. Topper's diminished fortune was revealed only after the wedding, and it was an open secret in Palm Beach that Lally now worked to bring in extra income to supplement the dividends from her small trust. Luckily, the pair lived in Lally's parents' guesthouse on their property on Middle Road, as it was rent-free and Topper was trying to get his wealth management company off the ground. Most days saw him playing polo and drinking at the club, to Lally's chagrin.

"It's been in the same family for years, but no one visits since La

Comptesse moved to France to live out her remaining days in Bordeaux."

Constance surveyed Lally's blond confidence with admiration. "No children or heirs forcing the sale?" She threw down her first card, trying to assess the urgency of the situation. Or, hopefully, lack of.

"Tragedy. Her only son died in an auto accident. The house is in trust for the Metropolitan," Lally opined.

"I see." Constance processed the seemingly casual information and went in for the kill. "Truly a white elephant"—she exhaled—"but someone with an eye . . ."

"Well, no one has a better eye than you do," Lally offered. "After all, not many women make the cover of *Time* magazine." Lally beamed at her friend and now famous client. It was interesting and satisfying to Constance that someone of Lally Stanton's social stature had finally accepted her and was even proud of her. A few years earlier, before her marriage to Van and her public success, she was very well aware that Lally Stanton, the Seward Oil heiress, hardly had given her the time of day.

"Oh, that . . ." Constance glowed proudly but played off her major win as a minor event. Her recent profile on the Gardiner Girls and her English Garden Collection, which had taken America by storm, had "unleashed the power of the female workforce" and was on every newsstand, making her a celebrity in her own right. Her ready-made kits allowed the average girl and wife next door to become her own full-time or part-time businesswoman, earning up to 40 percent of the profits. It was ingenious, and Constance's beauty armed forces had swept Middle America. The kit fees alone made her rich enough to afford the best Palm Beach had to offer. Even Van had put aside his skepticism with the *Time* cover and the fact that he was now married to one of America's most high-profile and richest women. It also afforded him more time at Piping Rock and less time on Wall Street, not to mention the slew of polo ponies and racing horses he and

Constance were amassing. It was the one thing they had in common, and it kept them on civil, if not friendly, terms.

"The ocean-to-lake vista affords breezes and the coral stone keeps it cool, even on the most humid days," Lally offered without trying to oversell.

"It's way too big and impractical. Isn't there anything smaller, Lally? What does one need with so many rooms?" Constance pulled on her rope of lustrous pearls, playing off the positive as a negative.

"Well, you asked for something that had presence. I'm not sure I see you and Van on the lake, but there is a Venetian palazzo coming on the market. But it's ghastly dark."

"How much are they asking for this . . . pile?" she said with shrewd disdain.

"One hundred and twenty thousand. Mizner brought over so much of it from Europe."

"Well, that's not in my budget."

"One can always make an offer." Lally lit up a cigarette in a nonchalant and somewhat sexy fashion.

"Make a low offer and see if they'll bite. I'm not sure I even *want* it, but for sixty thousand it might be worth my time."

"And if you get it, we can start talking about which of the clubs you and Van should join. As you know, the season is very social and it's a lovely tight-knit community. Van and you are shoo-ins at the Bath and Tennis," she said, dangling the ultimate carrot.

"Oh, that's so lovely of you, Lally." Constance flashed her best door-to-door saleswoman smile, knowing the invitation to the storied club was anything but an everyday experience. In fact, one didn't "ask" to join the B&T but had to be invited, and Constance was quite aware of the importance. While hiring Lally as her broker had been a given, thanks to Topper and Van's relationship, now that she was Mrs. Van Wyke the very closed iron gates of Palm Beach society had slowly started to open for her.

"Of course, everyone will be very welcoming since you and Van have so many friends here already. And remember, it's not only about who's here, but who's *not*." She laughed. "You know what they say, if the infidels are at the gates, in Palm Beach we just pull up the bridges." She gave a knowing smile.

"Well, that's music to my ears." Constance bristled at the thought of that parvenu Josephine and her Trojan horse to New York society. She would just go where Josephine would never be accepted, and Palm Beach was perfect. There was nothing more white bread, conservative, and restricted. Of course, she knew there was a smattering of old-money German Jews, such as the Schiffs, the Seligmans, and the Warburgs, and even a leading Jewish member of the Everglades Club, but those were exceptions and the club system was increasingly anti-Semitic. Even hotels were known to have selective quotas. And Constance knew many of the "our crowd" Jews who had places here would be the first to shun a new-money immigrant such as Josephine Herz.

Even though she knew deep down that *she* was new money, and Lally and Topper knew it, too, the Wyke name and her own tall blond persona had cleverly given her the old-money patina. Not to mention her ingenious respelling of Gardiner. Deep down she felt like a parvenu herself but was buffered by her looks, Van's family cachet, and her religion. She breathed a sigh of relief that she was able to pass on all levels. Suddenly she thought of CeeCee, then immediately banished the thought.

"Yes, I think I might want it after all." She looked out on the emerald-green lawn toward the sea and also realized that owning an imposing and storied mansion would give her more social cachet. "I have an office in Atlanta and one opening in Miami, so I might be down here a bit more."

"Fine, I'll put in the offer. I have a feeling you just might get it. There hasn't been an offer in over a year." Lally hooked her arm happily, calculating her commission with the knowledge that Topper was broke and her trust was dwindling. Constance immediately felt the electricity when the handsome strawberry blonde locked arms and wondered if she had the same proclivities. No, she couldn't. Constance banished the thought and put it down to a budding friendship.

"I'll have Van take care of the clubs. That's his thing. After all, I am working." She laughed.

"Well, that's what we love about you, Constance. You really are a thoroughly modern woman."

"You are, too, Lally. You're a working woman now, too." She smiled at her.

"You're right, but grudgingly." She shrugged.

"Well, I wouldn't have it any other way." Constance looked at the aqua waves, which suddenly calmed her, and thought of a place where she would never run into *that woman*.

"Put in the offer," Constance said softly, and then with fervor: "Today."

20

THE LAUNCH FIZZLES

New York City, 1935

It was a clear lesson that seared: one success does not always follow in the footsteps of another. The winter was charmed. The spring had seemingly thawed her luck. The next planned launch of Gardiner's "Moulin Rouge Lipstick Collection" was not the success Constance had planned. Met with lukewarm reviews and reception, it landed with more of a fizzle than a sparkle.

Constance steadied herself against her sturdy blond-wood desk at the reports. Numbers did not lie and she viewed the information as if anticipating a doctor's report, with nervous anxiety at the results. Word was the colors were too bright, too bold, and too brazen for her core customers. A meeting with her morose accountant did not brighten the mood. Projections had been overly optimistic, and production and marketing costs had been higher. She had been overconfident and overspent to compete given the success of the *Time* cover and had taken her eye off the ball with the purchase of the Palm Beach estate. She had misread her "woman" and what she was looking for in only a few months. In short, her customer wanted the sophisticated elegance of Claudette Colbert and not the brash look of Jean Harlow. The women shook their permanents; the colors were tinny, brassy, and bold. Their husbands, boyfriends, and children thought the look was too young, too exotic, that it made them look foolish.

"What are you wearing on your lips?" they would grumble. Instead of the compliments they were used to getting from her products, they were getting criticism. They may have bought once, but there were no reorders. From this, Constance learned one of the great lessons of her business career: her woman, her customer, wanted quality products that enhanced, made her feel and look younger—but not "too" young, which translated to foolish to her friends and family. While Harlow was hot and women and men admired her insouciance, not every woman could pull off the look of a "brazen hussy" and wise-cracking platinum blonde.

In short, the launch was an expensive bust. Still, Constance was never one to give in quickly, much less reveal her consternation on her perfectly creamed face. With a simmering smile, she dismissed her accountant and took in the clean lines of the city buildings visible from her window. Damned if she would be dwarfed by these statuesque shapes. She was one of them. A deep inhale fortified her, but reality was heavy right now. Deflating, Constance slid down into her chair.

Why did every blow feel like a step back? Had she put too much on the line for this product? The advertisements alone cost more than double the last campaign, as she was trying to keep up with that whirling dervish Josephine Herz, who seemed to have invaded and conquered New York. Her New York.

She flipped the pages of *Ladies' Home Journal* and studied Josephine's new campaign and tagline—"Yours for beauty, Herz for Beauty"— with rage. The single-page glossy ads featuring women of means seemed to be omnipresent, at every turn of the page. All her midwestern door-to-door sales meant revenue, but no one gave her the accolades or saw her ads or temple of beauty on Fifth Avenue, because she did not have one. She hadn't wanted to promote the rouge and lipstick in the press but felt she had to compete for her ego. She had hired an expensive ad agency and spent heavily on the Moulin Rouge Lipstick Collection, featuring the line "You Can, Can" and the tag "Choose from the Colors of Your Garden," which seemed to fall flat and appear banal next to Josephine's new and sophisticated ad campaigns. Herz's regal ads for her pretentious Parfum Empress Josephine broke at the same time, featuring a much younger photo of Josephine in a diamond tiara that had actually belonged to the empress and now belonged to Herz. Constance thought it vulgar and pretentious, but sophisticated women seemed to eat it up. Regardless, Constance punished herself for her own campaign's lack of sophistication, not to mention the fact that wherever she went, she seemed to smell the distinctive Empress Josephine fragrance: from powder rooms to the changing rooms in Lord & Taylor. She became nauseated at the scent and it seemed to be everywhere, enraging her and causing her to feel faint at the same time. She had to admit that every time she faltered, Josephine seemed to make an advance. She was like a vampire, feeding on Constance's lifeblood. Furious and renewed in her resolve, Constance turned to her fail-proof source of inspiration, her bar.

Now that Prohibition had thankfully ended, a bottle of Christmas gin peeked out of the amber mass, as though bedecked in a silver wrapper just to win Constance's attention. The office was empty, halls dark, the only sound the occasional rattle of the cleaning cart. It was, of course, time to head home. She imagined the vignette there: Constance sitting next to her doting husband, Van, the bore, whom she had deigned to marry solely because of his name. Van Wyke. She was now Constance Gardiner-Wyke, often described in the social columns as the new Beauty Queen of New York and Palm Beach society, married to the affable banking heir Van Wyke. Yet she had little patience for the balding and boring Van and his Ivy League friends, who placed squash and polo ahead of their finance jobs and who all stayed within a small fenced-in area of the Gold Coast of Locust Valley. It was all a bore, but at least she had an escape. Lit by a roaring fire, framed by the mantel she had found in Paris and shipped back to New York, she took a hearty swig of gin and became more angry. She imagined the way his head would nod as he listened to her recount her day, detail the latest market travail, the failure of her vaunted product. He always gave her his full attention, and yet he was so passive. How could a man be so patrician and yet so completely devoid of spark? Constance gave little thought to a generous refill. She had no desire to see her husband tonight.

The elevator stopped on the fifteenth floor and CeeCee stepped into the hallway, dark and silent but for the distant squeak of a cleaning cart's wheels. She hoped to find some silence and solitude to work on her pomade. She was close to having a presentable idea to show Constance, but she knew it had to be worthy of bearing the Gardiner name. Constance's approval was hard-earned and CeeCee had worked herself to the bone for her respect. She was not going to squander her boss's time on an incomplete or less than perfect idea. Her keys at the ready, she grasped the doorknob to the reception area and was surprised to find that the door was already unlocked. She entered slowly. The only light shone from Constance's office.

She was aware that these feelings were childish, but the anxiety and excitement of breaking a rule sent a sharp electrical current from her toes up her spine. Her reverence for her boss was not unlike a crush: sincere respect, admiration, and, of course, that something else. That something about Constance that made her feel on the alert when she was in the same room. She set her books down quietly and sat very still. Suddenly, the sound of rustling papers was like a whisper in her ear and she gathered up her books, walking slowly down the hall to inspect the subtle interruption. She paused in a corner and then peered into Constance's office to see Constance riffling through a movie magazine.

Constance remained poised, despite the nearly empty gin bottle beside her. She gazed at an image in a magazine of Carole Lombard. Now, she had the looks and the talent. What was it about her face that appeared both girlish and womanly, both fresh and flirtatious? The outmoded hoop skirt had been replaced by a sleeker, tighter line, a pencil skirt that both elongated the leg and accentuated the hip as Carole posed for the press against a Ford, a new blond icon: gorgeous, irreverent, and funny. There must be a way to tailor her cosmetics to this emerging shape, this emerging identity. This was the image she should have aimed for. Not Harlow. This was a look *all* American women could embrace!

From the hallway, CeeCee found herself staring inadvertently, admiring the way Constance's hands fell on the picture on the page. Instinctively, CeeCee leaned forward, craning her neck to catch a better glimpse of the image, and as she did, the floorboard creaked. Constance froze.

An uneasy silence circled the two women like a belt. CeeCee stepped back quickly and switched on a light to make her presence known. The metallic hum of the hallway's fluorescent lights struggled to fill the silence.

"Hello?" CeeCee called out. She felt like a child caught holding a stolen toy. Grinning with embarrassment. Busted with evidence in hand. A cheery disposition would surely hide her guilt.

"Hello, Constance. It's me, CeeCee," said CeeCee. She stepped into the light.

"CeeCee? Come in, dear," Constance chimed, her saccharine tone just barely saturating the gin. CeeCee did as she was told.

"How did it go?" CeeCee asked, pretending she didn't already know.

"I'm sure you could guess." Constance looked at CeeCee. Rather, she stared at CeeCee, stilled by the smooth, creamy color of her complexion. "You forgot something?"

"No, I had a few things I wanted to finish up."

"You wanted to spy on me?" Constance said.

"No. I had no idea . . . I didn't realize you stayed so late." CeeCee held her ground despite Constance's attempts to shake it. Constance approved of this. She admired commensurate strength.

"Well, I'm glad you've found your way back." Constance returned to her magazine, feigning interest. "Any brilliant ideas?" she said. "I'm open to anything. We need a miracle right now."

CeeCee did not pause. This was her moment and she knew it. The pomade. Of course, she knew it was not ready. She thought of her sketches and papers and the jars of shea butter and essential oils cluttered on her kitchen counter and in her bag. Still, she knew it was time. Opportunity did not knock twice. Formulating the beginning of her pitch, she smiled and began.

"Actually I've—"

Constance stopped her, extending her hand and taking CeeCee's notebook to see what she was working on.

"I'm working on a pomade for colored women. . . ." She trailed off to Constance's non-interest in the subject.

"What's this?" She opened to a page in the notebook with Egyptian-style drawings. CeeCee stepped toward Constance and saw the drawings and, in perfectly scrawled script, a long list of ingredients. Constance stared at the page. This was not the moment she had hoped for. She swallowed her sentence as she saw Constance devour the list. Coal. Dye. Ink.

"Things that are black," CeeCee explained. "For the eyes. I was researching Cleopatra. Do you know she used kohl on her eyes for mascara? She also perfumed her sails when she traveled by boat so she could leave or make an impression when she came into port to see Caesar. She used beauty to achieve her political goals," CeeCee said proudly of her research.

"Yes, like all of us smart gals," Constance said dryly as she looked at the page with interest. And then at the books in CeeCee's arms. Hardbound books and soft covers featuring diagrams, endless lists with potential ingredients, history books open to pages of ancient Egyptian men and woman with kohl outlining their eyes. The discovery of King Tutankhamun's tomb some years earlier had piqued the public's interest in Egyptology and reintroduced the idea of primitive cosmetics and coal-black eyeliner. Constance looked at the photography book of many of Tut's vast array of treasures and the funereal mask: the gleaming gold and dark black slashes around the eyes.

"This is good. This one might have possibility." Constance smiled, knowing deep down that CeeCee's idea was a winner and that she held another type of gold in her hand. "Would you mind if I kept this and kept the books? Such an interesting idea."

"Of course. I work for you. My ideas are your ideas." CeeCee smiled.

"We shall see." She cleared her throat. "You know, there's never enough time!" She smiled at CeeCee. "I'm so glad you believe in working late, too. Two working gals coming in late on a Friday night? I can't help but admire you."

CeeCee blushed. "Well, it's mutual, of course. I mean . . . you're an idol to me. Everything you've done . . . everything you do . . ." She paused, aware she was stammering. "I admire you, Mrs. Wyke. Many of us girls do. You're giving us all the right to be like the movie stars, to express our personality in the way we look. Who, besides you, is letting everyday girls get to feel so beautiful? And give them economic freedom."

"Well, you know I'm not the *only* one," Constance said, demurring, pointing to an ad for Parfum Empress Josephine on the next page.

"You are. She doesn't compare. She doesn't invent like you do."

"I think quite the contrary, she is rather ferocious in her passion."

"She's not like you. She wouldn't hire a girl like me. A black girl with no—"

Constance stood from her chair, unsettled and passionate and feeling overconfident.

"Don't do that. You are a woman. A brilliant, talented, caring, beautiful woman who shouldn't be overlooked because of the shade of her rouge!"

CeeCee stared at Constance. This kindness, this force, was totally unexpected and it took her breath away.

The two women now stood face-to-face.

CeeCee felt the warmth from Constance's body. Jasmine perfume from the English Garden Collection filled her nostrils. Her soft pink skin, flushed from the booze, her rose-shaped lips, moist and plump.

"Tu as de beaux yeux," Constance said.

The intense connection overpowered both. They felt a force pushing them toward each other. Their eyes closed and the two sets of lips gently rested on top of each other. They stayed like this, lips touching lips, for several seconds, until they fell, laughing, onto the desk.

The passion and lust that followed was unlike anything either woman had ever known—deeply erotic, wonderfully playful, and electric in its heat. They romped and rolled for hours, carried by lust and secrecy, exploring each other's bodies like young lovers, discovering the pleasures of another body for the first time. Of course, months later, the innocence and delight of the night would take on a different tinge, propelled as it was by disappointment, admiration, companionship, and a splash or two of gin. But regardless of the factors that thrust these two beautiful women together, it was lasting and powerful for them both. CeeCee had never been touched or desired in that way before, let alone by a woman. It was pure and intimate, devilish and hot. And, of course, sweetened by the sugar of secrecy and the honey of forbidden fruit.

This night would come to bookend Constance and CeeCee's working relationship, as it marked the end of the professionalism and distance that had characterized it before and the beginning of an intimacy neither had known could exist. Their partnership morphed into something neither woman could have imagined. Their trysts became a weekly event. Meticulously planned and structured, like everything in Constance's life. Constance went so far as to tell her husband that she had a client who could meet only after sundown. She let him wonder if the client was in some sort of religious cult.

Yet this rigidity, while ideal for Constance, left CeeCee feeling uneasy. For CeeCee, the liaisons grew increasingly predictable, almost rote, and never again captured the passion of that first night. Within a few months, CeeCee began to feel that her time was no longer hers. She often lied to Mickey that she was working late and could not see him. Upon getting home to her apartment, she bathed before he arrived to wash off any scent. Then she started to feel she was divided between Constance's new project and Constance's lust. A toy, another product penciled into Constance's schedule. It had been weeks since CeeCee was able to work on her pomade. And for CeeCee, lust paled in comparison with the force of her ambition.

It was a Monday evening and the sun had set and the office had emptied. Constance and CeeCee met at the appointed time and were sure to be alone. CeeCee gathered her belongings—her supplies, her notebooks—left her bag in her chair, and walked toward the office of her lover, her boss.

Constance was busy on the phone and didn't see CeeCee enter. CeeCee took advantage of her anonymity to analyze Constance as a stranger would. Her glossed and lacquered nails held the phone just away from her face, so as not to ruin her cosmetics. She threw her head back when she laughed, or pretended to laugh, and her neck moved gently in and out with each breath. Constance was the string dangling CeeCee from success. To be desired by such a powerful woman was an honor. But to be captive to her would not do.

Constance turned to CeeCee, smiling now, as though she had known she was there the whole time. She was putting on a show of not noticing. Putting on a show. Constance waved alluringly, mouthing, "Five minutes." CeeCee nodded and went back to her desk.

But CeeCee would not be deterred. She would not give this up. She sat and waited. Five minutes turned into ten. Ten minutes turned into a half hour. She was never one to waste time, and yet here she was, staring at a blank piece of paper in her notebook, sitting in an empty office, doing nothing but waiting. Infuriated at herself for her passivity, she turned to her pomade notes. On a lark, the night before in her kitchen, she had added a drop of peppermint oil to the shea butter and coconut oil. She'd mixed and watched the reaction. Then she'd inhaled. The scent was deep and intense, healing and invigorating at once. She had used it on her scalp and the formula had eased the itching. It had actually "relaxed" the irritation the lye had caused. The peppermint had given the treatment and her scalp a cool, calming sensation. She knew this was the secret. Now, at the office, her mind began to race faster than her pen. She felt inspiration. A eureka moment. That airless feeling you get only from a new idea. The water that evaporated as steam may as well have been CeeCee's spirit rising aloft. She sketched out a logo, as she knew she would need one, just as the Gardiner logo of assorted English flowers in a wreath had served the brand well. She wrote, "CeeCee Lopez's hair straightener." No, she thought. "Straightener" sounded too businesslike, too formal, and wasn't descriptive enough as it related to the product benefit. She thought of other words and in her mind liked the idea of the hair being softer, less stressed. Relaxed, even.

"Relaxed." She smiled. "That's it, that's the idea." Her spirits soared at the term. She would use the word "relaxer" rather than "pomade" or "straightener." The fine curls of the capital *C* she drew became lovely tendrils of silky, relaxed hair. She finally had the idea and the concept. CeeCee's Relaxer. That was it. She loved it.

"He doesn't stop. That man can go on for hours."

CeeCee looked up, shocked. Constance stood in her doorway. Her immediate thought was to tell Constance her discovery. It was time to make her move. But when she spoke, the only thing that came out was:

"What time is it?"

"Late. Thanks for waiting. Let's make it *rapide*." With a swift turn, Constance headed back to her office, her heels clacking on the hallway's hardwood floor. CeeCee heeded the command and followed behind. She looked at Constance with reignited fire, elated by the night's events, and that night, when they made love, the two held on to each other as if for dear life.

Lenny Ryan, the custodian of the building, expected to see an empty office. Sometimes, if the mood struck him, he would take a seat at the famous Mrs. Gardiner-Wyke's desk, pretending for a moment he was a different sort of man. After all, he was bitter at having to clean a woman's office. But tonight, there was not the usual empty spot that he found at the desk. For a moment, he watched with shock and a thrill as these two women entangled themselves with each other. Then he coughed.

CeeCee scrambled to cover herself. Constance slipped her blouse on with ease.

"May I help you? This is a *private* office," Constance snarled.

"You're Mrs. Gardiner-Wyke," he said, repeating her full name out loud as he had seen it in the various articles and magazine covers he had often tidied in her office. He felt emboldened, using her full name in a caustic tone.

"This room doesn't need attending to." She stepped toward him like a lioness intimidating her prey. She could take him down, if need be.

"This is a double dose of wrongdoing here," Lenny said. "You're married. And she's a . . ."

"Stop yourself now." Constance's neck, no longer gentle, hardened with rage.

He stared back, defiant. "This isn't right."

Pure barbarism flickered in his eyes. He was an older man, striped with veins, but it seemed possible he could harm them both. Even if it was two against one.

"I'm not—" CeeCee choked.

"Not what?" he said. "Not a dyke? Or a spic?"

Constance recoiled in revulsion.

"I want you out of this office right now. My husband will be hearing about this," she hissed. "I will not have such an invasive and vile person—"

"Mr. Wyke won't know anything, unless he has to," said Lenny.

Constance paused, understanding his inference.

"Oh, I see," she said, exhaling and rising slightly higher. Her mind raced as she thought back to the night she'd had to post bail for her brother, James. She knew that homosexual behavior was considered illegal, and one word to the police or the press could ruin her, socially and professionally.

"Perhaps we can work something out," she said.

CeeCee blinked and stared at Constance now with the same level of revulsion as she regarded the custodian.

Constance moved back toward her desk, having resumed the tone of a businesswoman.

CeeCee gathered herself and walked toward the door, still zippering her skirt. She inched past Lenny, who did not move but rather kept his eyes on her, as though he too had been promoted from prey to predator.

21

THE DECLARATION

New York City, 1935

She got off luckier than her checkbook thought. Constance had been prepared to write off at least $2,000 to silence the awful custodian. Of course, the vitriol he'd spewed at her when she'd handed him the check should have prompted her to rip it out of his hands and possibly slash her violent red nails across his florid cheek. Instead, she kept it to herself, the incident and the rage, and walked past him and out of the office. The next day, as she strode calmly past the newsstand on her way to her lunch at the Colony, she stopped in her tracks as she saw it. The newspaper bore the face of the woman she detested, Herz. Her smug smile and angular eyebrows looked lurid on the front page. The headline read:

> HERZ BEAUTY IS HERE TO STAY
> INTERNATIONAL BEAUTY BRAND
> PLANS TO OFFER STOCK TO PUBLIC

How many rubles had it taken for the *Daily News* to run that on the front page? was the first thought on Constance's mind. She was so glad she had snubbed that woman at the opera opening benefit. She had been introduced by their mutual friend Avery Fisher, the electronics mogul.

"Constance, have you met the *other* beauty pioneer, Madame Herz?" he asked her, as the diminutive Josephine had greeted him warmly in her green satin Vionnet, resplendent in a collar of emeralds.

"It is indeed a great pleasure." Josephine extended a white-gloved hand to Constance, which was immediately rejected by her tall blond counterpart.

"I don't believe I know or have ever heard of her." Constance gave a haughty laugh. "Avery, you are quite a card. Van, let's go inside," she harrumphed to her husband. "I don't want to associate with strangers. Or immigrants," she added for good measure, threw her foxes over her shoulders, and stormed off.

"I'm sorry, Josephine." Avery shook his head.

"Don't vorry. She'll get Herz." Josephine smiled at what had become a famous bon mot, but the smile masked her fury. And that Gardiner Girl was now a sworn enemy.

The next day, on the other side of town, Josephine knew the truth was more complicated. She sat in her conference room and thought back to her days at her uncle's shop. How little it took to satisfy the local women with her potions and cream. Before it became all about product introductions, launches, and marketing. She also thought back on her uncle's stern behavior and his misunderstanding of her goals— his actual thwarting of her goals. But of course, what man had not crushed the dreams of a woman he professed to love? Yes, she had nicked a few bottles to make a profit, but in the long run they were worth less than pennies to her uncle. Now that she was so successful, he had finally written to her for financial help, as she knew one day he would. She'd opened the letter carefully when she saw the Melbourne postage, savoring what she knew would be in the letter. It had been filled with rosy remembrances and platitudes and stressed how much he and Aunt Masha had helped her in the early days, and everything had a sickly sweet glow to the script. Aunt Masha was now sick, the store was failing, and the girls needed money for their weddings. Josephine had read the note with her own level of revulsion and then with great satisfaction. She had finally won. She had immediately sent him a check for $1,000 with a note that read, "Dear Uncle Solomon, Everyone gets theirs! Josephine Herz." That was her style. Cool, calculated, and blunt. Never one *not* to relish the win.

Sarah Collins, the tawny-haired chief marketing officer Josephine had recently hired, entered the boardroom. The meeting was scheduled for noon, but Josephine was always prompt. She had arrived a half hour early and sat at the head of the table where she always did, thinking about the upcoming board meeting as she reviewed the balance sheets. The numbers looked healthy and profitable and there were new products in the pipeline. Why, then, did she feel the future was always uncertain? The shtetl mentality, the years of scraping by and making do, had never left her. She couldn't escape it despite her jeweled trappings, which had grown only more extravagant over the years.

"I wonder what you think of this. . . ." Sarah laid down an industry publication reporting on the new effort from Gardiner Cosmetics. It was a bland feature on the new product line, entitled the "Moulin Rouge Lipstick Collection."

Sarah had been followed in by a European assistant, who was dark and had a Gypsy-like quality. Who was this new brunette in an ongoing line of nameless brunettes who were arriving daily? My god, was there ever any shortage of these busy brazen young women with their pens and pads? Where did these women come from? Josephine mused. Then, she remembered, many of them came from Eastern Europe, just as she had. With that inbred overbite, this one must have just gotten off the last boat from Minsk.

"Think of what?" Josephine tapped the table with her Van Cleef cabochon ring and turned her attention toward the new, eager young woman standing at the side of the table.

"Gardiner. Look at hers and look at yours." She placed the morning's newspaper headline in front of her. "Have you seen the papers?" Sarah placed both stories side by side to illustrate her point, Josephine could see only the vile photograph of herself that she specifically told PR to never use.

"Yes, I read it." She had not.

"Then I don't have to say that Gardiner is sinking. She came out with a line of European-inspired cosmetics to compete with you, with us. Word around town is it's a failure. You know what, I think you should buy it. We should make a low offer and buy Gardiner." She looked quite smug.

Josephine had several thoughts competing for her attention at that moment. First, what gumption and pride this young woman must have to speak to her with such a tone. Second, despite wanting to eliminate Gardiner from the playing field, she knew that Constance would never sell her business, no matter what the circumstances. Especially not to Josephine! It was an immature idea and she disliked the overt bluster. And third, it occurred to her that this CMO's name might be Polly, not Sarah. That was the last one. Some lasted only weeks. Months. Lately, she fired incompetent people within days.

"Now, my dear Polly. We don't engage in that sort of play here at Herz Beauty. Let that dragon sell to the housewives of America with her door-to-door *stuff*. I sell to the carriage trade and she knows it. That's torture enough for Miss Palm Beach," Josephine snorted, having read about Constance's new island mansion, a social coup. The photo spread of her estate and pictures of her and Van and their polo ponies in the social press made Josephine insecure and anxious, as she knew she would never be part of that set.

Sarah, aka Polly, appeared frustrated, as if she were explaining something important to a child who simply could not understand.

"If you buy Gardiner for a discount with cash or stock, you will remove all of our immediate competition. We get her products and the packaging. Change the name to Herz or keep it as a secondary under

Gardiner. She'll sell the name rights if she has any good sense."
Polly beamed at her boss and winked from under the frame of her
smart glasses. Josephine thought something was amiss that her new
CMO was so fixated on Gardiner, as if she were trying to make a
point . . . like the Shakespeare quote "The lady doth protest too
much."

"Let me tell you something, dear. As easy as it would be, the truth
of the matter is that I need her, as much as she needs me." She sighed
and dismissed the idea for good with a wave of her hand.

"Meaning?"

The door to the boardroom swung open and the board members
began to file in. The young woman assistant stared at Josephine and
scribbled something on her pad. And again, when Josephine spoke,
Polly's assistant took notes.

Once everyone was seated, Josephine's creative team began to
elaborate on the upcoming products for the launch. The calendar had
images of various new blushes, lipsticks, and powders with a "Greek
isles" summer theme. Fittingly, the marketing idea was "Grecian Goddesses." The advertising agency executive showed large boards with renderings of various glamour girls in tunics, their faces all sporting the
new Herz colors of the season. At the end of the calendar, before the
winter holidays, there was a large question mark.

Josephine, however, struggled to hold her focus during the meeting.
The thought of Constance Gardiner swirled in her mind. Constance,
a woman who had spurned her, insulted her, was her greatest rival, was
ironically the woman most likely to understand her. That said, she was
also Mrs. Van Wyke, the toast of the very restricted Palm Beach, where
Josephine knew it would be difficult to obtain a weekend invitation
or even a hotel reservation.

"Madame?"

Josephine assumed a regal look and fixed her eyes on Polly and the
eight men at the table. Eighteen eager eyes stared back at her with
vacant expressions.

"Yes?"

"What is the last product you plan to launch? What is the question mark?" Carl Epstein called out from the end of the table.

"Yes," said another. "Where is your golden goose, Josephine? We know you're hiding one somewhere." Her chief financial officer laughed.

Josephine feigned her most polite, flirtatious laugh, then pulled her mouth into a tight purse. "I *vas* going to tell you"—she looked directly at Polly and her scribe—"but now I have decided I am not ready. We have some further testing and development on this. But, I promise it vill be soon. We vill announce, and when I do, I promise we vill *crush* the competition."

Josephine stood up, smoothing her Mainbocher. The table followed suit. She walked out of the room without turning back. The assistant was still scribbling.

Before heading to the 21 Club for a late business lunch, Josephine swung by Polly Collins's office. She was not so much worried as perplexed by the appearance of the new young lady and the sudden disappearance of her other assistant and all the scribbling on the pad. Nothing escaped Josephine's gaze. When she reached the office, she was quite surprised to see Polly Collins with her feet up on her desk, which she immediately withdrew.

"Polly, that is a Napoleonic antique, I prefer you don't put your street shoes on it," she lectured.

"Sorry, Josephine . . . Madame Herz," she said in a guilty fashion.

"Your new young assistant, the dark-haired girl in the meeting taking notes. I would like to speak with her. Do you know her name?" she asked.

"Well, Suzannah, my assistant, is out sick today . . . perhaps they sent a temp." Polly shrugged.

"Brown hair. Glasses. Strong-villed. Looked European."

Polly shook her head nervously. "I can't think of anyone that fits that description. Was there something you wanted specifically?"

"I remember coming up with a name for the new lipstick shade in the meeting and cannot remember. If you see her I would like to see her notes." She looked at her face to see if there was any unusual expression at the request. There was. A subtle look of fear masked by polite confusion.

"Yes, of course." She nodded.

Josephine also nodded, realizing her hunch might be right.

"Would you like me to try and find the girl? I could call the temp agency."

Josephine paused, but barely long enough to answer.

"Good evening." With this, Josephine left the office and got into her chauffeur-driven Packard. An uneasy feeling grew in her stomach as she swung her mink over her left shoulder. Polly's talk about buying up the Gardiner line had clearly been meant to mislead Josephine about Polly's true allegiance. Combine that with the suspicious presence of the dark, unnamed girl, and it was clear that Constance had planted a spy or spies in her office and they had infiltrated her board meeting. Polly and the note-taking girl were plants who needed to be summarily ejected. War had officially been declared.

22

THE PLAY

New York City, 1935

Lenny Ryan always enjoyed the feeling of a wad of cash in the pocket of his navy slacks, and this one was thicker than usual. He had paid his rent on time and enjoyed himself with a girl he had met at a local whorehouse, since he hadn't had one in a while after his wife, Sheila, had died. And now he was finally going to buy himself the new hat he'd been coveting and thought was well deserved. He had one stop to make first before he could enjoy the perks of his haul.

He entered Gardiner's building at 9:15 a.m. This was strange for him. He had never been inside this building during the day. He was a nocturnal creature, condemned to roam this travertine lobby only when it was lit by moonlight, to drag his cart through the halls, accompanied by the buzz of fluorescent lights. So, while feeling out of place, he was shocked to see the army of people inside the lobby. As he waited for the elevator, he watched a man turn out his pockets, scattering lint and papers onto the floor. I'll get those tonight, he thought. The elevator dinged and he stepped inside.

It was clear he did not fit in with the crowd. His one suit, which he wore to his own wedding almost thirty years ago, now hung off him like hand-me-downs on the youngest sib in a big family. He was a larger man when he was younger, and he had worked himself to the bone. He admired the men's pressed tailored suits, and their heft, the muscles afforded by luxury and leisure time. The elevator opened on the fifteenth floor. Lenny stepped out and looked back. He went unnoticed. The doors closed and he walked into the home office of Gardiner Cosmetics. He found a hive of productivity. Women buzzed around the office as if they were pollinating a flower. He slipped through the crowd of desks, weaving in between women and ringing phones. He found himself in front of Constance's office. He knocked three times.

"Yes, come in," Constance called from inside. Lenny straightened his shoulders and opened the door.

The office looked almost empty compared with the state in which he had found it the other night. Constance sat at her desk, wearing one of her usual suits of heavy tweed trousers and matching jacket with well-proportioned shoulder pads. She gazed over stacks of paperwork, like a bookie studying scores. Her demeanor changed when she saw the face of her visitor.

"Close the door!"

Lenny obeyed and shut it quietly. He needed to regain his stance, the power he had embodied the other night. He was the man in the room, after all.

"Hello, I'm here—" he began.

Constance stood. "No. Absolutely no reason. I gave you money. Onetime deal."

"I came here to ask—"

"You came back for more?" she said, outraged. "What? Did you drink it all away in two days?"

"I'm not a drinker." Now on the defensive, Lenny grew mean. "But I did come here to thank you."

He might not have been a smart man, but he was a quick one: a street fighter who had learned the hard way to protect himself growing up in the mean streets of Hell's Kitchen. A photograph of Constance and her husband, gleaming from a silver frame on her desk, inspired one last idea.

"Thank you for letting me be the one to tell your husband. Or the police. You do know that it is a crime to be a queer. I checked and came here to give you a choice."

"You rotten bastard. I have lawyers, I have money, I have—" Constance heard her voice growing more manic. She knew—and he knew—that she had lost control. "You may not . . . ," she trailed off. "You cannot . . ." She stopped. "I have nothing left to say to you."

"Then I suppose everyone will know. That you're a whore and a dyke. . . ." He turned and strode near the door. He hung in the door frame for a moment. He turned back and hissed, "If you fly with the crows, you get shot with the crows." And with that, he left.

Constance stood, speechless for a moment. Her eyes darted back and forth, then she paced as she began to devise what must happen next. She picked up a paperweight and imagined the glass shattering out over Fifth Avenue, but in her other hand, she picked up the phone and dialed.

Within moments, CeeCee was in Constance's office. CeeCee would not survive the charges or the slander, whereas Constance, though terrified, knew in her heart that she would emerge alive. She'd be ripped apart in the papers or whispered about socially, but it would be easy for her to deny. CeeCee didn't have that luxury.

"We need to retaliate," Constance said.

"How?" CeeCee asked.

"We need to get rid of him. To end him. You can do this. You know how. I'm Constance Gardiner. He's . . . what? A janitor?" She paced.

Constance turned away from CeeCee, fixing intently on a paper on her desk. "Between the two of us, my dear, I'm afraid it's you who can do this best."

"I'm sorry. I don't understand," said CeeCee.

"You must know someone who can . . . well, in your circles someone who could . . . make him go away."

"I don't." She turned from Constance, bruised, hurt. Not only had Constance failed her, put her in harm's way, but now she had revealed her true colors, expecting CeeCee to mastermind some evil deed—and worse, assuming she could because of her race, her lowly station.

Constance saw the hurt immediately and hated herself for the slight. She wanted to fly over her desk and hold CeeCee close to her. CeeCee's doe-like eyes, her perfectly formed heart-shaped lips—she still sent a jolt of electricity into Constance's heart.

"He was bluffing," CeeCee said finally. "It'll go away." She took a step away from Constance.

"Ma jolie fille," Constance whispered.

"No," CeeCee said. "After this, I can't anymore." She turned and left the room without meeting Constance's eyes. Constance watched her leave, listened to the sound of her heels on the wooden hallway floor. Her heart sank as she knew this would be the last time they would be alone together.

23

THE ASK

He told the tailor time and time again that the collars on his shirts were too tight. But the old man would not listen. He had blithely insisted on English-made shirts; yet Mickey was now certain that the old *Schneider* had been buying English schlocks from Chinatown, not from Savile Row as he claimed. Ordinarily Mickey would have let it ride because the old man had been coming to his father's fruit stand for decades. Now, however, as he stood in this bar and pulled at the tight collar, he wished he had insisted that the tailor had made it larger or that he'd simply spent the money to buy real imported shirts. He would not skimp again.

Mickey ran his fingers through his mane and tried to tame his ringlets as he continued to stand at the bar. He didn't want to sit down, since he always flew to his feet when CeeCee entered a room. There were some risks to them meeting out in the open. He only wished that he could be with her. To think of it, he couldn't remember the last time they had been alone together in the last few weeks. CeeCee had dived into her work and the girl was hungry, persistent, to say the least.

The door swung open and CeeCee stepped inside. Her hair was a little wild from the weather—frizzy and emanating at all angles from her face—but to Mickey, she might as well have been an angel.

"Wasn't sure you'd find the place," he said with a charming grin.

"Mick. It's good to . . ." She paused, out of breath. She sat beside him on the bar stool. Across the bar, the bartender looked displeased.

"None of that here. We are a good Irish bar. The Spanish ones for your crowd are on the Upper West Side." Mickey and CeeCee looked at him, unfazed, with disdain. Mickey calmly spat on the floor and the two of them took off running.

They raced into the lamplit Tompkins Square Park, laughing and checking their backs to see if the bartender was after them, but he hadn't bothered. The two settled onto a bench as Mickey put his arm around her.

"Mick, I need something." She looked up at him.

"Cee, I'd do anything for you. You know that. God, you make feel—" He let out a loud roar.

CeeCee laughed and quieted him down. "I know. But we wouldn't work."

"Oh, *we* could. Maybe not with the world. But just you and me. We work. We work like a perfect machine."

"Mick," she said. Her laugh sizzled into a flat line. It was time to make her point known. "There is someone that is bothering Constance."

"The lady is richer than half the broads on Fifth! She can't toss him some dough-re-mi from her beautiful terrace up there?"

"He's bothering me, too," CeeCee said.

"Who is it? Where is he? I'll kill 'im myself!"

"Kill?" CeeCee's eyes widened. It was the first time she had heard the word out loud.

"Then what? You just want me to smack someone 'round? Maybe turn 'im into next week's dinner?" He shrugged.

"Don't be vile! But who should I turn to?"

There was silence for a moment. Mickey did not completely understand where she was heading. "I don't know, Cee."

CeeCee's face fell and Mickey frowned. CeeCee's pain was Mickey's pain. When she felt down, Mickey would do anything in his power to lift her up again.

"I do know a guy . . . ," Mickey began.

"Don't tell me any more." CeeCee winced.

Mickey wrapped his muscled arms around CeeCee. She felt the strength of his bulky arms, so different from Constance's soft, smooth limbs. The musk of his aftershave. A distinct contrast from the treacly sweet rose of her former lover. She leaned into his embrace, burying her face in the crook of his arm and breathing in the comfort and strength of this man she loved.

"Don't you worry. I'll take care of it," Mickey whispered into her ear.

CeeCee pictured a different life. One where she was never insulted for walking into a bar, one where she never had to pretend to be someone she was not, one where she did not have to stifle her dreams or siphon them off for another woman's ambition. She pictured a world in which she had never slept with Constance and the only thing she knew was the feeling of this man and his two strong hands.

24

THE BIG IDEA

New York City, 1935

Constance threw the latest edition of *Photoplay* magazine across the room. The George Hurrell photo of Joan Fontaine incensed her. How did he do it? Hollywood's master court photographer was able to highlight her eyelashes like palm fronds casting a shadow against her alabaster skin. How could she get lashes like that into a bottle? It had been years and they still couldn't achieve a nonclumpy, no-mess formula.

Staring at herself in her boudoir, Constance studied her own face. It was still peaches-and-cream beautiful, but she saw suddenly the creeping of fine lines. To hell with that. A stronger lip color would divert attention as she applied her own Cherry Blossom lipstick. She thought back to the anxiety of the other night. She hadn't heard a peep from Lenny since his eerie visit. CeeCee had been right. He was a big fat bluff. The whole ugly mess had blown over. Her full attention was back to the product at hand.

She pulled out a tiny brush from a clean and sterile white sample box her office had sent her. The prototype was finally finished. This was the beginning of her own reinvention, the next chapter of her success. American women wanted and demanded new. They all wanted innovation. Of course, they bought the creams, the powders, and the rouges. They had to have that. But the information she received from her earnest army of Gardiner Girls was what every loyal customer asked when they arrived monthly. "Do you have anything new? I want to look like [fill-in-the-blank Hollywood star]." They all wanted a bit of glamour in their everyday lives. Hopefully, this one will work, she prayed as she took out the sample tube. It simply had to work. Slowly and with relish, she dipped the brush into the thick black paste, wiping the excess off of the edges and spreading the mascara onto her eyelashes. Her blue eyes popped in contrast with the deep black. The result was easily smudged and very clumpy, but it was much cleaner than the effect of kohl paste around Cleopatra. It was striking and undeniably unique. Yet it still clumped. That said, she knew she was close. It needed an agent to make it smooth, consistent, even. And then it would be marketable. Women would buy it. Constance held the container of black paste in her hands as though she were holding a serum that could cure a disease. She thrust the brush back into the bottle, again wiping the excess off of the edge. The overflow stained her hands with unsightly black. If only the container and brush didn't allow for so much excess . . . so much mess.

Constance was on her feet making phone calls in minutes.

Several blocks away, Josephine was on her way to an art auction at Parke-Bernet. The French antiques in the catalog were sumptuous and she had her eye on a small writing desk that provenance suggested belonged to Marie Antoinette. It had to be hers. As she entered the already packed auction room, she caught a glimpse of one of the young socialites standing beside her boyfriend with the catalog at her side. Josephine began to make a mental count of every cosmetic product that would be needed to fix this young lady. Her skin was soft, still supple from youth, with a bit of baby fat and a scattering of unsightly acne, yet her eyes were wide and her strongest feature. Josephine walked toward her, trying to get a closer look at the girl's eyelashes. They were magnificent. Bold and dark. Supple and thick and black against aqua-blue eyes. . . . This was what made her eyes seem so vivid across the crowded room. The lashes were upturned long black fringes and more exciting than the desk, and Josephine lost interest in bidding.

"Anything we can help you with today, Madame Herz?" Reginald, the dapper Englishman in his natty suit, asked with deference. Although diminutive, Josephine cut a familiar figure in the auction rooms and was one of their best customers.

"Yes, her eyelashes!" she said to a bemused face as she stormed out to her driver.

"Damn it to hell!" Josephine screamed as she pushed a vial of dark liquid away from her. She was down in the labs of Herz Beauty, alone, playing with various formulas. This latest, a thick paste that looked more like fireplace soot than an eye cosmetic, was frustrating her to no end. The consistency wasn't right. The color was off. Too much mess. The texture was either too thin or too thick. *What was she missing?*

She had to get home to see Miles and make sure he had had a proper dinner and bedtime. She knew she shouldn't be working so late, attempting to do the impossible. In times like these she always thought of her husband. Her hapless husband, who had been of great use only once, when he gave her a beautiful boy. A man who hurt her as she had hurt him, over and over, with his words and his flings. A man who envied her business. A man who was finally *gone*. A gossip columnist she knew and who was on her payroll had called her a few days earlier. He had told her that Jon was having an affair and flaunting the woman, a client of hers, in public. She had confronted him and thrown him out. And worst of all, he hadn't denied it or seemed to care anymore. No apologies and no remorse. Damn him. Her mind fluttered back to the days when they had first met.

Jon wandered in Melbourne's Fawkner Park after a long day at the paper. He lit a cigarette and took a majestic inhale. He had just picked up the habit a week prior, but he did not look like an amateur. His feet shuffled against the pavement and he walked around with his head facing the darkening, orange-streaked sky. This was something he had always done. He would drift in and out of reality. She would simultaneously love and hate this about him.

Josiah waited for him at the fountain, which was their agreed-upon meeting place. He had wanted to pick her up at work and she had said no, not wanting him anywhere near her awful family. She would meet him. She was escaping yet another fight with her uncle—who had given her a bill for her stay—with a book and a head of steam. The warm air filled her lungs and reminded her of the summers in August back at home.

Jon looked at her as he had done in the teahouse: stalled, intrigued by this fiery and beautiful creature. As he walked toward her, he flicked the cigarette and took a deep breath of the warm spring air.

"Hiya," he said, in a folksy American tone. He gave her a brief kiss, then looked at the book she was carrying, "I read that once."

"You did? Vell, don't ruin it. I'm only halfway through," she replied.

"I would never tell you the ending. But I know what ours will be," he said simply.

She regarded him in the dusky light. He was very handsome, that was for sure. "So tell me my future?"

"No, next time."

"Tell me. You can do it," she insisted.

"Here, these are for you." He revealed a very mismatched bouquet of flowers. Speechless and touched, Josiah took a deep breath.

"I didn't know which kind you liked, so I got them all."

Josiah blushed. This was a new one for her. A handsome man she had just met, falling at her feet. A man straining to please her. She had never known anyone to show her affection in such an endearing manner. Taking the flowers, she held them close to her chest and smiled.

The two strolled around until the night seemed to envelop them. Jon told his war stories of school and his work as a young, hungry reporter. She spoke of her town in Poland and what she had learned from her travails, the journey from Europe. Throughout, he listened, rapt and engaged. And this garnered more affection in Josiah than any flowers he could buy. The night and their endless talking had faded into dawn and they found themselves in front of the boardinghouse. Every step she took, he was one step behind.

Finally, they reached the door. Josiah did not want to ruin it. She smiled and looked into his eyes. Deep, blue, and caring. Jon seized the opportunity. Their lips touched and the spark was like a circuit closing and lighting a bulb.

Josephine thought of the years that followed. The sweetness of their early love. The betrayal after she'd moved to London. The reconciliation. The flowers, the gifts of jewelry, the endearments. The promises never to . . . again. And then there was the whisper of a girl in Los Angeles and the call about his girlfriend in New York, a high-profile client whom he was seen dancing with at the Stork Club. Whoever could have guessed their love could become so tainted and so soured? She and Jon were doomed even as they recited their vows. He would help her launch and take flight, but then he would weigh her down, chasing his own success by shedding the weight of her business. He had cheated on her, it seemed, in every port they occupied, since she was always working and unavailable. And now she was done and he was gone, and he didn't seem to care anymore. Nor did she.

"Better without him." She shook her head. "He was weak and always a problem. Now he could go."

She took a deep breath to banish her anxiety. Her business was flourishing and she had recently gotten her American passport, and her son, Miles, whom she'd enrolled at Collegiate, was doing so well there. Who needed Jon? Now she could spend all her time on her business. Now she could really win without him. Damn him. She knew deep down she still loved him but refused the feelings. Renewed in her resolve, she left the lab and darted into the street in front of her Fifth Avenue office, finally heading home.

25

SUSPICION

New York City, 1936

The day before the New Year's Eve ball dropped, Constance had withdrawn the perfect amount from the bank. An amount she could draw legally without suspicion. She passed by a small card store and snuck in to purchase a cardboard envelope. She reached the office around a quarter to eleven. She did not even notice the inclement weather. She was too intent on the task at hand, the need to rid this nuisance from her life. Lenny had come back again with more threats and CeeCee had finally revealed her plan to scare him off and they'd sprung into action.

Inside, she headed immediately to her office without checking to see if CeeCee was in. She counted the crisp hundred-dollar bills and placed them inside the envelope. After several calls and a lunch with a client, she would place the package where CeeCee had instructed her to do so.

Before Constance checked the time again, the day had come and gone. It was near dusk when her phone rang.

"Constance?"

"Yes, who is—"

"CeeCee. I am grabbing a few things. Please leave it in my desk. Right side, lower drawer. I told him it would be there."

"He's coming tonight?"

"Yes. Leave it there and go home as soon as you can." CeeCee's voice sounded distant and panicked. "Happy New Year." She heard a sullen resignation.

Constance held the envelope. "I'll put it there now. CeeCee, can we—?" The phone clicked. Not knowing where she was, Constance made no effort to ring back. Instead, she quickly put on her coat—a luxurious mink with a belt—over her signature trousers, and holding the fattened envelope and with barely contained anger and terror, she walked out of her office to make the drop.

As she neared CeeCee's desk, she noticed the top was bare. Constance opened the desk drawer to find it emptied. Where were CeeCee's belongings? Her office looked sterile and abandoned. There was not a scrap of paper or pen inside. All that rested on top was a small, limp flower in a vase. Constance put the envelope inside the desk. Right side. Lower drawer, per the instructions. Then she continued down the brightly lit hallway and into the crowded elevator. Her unease grew with each step until she exited the building.

Lenny walked the halls and offices of Gardiner Cosmetics with a sense of grandeur. He knew Mrs. Gardiner-Wyke was convinced she had to put him on the payroll to gain his silence. The dirty dyke had no choice if she didn't want her fancy world to know the awful truth. This would be the very last time he would be in the building, but what he didn't know wouldn't hurt him, as he mopped the floor.

It didn't take much for Tony Morello to get himself into the building undetected. Rush hour all but invited outsiders to waltz into the busy throng. He made it to the fifteenth floor without so much as a request for his name. The instructions were simple: the money would be in the lower drawer of the desk with the flower on top. A simple, thirty-minute job at most. Tony was not entirely sure why Mickey had asked him to do this, but he was more than happy to oblige. The money was good and the job was easy, just putting the fear of god into the paddy. And Mickey was a friend and always got him laid from the best-quality broads in town. He had given him a lot of business over the years, not to mention access to the hottest women. And when Mickey got on a kick, especially with a pretty girl, there was no stopping him.

Tony could see the figure in the distance. An old man sweeping in the middle of the office. He stepped quickly toward him.

"Got a light?" Tony said. He pulled a Chesterfield out of the pocket of his jacket and let it hang in his mouth.

"The building is closed, sir," Lenny replied. "Opens tomorrow at six-thirty."

"Tomorrow, the person I'm looking for won't be here. That wouldn't do me any good." Tony began to circle Lenny, closer with each step.

"Who ya lookin' for?" Lenny asked. He gripped the handle of the broom. His knuckles began to turn white. Tony leaned forward and came into the light.

"Some lousy piece of shit that takes money from rich old broads." He punched him in the jaw.

In an instant, Lenny took the broom and hit Tony across the head. He was fighting Irish, after all, and had had plenty of scrapes with the guineas. Like an angry bull, Tony lunged forward, grabbed Lenny's collar, and started to beat his face. With a swing of his right arm, Lenny got Tony in the side of his face. Again, Tony went at him. Rage filled him to the core.

Mickey's phone rang in the middle of the night. He had fallen asleep with a bottle of single malt whiskey in his lap. He picked up the bottle, played with it for a moment, then answered the phone.

"Hello?"

"Mickey—I screwed it up." He heard Tony's voice cracking,

"What happened?"

"I attacked the guy, see. He hit me and then we fought. Then he got my wallet, which slipped out of my pocket, Mick. I had to run as someone saw us fighting and started yelling. So I ran down the stairs. He could call the cops, Mick."

Mickey sat bolt upright, knocking the bottle to the ground. He ran through his options as he tried to sober up. He could tell CeeCee he had struck out, and they could try again. Or he could muster up the courage to go and finish the thing himself. He would need a couple sips of fiery liquid luck, then perhaps he could go and teach the guy a lesson.

"Where are you?" Mickey asked

"At a diner on Broadway and Lafayette," he heard Tony whisper in a hoarse voice.

"Do you still have this guy's home address? I gave you that?" He recalled asking CeeCee to get his home address as well and was glad he had. He also knew the guy lived alone.

"Yeah. I was gonna put it in my wallet, but for some reason it was in my coat pocket."

"Then this is your lucky night. Hang up. And wait there. I'll be there in an hour. I'll have to call Charlie." Mickey hung up and swigged back the drink. He dialed the number he had for his friend Charlie, the wiseguy who handled the tougher jobs. Half of him was hoping that he wouldn't pick up.

"Do you have any clue what time it is?" Charlie's voice growled.

"It's Mickey. Tony and I got into some trouble." He was nervous. He never called needing this kind of help.

"Where and when?" Charlie said.

26

THE HIT

New York City, 1936

CeeCee's days at Gardiner Cosmetics were over. The women of the office were baffled. They stopped by all day to ask Constance what had happened since she was so integral to the operation, why she had left so suddenly and cleared out her office with no explanation. All Constance could do was lie. To be honest, Constance wasn't exactly sure what had happened herself but knew deep down it was related to the seemingly nefarious events at hand. She remained stalwart but felt clearly she needed to move on and to do so immediately. Luckily, shutting down her emotions was a Constance specialty, or a Canadian WASP specialty. She also wasn't quite used to or familiar with crimes and misdemeanors, but she was smart enough to know she needed to leave town for a few weeks. And a trip to Palm Beach would be the perfect tonic.

Her new mansion was the perfect getaway. When told, Van was thrilled at the prospect of two weeks in the sun with his elusive wife and a bit shocked that his Constance would take so much time from work. He just smiled and nodded, as he didn't want to risk bringing up the topic, lest she recognize it and limit her time there.

Within days of rail travel, she and Van were enjoying Constant

Gardin, their newly christened Palm Beach estate. She had been advised to hire renowned interior designer Elsie de Wolfe, Lady Mendl, to oversee the renovation and installation. It had taken months, but the mansion had been completely stripped, painted, cleaned, and reset with the regal antiques Constance had purchased with the house. Lady Mendl insisted on cutting down the thick tropical shrubbery that hid the glorious sea view and created a bold and iconic green-and-white–striped Florida room, replete with a whimsical circus tented–style awning that would become the focal point of their entertaining. Soon after, Constance came to the conclusion that stripes would now figure prominently in her packaging, shopping bags, and tissue paper. She was "mad" for stripes. Green and white stripes. Pink and white and yellow and white. All stripes. While she knew deep down it was Lady Mendl who had pushed her toward the striped motif, Constance was brilliant at taking ideas and making them her own. "Stripes, stripes, stripes this season!" she fired off in missives to her staff of product designers.

Constance felt like a princess with a staff of twelve to clean and polish the silver services, and she and Van had never been happier or better acquainted. They both settled into a congenial routine of polo matches, swimming, and rounds of tennis at the club and, of course, cocktail and card parties. Through Topper and Lally, their membership to two of the very best clubs ensured a lily-white environment in which Constance was able to study and hone her social skills and craft. She learned the proper way to hold a cigarette holder, and the word "dahling" was now peppered and featured prominently in her speech. She listened astutely and realized everyday words became an old-money code: couches became sofas and paintings, pictures. With her movie-star blond looks, aristocratic husband, renovated mansion, and novel business success, Constance Gardiner-Wyke had officially been launched in PB society.

Lally and Constance had become close on and off the court. And of course the commission from the purchase of her estate didn't hurt either. At the club, they were just finishing a late-evening game, tossing their wooden rackets in the air and laughing as they walked to the locker room.

It was late and dusky, and the locker room was empty of members, as they were all on the way to the terrace for cocktails. Constance watched as Lally stripped her tennis costume off to her brassiere and panties and felt the usual sensation in her chest and between her legs.

"Damn this heat!" Lally unhooked her brassiere, her alluring breasts freed and supple, freckled and rosy from the sun and the heat. "Here, let me help you." She walked over to Constance and promptly started unhooking her bra as well.

"Really? You're quite assumptive, Lally. . . ." Constance smiled as she felt Lally's hot breath on her neck and then her cupping her generous breasts with her hands. They fell into a heated embrace.

"I had no idea you . . ." Constance threw her head back in pleasure.

"I knew from the moment I saw you at the Stork Club. It's just like having another gin and tonic. Sweet, wet, and feels oh, so good." She shrugged.

"Does Topper know?" Constance asked as Lally nibbled on her neck.

"He's too stupid and he could care less about what I like or do. He's made that very clear. He is also sleeping with that tin heiress, what's her name? Jacqueline . . . something foreign. I'm sure it's for the money." She grimaced. "Does Van know?"

"If he does, he's never said a thing."

"I'm sure. A lot goes on in Palm Beach that no one talks about," she confided. "And that's the way we like it." After a half hour trysting in the shower rooms together, they silently walked back into the locker area as if nothing had happened. Neither woman commented on what transpired as they dressed for drinks and dinner. It was a brisk and businesslike exchange, and while their lust never generated as much heat as Constance had experienced with CeeCee, it was more functional and tidy. Constance felt as though she were back in college again, the secrecy and camaraderie of the forbidden pleasure from women of her class.

"Lally, I do like so much that color combination." Constance surveyed the sporty top Lally had slipped over her head. It was a vivid green and contrasted beautifully against her pink lace underwear. She also stepped into a bright pink pleated skirt. Pink and green. A fabulous color combination for one of her products.

"Oh, this. . . ." Lally shrugged. "It's veddy, veddy Palm Beach, dahling," she joked.

"Well, it suits you and your coloring." They hooked arms and walked to the clubhouse like conspiring sisters. At the bar, they nodded and waved to friends and both had gin and tonics and toasted their close friendship. Constance was pleased, as she now had a new home and a new "athletic" outlet on the island. And she also now had a new very pink-and-green packaging idea for her new mascara, soon to be called Eye-allure.

With great aplomb and speed, Constance returned to New York, tan and relaxed. She breathed a sigh of relief when she saw that Lenny was no longer at his job. CeeCee had obviously taken care of the nuisance with one of her uptown thugs. She would have called her to get the update but had no way to reach her. She never even knew where CeeCee lived. With a sense of confidence, Constance shifted her focus to a new product and her newest big idea: adoption. It had come to her on the train ride back to New York when she had seen a mother with a new baby handled by two capable British nannies. It all seemed to make so much sense. A baby would solve everything, given her tawdry inclinations and Van's silent demands for a family. And as usual, and with businesslike focus, within a few months after contacting the very best service, she and Van had the picture-perfect son, all blond and blue-eyed, and she had bribed plenty for it. Van was happy to have a namesake . . . Van Wyke Jr. While Constance could never be described as maternal, she hired her own two British nannies to do all the work and oversaw their care of him with punctual efficiency. She also knew there were side benefits to their new addition. At a moment's notice Van Jr. was camera ready, and she loved the occasional carriage push in the park with photographers in tow and the resulting press opportunities. Constance marveled at the whole thing. All it took was $25,000 to the unwed mother in Kentucky and she would give her child all the best that life had to offer: the elite schools, homes, and clubs. After all, what said "heterosexual" more than a new baby boy with platinum-blond hair who looked exactly like her? That she was never showing was not an issue to her public and army of Gardiner Girls, as she had stayed out of the limelight, always working. Close friends and acquaintances knew, but no one talked about it. It was unmentionable. Once the hand-engraved baby announcement went out, they received the proper slew of baby gifts and telegrams of congratulations.

Constance wheeled the baby back to the nannies, gave him a perfunctory peck on his blond forehead after a twenty-minute photo session with *Good Housekeeping,* and got down to the business at hand. She took a cab to her office and checked in on her number one project. She had ordered numerous tests from her cosmetics team on the mascara and was close. She gave detailed instructions on both the sample products and the containers that held them, ensuring that the box was just as beautiful as the product within. Slim, shiny boxes in all different shapes lined her office shelves. But none compared with her signature packaging, the inimitable peachy-pink and green. She thought about how different the color scheme had looked on Lally. It was nautical yet witty. Bold but elegant, fun even. She was excited that her internal product development team had promised that she would see samples later in the week. Constance told them it must be finished by the close of business on Friday. She had to play hard to stay in the game. The women of America demanded and wanted something new.

In the office atop Herz Beauty's Fifth Avenue flagship salon, a frustrated Josephine sat on the phone, listening to the banal excuses from her own development team.

"I'm coming back to the lab tonight to see the new samples. If it's not complete, I vill remove the lot of you." She banged the receiver down.

A knock on her door offered a merciful distraction from her distress.

Sheridan Sloane had been the head of Herz's legal department going on eight years. He was a rigid snob, if one took the time to know him. Josephine had always overpaid for the best, and she had thought a patrician, white-shoe, Princeton-educated lawyer would help her ease the way with national accounts. Such was her insecurity, she had thought lawyers also needed to look the part.

"Do you have a moment?" he asked. Before waiting for an answer, he sat himself down in the chair opposite her.

"Only one, Sloane." She always called him by his last name, and now with dismay he saw the turbulent look in her eyes and knew she would be in one of her famous moods.

"We have a problem with your *rushed* production on the new product line. I'm still a bit in the dark on this. May I ask what it is exactly?"

"When it's complete, you will have your answer." She had been fielding questions about the whole matter, from the press and her own employees, for months now, and she could not risk a leak from her own inner circle given her recent mole, Polly. Something about this man had always given her pause.

"Unfortunately, as you know, it's not a smart move to place the product in the stores if we haven't trademarked the name and have a patent. Especially if this is a newly designed item. We don't have the insurance in place, let alone the time to go through testing on this. When we have the trademark and/or the patent, then we can at least announce to the trade. One cannot put the cow out to pasture if one does not know if the cow can feed itself. Do you see my point, Madame

Herz?" He seemed too proud of his point and Josephine wished she could reach across the table and flick the glasses off the bridge of his perfect aquiline nose. Like lightning, she now knew why Sheridan Sloane gave her pause: he reminded her of Jon Blake. Good-looking, lazy, and . . . always a step behind.

"Yes, I am quite aware," she said in a bored tone.

"It seems rather unconventional," he said. "Are you certain you cannot reveal more?"

"I promise that when I do, all the hoopla and hype will be worth it. This is the next step in the future of our industry." She glared at him.

"Well, Madame, far be it from me to be the one to doubt you."

"Indeed," Josephine said. She made a mental note to fire this man and next time hire a Jew. She had already been working with an outside legal firm on the patent, and Sheridan had been too busy playing squash at his club to figure that out.

Sheridan stood up and collected his things. He pushed his glasses farther up the bridge of his nose. Before he left, he turned to her.

"Does it have a name?" he asked. "Or will we be waiting on that, as well?"

"Lashmatic," she declared. "I already have the trademark."

"I see," he said. "You used another lawyer for that?" He was confused. "Sounds like a wonderful new car."

"Since that woman, Gardiner, planted a mole in my office, I will be using different lawyers for different things from now on. I don't want any one person knowing too much." She looked away briskly.

"I see." He looked down. He knew she was right and couldn't argue but was displeased nevertheless.

"In fact, I trademarked the name months ago with an outside firm."

"Are you sure you don't trust me to do that for you?"

"I trust no one, Sloane, including my own soon-to-be-ex-husband, so don't take it personally," she said matter-of-factly as she dismissed him.

He walked out of the room with his silver-blond hair a perfect helmet, despite the fact that his confidence was in disarray.

Josephine managed a faint smile and remained silent for a while. She had just received news from the trademark office that Lashmatic was hers. *Herz!* Now that she had the perfect name, she needed the perfect product. And one that must work.

She laughed aloud.

Lashmatic. A wonderful new car.

What a fool, she thought about Sloane. She would hire a new in-house lawyer in the morning.

27

FALLOUT

New York City, 1936

CeeCee had called Mickey numerous times to discuss that night. Did the plan go as executed? Was there any fallout? The endless questions and anxiety swirled in her head. She figured it was best to find him at home and talk with him face-to-face. The problem was she would only allow him to come to her apartment and had never been to his. She had a rule that she would not go where she knew other women had been.

As she made herself up, she looked down at all the products spread across her dresser. Various half-used bottles and old trial samples of Gardiner Cosmetics took up most of the surfaces in her room. She remembered a box in her closet. All of the Herz Beauty products that Constance wanted to study, some that she had asked CeeCee to purchase and some that Polly and the other girl, Frieda, the spy, had stolen. Unopened products, most of them of a higher quality than the small samples she was allotted. Grabbing the waste bin, CeeCee dragged her arm across the dresser and dumped all the Gardiner products into the bin. Next, she went to the closet and grabbed the box. She opened it, brought out the products she needed, and started to apply the cosmetics the Herz way.

It was near noon when CeeCee reached Norfolk Street and Mickey's family fruit stand. A small older man was unpacking peaches and apples from wooden crates.

"Excuse me? I'm looking for Mickey. Is he here today?"

The old man turned around. "No, miss, he is not."

"He's a—" She stopped herself. "Friend" wouldn't be the right word to use in this case. Additionally, she had no desire to get into racial politics with the man. She needed information. "I'm CeeCee Lopez. He needs me to clean his apartment. He told me to meet him here. He never gave me an address." To others it may have seemed strange she had never been to his apartment, that she would see him only at hers. But she had never wanted to cross the line, no matter how much time they spent together. Now she thought it was odd that she had no idea where he lived.

"Oh, of course!" The man's tone changed as if he were now speaking with a child. "I will write it down for you."

The man went into the loading area to grab a piece of paper and a pen. When he returned, he began to write down the address.

"You like cleaning?"

"Very much, sir. Mama always said to keep a good house." She smiled sweetly and batted her eyes.

"You seem like a very pretty girl for a maid, but we know our Mickey." He laughed and handed her the address, and she smiled.

"Thank you, sir. Good day."

Mickey's apartment building was not too far away from the fruit stand, a few blocks south of Delancey, near Orchard. The old man could have just given her the street and building number, but was kind enough to take the time to write out a virtual map with arrows, perhaps underestimating her sense of direction. When she arrived, she climbed to the third floor and knocked on the fifth door. After a series of knocks, Mickey opened the door in a dirty wifebeater and holding a glass of whiskey. A mass of wiry black hair sprouted from the shirt, and dark thatches of hair were visible beneath the thin material. He looked as though he hadn't slept in a week and CeeCee could see, just by peering in the door, that the apartment was in a wretched state.

"Cee, how did you—"

"The stand. Why haven't you been answering my calls?"

"I didn't want to talk. You came looking for me?"

"May I come in?" She put her hand on the door and gave it a gentle push. He showed her inside, closed the door, and started cleaning up clothes that were strewn about.

"Apologies for the mess. Can I get you something?" He attempted to turn on his charm. "I'm so glad you finally came. You would never come here before," he said, making pleasantries.

"Mickey, what happened?"

"It won't be a problem anymore. You can count on that." His eyes darted around the room, looking anywhere but at her.

"He got the message?"

"Yes, one way or another." He still would not meet her gaze.

CeeCee removed her jacket to reveal a somewhat provocative dress. A plum cotton sundress with a sweetheart V-neck that was scalloped at the breast. She was not unaware that some allure might help her to get the facts straight.

"You're so beautiful," Mickey stammered.

"Tell me what happened." She sat on the couch and patted the place right next to her.

"The details aren't necessary. He won't bother you again."

"Tell me, honey. Please." She was willing to perform. The seductress, eliciting her answers. He'd open up in a moment or two.

"No, Cee. It didn't go as planned. Let's leave it at that."

Her smile dropped. "What do you mean, as planned?"

"I said leave it!" he roared. She couldn't have imagined his voice that loud before. He stood and began pacing the room like a tiger.

"Mickey, you tell me right now what happened. You can tell me what didn't go according to plan."

"I was drunk and it was Tony. He egged me on."

"Who is Tony?" she asked.

"It was like a nightmare. I can't rack my brain why I did it."

"Did what?!" CeeCee had enough. All the worst possible thoughts raced through her mind.

"My guy screwed up. Morello beat him up. But the guy took his wallet. We had to get to him before the pigs got involved."

"Morello?"

"The guy sent to get the guy that was messing with you." The more he paced the room, the quicker her heart began to pound.

"Morello called me in a panic. . . . Then I got Charlie on the phone. We went over to the guy's house and luckily he was there drinking beer. He was a greedy son of a bitch and I had a feeling he was thinking about *his* next move. So we busted in, beat him up, and threw him in the trunk of the Buick. And next thing I know, I'm at a shit motel a mile out of the city with the guy bleeding out in the tub."

"Who was bleeding, Mickey? Who was bleeding!"

"The guy. The janitor."

CeeCee shrieked. The sound of a wounded doe. This was not what she bargained for.

"Cee, it wasn't good."

"No more." She turned away, tears streaming.

"I did it for you, Cee."

She shook her head. "I didn't ask for this."

"I wish I could take it back. I do. I do." He sobbed into her chest and she held him. The two sank into the couch.

"I gotta get out of town for a while, Cee," he whimpered, which was an unusual sound for such a macho guy.

"Where?" She let out an anxious breath at losing him.

"L.A. My uncle Irving runs the numbers rackets out there. I'm going out to work for him until this all blows over." He shook his head, his glossy curls breaking free of the hair pomade.

"I understand." CeeCee lowered her head. "I'll miss you."

"Not more than I will." He gathered her into his muscled frame, and she felt his bulk and the sensual smell of his aftershave mixed with manly sweat. And for one wretched moment she let herself think of only one thing. Not the man who died, but the man who loved her.

28

REALIZATION

New York City, 1936

Constance and her team at Gardiner were having a different kind of launch plan. No big speeches in a boardroom on strategy. No grandiose talk of the future. Because the future was being cranked out as best they could, piecemeal and with the best of intentions. That said, everyone knew something was amiss. Constance had first approved the slim, cylindrical metal tubes chosen from an exposition in Paris a few years back. Then she'd decided to look at a new form of lighter plastic that was now available. The brush size kept changing as well, and the formula was either too thick or too watery. If all went as it should, everyone knew her eye product would be an instant success, but the project was plagued by indecision, a lack of control, and product formulation problems.

To take her mind off it, Constance was more focused on the marketing right now, the rollout plan for the product once it launched, as this was her favorite part: approving the advertising and promotion creative side. Then there were the more difficult budget decisions; how much to spend on brochures and radio versus newspaper and magazine ads to support her door-to-door army, and whether or not it would be the right decision to offer a small introductory gift with purchase.

As she finalized the list of stores to receive the first shipment, the door opened to reveal a familiar face. Although it had been weeks, the sight of her old friend immobilized her momentarily. She did her best to hide her surprise.

"Constance." CeeCee nodded as she breezed in. She wore a tailored navy suit that highlighted her lithe figure and a simple strand of white pearls. She had never looked lovelier.

"CeeCee." Constance formed a prim, professional smile.

"I hate to bother."

"You are never a bother, Cee. Come in." She quickly motioned to the lingering staff to give her a moment of privacy.

"I owe you an apology."

"The apology is mine."

"I lost my way."

"Oh, darling, we're all a little bit lost." She smiled nervously. She had missed her more than she'd thought.

Constance laughed, but CeeCee was not having it. Silence was strongest in the room. CeeCee had come now that the awful thing had been done, and she knew that Constance *owed* her. She was also without a job and feeling the sting of reduced circumstances.

"In all our time together I was never able to actually present my business idea to you. And now that everything is, well, fine again, since I delivered for you . . . I wanted to finally show you my idea," CeeCee said. "I'm planning to start my own business like you did and I need . . . an investor," she said with businesslike authority.

Constance looked at her friend's face, her bright doe eyes, her elegant cheekbones, then stole a glance at her perfectly curved body. Despite superficial differences, she saw herself in CeeCee. But it did not fill her with affection. It threatened her to no end.

"I have our new item launching next month and we are in a bit of a transition." Constance felt unhappy at what she considered a mercenary conversation. She was upset CeeCee had brought up the other topic as an exchange. It was all so beneath her.

CeeCee could sense the rejection coming, but she found herself smiling brightly anyway. "All of those months of trial and error, and you got my mascara project to work?"

"It seems that success comes to the one who stays latest in the office. And it's *my* mascara project," she said with an icy edge.

CeeCee tried to smile. "Yes, but it was my idea. I—"

"It was just a drawing on a page and you wanted to discuss your other idea. That is the difference. I see and spot winners. That is the talent. *That* is the idea. That is why I am a success." Constance beamed proudly. "And it's our next scheduled launch, once the kinks are worked out, of course. The announcement will hopefully be in the papers shortly."

"What did you end up calling it?" CeeCee lowered her voice and eyes, knowing she could not win.

"Eye-allure."

"Wow," CeeCee said. "Catchy."

"Thank you. You would have known about it and been involved, but *you* chose to disappear without an explanation. CeeCee, I wish you the best of luck with your business idea," Constance said in a clipped and frozen tone.

"After all we've been through"—CeeCee gathered her things—"I might have expected a bit more. Even a loan would do. The market for colored women will make us both millionaires." She gave one last pitch. "Not to mention I helped clear up our problem."

"CeeCee, I will have you know I am already a millionaire and I have no desire to work in the colored-women category. It would tarnish the Gardiner image," Constance said.

"So you can tarnish your image with me but won't bring it to the public?" CeeCee said, enraged, finally standing up for herself.

"That's right. You should go, CeeCee. We have nothing more to discuss on the subject." Constance looked back at her desk and resumed her work. CeeCee continued to watch as she processed Constance's second betrayal.

"Fine. And don't worry, I won't ever say anything about the other situation. . . ."

"Yes. You're the one who arranged it. I had nothing to do with it."

"Really . . . nothing to do with it . . . hmmm. . . . Constance, from here on out we are through being friends." CeeCee stood erect and walked out the door. She felt proud despite the betrayal. And she knew Constance had totally used her. Now she would need another way to raise the money. Why was life so unfair to her?

As she rode down in the elevator, CeeCee felt her respect for Constance dissipate with every sinking floor. And her anger started to build. How could Constance use and disparage her like that? How could she so easily turn her away? CeeCee had had the original idea for Eye-allure. Not to mention the sacrifices she had made to protect Constance's name. She felt so guilty that someone she loved had committed a crime for her and Constance to cover another one up. And there was no appreciation. Now, she was to end up with nothing after investing so much with her. She, being a young and enterprising woman, made up her mind right then and there. She knew exactly what to do next.

"Where to, miss?" the cabbie asked.

"Fifth Avenue. Herz Beauty Salon," CeeCee said. And she watched as the limestone giants of Fifth Avenue presided over the path for her, cheering her on.

29

SWEET REVENGE

New York City, 1936

No one waltzed into the offices of Herz Beauty unannounced. Not even its lead investors. But CeeCee knew she had nothing to lose—and so very much to gain. Without stopping, she burst through the famous large lavender-lacquered doors of Josephine Herz's office as her assistant trailed behind with a look of confusion.

"Miss, you cannot go—" she shouted after her.

"Madame Herz! I'm sorry to interrupt. I've just come from Gardiner Cosmetics. I need to speak to you about something very important." CeeCee looked around Josephine's office. She was now not only out of breath, but totally out of place. She took in her surroundings in awe. It was all so opulent, feminine, and regal.

Josephine gestured to the assistant to leave and close the door. She knew who this young woman was and had the feeling that she had something valuable to offer.

"You are the young woman that works over at Gardiner's," Josephine said, still sitting in her throne-like chair. "I hear you run the place. And to what do I owe this incredible pleasure, Miss . . . ?"

"Lopez. CeeCee Lopez. Madame Herz, I know what Gardiner Cosmetics is launching next," she said hurriedly. "A new product that is sure to change the market. A market changer. No, more than that. A market maker. But she's going to botch it. As she always does."

"Hold on," Josephine said, sitting back in her gilded chair calmly, not wanting a movement to signify interest or lack thereof.

"Stop right now. You've come here driven by revenge, my dear. I know you feel like it's the best thing to do right this moment. To run to her competitor and give me her most precious thing. But you will regret it and I don't need it. . . . Go home, darling." She toyed with the lustrous ropes of her white and black pearls like an empress in residence.

"You will regret this, Madame Herz."

"Miss Lopez, it's not worth—"

"It's an eyelash extender," she said in desperation, playing her final hand. "Comes in a tube with a brush. To darken and draw attention to the eyelashes. It can fit in your pocketbook," CeeCee said triumphantly. "Here, take a look at the prototype—" She walked forward and placed a crumpled piece of paper on the desk.

Josephine immediately snatched it up. "Where did you get this?" The drawing took her breath away.

"I drew it myself. It was my idea." CeeCee grimaced at the thought of her stolen baby.

That stopped Josephine in her tracks. "I see."

After the board meeting today, she was certain of her imminent success, a success that would forever eclipse Constance and establish her own control of the entire industry. She and Constance were so similar—beauty and brains, form and design, content and packaging. And of course, it was no surprise that they had devised the same product at nearly the same time. These next few words had to be calculated carefully, so as not to extend this girl's leverage. She needed to keep control of her emotions.

"It sounds like a wonderful idea. I'm happy for her. And you, my dear, are a very smart young lady." Josephine surveyed her beauty.

"I'll give you the details. Everything. The name. The formula. The packaging. But I will need something in return."

Josephine sat back, looked at the drawing, and then made her move.

"I only need one thing from you, and I will agree to anything you would like, my dear," she said quietly, running all the possible scenarios through her head simultaneously and trying to find the best outcome in record time.

"Yes?" CeeCee knew she was breaking through.

"Does she have a patent?" Josephine asked, clearly intent on hearing the answer.

"Not yet. I believe they are just applying for one. She couldn't get the formula just right and is still trying but is planning the launch anyway. The name is Eye-allure, I believe that has a trademark pending."

"Awful name. Is this the brush?" Josephine looked at the drawing again. "Straight?"

"Yes. I drew it myself and saw the actual prototype. It works well, but the product clumps, you know. Not to mention the overflow, the mess and staining."

"That is the issue we have all had. . . ." Josephine shook her head.

"I have the answer," CeeCee said softly. "I was going to give it to her, but since she is a thief, I am going to give it to you."

Josephine stared into CeeCee's exotic brown eyes. "Dear, it's all very tantalizing." She breathed deeply. "Now what do you want for it?"

"I don't want money, Madame Herz. I want to sell you something." CeeCee stood her ground.

"What else could you have that I would possibly want besides this? I don't want any of Gardiner's failed items. I certainly don't—"

"It's a new hair product." This was the first time CeeCee had said it out loud to anyone. Even Mickey.

"Darling, I'm in the cosmetic business, not the hair business."

"I thought you were in the *beauty* business? I hear you are the innovator. Please just let me explain. But before I do, I will tell you the secret for the mascara. Will you shake on it?" CeeCee stood tall, erect, like a formidable warrior.

"A deal is a deal and my word is my bond." Josephine shook firmly on it. "If you give me the secret, you can work for me and we will work out a deal for your product." She was on the edge of her seat. "Go on." She had made her decision. This girl was a winner.

"Good." CeeCee composed herself. Now was her moment. "Colored women use lye to straighten their hair, and that can create burning and itching and hair loss on the scalp," she started slowly.

"Go on." Josephine peered at her intently, intrigued, not knowing where this was going.

"I have created a pomade that straightens the hair called CeeCee's Relaxer. I have experimented with shea butter, peppermint oil, and . . . Vaseline. And it helps soothe the scalp. Relaxes it, even. One evening the sample brush of the mascara fell by accident into the open jar of Vaseline. Instead of wiping it off, I inspected the brush when I removed it from the Vaseline and it created a glisten to the paste—and when I applied it, it became smooth. Something as simple as Vaseline, or paraffin and iron-oxide pigment. The lab can figure out the rest. See, I am wearing it on my lashes as we speak."

Josephine almost fainted when she saw that CeeCee's lashes were long and glistening, like those of the young girl she had seen at Parke-Bernet.

"Not only do we have a deal, I will give you one and a half percent of sales on Herz Lashmatic. You are going to be a very rich woman." She caressed her large pearls in her hands like a talisman as she spoke. "Like me." She eyed her new star with good fortune. "You will come with me this evening? The latest samples of Lashmatic are in and I want to see if it's as good as what you have told me and are wearing on your lashes. Can you come? It will be at six o'clock."

"I am not leaving."

"Good."

"Oh, and one last thing . . ." CeeCee went in for the kill. "Constance's product colors for the Eye-allure package are pink and green. She said it was very 'Palm Beach.'"

"That's such a coincidence." Josephine paused and winked at CeeCee. "My packaging for Lashmatic is also pink and green. Great minds think alike." She laughed out loud.

"It is?" CeeCee asked seriously.

"Now it is," Josephine said with all seriousness, and uttered the words that would become famous: "If I can't go to Palm Beach . . . then Palm Beach will come to me!" And she banged the desk with her emerald ring with such force, it cracked the center of the stone.

After cursing the wreckage of her ring, Josephine agreed to all of CeeCee's terms. She was impressed with the young woman's ambition, her smarts, and her gall. And when she heard about the idea for CeeCee's Relaxer, she could not get over the concept. It was brilliant. She knew a good idea when she saw one, and there was no competition, a wide-open playing field, exactly the way she liked it. And CeeCee stood her ground as she insisted on maintaining a 51 percent control of the new company. It took a lot of temerity to speak candidly with a superior, an older man or woman. She knew this from experience.

Josephine agreed to everything CeeCee wanted. She knew CeeCee would be a success and a moneymaker because she was an outsider, driven by anger and fear, just as Josephine was. CeeCee Lopez was a star, and she was now in the Herz galaxy.

30

CITY OF ANGELS

Hollywood, 1936

Mickey woke up as he usually did: naked in rumpled sheets, the radio blaring next to the broad he had chosen the previous night at Madame Maude's, the elite Bel Air brothel that catered to Hollywood studio heads, stars on a bender, and the occasional celebrity mobster. The buxom, peroxide blonde next to him bore an uncanny resemblance to Ginger Rogers, but that was the gimmick about Maude's. Every hooker was made up to look like a famous star by hairstylists and makeup artists who worked for the Hollywood studios and freelanced for extra cash. They even had a wardrobe assistant who brought over retired costumes. The patrons turned the assortment of would-be actresses and working girls into somewhat believable imitations of Jean Harlow or Constance Bennett in the dark glow of the drawing room and under the haze of alcohol. Rumor had it a famous star moonlighted at Maude's pretending to be a copy of herself. It was a way to avoid the hot glare of her morals contract with the studio and have as much sex as she liked.

"Thanks, hon," Mickey grunted, standing bare-chested and withdrawing a thick roll of tens and twenties from his pants pocket. He peeled off a few and handed them to the awakening nymph.

"Thanks, doll," she said, yawning, one of her fake eyelashes from the previous evening landing like a butterfly on her cheekbone. "You're so sweet and handsome, I almost don't want to charge you."

"But you will."

"I'm not gonna say no to this." She kissed the wad of green he had handed her. "You're too cute, though. Ask for me again and I'll throw in some extras next time."

"That's what they all say." He shrugged.

She raised herself from the bed and walked on her hands and knees, unzipping his fly, expertly taking out his member. He immediately stood at attention as she started sucking.

Mickey's eyes seemed to roll back in his head as he stood firmly, his legs planted as she worked him over. He shuddered slowly and she smiled, knowing she had pleased him.

"Thanks, hon. That was a bonus." He looked down.

"You're welcome. You remind me of John Garfield." She wiped her mouth.

"So I've heard," he said, and laughed. It was a standard line for women who wanted to pay him a compliment.

He looked down and suddenly saw a red-gold ring around the base of his penis. It wasn't the first time he had seen this unique color after an evening at Maude's.

"What the hell is that?"

"Oh, my lipstick. All the girls here use it. We call what you have a rainbow." She laughed.

"No, what color is it? Where did you get it?" Mickey asked.

"The makeup guy here works at MGM. All the stars use it on camera. Doesn't smear."

He tried to rub off the lipstick to no avail. "Only for the movies, you say? What's it called?"

"What's it to you?" She shook her head.

Mickey answered with a hundred-dollar bill.

"Whatever floats your boat. Dax something, I think." She took out her lipstick from the side table and looked at the printed name on it. "Dax Shachter."

"Here, I'll take that." He snagged the lipstick as she slipped the hundred into her black lace brassiere.

"Don't tell your girl where you got it from." She smiled with a wink and fluffed her platinum hair. "She might get ideas."

Mickey smiled. It was an idea not for her, but for him.

31

THE RACE

The two women and seven men crowded around the large, burnished Napoleonic campaign desk that served as the conference table. Josephine always decorated her offices at Herz Beauty in an androgynous style, which is to say one that would please her and also let her male bankers and employees know who was boss. She had chosen a sumptuous lacquered lavender for her doors with the black moldings leading into a room with touches of mink—miniver—and walls hung with the thought-provoking art she had collected over the years. It was an unusual setting for business discussions about cosmetics, but it was perhaps more imposing and strategic than one would expect of a women's beauty firm once inside. And in addition to setting her male colleagues at ease, it filled Josephine with a sense of pride to see the artwork she admired so much and had purchased with her own earnings over the years. The new Max Ernst hung proudly on her wall, as did the Picasso. Yet no matter the masculine cues, it all still reflected a cultured woman's touch: translucent Limoges china (Princess Eugenie pattern, *bien sûr*) and an ornate sterling tea and coffee service with which she could sensually pour and serve a retailing magnate or press baron a cup of strong espresso as she had in the early days at the Melbourne tea shop. Yes, she knew deep down it was a stage set crafted to impress and intimidate and . . . if the office was a touch on the stuffy side, well, at least it was not like the leather-and-oak–paneled coffins where the Locust Valley bankers such as Van Wyke went every day to die.

Three lanky and well-appointed models formed a line in front of the table while a hygienist, dressed in nurse's white, stood at their side. The models wore contemporary, if slightly advanced, fashions, each one sporting not a full circle skirt, but rather the more daring slim pencil skirts of the new caste of "working women." The outfits were all in crisp, neutral, and clean skin-toned beige, and the models' hair was pulled back into tight, neat buns replete with matching headbands to avoid competition with the hairline: a totally clean palette to draw attention exclusively to the face. These long lines accentuated their handsome height, as well as drawing the viewer's eye upward as test lipsticks and rouges were applied. Today, however, would be all about the eye.

Their faces had been freshly powdered, giving them each a somewhat ghostly look and creating a fresh canvas for testing. Josephine turned to her staff: her Swiss head of product development, Ned Born; Carl Epstein, the silver-haired, Bronx-born founder of the ISS (International Scents and Salves), which executed her manufacturing and production; her chief financial officer, Ralph Levin; and the other heads of departments she had asked to attend—head of testing, head of marketing. Finally, Josephine introduced the newest member of her team, CeeCee Lopez. No one was surprised. And with a nod and clearing of her throat, she both ascertained and informed them that she was ready to begin.

The hygienist rose to attention. She applied the new product to the first model.

Josephine watched as she brushed the thick black paste over the lashes of the first model.

"Too messy," she said. "Much too messy." Her bejeweled wrist tapped against the tailored sleeve of her navy-and-white Chanel bouclé suit, while the layered ropes of her long pearls swayed.

The hygienist nodded meekly and moved on. She applied the next round of black paste from a second bottle to the second model's face.

"Too thick and clumpy, Carl." Josephine shook her head as Carl gulped.

The hygienist nodded and moved away from the model, as though she were scanning a conveyor belt for defective parts. She withdrew a third bottle from her wheeled cart and applied it to the third model, her hand gliding noiselessly back and forth.

"Stop." Josephine raised her voice like a crossing guard alerting an errant child who had ventured into oncoming traffic. She stood from her chair at the head of the table and all but leapt to the side of the third model. She leaned within an inch of her face, studying her eyelashes. She remained there, staring, her smoky, almost Asiatic eyes intense against the question mark of her arched and plucked brows as though assessing an impossible choice. No sounds were audible in the conference room other than the breathing of the model.

"Do you like this one?" Carl's tremulous voice from the table finally broke the silence.

"No," said Josephine. "Not . . . yet!"

The hygienist began to collect the bottles on her wheeled cart.

"*Vait!*" she commanded again. "I do like that shade of black." The room exhaled as Madame actually liked something. She turned back to the assembled group. "Please go back to the lab and start again, using that shade, and this time, let's try it with something that will make it smooth and glisten. Let's try CeeCee's idea of using petroleum jelly, paraffin wax, or some agent like this. Carl, your wife wants to shine when she is going to the club for a wedding or a bar mitzvah. And Carl, we all want clean, clean, clean." Her lovely, well-groomed hands sliced the air, punctuating each word with a staccato motion. "A recipe that doesn't make such a mess. Our customers do not want something to stain and tarnish their clothes. We want easy and clean and fantastic." She lifted her arms skyward to make her point. And that's when she saw it. It came to her in a flash. She fixated on a curved oval dental repeat pattern detail in the ceiling. It was all she could see. The curve. That was it!

"And *vhy* is the brush straight?" She looked at the applicator in the tube. "Why is it a straight brush, Carl? Is my eye straight?" She raised a well-plucked and penciled eyebrow, accentuating the upward curve.

"No, Josephine, it is not." He knew she was on to something.

"Thank you." She patted the arm of his tailored Savile Row suit. "I vant a *curved* brush as well. Apply for the patent today. Petroleum jelly or paraffin and the curved brush. That's the answer. Call my new lawyer and tell him to meet me at my office first thing in the morning."

"The curved brush. Of course, that's it," CeeCee marveled out loud.

"You have packaging? A name?" Carl asked.

Josephine walked over to an easel and removed a white sheet covering the large product illustration. Everyone gasped when they saw the rendering bringing the package to life in vibrant pink and green. The contrast of the color scheme was so different, so original, it brought forth a round of applause.

"This is Lashmatic." She said it offhandedly, as though she were merely wiping off confectioners sugar after baking a plate of chocolate cookies, not setting out to invent a product that would create America's billion-dollar beauty industry.

32

THE LOAN

Beverly Hills, 1936

Beverly Hills was running hot and cold mobsters, and Mickey was part of the flow. He'd been given the moniker "Handsome Mick" by his uncle's cronies, all Italian and Irish wiseguys with a few odd Jews thrown in for good measure, either quick and wiry or heavyset and dumpy. No one had Mickey's movie-star looks and six-foot-four-inch sculpted physique. And with his talents as a boxer, womanizer, and fashion plate, he quickly became something of a fixer for Hollywood stars who needed a loan or a girl. Hell, even a boy now and then. Not that that was *his* thing, but hey, everyone had different tastes in Los Angeles and he was more than happy to take the cash for other people's vices. If someone liked buxom blondes, a jock, or to be spanked, he would procure it all for cash. His posse was loud and colorful, and they spent all their evenings at all the right places: the Cocoanut Grove and Café Trocadero (simply known as "the Troc"), or the races at Santa Anita, where he would go with the guys and bet on the horses.

Mick lived by the motto "Broads, betting, and booze." All the wiseguys cracked up at that one. Mickey loved the glamour and the evening clothes. No one looked better in a white dinner jacket and slicked-back hair than Mickey Heronsky. In fact, Mickey was so good-looking with his piercing blue eyes and cleft chin that he had been approached a few times by casting agents, but his Lower East Side accent was so thick he couldn't get past calling girls "goils." He also had no desire to submit to the morals contracts of the controlling studios and the snooping press agents his actor friends had to constantly endure. Mickey was having way too much fun for that. He abided by CeeCee's rule: Never stay for breakfast with a broad. He would end his evening in a hotel or whorehouse and then wake up and leave pronto, shower at his house, and lounge in his monogrammed silk pajamas till noon, talking on the phone about all his ongoing deals. Twelve to one was tanning time by the Garden of Allah pool with an aluminum reflector for his Hollywood mahogany tan. As he slathered on the baby oil, he congratulated himself on being far away from the fruit stand and the smell of herring wafting from the fish store. He was now a filet mignon and lobster man.

Mickey's Mob ties were well-known around town, and he also befriended stars who played mobsters, like his great friend George Raft, who was one of the highest-paid stars in Hollywood. Mickey could not get over that his friend earned more than $4,000 a week and all he had to do was play hard-nosed people like his uncle and his friends in the movies.

Mickey had lipstick on his mind, not just on his cock, while he attended the opening premiere of the much anticipated movie *The Great Ziegfeld*. After the curtain calls and applause, they were all humming Irving Berlin's "A Pretty Girl Is Like a Melody" when they ran into Dax Shachter outside the men's lounge.

"Hi, Dax!" George Raft gave him a hearty slap on the back. "Dax here makes all the cosmetics for us actors in the movies. Needed sandpaper to get off the greasepaint yesterday." He laughed. "Hey, Dax, do you know Big Irving Heronsky's nephew Handsome Mick?"

"Haven't had the pleasure. Nice to see you both." Dax shook both hands and nervously exited quickly with his date.

"What's his problem?" Mickey said. "I wanted to meet that guy and he just walked away."

"Don't you know?" Raft gave him a scowl.

"Know what?" Mickey blinked.

"He owes your uncle Irv big-time. Irv lent him twenty-five thousand and he can't pay it all back. He might have to sell his house."

Mickey smiled to himself. What luck. He slapped his date's bottom to get her moving past the crowds.

Dax Shachter's imposing Mediterranean villa sat on one of the smaller lots of Canon Drive, but it lived up to its image as a Spanish fortress more than a home when the two mobsters arrived to say hello. The high, wrought-iron gates finally swung open and they drove their cream-colored Cadillac Coupe into the driveway and adjusted their hats, despite the sunshine, stepping onto the running boards and into the bright light.

"Mr. Shachter will see you now." The diminutive and elegant Japanese houseman took them through the Mexican-tiled entryway and into the study, which was bright with a row of Palladian French doors that opened to swaying palm trees and a lovely oval pool.

"Hey, Dax." Uncle Irv stretched out his hand. "You know my nephew Mickey?"

"Yes, we met last week. Hi, Mick."

"How have you been, Dax?" Irving reached out and lit a cigar with the heavy bronze lighter he plucked from the desk set. The small move without asking put Dax on edge.

"Busy. Working on a new movie with Busby," he said. "Trying to put together some waterproof eye shadow for this aquatic musical he wants to do."

"You're a brilliant guy, Dax." He puffed. "How smart are you about getting me my money?"

"Well, that's just it. The divorce cost me more than I thought and I had to sell my Picasso. I sent you fifteen thousand last month."

"Yeah, but where's the other ten?"

"I need some more time, Irv. Once the contract is signed for my new movie I can get you another installment."

"You won't be able to work if you have a broken leg." Irv grinned. "Any other ideas? I'm not in the waiting business."

"Look, Irv . . . I just sold the painting. The only thing I have of value is a house with a mortgage and . . . my stock."

"Stock?"

"Of cosmetics. You know—eye shadow, lipstick. I'm starting my own line, but I had to make a huge order and they needed a pretty hefty deposit," he explained.

"Hey, Uncle Irv," Mickey said, "can we step outside for a second?"

"Why?" He looked at him as though he had two heads.

"Uncle Irv, I am asking you to step outside." Mickey glared, his biceps flexing beneath his collared shirt.

"Sure thing. I guess my handsome nephew here wants a Hollywood tan." He smirked.

They walked through the doors to the pool area and took in the lounge chairs and aqua water reflecting the hot, bright sun as Mickey whispered in his ear. The scent of jasmine was overpowering.

Moments later when they walked in, Irv walked over and shook Dax's hand.

"Where's the product?" he all but barked.

"Product?" Dax looked confused.

"The lipsticks and nail shit, Dax. Where are they?" Irv demanded.

"Oh, in my garage out back," Dax stammered.

"We'll take 'em," Irving said matter-of-factly.

"Take them?" Dax looked both horrified and perplexed.

"Yeah. They're all ours now and it's a clean trade. You're off the hook."

"Sure. Of course." He was sweating. "But can I ask, what do you two want with my cosmetics?" He had turned as pale as the ivory elephant tusks on the fireplace.

"Seems my nephew here has a fancy idea about getting into the lipstick and beauty business. Has a girl he bangs who works in the biz and says they're all rolling in dough out there. And we like dough." Irv smiled.

"It's so much more than selling a few polishes. You have to know the products. You have to understand the women who will buy them." Dax had aged in minutes. "It's been my life's work to have my own cosmetics company," he pleaded.

"Yeah . . . feel good your life's work is keeping you alive," Irv snarled.

They loaded the boxes of cosmetics into the back of the coupe as Dax looked on, tears streaming down his cheeks. It would take five trips and a small pickup truck to cart away all the boxes.

And that was how Heron Cosmetics was born.

33

PATENT PENDING

New York City, 1936

Josephine paced as she waited for her new lawyer to arrive. She knew there was no time to lose and she needed a way and a strategy to stop and beat Constance. The shiksa who had insulted her with her haughty confidence. Of course she was launching a mascara. She was sure her spies had stolen and planted the idea.

She grew increasingly anxious with every passing minute as she waited. Suddenly, she saw Felix's gangly, looming figure emerge from the shadows. He was so tall and emaciated she had the urge to feed him some kasha varnishkes.

"We have a problem," she said. "One that is going to cost us."

"Is it a matter of a patent?" he said with nonchalance.

"What have you got for me?"

She had plucked him right from Harvard Law School. They now had some Jewish students at Harvard, she marveled. And best of all, he had even interned at the leading patent firm Kenyon & Kenyon.

"I filed the curved-brush patent when you called me," Felix explained. "It's pending and we're first in line so even if they filed, it would be rejected."

"Gardiner's planning on launching hers next month. Word around town is she is overconfident and has been pretesting without a patent.

Here, this is the prototype. Called Eye-allure." Josephine thrust the rudimentary drawings toward him, relishing in the victory.

"Terrible name." He looked at the sheet, marveling at her abilities. She was a master and he knew it. "Where did you get this?"

"From a new friend."

Felix zeroed in on the rigid, linear application brush.

"You know there's already a patent on a straight mascara brush." He smiled softly.

"So will that knock her out?" Josephine asked.

"I bought the straight-brush patent from the inventor. It cost about ten thousand dollars, but now it's yours. She cannot launch without a lawsuit from us. She cannot win since we now have both the straight and curved brush patents." He looked so young and, frankly, nebbishy, but she could have kissed him on the lips.

"Felix, you are brilliant. Now go home to your family, it's Shabbat," she offered, thinking it was high time she had the staff make a Shabbat meal for her and Miles, if she was ever home on a Friday night.

"Shabbat shalom."

"You see, I knew I needed a Jewish lawyer." She tidied her upswept chignon and applied another coat of lipstick. She reveled in how close she was to a win.

34

THE LASH

New York City, 1936

Some would later admit they only understood the power of the product the moment Josephine lifted her head into the light. The women did, at least. The men were perplexed. But then they saw the undeniable shimmer in Josephine's eyes and the graceful, extended lashes that framed her face like the divine Garbo in *Camille*. The men cast admiring glances and were doubly impressed as they saw the way the other women in the boardroom crowded around her, oohing and ahhing at the immediate and cinematic results.

After the haste and stealth of a presidential motorcade brought her to her corporate offices, Josephine checked the line of her signature vermilion lips, cinched her newest cape with its adorable fur paws, and bounded out of the limousine. This time, she gave her driver more than her typical "Thanks": a crisp hundred-dollar bill.

"Why, thank you, Madame." Harry looked astonished at the note.

"Enjoy it, today is a day of celebration." She dashed into the building and headed straight to the lab.

"Is it finished?" she asked the technician without offering any pleasantries.

"Yes, exactly as you instructed. The sheen, the brush, and all." The hygienist handed Josephine a small plastic tube. It was barely larger than a tube of lipstick, in a slightly longer green case, and the pink top twisted off like a bottlecap. It looked like a small multicolored bullet. She opened it and studied the tip, a brush connected to the cap. It looked like a *curved* furry caterpillar covered in a jet-black paste. This was something that would go in pocketbooks. This would make any woman in America look like a movie star. To Josephine, this was the future of the beauty business, right here in her hands. The ultimate marriage of form and design, perfect even before it had been applied. And it was going to change women's lives if it worked as she thought it would.

"May I have a moment?"

The hygienist nodded and stepped outside the room. Josephine glanced upward at the mirror on the wall. She looked beautiful already—her lip line flawless, the shade pure power and drama, her complexion creamed and porcelain. But she was missing one thing. She unscrewed the top, pulled the brush from the tube, batted her lashes, and held very still, applying Herz Beauty's Lashmatic for the first time.

The boardroom was buzzing when she arrived in large dark sunglasses as big as saucers. No one understood why. Did she have an eye infection? they conjectured. They had never seen her eyes covered in the daylight before, and it made them uncomfortable, anxious even, as Josephine's eyes were so expressive that they were a window to her soul, her moods. Now they had no idea what she thought, what she was up to. And it was frightening.

Most of the staff had assembled for the launch announcement, from secretaries to high-level department heads: lipstick, eye shadow, rouge, nail, and creams. Josephine entered quickly, taking her place at the head of the table, and the room fell to a hush. She stood behind her chair and took control of the room.

"We have achieved our dreams," she began slowly, her sunglasses giving her even more of a commanding presence, if that were possible.

"We are the leading enterprise in the cosmetics industry. We have made the cosmetics industry. I do not know a woman who has not owned, used, or heard of Herz Beauty today. We have given every woman the tools to help her be seen in this world. To be her best self, to find her own beauty—inside and out—to be admired. And we have offered this to women of every echelon: mothers and daughters, homemakers and working women, actresses and spectators. We have empowered women to be beautiful, admired, and coveted, and we have given them this invaluable gift at an affordable cost. This was always our plan and we have achieved it. Now the future will test us. Do we buckle under competitors and tightening competition? No. We press onward! To the future." She produced and displayed the green-and-pink tube. "This is the future," she said. "This is what the future looks like."

The assembled staff let out a collective gasp.

"Meet Lashmatic mascara. It is a simple black paste designed to enhance the eyes of *any* woman. It creates the perfect curtain to adorn the windows to our soul. Your lashes will shimmer, shine, and appear longer. Best of all, no mess or clumping."

Curiosity permeated the room.

"And don't you want to see what it looks like?" Josephine took a moment to let the drama build. She never had trouble working a room.

"It's Palm Beach for the masses!" Josephine's words had a hypnotic effect, casting a quiet, focused lull over the room as she presented the green and pink package to applause. No one could have guessed that she had never been to Palm Beach.

At the peak of her theatrics, she finally removed her sunglasses and everyone saw.

"And now for the results." She smiled broadly. Whispers grew into fully vocal chants. She looked different, softer, younger, more beautiful, alluring. Her eyes had the "Hurrell" effect of palm-frond lashes, casting a dramatic shadow of lines across her razor-sharp cheekbones. Then the clapping and ovation. It was the pairing of these two things—her beauty and her words, her product and her packaging—that would make Lashmatic the final jewel in Josephine's crown.

35

STAR-CROSSED

New York City, 1936

Constance and her staff were working overtime as they planned the launch like an attack ready to flank enemy lines. Check in with the warehouse that shipping would be on time. Notify the stores when the product would arrive. Follow up with the lawyers regarding the patent. The timing was perfect, the product even better now that her lab had worked to get the proper consistency. She could not fail now.

Far uptown, Mickey and CeeCee were having a late dinner at the Cotton Club in Harlem. He had come back to New York for a few days to pack up his apartment and sign the papers. He was selling the family fruit stand to his cousin Benny and moving to Los Angeles full-time. CeeCee had been in tears at the news, but she understood the circumstances. They would see each other whenever he was in New York and eventually when she could visit L.A. That didn't make it easier, however, and she consoled herself with her favorite steak sandwich, only this time as a guest taking in the show as opposed to being in it. The irony of being Mickey's guest in the all-white audience also did not escape her. No one said a word to him as the maître d' led them both to a prime up-front table after he handed him a ten-dollar bill. Then again, no one would dare to question a six-foot-four, seemingly Italian mobster at the Cotton with a gorgeous seemingly Latin woman on his arm. In a white satin evening gown, white mink shrug, and the diamond bracelet he had bought her, CeeCee had the bearing and accoutrements of an exotic Latin princess and bore little resemblance to the awkward yet stunning ingenue who had shown up years earlier. No one recognized her, and all of the girls in the line had turned over since she had been there. The club favored chorus girls no older than twenty-one, and she wondered what would have become of her had she stayed. She thought of Gladys Potter. Was she still in show business or a mom or a maid? She would never know, and she forced the thought from her mind. Mickey ordered a steak sandwich, too, and they toasted with champagne to her new company and to the future. She was now partners with none other than Josephine Herz, who was going to fund her hair relaxer business!

"Here's to my girl." Mickey toasted her with his flute, his diamond cuff link illuminated in the overhead lights. "You are going to rule the world."

"I thought of a slogan." She blocked out the slogan with her hands. "'CeeCee's Relaxer. Be Cool and Calm.' Get it? It cools and calms the scalp."

"You are a gorgeous genius." He leaned over and kissed her. They both paused as applause rose from the crowd when the energetic and talented Cab Calloway took the stage. Rudy had made the switch to Calloway's orchestra and they would go backstage after the show. The spotlight shone on Cab's slicked hair and elegant mustache as he started to scat.

"CeeCee, I have something to tell you." Mickey spoke in a tremulous tone as the applause died down.

"Don't tell me you're getting married to a nice Jewish girl."

"No."

"Then what?"

He lit a cigarette for her with his gold lighter. "I've been thinking. You and all these broads . . ." He sighed.

"Excuse me?" She laughed. "Broads?"

"I didn't mean you. I meant them. Well, they're making money hand over fist in the beauty business. And . . ."

"And what?" CeeCee raised a beautiful arched eyebrow.

"I'm getting into the business myself. I just started a cosmetics company too. For the modern gal who wants to be a star. Every broad does. It's called Heron. Heron Cosmetics." He looked down, his long, black lashes somewhat downcast and his demeanor somewhat embarassed at telling her the news. "Get it? Heron . . . Heronsky?" He looked at her as if he were a teacher giving a troubled student a test.

"Heron. I think that's an amazing name, Mickey," she said tenderly, sensing a more fragile ego than he usually displayed.

"Yeah. From now on I'm going by Mickey Heron. I'm getting rid of Heronsky . . . sounds like a funeral home. Who wants to be saddled with that?" He puffed out his chest.

CeeCee looked at him, appraising him somewhat differently.

"See . . ." He took out a business card. "I hired this Hollywood gal I know out there who does animation work for Disney. She said I should use a bird—the heron—as my logo. So I did. You like it?" He looked at her adoringly. "Never even knew there was this bird called a heron." He pronounced the word "bird" as "boid," which made CeeCee giggle. "There aren't any herons on Norfolk Street, I can tell ya that!" he wisecracked.

CeeCee looked at the elegantly illustrated long white bird on the white business card and shook her head. "Clearly she's talented. I hope only in graphic design."

"Don't worry. She's young, but looks like Marie Dressler." They both laughed at the image of the old vaudeville comedienne and popular film star who had a face like a female prizefighter.

"Mickey, are you serious? You're really going into the cosmetics business?"

"I am. What . . . what do you think?" He blinked.

"Well . . ." She paused. "I like the name and the bird logo, a lot. Heron. I actually think it's genius. You know women better than anyone. You know what they like." She shrugged. "How did it all come about?" She was truly curious.

"When I was in L.A. a few weeks ago, I noticed all the young actresses are wearing this lipstick and nail polish color. I never saw it before." He took out a crumpled page and showed her a studio publicity photo of the actress Joan Blondell wearing red-gold nail polish and lipstick. "There's a guy out there who makes the stuff for the film people. They all use it. It's smear-proof!"

"That's very interesting." CeeCee's eyes perked up at the news. "Go on. . . ."

He could tell she was interested. "Since my uncle Irv is a bookie out there he loans the stars and film people money. His friend is a big producer at the studio and we get him all the girls. I met Raft through him and his gang."

"Well, I can see what *you* were doing in L.A." She nodded her head in a mock disapproving manner. "Don't worry. I know you can't keep your pants on."

"Well, so here's the rub . . . all the stars and working girls wear the same makeup. There's a guy out there, Shachter, Dax Shachter. He's the one that makes cosmetics for the movies. He sells it only to the film people and it's ahead of what they're wearing in the rest of America. I'm telling you there is a business there."

"In going to whorehouses?" She sneered slightly.

"Yes. And don't worry. Not *one* of them can hold a candle to you."

"Gee, thanks." She sipped her champagne with a gloved hand.

"So here's what happened. Raft told me Dax borrowed money from my uncle and he couldn't repay old uncle Irv, so instead of having his legs broken he offered my uncle and me all his product. Now I have a garage full. Lipsticks in all shades, nail polishes in every color, eye shadows . . . the works. I told Irv I would take them, sell the stuff, and split the profits. It took us five trips in the car to pick up all the shit. I hired this Disney girl, slapped my new Heron logo on it, and I've been selling the lipsticks at seventy-five cents a pop. I'm making a fortune. And I'm down to my last twenty-five. Have to reorder. I'll tell ya . . . it's a helluva lot better and more profitable than selling peaches and plums. And it doesn't rot! Here, I got a few for you—" He produced a few small lipstick cases.

CeeCee's eyes lit up. "Wow, it even says 'Heron Cosmetics' on it and the name Ripe Cherry." She surveyed the package with a bit of awe.

"I have a slogan, too." His eyes glistened. "Every woman wants to get her Cherry back. . . ." He laughed.

"Don't be vulgar." She play slapped him.

"Don't forget it's smear-proof. Kiss me." He kissed her moist lips.

"Only you, Mickey. You sleep with whores and run with the Mob and turn it all into a business. Only you!"

"Better than being a gigolo!" He grabbed his crotch.

She giggled. "I never met anyone else like you, and do you know what?" She kissed him softly.

"What?"

"I'm going to help you any way I can, Mickey Heron."

"You will?"

"You can rip off the old gals. And Shachter. I'll get you all the new product information on what's launching and you can rip it off and manufacture to your heart's content," she said nonchalantly. "Like you said, the way I see it, the entire industry is one big rip-off game—except for CeeCee's Relaxer!"

"You'd do that for me?" He looked like a little boy.

"You were there for me." She kissed him hard on the lips.

"I like that. Your lips feel calm and cool," he whispered as she laughed.

"Come . . . let's dance." They rose to the dance floor, and in full view she kissed her white, Jewish man who looked Italian. And while across the ocean the recently instituted racial laws in Nazi Germany forbade interrelations between gentiles, Jews, and blacks, in the all-white audience in New York, for these two and for this evening, no one at the Cotton Club gave a damn.

36

THE WIN

New York City, 1936

Constance wasn't particularly fond of waiting on an answer from her own attorney. She had paid his firm plenty over the years and had not gotten even a return call. The fact that she, Constance Gardiner, was taking a taxi in rush-hour traffic to her lawyer's office to get an answer was absurd.

Yet here she was, getting out of the cab, crossing Sixth Avenue, heading to the building, riding all the way to the top floor, and waiting patiently for her turn. Like a common, low-budget client. She was here to discuss the patent and she wanted answers, as the timing for the launch was crucial. She knew Josephine was working on the same idea, and she had to launch first and win. She knew it was an idea so big it would take her entire company to the next level and cash in on what she thought would be one of the biggest successes of her career. And time was money.

From the moment her lawyer entered the dark-paneled conference room with the air of a pallid mortician, she knew something was wrong. He sat and placed a large document on the table and stared into it, fixed and morose.

"We have a problem," he said. He rustled the top page of the document.

"Peter, I know I have pushed you on this filing." She removed the pearl-topped hat pin and her diminutive pale pink, silk couture hat with the lace veil and put it next to her white kid gloves and crocodile purse on the chair in a ladylike fashion, and then took the bull by the horns. "And when all goes well, I will make sure you get credit where credit is due," she said in an animated voice, hoping her optimism would banish any lingering issues.

"The initial patent application was denied." He looked down and continued to stare into the page. He could not meet her eyes.

"What?" She actually lowered, not raised, her voice in a hoarse whisper. "We had everything in order. There's never been a problem with the patent office before. Why now? Why this patent?" She stood and paced the room, utterly confounded, distraught.

"Can't we reapply?" she demanded.

"Unfortunately not."

"Why not? You said it was merely a rubber stamp. Why?" she repeated, sounding increasingly like a petulant, thwarted, spoiled child.

"There is already an approved patent on a similar product."

"But, that's not possible," Constance stammered.

"Someone pulled strings. Someone swooped in and bought the patent for a similar straight-brush mascara product. Someone . . ." He trailed off. "Bought the patent out from under us."

She got the point, loud and clear.

"No. Out from under *you*," she said angrily. "Did they say her name? Did they dare?"

"Not by name. Only by organization. Herz. And they already called the trademark office to let them know they would defend their patent against any new applications. I am afraid we are done." He sat back in the walnut Queen Anne chair, his suspenders sagging as woefully as his expression.

"Then can't we change the brush? Why does it have to be straight?" She banged the conference table, her large gold charm bracelet jangling and scratching the veneer.

"They had the same idea. They already filed a curved-brush application as well. I am afraid we have no choice but to abandon the launch for now," he said in defeat.

Constance lost her breath for a moment. The room actually spun. In her fury, she left the room without saying another word to her vapid lawyer. She had heard that Josephine had fired her WASP lawyer and hired a Jewish one right out of Harvard Law School. She had mocked the decision in public at a cocktail party in Palm Beach at the B&T, laughing that the "immigrant just needed someone to speak Yiddish to," and her group broke up at the thought. However, now she knew Josephine had bested her once again, in the legal department. In her shock, she missed the elevator and began to walk down the gleaming white-and-grey–streaked marble stairs, holding on to the wrought-iron banister because she was wobbly. Her thoughts raced. She would miss her launch, and all the money she had spent on development was now down the drain, and all the while Herz would be launching her very own mascara product and getting all the credit. Her product. It was *her* product, properly developed and perfectly polished. And now she would be number two. Days later when she heard the package color scheme was actually pink and green, she went into a two-day alcoholic rage in which she was unable to rise from her bed, which was littered with empty gin bottles, all of which unleashed a massive and painful migraine. Even Van commented that he was concerned. He had never seen her so angry and distraught, and he hardly ever noticed anything.

It took a week to get back to herself, and when she looked in the mirror she found herself pale and drawn and had lost several pounds in the process. Weak and upset, she forced herself each morning to get up from the bed and into a cold shower to perk herself up. That was the Canadian way: she fought her demons with freezing water and frigid emotions. Yes, she was a fighter, and despite her paralyzing anger, deep down she knew she would live to see another day. She also knew she had a full slate of obligations and needed to regain her power and composure to lead. Her office had called and reminded her she had a couture fitting for opening night at the *Follies*. She had been invited by Florenz Ziegfeld's widow, Billie Burke, to the Broadway opening of the *Ziegfeld Follies of 1936* and the after-party and wanted to look her best, as she knew it would be one of *the* social events of the season. She personally had been doing Billie's makeup over the years, flattered that the huge Broadway and film star trusted her and her alone with her maquillage. She knew *tout* New York society and the social press would be there on opening night and she bristled at the thought that her nemesis, Josephine, could be there, too, invited not by Billie . . . but most likely by the *Follies* headline star Fanny Brice or the great Balanchine, who she knew attended her salons and was doing the show's staging. She forced it all from her stormy thoughts as her driver deposited her at Hattie Carnegie's atelier at 42 East Forty-ninth Street and Park. The made-to-order department was headed by the talented designer Jean Louis, who greeted her with kisses and whose assistant brought her an elegant, slim flute of champagne. He had chosen a white crepe gown for Constance, one that looked best on their new blond in-house model. Carnegie always was able to attract the best models, especially as her former one Lucille Ball was becoming famous. Carnegie had been the one to order the ingenue and actress Ball to dye her brown hair blond to great results, and what looked good on the tall, striking blonde would look good on their top client Constance Gardiner, as they had almost the exact same measurements. Jean put the crepe gown aside for her before any other client could see it. Constance appreciated the gesture and actually enjoyed her fittings. It provided her with a creative respite where other people were doing all the work and she didn't have to do much aside from being fussed over. Hattie stopped in, kissed her briefly, and asked after Van. Soon after, another young designer she had hired, Norman Norell, brought her the crepe de chine garment on a straight wooden hanger.

"It will look ravishing on you, Mrs. Wyke." Norman nodded as he handed her the gown and surveyed her tall, blond lean looks with admiration. She thanked him and took the gown into the dressing room behind the fabric curtains.

"Call me Constance, Norman," she said.

"It will look as good on you as our model. Not many civilians could carry this off." He marveled at her height and perfectly proportioned figure.

"Here, try this brassiere under the gown and use these shoes," Jean Louis directed her as he handed her the undergarment and the *peau de soie* pumps through the curtains. After pulling the fabric panels closed, Constance breezily disrobed and put on the new strapless brassiere and gown and then slid into the slightly oversize shoes. The gown fit her like a glove and gave her a clean, streamlined look, like a blond racehorse. The stress and the weight loss had even yielded a more mannequin-like figure. She knew she looked like a movie star as she held the hem of the gown, walked toward the three-way mirror, and stepped up on the wooden box so that Jean could pin and use chalk to make the final adjustments.

"It looks divine on you." They both thrilled at the sight of her.

"She could be the model." Jean smiled brightly. "But she has beauty *and* brains."

Suddenly, across the room she heard a commotion as another customer emerged from an identical dressing room in an emerald-green satin sheath. She was diminutive and dark, but extremely sexy and alluring, her raven hair cascading against her dove-white skin, her substantial bust spilling out over the satin strapless garment. Constance almost fainted when it registered that it was Josephine Herz. Jean walked over and fussed over her as well.

Constance saw Josephine stop briefly and also regain her composure when she saw her, yet she just marched forward in defiance and stepped up on the wooden platform as though she were leading a marching band.

"I assume you two ladies know each other?" Jean said cheerfully, unaware of their feud as the two women stood in stony silence, looking at anything and anyone but each other.

"That would be an understatement." Constance gritted her teeth.

"Or overstatement." Josephine rolled her eyes.

"Oh, I see." Jean detected the chill and withdrew slightly.

"Darling, can you bring me my emeralds?" Josephine commanded her ladies' maid, Valentina. "I want to see them with the dress. Not the Riviera, the parure . . . ," she said for effect.

Neither woman said a word, as the oxygen had seemingly been sucked out of the room. Jean and Norman knew from the *froideur* that they also needed to stay cool, calm, and out of the way in the midst of the dueling titans.

Suddenly Constance could not stand the silence anymore.

"Well, she looks good," she said icily. "For a thief!" she hissed under her breath.

"She looks fabulous." Josephine's eyes had a volcano of fire under the lids. "For a sleazy spy!"

"You stole Lashmatic from me. And you know it." Constance turned to her and threw the first direct grenade.

"You should know that I was working on my mascara project years before you infiltrated my company with your cohorts."

"Don't think I don't know that CeeCee gave you my color scheme . . . mine. It's Palm Beach, dahling, somewhere you have never been and your kind would never be accepted." She smirked.

"The color scheme is all mine . . . it's pink for the color of my lips, smiling as I see green, the color of money piling up in my bank account. Not yours."

"You're just a . . . new-money parvenu," Constance said in an exasperated tone.

"Darling, I thought you had no idea *who I was*," Josephine taunted her. "And by the way, I would wear a girdle if I were you. You may be thin"—she sniffed—"but I can see your cellulite, dear. Jean, the crepe is not very forgiving for women with that issue. I do have a cream for that problem should she want it."

In her fury, Constance, walked off the wooden platform and up to her. Josephine recoiled, not knowing if she was going to get physical.

"You're short and fat. And that fur is mine." She ripped the mink shrug right off of Josephine's shoulders. Without so much as a thought of a reprisal, Constance marched off to her dressing room with her prize, seemingly the victor.

"Well," Josephine shot back, glaring, "you take it. It's not mink, it's rat, like you." She stood her ground as Constance turned.

"You listen to me, you Polish bitch," she hissed in front of Jean and Norman, who were now actively cowering in the corner. "I am going to do to you what you did to me if it takes me an entire lifetime. You wait. You will get yours." She raised her voice, clear, clipped, and modulated in anger.

"You think I am vorried about you?" Josephine laughed out loud and stood firm, her hand on her hip. "Miss Palm *Bitch,* I have CeeCee and all your secrets. I *vould* be very careful, though." She wagged her finger, her accent emerging in anger. "Don't overstep your bounds, Mrs. Gardiner-Vyke. I vould advise you, like the little Dutch boy, to just keep your finger in the Dyke-Vyke." She laughed out loud. Her assistant helped her off the box as the seamstress unhooked her green satin gown. She stepped into the dressing room and pulled the curtain in a flash of anger and energy.

The next day, in a fury, Constance manned the phones and hired a new Jewish law firm and a new advertising agency. This gave her some solace, but the patent situation was already locked down, and she knew that even if she could develop something new, it would take months, even a year, to redevelop a competitive product. The worst thing was she knew she would have to have a mascara product for her woman, her middle-American customer, so there was no going back. Gardiner would have to develop something new and patent-worthy, and she knew when she did that Herz and Lashmatic would already be famous for the single greatest breakthrough in the cosmetics industry and synonymous with the industry herself. Worse than that, she would have to rub shoulders with Josephine Herz in competing Jean Louis evening gowns at the *Ziegfeld* opening on Broadway. In a city of millions, New York was just too small for the two of them.

37

WITH THE WIND

New York City, 1939

Josephine sat alone in the darkened movie theater and did something she hadn't done in many years . . . she cried.

Never one for light entertainment or emotional entanglements, she allocated little time for everyday diversions or frivolities. Trips to the theater, movies, card parties, tennis games, and affairs of the heart held little or no allure for her. Small people were occupied with such things, she thought, not her. "Work, work, work" was her motto. It was all-consuming, and the seasons flew by with few markers and any sort of emotion was never investigated, only flung to the side into a pile of yesterday's dirty laundry. Even the limited time she spent with her son was about making sure someone had fed him and gotten him off to school on time. Perhaps a dinner occurred once a week, and when it did she peppered him with questions and demands for academic excellence. His emotional state held absolutely no interest for her; if that was something his father wanted to explore with his twice-monthly dinners, so be it. Josephine was often quoted as saying she was not interested in "wasting time with nonsense."

That said, despite the monumental success of Lashmatic, she had recently read about a new cosmetics company called Heron Cosmetics that had surfaced in Los Angeles and was starting to get real attention and traction in the marketplace. Its dashing founder, the playboy Mickey Heron, was often photographed in the press squiring around young, nubile Hollywood starlets at the Cocoanut Grove and Café Trocadero. His savvy association with stars and his ever-present product placement within films had created a new niche in the marketplace.

From the black-and-white newsprint photos in the *Daily News* and other assorted papers, she gathered he was a handsome and sexy bachelor; she couldn't deny that. He had dark movie-star looks, that was for sure, but what was his motivation? She couldn't begin to understand, because he was a man and she had given up trying to understand them. Earlier that morning, she looked in the mirror and found and then plucked at an errant grey hair. The singular hair was coarse and unruly and made a bold statement. There! it said. Age is upon you, and it's not pretty. She was turning forty and laughed bitterly that the last movie she had seen must have been a silent reel starring Theda Bara. Was it that long ago? She thought back. Nonetheless, Heron's success and promotion with *Hollywood Hurrah,* the Technicolor musical, and the resulting Hurrah collection of lip glosses prompted her to take what was happening on the West Coast and the silver screen a bit more seriously. She knew she needed to see what was currently playing in the theaters and who the latest stars were, as she was completely uninformed. She had spent years educating herself on French antiques and modern painting and was so knowledgeable about jewelry she could have been a lapidary. She didn't often punish herself, but it pained her that she had been wrong to put her head in the sand and ignore the film industry. How could she have been so stupid? Even that dragon Gardiner had her eye pencil product in a new film. As Josephine had done before, she treated herself harshly for a day or so and then moved on. She would now embark on a Hollywood tutorial to take Herz Beauty to the next level. She had her assistant order all the movie magazines. Her star employee, CeeCee, had contacts in the film and theater worlds and she had tapped her to keep current. CeeCee had casually mentioned she knew Mickey Heron, and Josephine decided in the next coming months she would send her to Los Angeles so she could meet the locals and see if there were opportunities for Herz Beauty, not to mention a location for a Beverly Hills Herz flagship shop and salon. She was thrilled that CeeCee seemed eager to uproot herself and venture to the West Coast, since Hollywood and the trip out west held little or no appeal to her.

The film adaptation and enormity of press surrounding the premiere of *Gone with the Wind* had piqued her interest, and she decided that on a Friday afternoon between work and dinner with Miles, she would see what all the fuss was about. Her driver brought the gleaming limousine to a halt in front of the box office, where she bought a ticket and entered the vast, ornate Capitol Theatre. After buying a bag of popcorn, she spied an empty end seat toward the front and then quietly draped her mink coat over the chair and settled into her seat without much fuss. It seemed odd to her that she was seeing a movie while it was light outside, but it was now deemed work, and therefore it was acceptable. Her secretary had advised her to time her arrival to avoid the stage show, for which she had little patience, the movie being long enough.

The moment the opening title sequence appeared on the screen, Josephine sat back and watched the epic movie in awe. The screen proclaimed "A Selznick International Picture." A fellow Jew, she thought, and felt a moment of pride that the producer David O. Selznick was associated with one of the great American stories. Leave it to a *yiddishe boychik* to bring the book to the big screen. The period piece about the Civil War based on the book by Margaret Mitchell was riveting and she related to the feisty main character, Scarlett O'Hara. Engrossed, she ate her popcorn, slowly savoring each piece. It was the longest movie she had ever seen, and it seemed to fly by. The Technicolor screen cast an illuminated glow on her face, like an immense makeup mirror. Suddenly, she felt a lump in her throat as Scarlett visited Melanie on her deathbed. She couldn't understand why, but within minutes a torrent of tears fell from Josephine's face. Perhaps mortality stared back at her from the celluloid. The year 1939 had turned out to be a tumultuous one for her, with the Nazis invading her native Poland. She feared for her remaining relatives and her youngest sister, Chana, who had been a small child when she had left for Australia. What would become of her? She had a top lawyer working on trying to locate her and bring her to New York, to no avail. And then there was her former husband, Jon, remarrying to her shock and surprise. The events had shaken her to the core, and she felt more vulnerable than usual. Not to mention she was also turning forty. Forty. How could she be forty? And so alone.

"Look after him for me. . . ." Melanie's kindly face and words to Scarlett about her husband, Ashley, knifed her to the bone, and tears fell from Josephine's eyes as her body convulsed in emotion. It was as if a garden hose had suddenly sprung a leak and then another and another as the water seeped out. Miles was growing like a weed and he was always off at school events with his friends. How much longer would he be home, even for their sporadic weekly dinners? Her sister Sybil was running the London operation and they rarely spoke unless it was a business issue. Jon, who had run off with the former showgirl and radio announcer Sylvia Shore, was now an omnipresent part of New York café society. As the film concluded and Scarlett uttered the famous words "I'll go home and I'll think of some way to get him back. After all, tomorrow is another day," Josephine related to a strong woman in pain and the emptiness she was feeling.

She may not have wanted Jon Blake back, but she knew she was more alone than ever. She had started to resent going to evening events without a date and when she ran into Jon and Sylvia at two social gatherings, she decided enough was enough. She knew that despite her fame, success, and fortune she needed another man, another husband. It was as simple as a woman knowing she needed another black cocktail dress in her closet, as the old one was worn-out or last season's design. As with her new mission in Hollywood, she also knew she would have to make the time to meet a man now that she was turning forty. With the success of her iconic Parfum Empress Josephine and Lashmatic mascara, which had swept the nation, Josephine had become the richest woman in the world. How come, she thought, she felt poorer than before? It was all catching up with her. She wanted a man, needed a man, and would find one, even pay for one. She was a realist. After all, she thought, as she raised herself and wrapped herself in her creamy mink at the conclusion of the film, she was Scarlett and not Melanie, and tomorrow was another day.

38

THE VISIT

Los Angeles, 1940

"Why the hell are you staying *here?*" Mickey looked around the lobby of the Dunbar Hotel with slight disdain after coming up for air. It had been one of the longest kisses in history. The zinc deco elevator doors had opened and CeeCee caught sight of him across the lobby, standing like a little boy in the corner, as if he had been waiting for his mother at school pickup, tapping his foot, with crimson roses dangling and hanging down at his side, the soggy paper staining his pants leg. When he caught sight of her he smiled brilliantly, crushed the cigarette in the sand atop the standing bronze ashtray, and surveyed her like a carnival prize. She walked shyly and then, as if to betray her outward stance, quickly across the room. They stood facing each other at first, only a slight separation between them, only a sliver of air. Was it a dream? she thought as they forced the air away and touched lips. She melted into him and swooned at his distinctive scent of aftershave masking manly sweat. It was the hint of animal that always did it to her, and she felt the usual heat between her legs.

"Should we go upstairs now?" Mickey nibbled on her ear.

"What kind of girl do you think I am?" She gave him a subtle, playful whack.

"You're exactly like me and you know it." He softly kissed her neck, which was pure velvet. "The way you smell is . . . well, you know."

She wanted to admit right then and there that she was exactly like him, that his smell was an aphrodisiac as well, and that she would take him up to her room at that very moment and open herself up to him over and over. But she withdrew and took a deep breath of fresh air. She was in L.A. for business, not for pleasure. Pleasure would come later.

"Dinner and dancing and then we'll come back. I promise." She kissed her fingertips to his lips.

"One more kiss before dinner." He lunged at her and they seemed to cling to each other for dear life. Within moments they were wrapped around each other, the intensity of a Venus flytrap and its prey.

"And for your information, this is the best hotel in town, where I can stay," she said without bitterness at the whites-only hotel policies she was used to.

"You know I can get you into a regular hotel, CeeCee—with my help and with your last name. No one would think twice, especially in this town." Mickey cocked his head.

"I don't like lying, Mickey, you know that." She caressed his brow and moved a tendril to his forehead. "You know that," she repeated her words, and smiled faintly.

"You're too by-the-book. Why the hell aren't you staying with me? I have a house and a pool now. For chrissakes, I even have a guest-house." He crooked his finger at her.

"'Cause I never want to cramp your style, baby," she said slyly. He knew she was lying. She wouldn't stay anywhere other women had been, and he didn't push it, since if there were a box office to his bedroom, it would have been one of the biggest hits in town. He put his hulking, defined arm around her shoulder and walked her out to the car. The California evening was bright and balmy, like a silk shirt on a sunburn, and CeeCee was enjoying the weather, knowing back home it was sleeting and snowing, while here the palm trees were performing a line dance for her in the sky. She looked back toward the hotel lobby as a group of famous jazz musicians and singers passed them, entering the hotel. They all nodded. The Dunbar was well-known for catering to the black elite, and on their way to the bar and lounge two jazz musicians nudged each other and looked back and appraised CeeCee while she ignored their glances. She could get used to this, she thought. Mickey took her by her white-gloved hand and led her to his waiting cream-colored Cadillac convertible. CeeCee slid up against him in her ivory satin evening gown.

"Also, the music is better at the Dunbar," she added, and laughed as he opened the door to his convertible.

"We'll come back later for a nightcap," he said. "Who's playing tonight?"

"Lena Horne and Sissle's orchestra." CeeCee reapplied her Herz Capri Coral lipstick in the shimmering gold case and put it back in her evening bag.

"Word around town is she's going to be the first black female movie star." Mickey put his arm around her. "Maybe you should go backstage and talk to her about CeeCee's Relaxer," he offered.

"Maybe I should," she said. "And it's not called CeeCee's Relaxer anymore, Mick." She smiled as he drove down Central Avenue, hitting all the lights.

"It's not? What happened?"

"I changed the name. It's now called Queen CeeCee's Hair Relaxer. What do you think?" She stared at his handsome face intently to gauge the reaction.

"I love it." He honked his horn at a straying Ford. "Damn L.A. drivers. Fuck you!" he yelled, giving the driver the New York finger.

"Mickey, you never change. You only get better looking." She ran her hand against his slicked-back curls and took in his glowing L.A. tan offset by the white dinner jacket.

"You are my queen." He pulled her closer in the auto's front seat.

"The girls at the Cotton Club used to think I was uppity 'cause I wouldn't socialize with the stage-door Johnnies, so they would call me Queen. 'There's Queen CeeCee,' they would say, and roll their eyes. 'Too good for the likes of us.'"

"Well, you are." He smiled.

"So it came to me one night that I wanted to create a positive image for my black girls, and voilà . . . Queen CeeCee. Turning a negative into a positive. Sales are off the charts," she said with pride.

"Of course. . . . You know"—he looked at her—"you could be in movies. You're prettier than Lena Horne and you'd be a big star."

"Yeah, playing what? Maids? At least Lena can sing." She looked into the side-view mirror. "Congrats on your lip gloss. It's all the rage, Mickey. I'm so proud of you."

"Yeah. I did the deal with the studio and Hollywood Hurrah glosses are off to the races. I paid Dax to develop it, but now he wants his own company." He steered the car into the right lane. "At first, I tried to stop him, but then I had an idea—I would fund him and own half his business. Like I did on Norfolk Street. Same concept. Old lady Grossman was selling her loaves of breads, challahs, and fruit pies out of my stand and wanted her own place. So I set it up, gave the old broad the up-front dough, and we were fifty-fifty. And I was up to my ears in pies."

"That's why you're brilliant, Mick." She snuggled into him.

As Mickey and CeeCee entered the Troc heads turned and swiveled. Who was the exotic, dusky beauty on Heron's arm? Was she a new starlet in the studio system, a tawny singer in a soon-to-be-released opulent Latin-themed musical, or a married South American socialite on the town for a lark? Clearly she was someone, as CeeCee's New York sophistication, couture, and diamond jewelry conveyed a more polished look than the usual corn-fed contract players who squeezed into a loaned studio gown from the costume department and wore paste jewelry. For CeeCee it was heavenly. They wined, dined, and danced the night away, Mickey nodding and introducing her to a wide array of familiar faces and Hollyood players. They kissed tenderly in the car and then returned to the Dunbar for a late-night drink and to listen to Lena, L.A.'s newest songbird. After a whiskey and a cigar, they made their way up to her room. In an explosion of arms and legs, they made frantic and passionate love over and over until they slipped into a trancelike sleep and reverie. In the morning light, he looked over at her and imagined them together like this, always. He slipped out of bed quietly so as not to wake her and put on his crumpled white shirt. He then walked over and kissed her gently on the forehead before leaving.

"I'll call you later. I'm setting up all your meetings." She heard and smiled and shook her head, still half-asleep and savoring the night before, awake but not fully awake, that beautiful moment of half dream and reality.

Mickey drove back to his new house in the Hollywood Hills, showered, dressed, and had his Mexican housekeeper, Maria, make him a lox, eggs, and onion omelet the way he had taught her to do, making sure the minced onions were golden brown before pouring in the frothy egg mixture. He loved the smell of it, as it reminded him of his *bubbe* when he a small boy. He then took to his phone and started dialing. He knew that CeeCee needed to meet some real L.A. players to try to set up some cross-promotional deals with Herz, and he was there to help her. He sat at his expansive wooden desk and flipped through his address book, his solid gold cuff links reflecting off the high-gloss veneer like a mirror. He came across the names of a few important industry players who owed him favors and he started making calls to set up introductions to leading up-and-coming actresses, producers, and their movie projects. He did this good-naturedly, with his usual flair and aplomb, and everyone he spoke to agreed to meet Miss CeeCee Lopez, vice president of Herz Beauty. CeeCee was also savvy enough not to talk about her Queen CeeCee line. That was for her accounts in Harlem and the salons near the Dunbar. CeeCee had two sets of business cards and could easily switch back and forth depending on whom she was talking to. Even her business cards were segregated, she thought, shaking her head. Each day, after a slate of meetings they would meet at the Dunbar for a romantic evening in bed together. They fell into a loving ease, where CeeCee would fill him in on her meetings and then exchange ideas about the latest product development on the Herz Beauty lineup or what she knew was still happening at Gardiner.

Mickey marveled at CeeCee. She took to L.A. like the Santa Ana winds, whipping things up. Within days she had found a wonderful location on Rodeo Drive for the L.A. Herz Beauty flagship salon and started researching the current slate of movies in production. Mickey set her up with a top meeting at MGM to discuss Hedy Lamarr's newest vehicle and partnership opportunities. Considered one of the most beautiful women in Hollywood, Hedy was the perfect choice for their next advertising campaign. A few years earlier she had fled Austria to escape both the Nazis and a wealthy, overbearing husband and while in London was noticed by MGM mogul Louis B. Mayer, who signed her up immediately and brought her to America. Her Hollywood film debut in *Algiers* opposite Charles Boyer had created a sensation. It was written that her beauty literally took one's breath away. Josephine was delighted when CeeCee called her in New York with the idea.

"Tell MGM we want her!" said Josephine. "She's today's version of Theda Bara. Her European sophistication is exactly what our brand stands for. You say she's Jewish to boot?"

"Yes, and originally from Vienna," CeeCee explained. "She was married to the richest man in Austria, Fritz Mandl, and had to escape him."

"Perfect. We'll take her and let Miss Palm Beach over there have that perky Janet Gaynor." Josephine laughed. Now that she was reading the movie magazines, she was more conversant on the subject of stars.

CeeCee smiled. Her L.A. trip had been quite successful; it had taken her only two weeks to get the lay of the land, and she knew that

Josephine would want her to come back again, fully paid. That would give her the opportunity to see Mickey again. She was starting to feel melancholic, as her trip was coming to a close.

"Why are you leaving me, baby?" Mickey looked at her like a lost little puppy in from the cold after the two weeks flew by like a lightning storm. "Can't you stay any longer?"

"Josephine wants me back for the big new product development meeting, and I'm making an appearance at the Apollo Theater, where Queen CeeCee is sponsoring Talent Night." She smiled.

He shook his head and knew it was a lost cause, but he promised to see her in New York.

When the time came for Mickey to drive CeeCee to the train station, he trudged slowly to open her door, as if his plodding would delay the waiting and hissing train. He removed her luggage from the trunk and tipped the dapper black porters to take it to the first-class car. He had hated the idea that she would have to sit in the colored section and had made plans through his connections to get her a seat in the whites-only first-class car. A call had been placed by the press agent of one of the most powerful Mob families in Los Angeles, indicating that Miss CeeCee Lopez, a new Brazilian actress signed by MGM, required a first-class ticket to New York City; under the circumstances, no one made a fuss. CeeCee knew she couldn't fight Mickey about it and agreed to his parting gift. After what seemed like an eternal kiss, she sat back in her train seat, feeling lucky as she saw L.A. pull away. First class. She thought back to her first train trip from Virginia, where she'd had to stand half the way. Now she was in first class and a well-respected business executive. The African American porters were extra helpful, as they thought she was the most beautiful Latin woman they had ever seen. CeeCee also knew one more thing as she settled into her first-class seat. Sometimes a girl just knew, had a feeling, an intuitive moment. She knew she was pregnant with Mickey's baby. And she wasn't about to say a word to anyone. Not just yet.

39

SWEET REVENGE

Beverly Hills, 1940

PARIS FALLS—BRITAIN NEXT, the headlines screamed. Constance, like most Americans, stopped in her tracks and felt a cold chill travel down to the base of her spine as she read the newspaper. In Los Angeles it was all sunshine, screenings, and swimming pools. Was she living in an alternate universe? She knew things in Europe were bad but now knew it was worse than she could ever have imagined. In her mind she could process the fall of remote places such as Poland or the annexation of Austria, since they seemed so out of the way, even "second tier." But Paris? Paris was the center of the world. Paris was everything. She couldn't imagine her beloved Paris overrun by the Germans. Was she dreaming? She stopped in her tracks at the news concession in the Beverly Wilshire Hotel and bought the paper, as if the purchase would confirm the reality. She stood in the lobby and read as did others, standing, reading, and in shock. The proud and haughty French reduced to the conquered, the helpless. She shook her blond locks in disbelief. She recalled her trip to Paris years earlier, as her business was taking off and she had splurged, staying at the Ritz. She had saved up and booked passage to see the sights but had gone to learn the secrets of French beauty and massage techniques and, of course, to order couture. She had met a lovely brunette treatment girl in one of the better salons. What was her name again? Madeleine. She had lovely soft hands, and after her facial and cool caresses, Constance had invited her to lunch, sensing a subtle attraction. She immediately accepted and they went to a lovely café in the Marais. She remembered feeling giddy at being in France and suddenly free, just as she had when she'd first moved to New York. She had sensed a similar sisterhood with the young French girl, who seemed so nonchalant and open about her sensuality. After a simple lunch of a croque monsieur and a carafe of white wine, they walked arm in arm back to her small garret off the place des Vosges and had spent the afternoon and then the weekend making love and drinking wine and smoking cigarettes. It all seemed so decadent, so wonderful, and it had lingered in her memory the way one registered the beautiful burning sensation of an after-dinner liqueur at the back of one's throat. Beautiful bliss, she had called it. It was only the third time she had performed oral sex on a woman and could still decipher her distinctive smell and taste: rosemary, musk, and a hint of vanilla. Where was Madeleine now? A wife, a girlfriend, a mother? Was she safe from the invading troops? She could only imagine the panic and the fear she must be feeling and hoped she was well and protected. And then, just as she always did when emotions became too raw or fresh, she banished the thought from her mind and focused on her business. The Canadian way.

Despite the awful international news, Constance and Gardiner Cosmetics were riding high. Through her fame and company profits, she and Van had indulged in another pastime for the wealthy: horse racing. Constance and Van had become stockholders in the Thoroughbred Santa Anita racetrack, and their horse, Constant Gardiner, had come in second against the famed Seabiscuit in the Santa Anita Handicap. Just as she had used her mansion in Palm Beach to gain entrée to PB society, Constance started to cultivate the horsey set in Kentucky, where she now owned the fabled stable the Lucky Eight, recently renamed Constantly Gardening, and to mingle with the stars and Hollywood elite on the West Coast. She loved nothing more than an afternoon at the track, with a flask of gin and a good bet; she felt like a little girl at the races, satisfying her tomboy side by yelling and cheering in the owner's box to her heart's content. It was the one area in her life where she could scream and curse and no one would take notice or pass judgment, since she was a proud owner. Taking in the stunning San Gabriel Mountains in the background through her binoculars, watching her Thoroughbred Constant Gardiner, was a thrill. Although she played at being nonchalant, she got a kick out of mingling with such leading box office stars as Clark Gable and Lana Turner as she became a familiar face at the track. Spending time out west had also led to a few product breakthroughs. The latest beauty trends in Hollywood led her to create her incredibly successful "Garden of Allah" brow pencil collection: a movie-star eye kit that included a tweezer and colored brow pencils for the plucked and arched brow that was in vogue during the late 1930s. Her women loved kits, and there was even an instruction guide on how to pluck the brow and apply the pencil in a strong arc. Kits and guides were important to her women, as she knew they craved an easy way to achieve a current look and the information on how to get it.

However, that latest winner product wasn't enough for her. The triumphant commercial success of Josephine's Lashmatic had taken her months, even years, to process. She had been so close and had been crushed at being the loser and Herz the winner. And Constance was not one to take it lying down. She had to admit her Eye-allure product would have been good, but when she tested Lashmatic she went into a rage. Everything about it was better: the curved brush, the consistent, mess-free shimmering liquid, and the now iconic package with its modern plastic twist-off top. The green-and-pink motif, of course, drove her to the edge of insanity and always set her teeth on edge when she saw a woman retrieve it from the bottom of her bag. It had given her more sleepless nights than she could possibly count. The rivalry and intensity had created such a powerful enmity that now decisions were being made out of ego and how to get back at her Jewish usurper.

If only Josephine had been visiting her family in Poland, she would have been blitzkrieged, she would joke with her friends at the club. The idea that CeeCee had gone over to work for her archenemy also tormented her and was almost all she could think about.

Ordinarily, product and retail innovation came from consumer need or desire. Now it came from revenge. What could she, Constance, do to wound Josephine as much as she herself had been wounded? It was a formidable question and one that kept her thinking and scheming till the earliest hours of the morning. Despite this constant ache and anxiety, she literally put on a good face and went about her business. The sun, the beaches, and the horsey sets of Palm Beach, Kentucky, and Los Angeles were always a fun diversion to take her mind off her aggravation.

Constance and Van, having drifted even further apart, at least had racing in common and had attended the races with one of their friends, the pharmaceutical heir Jock Ashton. Jock was the L.A. version of Topper: a dashing womanizer and bon vivant. He had invested heavily in Santa Anita as well, and they were all driving back to Los Angeles in his navy Packard. They stopped for gas at a small, out-of-the-way service station when Jock nudged Constance. Near the gas station and the grocery store he had spotted a small hair salon.

"Constance . . . pretty soon you'll see a Herz salon opening right there . . . ," Jock said sarcastically. "She's everywhere, that woman."

"Spreading like cancer." Constance lit up a cigarette, her hand shaking slightly.

And as she inhaled the purple swirling smoke, it suddenly hit her. That was it! What she had been searching for. She would steal *Josephine's* idea the way Josephine had stolen hers. A low-cost, mass-market version of Josephine's high-end salons for the average woman in more local environments. A place where her customer could go and buy Gardiner Cosmetics but also get her hair and nails done, all at a reduced cost. And she would paint the front door lavender just as Josephine had painted the lacquered doors in every one of her personal offices. She laughed out loud. That was it. She would call it the Gardiner *Lavender* Door Salon to boot!

She knew Josephine would feel the same way she had when her Palm Beach pink-and-green motif had been stolen right out from under her nose for Lashmatic. Lavender and black! Perfect. She also loved the play on lavender from a garden, and she knew that her customer would not only appreciate an affordable place to have beauty treatments but also be happy to pay less for everyday indulgences. She would trademark the name and own it first before telling anyone, even Van. Best of all, she knew the low-priced competition would drive Josephine Herz insane.

"Oh no, Jock . . ." Constance tapped her cigarette in the back of the car, the ashes dropping onto her mink and settling on the fur. "It won't be a Herz salon over there but mine. Wait and see what I have up my sleeve next." She raised a well-plucked arched eyebrow outlined with her sable-colored brow pencil.

"I'm not betting against you, Constance"—Jock nudged Van—"in horses or in business."

"That's right, Jock, better you don't. But I will quote Josephine Herz herself and say, 'Never discount a *vinner*!'" She laughed out loud as she mimicked and mocked her Polish accent, breaking up everyone else in the car.

40

THE LIST

New York City, 1940

Everywhere one went on the Upper East and Upper West Sides, it seemed one heard German-, French-, or Polish-tinged English. The wealthy and the lucky few who had escaped war-torn Europe had arrived in the nick of time—once confident, now somewhat unhinged, bringing their few assets and their specific accents to the English language. Years earlier, an accent would have been considered exotic in the city, but now the sound of a foreign tongue in New York or Los Angeles received either sympathy or derision. Most arrived by liner through Ellis Island, although one heard the occasional story of making one's way to Cuba and then Florida or Los Angeles via Mexico. Some families broke apart altogether and would not see one another again for decades. Fractured families and spirits that needed to be rebuilt. Émigrés, all trying to make sense of a new life, new language, and a new land, and forced reinvention. The clothes and English were alien and disruptive. No one knew what to do with an Austrian tweed loden jacket in the Los Angeles heat. Once-famous German movie stars were reduced to waitressing and lauded European auteurs assigned to B movies or film trailers.

Though these displaced people would form their own community and meet weekly at the Automat or a neighborhood teahouse to commiserate and reminisce about their former fame and riches in Berlin or Vienna, they knew they were lucky to have what little work was available. Most were Jewish, rich, or formerly rich, and a few were titled, like the Rothschilds and branches of the de Gunzburg family. There were downtrodden intellectuals of every stripe and religion, Catholic and Protestant homosexuals, and rangy, gap-toothed Romanians and Hungarians. One special group, the Russians, had been uprooted not once but twice, first fleeing to Paris during their own 1917 revolution and now having to abandon Paris for New York to escape the Nazis. These White Russian aristocrats were more often than not objects of pity, with their outdated evening clothes and medals to prop up their diminished self-confidence. That said, Americans always loved a good title, and if a former prince or princess attended a soiree, it still rang the cash register of prestige. There were also the odd, expat Americans returning home to safe shores.

This new influx of elite émigrés would also redefine New York's and Los Angeles' creative culture with a wave of out-of-work artists, writers, and film directors bringing frenetic energy, raw talent, and vision to film, theater, music, and dance. They had been rewarded for their foresight, as doers who had been smart enough to read the tea leaves and uproot themselves. Josephine embraced this chic set at her weekly salons and felt a special kinship with adults in search of freedom who would have to remake themselves as she had. It was also good for her business, the cream of European café society adding a sophisticated flavor to the stolid Americans who showed up weekly for an exotic blini and vodka. There was nothing Josephine liked better than an eclectic crowd, and she knew it would be a more successful evening with the addition of a stray White Russian princess, a Jewish baroness, or a famous German theater director such as Max Reinhardt. She had been a guest at Schloss Leopoldskron, his palace in Salzburg, and knew what a comedown it was for him in New York after the countless rooms of his palace. She even offered him the use of a guest room on Fifth Avenue. With so much talent on the street, she also boosted her ranks with top people who were available for less. Claudine Lelong, who had run the atelier for Chanel before the invasion, had moved to New York a year earlier after a difficult divorce. She was in her forties, brunette, chic, and smart and had been married to a French count before he left her for a German film star. With her ex-husband involved with a German ingenue and Chanel herself dating Hans Günther Von Dincklage, a high-level Nazi intelligence officer, Claudine was smart enough to know that the cards were not in her favor, especially when Chanel closed her shop and moved with her lover to the Ritz. Josephine snapped her up and had her overseeing the salon business and her soirees. Within months Claudine became a trusted adviser. Chanel had not been easy; Claudine knew what powerful, enigmatic women needed, and she delivered. After a few business meetings, Josephine sensed a kindred spirit and also opened up about meeting an eligible man, as American men had a limited appreciation for Josephine's charms, except perhaps for her wealth. Thus far, she had accepted dinner invitations with a doctor, a trial lawyer, and a WASP heir who had lost his fortune, but there was always a cultural divide and little understanding of who she was and how she lived her everyday life. "Everyone in New York has a bourgeois mentality," she complained to Claudine, igniting her cigarette with her gold Cartier lighter. "At the end of the day they would all rather have me stay home and be a hausfrau."

"Then find a European. The city is overrun with them, and who wouldn't want to be with you . . . beautiful, successful, and wealthy." Claudine laughed as she observed Josephine's stack of glittering diamond bracelets, which were enough to awe a pasha.

"Not just wealthy, my dear, enormously rich. What do you think, Claudine? What should Josie do?" She smiled, talking about herself in the third person. She felt she could be honest with Claudine.

"Do it *à la française.* You don't need a successful man, or a rich man." She smoked a smuggled Gitanes at the Plaza bar and blew smoke rings that resembled musical notes. "Do what men do. Meet a handsome young one who has nothing. You can own him mind, body, and soul. I have one myself and would gladly give him to you"—she paused and laughed—"but he's married."

"You know, Claudine, you're smarter than I thought."

"Wait . . . you didn't think I was smart?" She looked up with a question mark on her forhead.

"I didn't say that, I said I think you are smarter than I thought. Take it as a compliment." Josephine knew having the well-brought-up French society matron on her staff had added an extra dash of polish and élan to her business meetings and soirees.

"*C'est bon.* There are a few I can invite on Thursday evenings. . . . There is Ducalet. He's a very intense poet, dark, brooding."

"I hear he likes young girls. And boys." Josephine looked at her intently.

"Who doesn't?" she said with the resignation that comes with disappointment and age.

"Who else do you have on your list?" Josephine scrutinized Claudine's navy Chanel slacks admiringly. She would have to get a pair.

"What about Ludwig Grunewald?" She went down her mental list.

"The painter? He's neither young nor handsome, and he smells like mothballs. Next." It was as if she were giving comments on a new product line.

"Don't be so picky. He's quite famous. He had a well-received installation at the last *biennale* in Venice." Claudine puffed on her Gitanes.

"I liked your first idea of young and handsome. Who else? Anyone with a title?" She blew air out of the side of her mouth at the thought: a prince, count, or baron. It would drive Constance Gardiner crazy if she had a title.

"You know . . ." Claudine applied a thin veil of face powder from her circular gold Herz compact and eyed herself and Josephine in the compact mirror with a knowing smile. "I think I actually might have someone for you." Claudine's eyes sparkled.

"Go on." Josephine seemed a bit overeager at the prospect.

"I'm not going to say anything more. I'll just bring him to one of the Thursday evening soirees." She paused. "He's new in town."

"So is everyone else." She sighed. "Straight off the boat? A real greenhorn you're giving me?"

"Don't worry, Josephine. I thought you said I was smarter than you thought."

"Yes, and I pay you well for it, darling." Josephine appraised her. "Remember, I want someone who is young, handsome, and will take orders."

"Perhaps you don't want a husband, you just want a gigolo."

"I don't have the time for trysts and love affairs. I just want a man in my bed and at my side at events, holding my drink and my purse. That's what I want."

"And you'll get it. Be patient."

"I have no patience for such things. But remember, I want younger and handsome. Perhaps a faded title."

"That's what I adore about you, Madame Herz. You are a woman who knows exactly who she is and what she likes."

"One thing for sure. I would rather be a nanny than nursing the elderly any day of the week," she quipped as she smoothed last year's Chanel.

Although it had flown by, it had been a grueling and upsetting week, though it hadn't started that way. CeeCee had returned, excited to have found a prime Beverly Hills flagship location in an up-and-coming shopping area. Yet the negotiations for the Rodeo Drive store had stalled and then fallen to pieces once Josephine's offer to buy the property had been turned down. She had never had someone decline an offer for one of her stores, and she couldn't understand why. The offer was more than generous. She put Felix, her lawyer, on the case to discover what had transpired and he visited her a few days later, looking none too pleased. He just placed a file on her desk and indicated that she review it. Her face fell when she read the document. He had uncovered an anti-Semitic covenant in the deed, prohibiting Jews and other minorities from buying the property. Felix explained that California had pioneered these racial clauses as far back as the 1880s, initially to restrict Asian Americans from buying property. Even though all he needed to do was set up a shell company that would buy it and then sell it to Herz Beauty, it disturbed her when she saw the words in black and white: "The said premises should not be at any time sold, conveyed, leased, or sublet or occupied by any persons who are not Caucasian, full bloods of the white races, including Asian, Jews, Negroes. . . ." And the covenant brought home more terrible reports she was hearing from her émigré friends from Europe. Jews were being systematically targeted, stripped of their rights and possessions and herded into ghettos or shipped off to something called concentration camps. For the past two years, Josephine and her sisters had tried everything to get their youngest sister, Chana, out of Poland. She had had more than a few opportunities in 1937 and 1938, when they secured her passport and papers to London and New York, but Chana was headstrong and would not leave. She wrote that she was in love with a gentile university student she met while she was finishing secondary school. Every time she said she was leaving, she demurred. To some extent, Josephine understood what it was like to not want to leave and remembered back when the day arrived for her to make her own journey. She had cried uncontrollably and fought with her dear, dear mother about going. Chana, at sixteen, had no such support. And now the window of opportunity had closed. Despite her money and connections, Chana was just another Jewish girl in Nazi-occupied Poland. Josephine shivered at the thought. It was evil and depressing and she was afraid for herself and Miles's future. What was the world coming to?

Later that evening, she tried to banish her anxieties as she walked into her capacious closet and chose a black-and-white taffeta gown for the salon she was hosting. Black and white. That was how she was feeling. After Max, the head stylist from her salon, had arrived and finished her hair and makeup, she took off her smock and stepped into the gown; Maria, her maid, helped her with the hooks, eyes, and buttons. The gown had an off-the-shoulder fitted bodice, a lovely A-line skirt with a crinoline, and a small white bustle bow in the back. She chose a diamond necklace in the shape of a repeating bow pattern from her formidable jewel box and surveyed herself in the three-way mirror. The stress of the week had caused her to skip a few meals and she had lost a few pounds thanks to her lack of appetite. Her naturally curvaceous body had responded well, though, and the corset and boning in the gown gave her an uplifted décolletage set against her small waist. The cinching really set her off to great advantage, and she looked a decade younger than her forty years. After touching up her Herz maquillage, she put her lipstick and compact in her evening bag, put on her white satin opera-length gloves, and walked slowly down the glamorous curved staircase to the oval black-and-white marble-tiled entry foyer. She often came down a bit earlier to survey the enfilade of rooms and to check that everything was in order for the evening's festivities. It was 7:15 on the dot and a few guests were already starting to trickle in.

"Darling, I'll have a glass of champagne with a small cocktail napkin, thank you," she told the handsome, dark-haired waiter at the bottom of the stairs.

"Of course, but where is the bar?" he said in a pleasant, accented tone.

"Don't you know? That is your job." She was not happy about having to tell the staff where the bar or service was.

"It is every man's job to get a beautiful woman a drink, but this is my first time here," he said softly, smiling at the glamorous vision descending the staircase.

"So that's your excuse?" Josephine fumed.

"Excuse? It's the truth." He looked at her with penetrating, deep-set sea-blue eyes set against the palest skin and longer blue-black hair. Josephine was taken aback, as she could have sworn he was wearing Lashmatic, his lashes were so long, dark, and lustrous. He would have looked feminine if he didn't have such a large, handsome physique and five o'clock shadow. She had never seen a man with such lustrous lashes and took a step forward to evaluate. They were natural. Figures, she thought. Women had to pay for it and a waiter had it for free.

"If you're going to do a job, get here earlier and make sure you know where everything is." She shook her head at him and his abundant lashes.

"It's seven fifteen," he said, looking at her a bit cockeyed.

"I don't expect back talk in my house." Josephine opened her evening bag and held the Cartier lighter out for him, indicating she needed a light as she rummaged for a cigarette.

"Oh, so I see you both have met." Claudine Lelong walked over and saw them both talking and kissed the handsome young man on both cheeks.

"Alexei, what have you said to Madame Herz?"

"Madame Herz?" He cocked his head in confusion. "Oh. Nothing. Nothing at all. I just didn't know where the bar was." He looked down sheepishly, realizing she was his hostess.

"He's not a waiter?" Josephine asked brusquely, and realized her mistake at once.

"No, this is my friend Alexei I was telling you about. Alexei Orlove?" she said in a questioning tone. "Prince Orlove?"

"Oh, my dear, I thought you were a waiter." She laughed out loud.

"Josephine, really?" Claudine shook her head.

"Is there a job available?" Orlove smiled widely, his charming, slightly crooked white teeth setting off an impish grin.

"It's because he's too young and handsome. And when they are young and handsome and wearing evening clothes, I assume they are the staff." Josephine shrugged and smiled as well.

"Don't worry, Madame Herz. It's a pleasure. Here, let me carry your evening bag and I'll be back in a moment with your champagne." He kissed her gloved hand European style and started to walk away, then stopped and suddenly turned.

"I have a confession as well." He smiled.

Josephine was charmed. "Yes?"

"I too had no idea who you were. I assumed my hostess would be a much older woman, not a young beauty like you," he explained.

She blushed. "You're too kind. Isn't he, Claudine?"

"Entirely. Josephine, really? A waiter?" She shook her head at her again as he walked away in search of her bubbly with her evening bag.

"You told him to carry my bag as well?" Josephine scrutinized her.

Claudine shook her auburn mane. "No. I did not say a word."

"Really." Josephine blinked. "Claudine, did I tell you I am giving you a raise?" She looked at her with a sly smile. "Orlove. He's a real prince?"

"Yes. A very distinguished White Russian family. His father was a military man, but his grandmother was a cousin of the czar. Irina Yureivskaya."

"And he's poor?"

"Poor as a church mouse. All he came over with was one tuxedo, some medals, and a signet ring."

"Well done." Her large eyes lit up the room.

"Really?"

"Yes, I think young Prince Orlove is exactly what the doctor ordered." She exhaled a smoke ring in the shape of a kiss.

41

CHESS

New York City, 1941

The stately Georgian town house on East Seventy-third Street between Madison and Fifth had always been cold and imposing, not unlike Constance's persona. Now it seemed enormous and empty after weeks on the road in contrast to the many sterile hotel suites she had endured. Constance was relieved to be back home and nodded politely to Gerta, her severe German maid, who silently nodded back as she took Constance's coat from her shoulders in one fluid motion, carried it to the coat closet, and arranged it on the wooden hanger, as her husband, Gunter, brought her suitcases up to her bedroom. German efficiency: just the way she liked it and had instructed them in the initial interview. Quick and silent service, with absolutely no chatter. Now that Van Jr. was off at Milton Academy the house seemed to lack the cacophony and chaos it once possessed, and that was heaven for Constance. It was finally quiet enough for her to think. There were no more annoying toy trains to trip over and awful fingerprints the staff had to wipe off the walls. No more invasive, unattractive nannies who invaded her space. She sighed and walked into her bedroom, delighted that Van was not at home.

She pulled out her new Gardiner scented bath oils and drew herself a hot bubble bath. The lavender and rose fragrances had been particularly successful sellers and she decided to mix the two. Just as she slipped into the claw-foot tub, savoring the warm water and luxurious bubbles, she heard the familiar footsteps. Even his footsteps lacked oomph and vitality, she groaned silently.

"May I come in?" Van knocked softly on the door and poked his bald head in. This was uncommon, as he usually knew not to disturb her.

"Yes, of course." She placed a terry washcloth over her luminous breasts. The bubbles in the water hid the rest.

"Hello, Van, how have you been?" she said with a wilted sigh.

"Fine," he offered. "How was your trip?"

"A whirlwind, but a success. We opened up the salons in record time. We had lines around the block. I despise Chicago, but the sales are leading. Clearly, they have nothing better to do in the Midwest. All those solid, farm types. Reminded me of Canada. I couldn't wait to leave," she griped. "You are looking well. The tan suits you," she said. "How was Palm Beach?"

"Very well, thank you. Lots of commotion with Topper and Lally divorcing. It's all anyone is talking about." He leaned against the marble-topped commode and lit a cigarette. She noticed his hands had a slight tremor to them.

"Another typical Palm Beach scandal." She yawned.

"Listen, Constance, I have wanted to speak to you for a long time now." He fumbled the words. "But since you are always traveling and working it never seems to be a good time. Especially now that Van Jr. is in boarding school." He paused, trying to find the proper words. "It's been quite lonely." He looked lost and she did not know where he was going with his rambling lecture. "I still think he is far too young to be sent away."

"He's lucky to be adopted and he will benefit from Milton and later Groton, just like you did."

"Yes, but I am now totally alone much of the time."

"I understand, but some of us have to work, you know."

"I know all too well." He nervously rubbed his red, chapped hands together.

"And what is on your mind, Van? You always seem to beat around the bush."

"We're not all as direct as you are, Constance."

"Clearly—"

"I'm leaving you," he said in a whisper.

Constance sat up in the bath and actually laughed out loud as she processed the shock of the news.

"Leaving. You are leaving *me*?" She was incredulous.

"Yes. This just doesn't make sense. We hardly see each other."

"I am working to pay for our lifestyle, *dear*." Her words dripped with malice.

He sighed slightly. "I am well-to-do in my own right."

"There's a difference between well-to-do and rich, Van, and you know it. The mansion in Palm Beach, the yacht, the horses, the clubs. It's all Gardiner money." Her eyes were poisoned darts.

"Yes, but I have invested my trust and I have done quite well. I've made up my mind. I have to leave."

"Really. And where do you think you are going?" She laughed bitterly.

"I'm . . . I'm going to marry Lally," he blurted out.

"Lally? This is a joke, right?" She was incredulous at the news.

"No, Topper is divorcing her to marry Jaqueline de Cuevas, the tin heiress." He tapped his cigarette into the heavy cut-crystal ashtray. "I spoke with him and he is all for it. Said it's all very tidy and friendly and he won't have to pay alimony."

"So it's a game of musical chairs, is it. That's so wholesome and convenient and just inbred of you all."

"Perhaps." Van nodded.

"And why is it that every time someone mentions that damn woman's name they have to follow it up with the words 'the tin heiress'?"

Constance said angrily, furiously scrambling to light a cigarette from the pack on the white stool next to her.

"Perhaps because she is. And don't think they don't say the same thing about you, dear. Constance Gardiner, 'the cosmetics queen.' 'Aren't you married to the cosmetics queen?'" He rolled his eyes. "Well, Lally and I have spent quite a lot of time together and we get along quite well. We're actually very well matched. She doesn't like to be alone either," he said matter-of-factly.

"But Lally is my closest—"

"Lally told me some disturbing things."

"What are you saying, Van?" Constance raised herself from the bath totally naked, the suds floating down her glorious toned physique like liquid clouds. Here she was, famous, successful, and beautiful, and this mouse of a man was leaving *her*? And with her best friend and lover, no less. It whipped her into a quiet fury.

"I know what's been going on, Constance."

"What, what's been going on?"

"Lally told me you made passes at her."

"I do think it's the other way around, Van," she said, wide-eyed with fear that she was being exposed.

"She said you'd say that. Do you really want me to verbalize your condition? Must run in the family." He nervously lit up another cigarette. She could see his hand tremble a bit.

"Oh please, it was all just a schoolgirl crush." She looked away.

"It's illegal, Constance. And there have been whispers about you since we married. I think it's far better if we finalize the divorce and let sleeping dogs . . . sleep. Don't you agree?" He puffed and found his nerve. "I really don't want to have to go public, I mean in the court papers, with your inclinations. You're not a wife to me and I've lived with you despising me for too long. So you will settle five hundred thousand dollars on me and we'll split custody of Van. This is going to be a very civil divorce."

"You signed a prenuptial agreement." She reminded him.

"That's entirely up to you."

"So"—she put on her robe—"you and Lally seem to have thought about everything. Including blackmail."

"It's not Lally, it's because you deceived me."

"Now I truly know that most people would do anything for money."

"And you would do anything for your image." He paused. "Look, Lally and I are just cut from the same cloth."

"Meaning?"

"Meaning you weren't brought up in our world. There's a kind of code."

"You think you're both better than me?"

"I didn't say that. But don't think I don't know you enjoyed being Mrs. Van Wyke."

"Fuck you and your old-money name."

"You know what, Constance? You're just a climber. No better than Josephine Herz."

Constance walked over and slapped him in the face. Van hardly flinched.

"At least she has sex appeal." He was finally loud. "And do you know what? I hear she's dating this Prince Orlove. She even found a better name than you did."

"Get out!" she shouted. "Go to your dyke." She picked up her glass filled with Lillet and threw it at him. It grazed his head and hit the sink and shattered into a galaxy of pieces.

"I have copies of James's arrests to make the case it runs in the family. Just agree to the divorce settlement."

"You'd never do it." She gave an unconvincing laugh.

"You've made a fool out of me all these years. I doubted myself, thought it was me. Maybe I was too ugly, too stupid, too worthless. And I finally found out you just prefer women. Don't think I'm not angry about it, and don't think I won't go straight to the press for a half a million dollars. You'll never be able to step foot in Locust Valley or Palm Beach again. And as for the Gardiner Girls . . ." He gave his parting shot. "How would *they* feel?"

Constance felt icy. She just stood there with nothing left to say. Finally, the man she thought so little of had beaten her at her own game. She was furious, and yet for the first time—she hated to admit it—she was impressed.

42

LAVENDER DOORS

New York City, 1941

The country was in collective shock at the invasion of Pearl Harbor. The surprise attack by the Japanese to destroy the Pacific fleet had caused so much loss of young life and unleashed a patriotic fervor that had immediately pulled the United States into what had been previously marketed as an unwanted war. Constance was dismayed, for she had been a proud, card-carrying member of the America First Committee, which was the largest noninterventionist group and whose most famous member, Charles Lindbergh, had been accused of fascist and anti-Semitic leanings. Like many of the members, she not only believed in the isolationist platform, but also knew it had been a convenient and not-so-subtle way for her to criticize outsiders—people like Josephine Herz—and to delegitimize them as warmongers and ungrateful immigrants. Just the way that Chanel, in the same year, would try to take advantage of the new anti-Semitic legislation in Paris and wrest control of her perfume business from her Jewish partners. After the surprise attack, when national pride and patriotism had galvanized, Constance and her friends had to revise their narrative. She was mortified that she had chosen the wrong side. She never liked to bet on the loser.

Down on Fifth Avenue, in her sumptuous and feminine lavender bedroom, Josephine was in shock. Pearl Harbor had brought the world and the Axis powers home, and like most other Americans, she was now gearing up for the Second World War. It did not escape her that what was at stake was not only democracy but her future—and that of her eleven-year-old son. Only a week earlier Felix had presented her with the news that her avenue Montaigne Paris salon had been requisitioned by the Nazis and stripped of all its products, which had been sent back to Germany for the officers' wives. They subsequently turned the limestone mansion into a French branch of the Luftwaffe. As an American citizen and a Jewess, she had no legal recourse now that the United States had entered the war. They had made much of it in Nazi propaganda PR that Jewish-owned Herz Beauty was now under their control. Would London be next? She actually felt sick to her stomach as she thought of how much time, money, and work had gone into the Paris salon. It was also ironic that the Nazi Party wives couldn't get enough of Parfum Empress Josephine and her sought-after slim and chic gold compacts and lipstick cases. It was even more ironic that her top-selling Chinois Rouge was the color of choice for top Nazi wives. And then to add insult to injury, just a few days before Pearl Harbor, her nemesis, Constance Gardiner, had planned her own more subtle attack, opening three Lavender Door Salons in New York, Chicago, and Los Angeles, lifting her color scheme the way Josephine had with Lashmatic. Checkmate. Josephine was angry but impressed nevertheless. All of it had thrown her into a depressing tailspin when she should have been on top of the world. Josephine knew that Gardiner had stolen her idea, but she had also created a low-cost, mass-market version of it . . . which she knew would be successful, especially in cash-strapped wartime. She predicted that her own high-end salons would suffer. Everything, it seemed, besides her young prince put her in a foul and sour mood.

While the outside world was going mad, Josephine's inner sanctum, her bedroom and boudoir, was a cloistered hideaway of silk, satin, and down. It was designed to reflect the ultimate in femininity, offering a tactile, relaxed, and intimate sensuality. Josephine knew a great deal about lighting, and the soft golden glow showed her to her best advantage. Usually she was relaxed after sex, but tonight she was on edge.

"What is it, Josephine?" Alexei stroked her cascading hair.

"I've had a difficult week. Here, let me massage your neck." She reached over and kneaded his taut, sculpted shoulders.

"No, let me do that for you. You're the one who had a hard week." He moved to the edge of the bed and started massaging her foot, and Josephine fell into a state of bliss. No one had ever connected with her this way before, knowing exactly which spots to touch. It was as if he had a psychic sense of what she needed. Alexei then curled up next to her in bed and kissed her neck, tasting her skin in a sensual way. Josephine looked intently at him and marveled at her gorgeous young boyfriend. He was an incredible specimen of manhood. A six-foot-four Adonis, he was perfectly muscled without an ounce of fat. Every appendage was beautiful, from his lovely, well-proportioned ears to his smooth, hairless feet. Not to mention the lush dark lashes that never ceased to amaze her. Although nudity had been offensive to her in the past, his was not: it was artful. He was a well-endowed version of the statue of David. That was it. She had the Florentine statue of David come to life in her bed. Not to mention he was sweet, and kind, and, best of all, made her feel beautiful.

The chemistry and frisson between Josephine and Alexei had been both inevitable and volcanic. It had erupted after their first dinner at the Russian Tea Room, which had been founded by members of the Russian Imperial Ballet in 1927. It was the perfect first date, as Josephine's Slavic features were highlighted by the opulent decor and Alexei proved to be a courtly gentleman. He held the door, took her sable coat and checked it, pulled out her chair, and ordered for her. He seemed to be able to read her mind.

"We may be at opposite ends . . . but we meet in the middle at borscht," Josephine joked of their commonalities. He laughed at all her jokes and mannerisms, and she could see as his eyes sparkled that he was thoroughly entranced by her. After he ordered for her—chicken Kiev ("Of course, how did you know that's what I wanted?")—he leaned over and gently kissed her by candlelight. She felt both an electricity and a comfort she had never felt with any man. It was almost as if they were twinned and separated and then brought back together again. At the end of the meal he had insisted on paying for dinner. He didn't tell her it was more than he could afford. She knew it, though, and was touched, but he wouldn't accept a sou from her. She would later find out he had borrowed money to take her out and had paid it back weekly with his earnings as a draftsman and illustrator. After dinner, when he dropped her off at her apartment, she invited him in, and in a most natural way they came together, as if destiny had split them and then brought them together when they needed each other most. They celebrated their spiritual reintroduction by making slow, passionate love. Usually in a rush and most always in control, for the first time in her life, Josephine allowed a man to take the lead, let herself slow down and enjoy real pleasure. True, she had participated in the sexual act many times, but she'd never actually made love before. It was a different experience to be touched with love and reverence. Afterward, Josephine would open up as she never had before about her issues, hopes, and dreams, and Alexei hung on every word, thrilled to be in her orbit.

"This woman, my competitor . . ." Josephine pulled the silk sheets to her chin. "We are locked, have been locked, in a war, a competition. Sometimes I best her, and she just bested me." Her pale skin flushed and grew dewy with a slight sheen of perspiration as she explained the situation. "She stole my idea and made it better and less expensive for her customer."

"And as you said, you've done the same to her?"

"Of course, but I am not a good loser."

He shrugged. "I think you need each other."

"That's so smart of you, I often say that." She marveled and kissed him gently.

"I think you should look at the situation differently."

"How so?"

"View her less as an enemy and more as a friend . . . she is giving to you, making you better."

"You're more mature than I am. It's hard, but I understand."

He rose from the bed and stretched skyward. He could have been an Olympic athlete, a discus thrower. How did someone get so genetically lucky? Josephine thought.

"Where are you going?" She didn't want their reverie to end. To her dismay, he put on his robe, obscuring his magnificent body.

"It's Sunday. I have to get the drawings done for the new puff powder line," he said earnestly. Alexei was a talented artist and illustrator, and Josephine had introduced him to the head of the art department to help with packaging. At first the existing team had rolled their eyes at the thought, but within days they were all impressed by his incredible talent and work ethic. Josephine always knew how to pick a winner.

"Don't go yet." She reached over.

"I'm new on the job, Josephine, and I don't want to be late with my drawings. Everyone is presenting ideas for the packaging and naming tomorrow. I want my ideas to win. It's important to me." His eyes had a pleading quality.

"So what do you have? Show me and I will help you," she said like an eager child at the hint of chocolate, raising herself on her elbow.

"Absolutely not. I will do it on my own and then I will show you. *After* the meeting."

"I understand." She nodded enthusiastically. "That's one of the reasons I adore you. You have pride. You don't take, you give, unlike the other men I have known." She looked at him with astonishment.

"I don't want just to be your boyfriend. I am grateful for the work. I want you to be proud of me." He looked at her, his eyes welling up.

"But of course I am proud of you," she said. "I will give you a raise to prove it."

"Please don't." He looked at her, his eyes silently pleading. "I don't want a raise. Not from you."

Josephine couldn't quite fathom a man who didn't want an open checkbook from her.

"The job introduction was more than enough. I want to work hard and succeed on my own merits," he said matter-of-factly. "I want you to know your money is your money and my money is your money."

"What?" She looked at him wide-eyed. "Where did you hear that?"

"I just made it up. Why?"

"It's just something I said to someone a long time ago." She touched his cheek with her hand. "We say the same things. A lot."

"I know." He gazed at her. "I love you, Josephine."

"How can you say that? It's only been a year." She scrutinized his face, bracing for a lie.

"I'll say it again. I love you, Josephine. I don't want anything from you. Just you," he said earnestly.

"And if I married you, you would sign a paper saying you would get nothing from me, or Miles, not a thing?" she challenged him.

"Of course. You don't understand, getting you is everything. Things are meaningless. I left Russia for Paris and now Paris for New York with nothing. Now I have everything. You, a job. Miles. Show me where to sign."

"You really are a prince of a man, Alexei Orlove." She kissed him.

"And if I get my way, you will be my princess. . . ."

"Our love, Orlove," she whispered as he left the room to work.

43

THE NEWS

Harlem, 1941

Blaring ambulance sirens. Punctuated shrieks. Tinny laughter, slamming car brakes, and roaring buses, the rumble of the el on Third Avenue and 125th Street. All of the noise, like ingredients in a stew, sounded like so many familiar friends outside her window. CeeCee had gotten so used to the menu and cacophony of city noises in her small walk-up, it actually seemed comforting and lulled her to sleep. Her place wasn't fancy, but it was hers. She was currently living in a one-bedroom apartment on the third floor but had given her landlady a deposit on a larger two-bedroom that was soon to be available, since her pregnancy had almost passed the three-month marker. She hoped and prayed this time she would carry the baby to full term. She had miscarried early after her first trip to the West Coast. The last time she had seen Mickey in New York she had thrown all caution to the wind and they made love with wild abandon without using anything. It all seemed inevitable, and when she missed her period she knew. This time she felt different, as if she could feel the baby taking hold of her. She seemed to tire a bit more easily and felt foggy and spacey in the evenings. After a full day of work she lay on the bed and drifted into slumber without taking off her hosiery and slip.

When the phone rang well after midnight, CeeCee knew exactly who it was. It was three hours earlier in L.A., and Mickey hardly had any concept of time. She smiled at his somewhat juvenile behavior. She picked up the receiver and spoke with a groggy haze, without bothering to get confirmation of the person on the other end of the line.

"Hi, baby," she breathed into the receiver.

"Are you sleeping?" Mickey asked.

She imagined him walking around his house with a bottle of whiskey in hand, naked except for the silk Japanese robe she had given him. She curled up, wishing he were there to caress the small of her back in the moonlight, as he often did. She reached down and felt the tautness of her stomach. She hadn't told a soul except for Josephine. She had been nervous about breaking the news to her and thankful she hadn't asked too many questions, although CeeCee intimated that she was engaged to the father, who lived in Los Angeles. Josephine was incredibly businesslike and supportive. She revealed that she and her husband had been separated when she found herself pregnant with Miles. She understood what it was like to be a single mother. Of course, she added, "I worked up until I went into labor, that very day."

"I will too," CeeCee promised, honored that Josephine had been so personal and honest with her. And that was that. Tonight she would break the news to Mickey. She smiled, thinking about how happy he would be.

"Listen, Cee, I have to talk to you about something—before it hits the papers."

"A new launch? I thought of a good name for a fragrance for you, 'Heroine' by Heron," she whispered.

"Hey, I love that, Cee. That's really good."

"I also have something I've been dying to tell you too," CeeCee said, sounding like a little girl who had just won a stuffed animal at the carnival and couldn't wait to tell her parents.

"You first?" Mickey asked.

"No, you go ahead!" CeeCee stretched in the bed like a silky cat.

"First, I want to tell you how much I love you. You know that, Cee. . . . You do know that, right?" The pitch of his voice seemed to waver.

"Yes, of course. I love you, too, Mick." She picked up on it. "Wait, is something wrong? It's not about a launch, is it?" A sinking feeling settled into her chest.

"I got myself into a bit of trouble out here, Cee."

"I'm not surprised," CeeCee said as a way to protect herself.

"Gee, thanks."

"Go on." She sat upright, forcing the sleep from her eyes.

"There's this powerful guy out here, Moe Stein, and he runs the numbers. I mean, the top guy running the numbers, get it? He's the *guy*—" His voice cracked. "Majority of guys are Italian, but a few of us in the ranks—"

"Okay, Moe. I get it. Go on. . . ."

"And Moe has a daughter. You know, one of these zaftig Jewish broads. Pretty face, but nothing compared to you, Cee, and . . . well, one thing led to another. She threw herself at me. I . . . shouldn't have done it . . . but I did . . . and now . . . she's pregnant. Moe was furious at first . . ." It all came tumbling out like an unfurling sail.

"And . . ." Her heart was beating so fast out of her chest, she was actually afraid for her own baby's well-being.

"And I have to marry her . . . or else," he whispered.

"Or else what, Mick?" she cried.

"Or else I won't be going to Santa Anita to bet on horses, I'll be buried under the racetrack." There. He had said it.

"What's her name?"

"Myra," he whispered.

"Figures. Do you love this Myra?" She was enraged.

"I don't even *like* Myra. But she's Moe Stein's daughter and she's knocked up and I have to do the right thing or I am a dead man walking. I'm sick about it, Cee."

She was stunned, her world crashing in. The room spun as she gathered her thoughts, which came tumbling out like marbles and jacks in a child's shoebox.

"I'm not going to rub it in that you're a fuckup and a pig and a dope. Or that you ruined my life. I'll just let you imagine what could have been." She began to sob.

"I don't know what got into my head."

"It's your other head, you asshole." She gulped for air. "Why did you have to ruin everything?"

"I'm so sorry, Cee, more than you can ever imagine."

She paused. "When?"

"We're eloping to Las Vegas this weekend. Then we'll have a reception in town."

"Well, at least she's Jewish." CeeCee laughed bitterly.

"There's only one girl in the world for me and it's you, Cee. I'm so sorry. I'm such a fuckup."

CeeCee tried to wipe away her tears. "Why did you have to fuck it up, baby? I never said you couldn't be with other women. Just to be careful."

"I was drunk."

"That's been your excuse for everything. Look, you play with that crowd, you live or die by the rules." She was nothing if not realistic.

"I didn't want you to read about it in the papers."

"There's nothing more to say on it, Mick. I wish you and this Myra . . . what do you folks say . . . mazel tov?"

"Don't say that, baby. It's breaking my heart."

"Mine too."

"What did . . . you want to talk with me about?"

She felt her stomach. "Nothing important, but . . . Mickey . . ."

"Yes, Cee?"

"Please don't call me again. Please. Maybe one day when you are older and wiser and Myra is fat and you're through with her and the kids are grown—call me then. Don't ever call me until you can be with me and I mean be with me fully. Do you understand, you thick-headed, muscle-bound piece of shit? I love you more than myself. I can't be in the same room with you because your smell makes me weak. Please, Mickey. Do me a favor and never call me again. Please. I couldn't take it." The tears were streaming now.

"Never"—he was crying, too—"say never."

44

PAIN AND PLEASURE

New York City, 1943

It may have been another dead, grey, overcast day in New York City, but for Constance it was as sunny as a day in Palm Beach.

"Forty cents, ma'am," the gaunt, thirteen-year-old newsstand boy said as he handed Constance the two copies of *Glamour of Hollywood* magazine she requested.

"Yes, of course." She reached into her small leather change purse in her handbag and took out four small silver dimes and laid them on the counter one at a time, appreciating the clicking sound against the white marble counter.

"Are you . . . ?" He looked at the woman on the magazine cover and back at Constance.

"Yes." She nodded; her delicate hat with the tiny lace veil did little to obscure her face, and she looked directly at the newsboy with pride.

"Well, congratulations, ma'am. I never met a celebrity before."

"I'm not a celebrity." She smiled. "I'm a businesswoman." She took the magazines and walked efficiently into the lobby of her office building and pressed the button for the fifteenth floor. She was excited to see the cover story on her Lavender Door Salons, which had been an immediate and ongoing success. As the elevator doors closed, she perused her face on the cover. Just the perfect amount of lipstick, she thought. She flipped through the magazine and had a rush of energy. The story and photos were perfect. The headline read, BEAUTY PIONEER'S NEW BEAUTIFUL CONCEPT OPENS: THE LAVENDER DOOR SALONS.

The subhead read: "Now *every* woman can be beautiful." Perfect, it was a direct hit against Josephine's upscale and expensive salons. She walked into her office with the gait of a conquering hero as she lifted up and waved the magazine at the three secretaries. "We have the cover!" she said to applause.

A chorus of congratulations was heard as she made her way into her new private office. Marjorie, her assistant, hung up her mink and then hustled to bring out a tray of tea, milk, and honey. She laid the usual morning newspapers on her desk as Constance sat back and read the profile to her delight. *Glamour* had said the "Lavender Door concept will change the way American women feel about themselves." That Constance Gardiner had "created a shift in American culture where every woman is celebrated for her beauty and her brains at the right price." She loved that! The fact that each Lavender Door Salon would have a beauty school training program was noted in the article as well. The school allowed young women to educate themselves and have a career. Constance had single-handedly created a self-selecting and -trained low-cost workforce. It was genius, she had to hand it to herself.

"May I?" Marjorie picked up the extra issue of *Glamour*.

"Of course, Marjorie. What do you think of the photo?" Constance asked, already knowing the answer.

"You look just wonderful, Mrs. Wyke. Just beautiful." She beamed at how statuesque and elegant her boss was.

"Please call me Miss Gardiner now."

"Of course. I love that you are wearing a lavender gown in front of the lavender doors. It's so chic and catchy."

"Thank you." Constance smiled. She could only imagine what

Josephine Herz would say when she saw the story and layout. She was in a jubilant mood. This, of course, would only be temporary.

As she scanned the *New York Daily Mirror* she came upon Walter Winchell's gossip and social column. She immediately felt a shock to her system as she digested the headline: TWO FAMOUS BEAUTIES REMARRY. The subhead screamed at her: "Josephine Herz becomes Princess Orlove." The photo of Josephine, dripping in diamonds, dancing with her handsome young prince at their Russian Tea Room reception, made her visibly weak. To add insult to injury, there was yet another dagger to behold. The next bold-faced paragraph read: "In other beauty news the former Mr. Constance Gardiner, the very swell Mr. Van Wyke, marries oil heiress Lally Stanton, the former Lally Seward. A match made in blue blood."

Constance slammed down the paper. Bested again! On the very day her cover story had come out. She could never, ever, it seemed, catch a break. She walked over to the bar with her teacup and poured a heavy dose of gin, her hands shaking.

Marjorie appeared at her door. "Miss Gardiner, the *Daily News* is on the phone for you. They would like a comment on Mr. Wyke's remarriage."

"Thank you, Marjorie. Tell them I am indisposed. Rather, tell them I am celebrating my new *Glamour* cover and I cannot be disturbed."

"Yes, of course."

"Oh, and Marjorie . . ." She forced a frozen smile as she tried to keep her composure.

"Yes, Miss Gardiner?"

"No further calls for the day. I am not available. I have an appointment uptown," she said as she took a copy of her magazine, fetched her fur, and made the decision to go home. Her bed seemed the only solution.

All the way downtown, on the other side of the tracks, the depressing office in a cold-water flat on the Lower East Side had none of the glamorous trappings of Herz or Gardiner. No limestone façade, no Fifth Avenue address or perfumed air. The air, in fact, was rife with the smell of opened corned-beef sandwiches with mustard on waxed paper. Not to mention the dank body odor of groups of young and old men working shoulder to shoulder in a cramped dark space. Josephine and Alexei were ushered into the poorly paneled makeshift office with an overhead fan whirring.

"Princess Orlove, Prince Orlove, please have a seat." Eduarde Finkelstein's haste, and the overwhelming files on his desk stacked so high as to obscure his stained tie, indicated that despite his humble office location and lyrical Argentine accent he was a top immigration lawyer, with deep connections in Europe and South America. Josephine saw the pained look in his eyes and immediately knew his ongoing search for Josephine's sister Chana had once again turned up empty. With Sybil in London and Rachel running the Australian operation, other disturbing thoughts were present. The lawyer had said the last known report of the twenty-year-old Chana was that she had received her papers and a passport in Warsaw two years earlier and at last sighting had made her way to Gdansk but had virtually disappeared, as if she did not exist.

"I am terribly sorry to report that with the war raging we only have secondhand information at best and none of it is good." Finkelstein looked over at the crestfallen Josephine. Her new husband, the handsome Prince Orlove, reached over and touched her hand tenderly. Josephine took out a small lace handkerchief and started to weep. Here she was, the richest woman in the world, and she had no power to find or help her youngest sister.

"How could she just disappear? I don't understand. People don't just disappear." Josephine would not listen, her glittering fifteen-carat diamond a bit out of place on the Lower East Side.

"Josephine, I—I didn't want to tell you, but I have a responsibility, not only to you but to let people know, and certainly, you and Prince Orlove are people of influence who can get the word out. The reports from those who have been lucky to escape Poland are unimaginable. Much worse than we thought. In fact, we have just had a report that the Nazis have liquidated the entire Krakow ghetto, sending the Jews to concentration camps, and those unable to go were killed in their homes or in the streets. We are talking about seven thousand people. The numbers are sheer madness. The largest mass shooting, we are told, was forty-three thousand people in Lublin."

"I—I don't understand. How can they kill that many people?"

"One by one, I'm sorry to say. They had to dig their own graves in trenches. It's unimaginable but true. We have eyewitnesses."

Josephine shook her head in horror. It was a nightmare come to life.

"And Chana?" she whispered.

"We cannot be sure. Maybe she married this young man and has the protection of a gentile. Maybe she has been rounded up. Or maybe she got lucky and got on one of the last ships out. We have no idea. There is really nothing more to say. We will continue our search, but do know I'm not hopeful."

"I understand." She wept.

"I'm not sure I can continue to bill you with the latest news. It wouldn't be fair." He looked grey and pale at having to tell her the truth.

"No, I insist. View it as a donation to what you are doing. You're helping people get out." Josephine sniffled.

"Thank you. That is very kind of you. I can honestly say we are overworked and understaffed and thoroughly unprepared for the work we are doing."

"I will make a larger donation as well." She hung her head.

Alexei silently helped Josephine to her feet. After thanking Finkelstein and offering the appropriate handshakes, he led her out of the office to the waiting limousine. He knew what they would do next and where they were going. Often loquacious and happy, Saturdays had turned solemn. The car drove down Essex Street into the heart of the teeming Lower East Side. Each weekend, he would accompany Josephine as she silently searched for Chana in the haunted faces of all the immigrants. She would scan the vast sea of young, middle-aged, and old women as her limousine drove ever so slowly. They all gawked at the gleaming black car, never having seen anything so large or fancy. Then they went about their business: the fruit stands, the kosher meat store, pushcarts carrying pots, pans, and housewares. And she would search. Search for a familiar face in a crowd, someone with absurdly high cheekbones, large soulful eyes, a resemblance, anything. She searched for a twenty-year-old girl who may have come over, maybe in the lucky flood of immigration before the doors slammed shut. Parties, soirees at night, work by day, weekends . . . and then . . . Saturdays searching for Chana. She would also go this Sunday as well. She needed to do it before they left on their honeymoon, which had been delayed multiple times due to work. She had finally agreed to take the time and was actually looking forward to it, now that they had changed it from Miami to . . . Palm Beach.

45

QUEEN CEECEE

Harlem, 1943

Gate Number 6 discreetly but boldly proclaimed, "PRIVATE ROAD—walk your horses." CeeCee always got a kick out of it when she passed through the stately gated entrance on elegant and private Strivers' Row, considered by many to be the Fifth Avenue of Harlem. Her newly purchased yellow-and-tan Federal Renaissance–style brownstone near 139th Street was home to the rising African American elite, such as Bill "Bojangles" Robinson and soon-to-be Congressman Adam Clayton Powell Jr. However, she was the only woman owner in the mix. It was interesting and poignant to all the residents that when the homes were built in the late 1800s there was a refusal to sell to blacks. It made CeeCee savor her elegant and prestigious address as much as Josephine did when she overcame the opposition from those living on Fifth Avenue. CeeCee rushed home after work each night, frantic to see her baby, Layla. And yet she knew that through her sacrifice, hard work, and business acumen, Layla Lopez was going to have a different sort of life from her mother's. She walked past the artfully designed wrought-iron railings and entered the brownstone.

"Gardenia, I'm home," she called out as she hung her steel-grey Persian lamb coat on the coatrack, placed her briefcase on the console, and ran upstairs to little Layla's room. The heavenly smell of freshly baking biscuits seemed the ultimate perfume.

"Now you go and wash your hands, you hear?" Gardenia Ray Gordon commanded at the sight of CeeCee, blocking the crib like a linebacker with her huge frame. She wiped her hands on her white lace apron and shook her head. She was used to young mothers barging in, and she was having none of their citified germs. CeeCee waved to little Layla in her crib and without dissent or a contrary word dutifully went into the bathroom and scrubbed her hands with the French milled lavender Herz soap as Gardenia had insisted. Gardenia had been the fifth woman who applied for the baby nurse job, and the moment she walked into her home, with her jaunty black velvet hat and wide sunny smile, CeeCee knew she ruled the roost. Gardenia offered a verbal résumé: she had raised scores of children in her career as a baby nurse, nanny, and housekeeper and knew every home remedy, from the varying teas with just the right amount of brown sugar to get the baby calmed and cooing, to the preparation of freshly mashed baby food. Her duties also included cooking late-night meals for the working mother, since she needed her strength to pay the bills. Her honey-dipped fried chicken and smothered steak were second to none, and some of her neighbors conveniently dropped by to see Layla at dinnertime in hidden hopes of being offered a stray drumstick or a side plate of mashed potatoes hand-whipped with farm-fresh butter and heavy cream with piping hot biscuits. Gardenia was a commanding force, with a boisterous laugh and large, capable, loving arms to hold Layla. Best of all, when CeeCee was at work she never worried about her daughter, knowing that the churchgoing Gardenia would have the best solution to anything that might happen.

The painful day that Mickey's elopement was announced in Winchell's column, CeeCee made a pledge that from then on she was going to focus on work and raising her child. She had little interest in being distracted by disappointing men and their foolishness. Her promise to herself and her unborn child was that she was going to work harder and longer than ever before. Josephine was duly impressed and found her more determined and strong-willed about building her business, given her existing new product responsibilities for the Herz Beauty brand. After her first week back, CeeCee requested an in-person meeting with Josephine, as she truly respected her acute and probing business mind in a way she never had with Constance.

CeeCee walked into Josephine's office with a pen and a pad to take notes. She knew she was in the presence of an entrepreneurial genius and was grateful. Josephine was as thoughtful as she was tactical and asked pointed questions about black women, their specific needs and desires. She was a sponge, eager to know and share. Since sisterhood and community played such an important role in the brand, they decided to build Queen CeeCee the way Constance had built Gardiner: with a door-to-door sales force, giving women in her community the ability and opportunity to earn money by becoming ambassadors called "CC Princesses." Josephine thought this was a marvelous idea. The starter kits alone would guarantee significant revenue over time. CeeCee gave her an update on the program now in place. Earlier that year, she had needed someone to run the newly formed CC Princess program and had turned to her cousin Rudy's wife, Lorene. A pretty and vivacious girl from South Carolina, Lorene had been a featured singer in Cab Calloway's orchestra, but when Lorene and Rudy had twin boys, she knew life on the Chitlin' Circuit was not for a young mother and made the difficult decision to retire. However, like CeeCee, Lorene had tasted freedom, and the idea of being just a stay-at-home mother after a glamorous but difficult career on the road held limited appeal. When CeeCee spoke to her about the idea of running the franchise division, she jumped at the chance. After all, Queen CeeCee was already profitable, with CeeCee herself having put in place a network of small but influential black-owned salons whose customers were wowed by her product. With the backing of Herz manufacturing and the scale of their buying power, Queen CeeCee's Hair Relaxer used the highest-quality oils and shea butters for moisturizing the scalp and taming the curl. All had instant results and none of the harsh, drying elements that had been used in inferior local products before. Since she also had the experience of running and building the Gardiner Girls program, CeeCee implemented many of the basic, hardworking concepts that had proven successful. Josephine loved the idea of building a brand for outsiders; she decided to invest in the concept and took pride in mentoring CeeCee.

CeeCee also wanted to better the lives of those women who had little opportunity for advancement. If someone became a CC Princess, she would receive training and a starter kit. The starter kit cost $10, but if a woman could not afford the kit's down payment, CeeCee offered to loan her the money. Josephine loved the idea so much, she funded the loan program personally and was satisfied to be paid back eventually through revenue sharing. Additionally, CeeCee pioneered the concept of a member making commissions on their own sales and also based on recruiting other women into the network and receiving a percentage of their overall sales. It was a forward-looking idea that would eventually position Queen CeeCee as one of the first modern multilevel marketing companies where non-salaried employees could make money through direct selling, and commissions on recruitment of new representatives. Top winners in revenue would also receive prizes, starting with a raccoon coat to a customized Ford coupe. With these generous incentives, women in the community clamored to become a CC Princess. Lorene would interview the candidates, and only the very best would be admitted to the program.

Working with Lorene was a joy. From the start, she also brought her own ideas to the table. For instance, she felt that CC Princesses should wear hats and gloves and be the ultimate ladylike ambassadors. She created a manual that stressed hygiene, cleanliness, and good manners, all important to fostering self-esteem and a respectable public image. Soon there were twelve CC Princesses operating in different regions, going door-to-door to local black-owned salons that were central to the community. These salons provided a place where hardworking women could gather socially as well as help one another with their hair care needs. Constance may have thought these ethnically diverse customers were beneath her, but Josephine saw an opportunity for both sales and female empowerment. Within the year Queen CeeCee was bringing in more than $150,000 in revenue. Following the birth of Layla, and in appreciation of her product's robust sales, Josephine surprised CeeCee with a large raise and bonus, which allowed her to purchase the Strivers' Row town house and hire Gardenia full-time. CeeCee Lopez was on the rise as Harlem's leading female businesswoman, inspiring those around her. Word quickly spread, and well-meaning friends and neighbors tried to set her up on dates with eligible men. She soon became tired of being approached on all sides by some of Harlem's most handsome and dashing bachelors. Each was smoother than the next, with compliments that rolled off the tongue like pearls and a keen interest in her business and especially her revenue. She knew such men represented a time-consuming and fruitless diversion, a waste of energy, each and every one of them eventually disappointing her or trying to get her under their thumb. Whatever the approach, from smooth come-on lines to persistent calls, CeeCee Lopez was having none of it. For now she enjoyed being queen of her castle. One without a king.

46

THE SANDBOX

Despite the social annoyance and idle chatter about Van and Lally's union, or even just the idea of it, Constance had to admit she was far happier than she had ever been. Her former husband, she thought, had actually done her a huge favor. She no longer had to tolerate living or spending time with an unattractive bore and his circle of entitled and arrogant friends she'd had to pretend to like. Now, she could come and go as she pleased, without having to make lame excuses. The luxury of the silence she preferred at home allowed her to fully dedicate herself to her one true passion: her business. She also had to admit that although divorced, she was still technically Mrs. Wyke, and there was no doubt the family name still held sway in some circles and came in handy whether it was related to banking relationships or her son's education. All in all, it was quite tidy, and she liked everything tidy and ordered. If she ever was in need of an appropriate male escort for a black-tie or cultural event, her brother, James, was always on hand and a dapper date. Charming and sophisticated, he had grown into his role as an event planner at Gardiner, and he was certainly a more engaging and witty dinner companion than Van. He had found a pale young ex–Broadway dancer, Gregg Stephens, who after a knee injury now worked in an antiques store, whom he occasionally brought

around. Constance was glad about it. He seemed to have finally settled down after two more unfortunate brushes with the vice squad.
These errors of judgment had cost her time, money, and embarrassment, and she had finally put her foot down, telling him that he
needed some stability, with someone. Anyone.

Gregg, a slight but muscular and ghostly pale ash blond from
Richmond, Virginia, seemed to be a suitable solution, and although
somewhat bland and nondescript, he was always pleasant, available as
an extra man for a seated dinner or for helping with the tree trimming
at Christmastime. "The relationship doesn't have to be all-consuming,"
she advised James, "just convenient and efficient." She always stressed
the word "tidy." "Tidy it up, James," she would counsel.

For her part, Constance had spent the latter part of the year totally
alone, just attending a gala or seated dinner now and then. She found
many of these evenings tedious but knew it was important to be around
the right people and accepted the important ones. Then, while in Los
Angeles for the Santa Anita Handicap, she stepped outside her carefully
orchestrated comfort zone. She was at the races when she accepted a
casual invitation to afternoon tea at the home of the well-known poet
and author Mercedes de Acosta, who was rumored to be the lover of
the bisexual Marlene Dietrich and Greta Garbo. She had heard the
rumors, of course, over the years that this was Hollywood's discreet
and elite lesbian circle, dubbed "the sewing circle," but she had always
declined the invitations to these events when she was in town with Van
and his set. Now, with him out of the picture and remarried, and herself fairly autonomous in Los Angeles, she decided to take the risk
and the plunge. Mercedes was another like-minded woman ahead of
her time, and her ideas were as revolutionary as Constance's. Rumored to have been the lover of Isadora Duncan and Alla Nazimova
after her divorce, she toyed with Hinduism, became a vegetarian, and
refused to wear fur out of respect for animals. Her gatherings at her
Spanish-style home off Sunset Boulevard was a mix of the most free-
thinking women of their time, and Constance immediately felt at

ease with the eclectic mix of actresses, authors, and writers. The women were welcoming without being overly forward, and she knew she could hold her own as one of the world's foremost female entrepreneurs. Her New York status and tall, lean blond good looks also made her an attractive addition to the Sunday afternoon high teas.

The day was warm but breezy as she lounged by the Mexican-tiled pool sipping a Lillet, adjusting her sunglasses, and toying with her gold charm bracelet. She had walked into the gathering alone and made her way to an outdoor lounge chair to take in some sun and her surroundings. A younger blond actress made polite conversation from the opposite chair, but Constance found her flighty and annoying. She casually dismissed her when a woman with a Hepburn persona caught her eye. She was having an animated conversation, debating the women's rights movement. "When I first moved to L.A., I sometimes put 'Marvin Rollins' on the script because when they saw 'Marilyn' they offered me a quarter of the price," she said, the color rising to her cheeks. "When I got my first agent he just advised me to put 'M. Rollins' since he didn't want me lying. So that is why I sign everything 'M. Rollins.'" The other women shook their heads in a knowing fashion, understanding the gender and pay inequality they all had to deal with.

Marilyn Rollins was neither shy nor retiring and may not have been traditional, but she always had an opinion and a stinging bon mot on hand and did not tolerate fools lightly. An established playwright and screenwriter, she was exactly the kind of woman Constance liked and admired. Tall, lanky, and striking, a Columbia University–educated tomboy like herself, she smoked, cursed, drank, and shot, and she wore trousers and spectator shoes without socks, which highlighted her long, shapely legs and high, slim waist. Although quite attractive without being beautiful, she never gave a moment's thought to her short-cropped auburn hair and had an innate intelligence and lovely hazel eyes that were both tough and vulnerable, condescending and sparkling. She eschewed makeup, which was also somewhat amusing to Constance.

And then as Marilyn passed by her lounge chair on the way for a refill of tea with a splash of whiskey, Constance raised her sunglasses.

"I have some advice for you." Constance smiled.

"I usually don't take advice from blondes," she quipped. "Only caresses." She put her hand on the hip of her cream trousers and scratched her upturned nose." I know who you are, though, Constance Gardiner. I'll take advice from *you*, Miss Makeup. Shoot," Marilyn dared her. Constance stood.

"I overheard your conversation," Constance started, and Marilyn lit her cigarette.

"I was having it for your benefit." She inhaled.

"That's nice to hear."

"Your advice?" She motioned. "Time is money."

"Start your own production company. M. Rollins Productions. Just like I did when I started Gardiner Cosmetics. You'll command more money when you're incorporated."

"You're not really blond, are you?"

"Why do you ask?"

"Because your advice is too good. Can we continue this over dinner at the Brown Derby? I'm dying for some corned-beef hash." She led Constance by the elbow, to knowing and appreciative glances. Marilyn and Constance. Formidable! the other women thought. An early dinner led to drinks and dessert at an out-of-the-way French bistro, which led to a visit to Marilyn's cottage in Santa Monica and then her bed for an active round of energetic lovemaking. Aside from their vastly differing views on politics, since Constance was a card-carrying Republican and Marilyn's views were more Marxist, Marilyn was her perfect ideal, smart, sassy, clever, and enigmatic. They made an immediate pact not to talk about politics since it would only lead to trouble. Best of all, she wasn't demanding. In fact, over the next few weeks, Marilyn wasn't around long enough to become annoying, always back and forth between the lot in L.A. and Broadway in New

York, where she was writing the book for a new musical. It was a lovely and mature friendship, with occasional and heated acrobatics and very few strings attached. It was functional and serviceable, just the way Constance loved to compartmentalize her time. And just when she needed a fix, Marilyn seemed to call. And then disappear and then call. Disappear and call. Back in New York, Marilyn had just called: she was in town for rehearsals and extended an invitation to spend time with her for a long weekend at Tallulah Bankhead's weekend house in Pennsylvania. Constance had paused but had been more excited by the invitation than she wanted to admit, admiring the avant-garde stage and film star whom she had seen in her tour de force *The Little Foxes* on Broadway and who was known for her bawdy sense of humor and outrageous off-screen antics. Bankhead was the epitome of glamour, portraying society bad girls to great advantage, and Constance was a moth to the flame. She canceled a Friday afternoon products meeting and had her driver navigate the back roads to rural Pennsylvania.

"Dahling!" Tallulah met her at the door with her legendary husky voice and a ready martini straight up. "Welcome to Bankheads, where every woman is a man . . . and every man a woman."

Constance was giddy at the risqué crowd and spied Marilyn across the room, who looked striking in a snug double-breasted man-tailored suit. Marilyn walked toward Constance with a bright smile and tried to kiss her on the lips but received her cheek as she turned away.

"Don't worry, Gardiner. Everyone here is queer . . . or wants to be."

"Ah, the two lovebirds." Tallulah raised an eyebrow. "You know, dahling, I'm from a long line of Dem-o-cratic senators in Alabama and cannot abide the Commies. But I forgive Marilyn her politics because she's not really red down there, she's *pink*." She emitted a throaty laugh.

"Opposites attract, apparently. I never tolerated Republicans before, let alone fucked them," Marilyn shot back.

Constance pursed her lips. "I don't approve of this kind of talk."

"Then call back your driver, dahling. Bankheads is all about trash talking. It's not only encouraged but expected." Tallulah rolled her eyes.

"Look at the two of you. Just gorgeous," a young man with beautiful features broke in. "Miss Gardiner, I presume?"

"Constance, do you know Keith McKeith? The choreographer?"

"I haven't had the pleasure. How do you do?" Constance extended a lily-white hand.

"I just adore your 'How do you do.' So very Palm Beach. Marilyn, you're really dating *up*." He arched a brow. "And I feel like I know you because I am one of your biggest customers." He smiled.

"Customers?" Constance looked confused.

"Keith is one of the most famous drag artists, dahling," Tallulah said. "He does me better than *me*! All the queens use Gardiner, you know . . . they prefer it over Herz."

"Yes, it's cheaper and stays on longer after a blowie." He laughed.

"I'm not sure what to say." Constance was reeling.

"Say thank you. He buys your product, *dearie*."

"I don't *buy it*. James, your brother, gives it to me. He gifts all the queens after we service him." He laughed out loud and walked away. Constance blushed, clearly uncomfortable.

"Constance, really? This isn't Palm Beach, it's Bankheads," Marilyn whispered. "You must have known."

"I'm sorry, I'm just not used to this."

"Here, have another martini"—she grabbed one off a passing tray—"and take the proverbial stick out of your ass. What? You think people here don't know I'm fucking you?"

"It's just so . . . overt?" She tried to find the right words to express her discomfort.

"Well, get used to it, chickadee. We are bunking together, you know." Marilyn blew her a kiss, and Constance finally relented and laughed.

"You see? I knew you could lighten up like everyone else. There's a famous story about our hostess. When she first arrived in Hollywood, she went up to Thalberg, can you imagine, and said, 'How do you get laid in this dreadful place?' And he said—"

Tallulah broke in to finish the anecdote herself. "And he said, 'I'm sure you'll have no problem. *Ask anyone!*'" Her throaty laughter was contagious, as her guests all laughed with her.

While loath to admit it, Constance hadn't been mentally or physically challenged or stimulated in quite some time and tried to fit in despite her innate prudishness. However, as much as she tried to laugh and be lighthearted and clever, the initial excitement receded once she had arrived. Now she knew why she never accepted weekend invitations. She always felt somewhat trapped and having to sing for her supper and entertain her hosts. Not to mention the fact that her feelings for Marilyn were actually growing, to her dismay. After a day and a half of witty repartee, country air, and more gin and tonics than she could count, Constance was feeling the claustrophobia of their togetherness, despite being stirred by their closeness. And when Marilyn pulled her near her on a path in the woods and declared, "I'm falling for you, you damn virgin," Constance froze and walked in front of her and then immediately begged off, claiming a new product meeting in the morning, deciding to leave early. Marilyn was upset and perplexed, since their chemistry in bed was so passionate that the chorus boys in the next room banged on the wall to keep it down, to her horror. That evening, after her thanks to Tallulah and excuses to Marilyn, as the local taxi picked her up and drove down the long tree-lined drive, she was relieved and happy to be away from the bitchy chorus boys, messy leaves, and seemingly growing overt affection between her and Marilyn, which was disquieting.

She breezed into her office on Monday, and Marjorie nodded silently and put her tea service and newspapers on her desk. To her continued dismay, she digested the bold headline about Roosevelt's win over Dewey, whom she had supported. A fourth term with him again! she griped. Marilyn had been jubilant at the outcome, toasting with the weekend guests to Constance's stony silence on the subject. The more she praised Roosevelt, the more Constance seemed to retreat. Had she been doing it on purpose to elicit some sort of response?

Marjorie buzzed. "Miss Gardiner, Mr. Wyke is on the phone for you. What shall I tell him?"

Constance hesitated before picking up the phone. She knew if Van was calling, it was either about money or some sort of annoying issue. She wasn't wrong.

"I'll take it." She sighed dramatically "Yes, Van . . ." She paused. "How can I help you?" She twisted her multistrand pearl bracelet with anxiety.

"Hello, Constance. First things first. I wanted to know if you or I shall be taking Van Jr. for Christmas holiday. I assumed we would," he said softly.

"We?" Her voice was laced with ice.

"Well, Lally and I. We would have him in Palm Beach for Christmas break."

"I actually plan on taking him this year. We will be in Palm Beach through New Year's and you can see him for a few lunches or dinner. I prefer Lally not be there, if you don't mind."

"Of course." He paused. "I do think, though, you are going to have to get used to the idea, Constance. Lally is my wife now and she has her own children." He tried to offer up a perk. "Van Jr. might enjoy the company of other kids his age."

"I am quite aware of that. How else can I help you, Van? I am quite busy." She paced beside her desk.

"I think it's time you sent over the remaining two hundred and fifty thousand you owe me," he finally blurted out. "I only received the first half."

"Well, that's just it. I am a bit cash strapped for now, so I will be sending it to you in installments. Five thousand a month."

"Constance, I think you need to reconsider," he said firmly.

"And why is that? You're getting your money, just not all at once."

"Lally and I just received a dinner invitation from the Louis Kaufmans. They are hosting a celebratory dinner at the Everglades Club for Prince and Princess Orlove, who happen to be at the Breakers for their honeymoon." He paused. "We are thinking of attending." He had dropped the bomb and now waited for the explosion.

"I see," she reflected. "So the one Jewish member is hosting a dinner for her. They do stick together, apparently, their little tribe."

"Come now, Constance. I am sure Kaufman is advising her. He was president of Chatham Phenex National Bank, on the board of General Motors, and is one of the members that saved the club from foreclosure in the twenties. His daughter Joan, whom you've met, was married to George Drexel Biddle. And Mrs. Biddle is also on the host committee, so it will be quite the crowd, I can assure you."

"I see. Well, it's all very convenient."

"Shall Lally and I attend . . . or send our regrets?"

"Yes. I rather think you should send your . . . regrets." She chose her words carefully. "The next installment of one hundred twenty-five thousand will be sent this week."

"I thought so. It's always a pleasure doing business with you, Constance. I will see you down in PB over the holidays and I will make sure Van Jr. and I spend some good quality father-son time together."

"Thank you, Van. Best to Lally." She slammed the phone down.

Of course *she* was in Palm Beach! It didn't take that woman five minutes of having a second-rate title to start throwing it around, and on her turf. Nor did it take the conniving duo Van and Lally two seconds to blackmail her with her rival. Outwitted again, she fumed. It did, however, prompt an idea.

"Marjorie . . . ," Constance called out for her secretary.

"Yes, Miss Gardiner."

"Can you get me Avery Fisher on the phone? I think it's time Gardiner Cosmetics got involved in some cultural events in New York.

I think we should sponsor the opera this year. You did accept my being on the benefit committee?"

"Yes, and I made clear that you would consider it only if, well . . . if *she* was not on it this year."

"Perfect." She smiled to herself. "If she is going to play in my sandbox, then it's high time I played in *Herz*." She laughed out loud.

47

NEWLYWEDS

New York City, 1945

The triumphant glow of Josephine's honeymoon in Palm Beach remained long after her slight sunburn receded and the newlyweds returned to Manhattan. Deep down, Josephine actually preferred the action and nightlife of Miami, but she had been thoroughly pleased by the welcoming staff at the imposing Breakers and the attentions of the cream of Palm Beach society, who were more than happy to overlook certain prejudices when it came to money and exotic titles. Certainly the men were impressed by Josephine's business savvy and her dark, innate curves and overt sex appeal, which was in contrast to the cool qualities of the languid blondes who occupied the grass tennis courts and charity balls of the island paradise. The women, young and old, were flushed and gaga over Alexei Orlove's dashing good looks and White Russian title. No one was born to the tuxedo more than the youthful prince, with his broad shoulders and tapered waist, and few women had as impressive a décolletage and famed emerald and diamond parures, which had belonged to the original empress Josephine and been reset by the current one. Most had to admit that despite their reservations, sheer glamour had descended on the insular and lily-white crowd. While many gossiped that she had married him for the title, and he for her riches, it took only a moment in their presence to see how happy they were together. A few bored members of the Palm Beach set even tried to curry favor with Josephine in order to receive an invitation to her famed weekly Manhattan salons, which had gained attention among those looking for more of a mix and a thrill. "Do you know she even hosts black dancers from the Cotton Club?" Women would raise a plucked eyebrow and men would give one another knowing glances, salivating at the thought of a more interesting and looser set.

For her part, Josephine had always been running, running, running . . . trying to succeed in life and in business, never slowing down to smell the roses. On her oft-delayed honeymoon, which Alexei had convinced her to take, she finally relaxed with him at her side. The ever-present anxiety and intensity receded and she felt calm, centered, and somehow complete. While the trimmings of his youth, good looks, and title were obvious attractions, his easygoing and low-key demeanor worked to soften Josephine's edges, and everyone found her looking younger, more attractive, and relaxed.

"A new youth serum?" those who knew her asked, and smiled at the refreshed and improved Madame Herz with a hint of youthful ardor. She just smiled. It would, however, eventually lead her to a new treatment line and a fragrance called "Our Love by Princess Orlove."

"Darling, look what I got you." Josephine wrapped her lovely, creamy arms around her handsome husband at his drafting table, her crystal-and-diamond cuffs jangling, and handed him a small bag from Gimbels department store.

"If this is what I think it is . . ." He eagerly opened the present, and his eyes laughed and sparkled. "I cannot believe you got this for me . . . it's so expensive, Josephine." His sea-blue eyes pleaded.

"You had to have one. It's the latest invention," she said as he marveled at and inspected the first ballpoint pen available for sale.

"But"—he looked at the receipt in the bag—"it's twelve fifty . . . for a pen?!" He looked at her as if she were insane.

"I know, but what do you think—I can't afford to buy you a pen? You won't take anything else . . . and after all, the pen is mightier than the sword."

He swiveled in his chair and kissed her on her pillow lips.

"You are crazy, you know that?"

"Well, now that the war is over we have to celebrate. What are you working on?" She looked at his renderings over his shoulder. He was drawing a new line of lipsticks called "Victory Rouge." The color scheme was red and gold, all vivid and bursting with excitement owing to the German surrender. The enemy had been defeated, and the mood in the country was now confident and jubilant.

"That is beautiful," she commented, studying his product drawings and vibrant watercolors as she ran her well-groomed hands through his dark, lustrous hair. "I never asked you. Where did you learn to draw and paint so beautifully?" She nestled into him. Her outward affection had become deep and uncharacteristic. He looked at her and smiled, putting aside his sharpened pencil to examine the new ballpoint pen.

"I'm not sure I told you, when I was a child I had rheumatic fever and was in bed for months. I had nothing to do for weeks on end, so my mother gave me a drawing pad and some watercolors. Once they were in my hands my health and spirit improved. It changed my life."

"I didn't know that. Well, you are very strong now. My handsome prince. . . ." She marveled at his strong physique.

"They thought I didn't have long to live, so I drew my way out of it." He gave a wan smile. Josephine processed the news about his early illness without saying much, only hugging him tighter. She knew that there must have been side effects to his heart but decided not to say anything, just mentally filing it away.

"Come. I've decided to take you and Miles to Lüchow's for dinner." She was in the mood for some schnitzel and potato pancakes and also wanted to fatten up Miles now that he was fifteen and still skinny like a string bean.

"That sounds like fun. I just need to finish this up and I'll get ready."

He kissed her. Josephine, for her part, had never been an overly involved mother and trusted Alexei when it came to opinions about Miles. A shy and reserved boy who was deeply affected by his domineering mother and his parents' divorce, he had developed a stutter and lack of confidence when he turned thirteen. Josephine had no understanding of his condition and often yelled at him to stop stuttering, which only made the situation worse. Now that Alexei was a permanent part of the household, he tried to build Miles's self-confidence and be a sounding board for the sensitive adolescent. His admonishment of his wife's unfeeling treatment of her son had moved her. She gave in to him, especially given Jon Blake's lack of involvement now that he had a new wife and two young children of his own, something she was bitter about after settling so much on him.

For his part, Miles was originally suspicious of the handsome younger man who had stolen his mother's affections, and shortly after they were married, at a Sunday night dinner, he exhibited a rare moment of rebellion with a caustic remark directed at Alexei. In a fury, Josephine pulled him into her office and instructed him to sit while she went into the wall safe behind the the Picasso portrait of Dora Maar. After cranking the safe dial, she opened the door and threw a sheaf of papers at him.

"Do you know what this is?" She raised her voice as he visibly shrank in his seat. "It is a prenuptial agreement that Alexei signed before we got married. It protects you and me from him getting anything, do you hear me? He gets nothing if there is a divorce or something happens to me. You, you spoiled young man, get everything just by virtue of the fact that you are my son. He wants nothing but to be your friend. To help you. When you are rude to him, you are rude to me. Now you go apologize to him, and if I hear you are rude to him again, I can assure you," she commanded, "I *vill* change the vill and he vill inherit. Do you hear me?"

"Yes . . . M-M-Momma," he stuttered, looking down.

"Now stop that stutter and get out and go apologize," she said in a fury.

The dramatic outburst and dressing-down seemed to work. Perhaps Miles needed to see in black and white that he was, after all, the heir to his mother's attentions, and he softened considerably over the next few weeks. Within the month, Miles and Alexei were closer and co-conspirators, to Josephine's delight. And while Alexei would never take a penny, the next day there would always be a new Cartier tank watch or a pair of gold-and-sapphire braided cuff links from Verdura on his drafting table. It was her way of gifting him and making sure he knew he was appreciated and loved and that he had a growing list of assets. As they made their way downtown to Lüchow's in the back of the limousine, Miles filled them in on his tests and studies, and to Josephine's delight his grades had been slowly improving.

"Good. I will only accept the Ivy League!" she commanded.

At the ornate entrance, they were greeted by the owner, Victor Eckstein, as all heads swiveled. Josephine was something of a local celebrity, and she and Alexei made a stunning couple. "Ah, Prince and Princess Orlove. So good to see you."

"Say hello to Mr. Eckstein. This is my son, Miles." Miles shook his hand firmly.

"A handsome boy." Victor surveyed the clean-cut private school boy.

"We're in dire need of some schnitzel to fatten him up," she proclaimed to laughter.

"I'll send the waiter immediately, Madame Herz. A pleasure." He kissed her hand in the European style and led them to his finest table.

Dinner was a convivial affair. The awkward silences that had once existed between mother and son were now peppered with animated conversation and laughter, and it made the weekly meals more agreeable and pleasant with Alexei leading the conversation. "He's only going to be home for two more years before university," Alexei kept saying, "so enjoy it while he's still living at home."

The opulent dessert cart was wheeled over, the layered cakes and torten stacked high like treats in a Turkish bazaar. Josephine ordered a linzer torte and then heaping portions of apple crepes with freshly whipped cream and cinnamon for the boys. Suddenly, a slight, bald-headed man approached the table and gave a short, courtly bow. While he was a stranger, he had the familiar look of a landsman, his Polish Jewish looks comforting to Josephine in a welcoming way.

"Are you Madame Herz? I heard the owner mention your name." He was tentative and ill at ease, and his emaciated frame was swimming in a suit two times the appropriate size. Josephine was unsure of why he had come over to the table but thought perhaps he might have known her from her childhood.

"A pleasure to meet you. I am Izaak Frydman. I am sorry to disturb your dinner, but I vanted to give you this number," he said in Polish-tinged English. "I am sure you vould vant it." He handed Josephine a small, crumpled piece of paper with a tiny phone number scribbled in faint blue ink.

"Yes, how can I help you? What is this?" She looked at him, confused.

"My . . . my sister Sarai vas in the camp with your sister Chana. They vere together till the end. I am so sorry," he said, a tear welling up at the corner of his eye.

"Camp?" Josephine uttered the unimaginable.

"They vere at Bergen-Belsen together vhen your Chana died of typhus. I am so sorry. I am sure you vill vant to speak to Sarai, who is still recovering. She said Chana vas an angel." He placed a kindly, gentle hand on her shoulder as he saw her register the shock and grief. That was, of course, before Josephine Herz, the world's richest woman and the Princess Orlove, promptly fainted.

48

BROKEN GLASS

New York City, 1946

The opalescent Lalique vase crashed with such force that a chunk of glass was now embedded and suspended from the wall. Despite the crash, the shattering glass was less piercing than the screaming.

"You no-good lyin' *son of a bitch*!" Myra Heron shrieked. "I'm tired of your cheatin'! You're a lowlife, do you know that?"

She stood firmly, facing Mickey. All he could see were big, glossy red lips, as if her lips and mouth were a screaming machine detached from her body. The timbre of her voice was usually loud even when she was just speaking, but when she was screaming, it was a world war–worthy event. Mickey tried his best to calm her, saying they were in a fancy hotel on Central Park South and that the neighbors could hear and "they could get kicked out." This only seemed to enrage her more.

"You're nothing more than a low-class fruit peddler! How I married you, you piece of shit. Look at you. Lipstick on your T-shirt and you don't even bother hiding it." She was going nuclear and her voice only kept getting louder. And louder.

"Myra, it was from a new lipstick we're launching. Some of it got on my clothes. I'm in the fuckin' lipstick business!" He tried to reason with her, although the child was now starting to scream as well. "You've already woken up the kid with your big trap!"

"What real man is in the lipstick business, anyway?" She walked up to him, screaming in his face, getting closer, assaulting him with her accusations. "Maybe you're really a fairy?" She poked him. "You should be ashamed of yourself. My cousin Essie married a doctor, Sarah Kaplan, a lawyer, and you . . . the big *macher* Mickey Heron . . . the lipstick king. You're an embarrassment. A mobster is more respectable. You run around with your models and your whores. I hear you like darkies too."

"Don't you . . ." He couldn't believe she had brought up the likes of CeeCee. How did she know?

"Don't I *what*? Or maybe you like boys, since you care so much about makeup. Maybe *that's* the reason you don't come near me anymore, 'cause you're a *queer*." Her voice quivered as she lobbed the crazy accusations at him like tennis balls, one after the other, although she knew none of them were true.

Mickey tried to control his temper, but she was pushing him toward war. And she couldn't help unleashing more and more epithets like the German Blitzkrieg, each one designed to devastate.

"You gotta be kidding me. I love women, but you think I'm attracted to the likes of *you*? *Just look at you!*" he screamed back with venom. "You're a fucking whale, Myra. You had the baby years ago and all you do is stuff your face. You think I want to sleep with *you*? Your mother is more attractive. Keep eating them doughnuts." He pointed to boxes of half-eaten doughnuts and chocolates that littered the hotel room.

"My father was right. He should have knocked you off when you got me pregnant. How did I end up like this?" She threw her hands up in the air, bemoaning and bewailing her fate as the fat on her arms jiggled unattractively.

"You're lucky he kicked the bucket before he saw you blow up fat as a house!" Mickey screamed, beet-faced. Her father, the hefty and ever-expanding Moe Stein, hadn't been felled by a mobster's bullet, but expired a year earlier from a heart attack after consuming a few extra-hearty portions of brisket and stuffed derma at the prime L.A. delis. Mickey would have been out of there the next day if it weren't for Mickey Jr.

"My father was a saint. Don't you ever talk about him." She slapped him in the face, gashing his cheek in the process with her razor-sharp red nails. Mickey Jr. was crying loudly from all their screaming. Being incredibly vain, Mickey became even more enraged when he saw the blood on his hand.

"Here, have another doughnut." He picked up a glazed one, then rushed forward and in anger shmushed it, grinding it into her face. "And you know what he said? He told me he was lucky I took you off his hands." Mickey laughed. "You . . . you fat slob."

"Take your hands off me!" She ran after him and pummeled him. Mickey was impressed; her punches felt like those of a prizefighter, and he actually emitted a laugh as she socked him in the stomach.

"You could fuckin' box the Golden Gloves. What woman packs a punch like that? You're a fuckin' fat beast."

"I eat because I *hate* you!" she yelled at the top of her lungs. "And I hate you more than I hate myself. I am going to get as fat as I can, so you can be Handsome Mick with the fat, ugly wife. That's what I've been up to!" Her face was contorted with rage.

"Well, you're doing a great job because *I wouldn't fuck you with Uncle Irv's dick!*" He picked up a heavy crystal ashtray and with one swift motion threw it like a talented quarterback into the onyx fireplace.

"You think I want to be married to you, you hairy, ugly animal? And to top it off you're as stupid as a brick." She pushed him.

"I'm stupid? *I'm* stupid?" He rushed her and pushed her back. "You have a fuckin' bagel between your ears. You're a disgusting pig. I'm *outta* here."

"Outta here? You walk out, you'll *never* see Mickey Jr. again. Never."

"Don't threaten me."

"You see this . . ." She twisted off her round, five-carat diamond ring. "It means nothing. You know what I'm gonna do with this?" She ran toward the windows facing Central Park South.

"Are you *crazy*?" Mickey rushed her. "That ring cost me twenty-five grand. You're fuckin' ugly, but stupid, too . . . ?" He pulled at her arm and twisted it. She whimpered in pain.

"You're stupid, you fuckin' moron. You think I care about your low-grade diamond that's probably hot and fell off a truck? It's fake like you. Probably glass. You think I care about your piece-of-shit low-grade junk of a diamond? Here's what I think about it!" she howled. She made it to the window as he was grabbing her elbow . . . and twisting her arm. He backhanded her as she fell against the window, moaning in pain.

"Help me—police! He's beating me!" she wailed. With one hand she managed to open the metal latch of the window.

"Don't you dare!" he screamed. She just looked at him with hate as she threw the engagement ring out the window onto Central Park South, twelve stories down. He slapped her one more time for good measure . . . just before the police broke down the door.

The wind was brisk and howled liked a stray dog at the moon and the trees shuddered under a grey-canvas sky that looked as if it had only recently been gessoed. Mickey pulled the collar of his navy cashmere coat up under his chin to try to block the chill. He hadn't shaved and touched the ointment on the gash by his cheek and winced. It was deep and raw. The thought of Myra's nail sinking into his cheek only angered him more. Central Park was dark, cavernous, and empty, even though it was only seven P.M.; no one, it seemed, wanted to brave the elements. Mickey just walked, still in shock from what he had seen. What he now knew. And what he had to do.

He knew the divorce from Myra would come. He knew that it would be painful and expensive and that Mickey Jr. would be used as a pawn—a virtual tug-of-war between the two battling factions. That his own son would be turned against him by his bitter and unrelenting mother. This he knew and expected. He also knew that since Moe's death he had nothing to fear. Everyone in his network knew that Mickey was a stand-up guy who had honored his commitment, and at Moe's funeral the men all patted him on the back with compassion when they saw how obese Myra had become. No man was expected to stay with that, or at least not have the freedom and the blessing to play the field. Especially Handsome Mick. There was even an ongoing bet on how long Mick could last with a sumo wrestler in his bed. They all chuckled and shrugged. "Poor Mickey, especially with all the talent he's had." What he didn't know was what he had seen the previous evening, and it rattled him to the core. He knew he had a rip cord and he had pulled it. He had called CeeCee in the middle of the night and asked her to come and bail him out. Said that he and Myra had come to blows and a divorce was at hand. He thought she might have been petty or joyous or nasty, but she was only sad and silent. She would come, she said, and she would do for him what he had once done for her: bail her out. But she'd told him not to expect anything and that she would be introducing him to someone. Not to be shocked or surprised. And then she hung up. He waited in the holding cell, and when they came to release him, he had fully expected a handsome boyfriend or a husband who was angered and jealous and fuming or steaming at having been awakened and summoned to a police station. He was soon to find out it was none of those things. It was a beautiful four-and-a-half-year-old girl with light skin, green eyes, and a mop of curly black hair, holding hands with her mother. "Layla, meet my friend Mickey. Mickey Heron, Layla Lopez."

"So nice to meet you." He took her little hand in his and tried to be charming, although he knew his eyes were bloodshot, his face gashed, and his chin sprouting stubble. He knew he didn't smell good either. He was so embarrassed to see CeeCee this way. Like a good-for-nothing. Like a bum. What man, no matter how angry, would hit a woman and get locked up? He was kicking himself. And there was CeeCee looking silky and beautiful as ever, and with a baby. And as he looked at Layla's little face and told her just how pretty she was, that's when he saw it and knew for sure.

"You, Layla, are as beautiful as your mother, and my, you have dimples." He paused. "Oh, and you have a cleft in your chin. Just like *me*." And in that instant Mickey *knew*. And he also vowed he would do anything in his power to get CeeCee and Layla back.

49

MIRIAM

Constance shook her perfect blond coif and sighed as she read the morning paper and groaned at the news. "What's the world coming to?" She felt a cold terror. Staring up at her was the black-and-white photo of the Hollywood Ten in *The New York Times* and an accompanying list of those having Communist sympathies and ties. She read the names of more than 150 actors, writers, and directors who had been accused by the House Un-American Activities Committee and effectively blacklisted, and just her luck, there was the name, featured prominently on the list. And not even M. Rollins, but good old Marilyn Rollins, her sometime lover, who was now a bona fide card-carrying member of the Communist Party. Constance blanched at the potential scandal on all levels of being associated with such a person and deep down knew what she needed to do. She shook her head and frowned. The news seemed to reflect an ever-changing world and brought home conflicting issues. It was the same feeling she had had months earlier with the headlines of Jackie Robinson, the first African American to be admitted to the Major Leagues. The controversial decision had her thinking about CeeCee. It seemed she couldn't escape her inner passions despite her outwardly conservative views. Yet, her ties to

Marilyn were even more concerning. There had been one frantic late-night call, then a silent period where Marilyn had all but disappeared before the news broke. She'd had no idea where she was until she received a call from Mercedes de Acosta that Marilyn had officially been blacklisted and summoned to appear in Washington before the committee. She was hiding out at her apartment on Twelfth Street in the city and Mercedes gave her the phone number. Constance decided to wait it out, knowing that Marilyn would eventually reach out to her when the time was right. Marilyn finally rang the following Monday and asked if they could meet at a small bar in Greenwich Village. She hadn't wanted to, but felt she needed to handle the potentially explosive situation carefully. To "tidy" things up. Her car ride downtown was met with a bit of anxiety mixed with nostalgia as she remembered James's apartment on Ninth Street. How young, naive, and hopeful she had been then. Now she felt as if she were going to a wake, not to see a lover but to meet a dead woman walking.

Marilyn was already sitting in a booth of the Cedar Tavern on University Place, drinking with the guys. She was wearing their uniform: a pilled black turtleneck, cuffed blue jeans, and black ballet flats . . . inhaling a cigarette like a water-deprived bedouin and downing a dirty glass of whiskey with two local artist friends she had collected, Willem de Kooning and Franz Kline.

"Modern trash art." Constance shook her head, remembering the canvases she'd seen stacked against the wall in Marilyn's Santa Monica cottage and adorning the walls. "A child could paint those," she had declared upon learning that Marilyn had purchased them from the group of surly men known as abstract expressionists. Always on the cutting edge, Marilyn embraced the new, buying future masterpieces at $100 a pop or for drinks when the crew couldn't afford the bar bill and she had sold a script. Her nonsensical and capacious drip canvas by little-known artist Jackson Pollock inspired particular ire. "A kindergartner could do that!" Constance had hissed.

"And only someone with *infantile taste* wouldn't appreciate it, Miss

I-Only-Like-Art-with-Bowls-of-Fruit," Marilyn had retorted. And so they had sparred and then had fallen into bed.

The Cedar, Constance thought, was as good an out-of-the-way bar as any in the decidedly down-market Village, and she knew she wasn't going to see any of her uptown friends. Hopefully! Constance gave a nod to Marilyn and thought she looked even more attractive in her beat costume. She rose when she saw Constance and walked over. Constance was her formal self and gave her a brief and unsatisfactory kiss on the cheek. She didn't want to feel any attraction to this woman any longer. After a quick introduction to the artists, whom she knew she would never see again, and the particularly drunk one, Pollock, who called out, "The debs are invading," to raucous laughter, they settled into the wooden booth. When Constance threw her mink beside her like a bundle of laundry, they all looked her up and down as if she were visiting from another planet with her Chanel suit and triple strand of pearls.

"Thank you for using your passport and coming downtown," Marilyn quipped. "I see you dressed *down* for the event."

"I'll have you know I used to live on Ninth Street. Just two blocks over." Nearly overcome with the smell of stale beer and cigarettes, Constance scanned the crowd of degenerate artists and writers to see if she knew anyone. She was relieved to find that she didn't.

"Yeah . . . in your salad days!" Marilyn raised an eyebrow as she nursed her whiskey. "I took the liberty of ordering you a gin and tonic since they don't serve Lillet and caviar here."

"So we're being snippy, are we. Is that it?" Constance lobbed it back at her. "Well, it's better here than at the Monkey Bar."

"Yeah, better for *you*."

"Perhaps. How are you?"

"You know I am not in the best of moods since I was just fired off the Gable movie and am officially blacklisted. I cannot get work. No one will return my calls, including my agent. I am what's known as Hollywood *poison*. Oh, let's not forget being summoned to Washington, where I will be raked over the coals in public: 'Are you now or have you ever been a member of the Communist Party?'"

"And have you?" Constance blotted her lips with the napkin.

"You're damn right. I'm as red as a Maine lobster on a summer day. With *drawn* butter. Tallulah was right. The only thing pink about me is my pussy."

"Don't be vulgar," Constance huffed. "Well, I told you that your politics would get you into trouble, but you wouldn't listen."

"Okay, Mrs. Lindbergh 1939. What else do you have for me? He gets rebuked by FDR for his war views and is living the high life in Darien and I can't get arrested. Well, maybe I can!" She laughed bitterly. "They are throwing us into jail now, you know."

"Here." Constance thrust a Gardiner Cosmetics bag at her. "There are some lipsticks, rouges, and eyeliner in there. Perhaps when you make your debut with the House Un-American Activities Committee you'll try to be a bit more feminine. I can assure you they'll go easier on you if you wear a dress and some lipstick. Not if you look like a beat poet or a dyke."

"Oh, so you want me to dress the part of the lipstick lesbian, is that it?"

"Marilyn, I adore you and love the term. Very clever. And clearly, you are one of the smartest women I have ever met. But you are a stubborn bitch and you dig your heels in. You need to rethink your strategy if you ever want to work again."

"Maybe I don't. Maybe, just maybe, I don't want to live in a world where I can't be me." She paused.

"Don't say such things, Marilyn. Just put on the lipstick and rouge, wear a dress, and be polite and forget the fire and the fury and you'll get back to working again."

"Yeah, maybe if I was like you—blond, Republican, and"—she blew smoke out of the side of her mouth—"a Christian."

"Wait . . ." Constance was wide-eyed at the revelation. "Don't tell me you're also . . . Jewish to boot?"

"Yeah, and so was Mary. The first famous Jewish mother. What's it to you?"

"Nothing, you just never told me." Constance tried to remain composed as she processed it all. Her world was unraveling. After all this time, she had been in love with a Jewess!

"Given name"—she hand-blocked it—"Miriam Goldstein. Problem with that too?" Marilyn said point-blank.

"As a matter of fact, I do." Constance puffed on her cigarette. "I don't like liars."

"And you? Miss Palm Beach with your marriage *blanche* and your adopted Aryan son whom you never see. You think you're truthful?"

"I'll have a whiskey, too," she called out to the passing bartender.

"Trouble with the truth?"

"We don't have conversations like this"—she gulped—"in Canada."

"And you think you're really that much different? Miss dyed-blond, the carpet doesn't match the drapes, Miss Gardiner with an *i* and not an *e*. Give me a break. You wanted Palm Beach and Locust Valley and you got it. All with the cleverly inserted and aristocratic *i*. And I wanted to be taken seriously and work in L.A. Do you think I would have been nominated for an Academy Award for *The Gentle Path* if it was written by Miriam Goldstein and not M. Rollins? Do you?" She raised her voice.

"How did you know?" Constance nursed her drink.

"Well, it's not too hard to see you're a brunette when I'm down there, lovie. . . ."

"No. My name."

"Oh, everyone knows and talks. It's all your brother James's boyfriend can talk about to the chorus boys. . . . It's a small world, Constance. And just because your transformation was, let's just say . . . 'more subtle' doesn't mean you didn't do it for the same reasons I had a nose job and a name change. Right? G-a-r-d-i-n-e-r?"

Constance was silent.

"Right?" Marilyn pressed her.

"Right. Touché. You won. Does that make you feel better, Miss Goldstone?"

"Goldstein." She laughed out loud. They both did.

They both sat silent in their revelations and raw truth.

"Look," Marilyn started as she ordered another Jameson, "despite our differences . . . I wanted you to know I love your mind and your body. It's very *endearing, dearie.*" She dragged on her ciggie. "But you can't handle the truth."

"Maybe I can't." Constance took a puff of her own cigarette. "I'll have you know . . . I have feelings too!"

Marilyn burst out laughing and blocked out the word with her hands again. "News flash . . . the great Constance Gardiner has"—she imitated the dramatic Tallulah Bankhead and spread her arms in a grand Broadway gesture—"*feelings!*"

"Of course you would laugh, but I do."

"Well, feelings seem to be in short supply between Park and Fifth Avenue these days."

"That's because you hate it and have never lived there. Look—" Constance reached into her purse and withdrew an envelope that was thick with cash.

"What is this, hush money?" Marilyn laughed again.

"It's money to help my friend Miriam Gold*stein* through a difficult period. Take it, you're going to need it."

"It's also a goodbye, isn't it."

Constance just looked down.

"Isn't it? Just say the truth out loud for once, you damned cunt."

"Yes—" She raised her voice. "It's goodbye because you are stubborn and brilliant and would never, could never, change."

"Change my stripes? . . . Reds, Communists, Jews, Marxists, leftists, lesbians, the media elite," she hissed, and threw the envelope back at her. "I understand. It's a witch hunt and they are coming after the coven."

"It's not my world. I have to leave." Her eyes welled up with tears.

"Oh. A new product meeting. Under-eye *cover-up,* perhaps?"

"I have to go." Constance stood. "Here, take this." She threw the envelope at her.

"Keep it! I'll only donate it to the . . . Bolsheviks!" she said, cackling. Constance just stood there and shook her head.

"Before you go . . . I have just have one question." Marilyn downed her third whiskey.

"Yes, go on."

"Go on? I'm not an employee . . . will you for once in your perfectly arranged life be truthful? Just once? Can you manage that?"

"Yes. Yes, I can." She tried to rise to the occasion.

"Did the cool, blond goddess Constance Gardiner with the *i* ever have feelings for Miriam Goldstein, real feelings for the caustic, the cutting, the *red* Marilyn Rollins? When we were in bed together, was it just sex or did you ever have real feelings for me? Real intimate, intense feelings for me the way I had them for you? Loving and passionate feelings. The kind that don't happen often but are based in the physical and the intellectual. Like when we made love and laughed together and you told me all about your stupid product launches and I pretended to be interested in rouge—" She suddenly emitted a lone sob and crushed her cigarette into the ashtray. "I . . . I just need to know. If it was . . . real like I thought it was, or was I just a damn stupid *fool* about everything in my life?"

Constance hesitated and then said with a slow gait, "You may find this hard to believe, Miriam *Goldstein,* but I love you. I loved you. I will always love you." She looked down and stood up. "I just don't *like* you . . . who you are."

And then among the abstract expressionists, they kissed in the most tender fashion. When they broke apart, Marilyn handed back the envelope as Constance shook her head and in her organized fashion put it back in her shiny black crocodile Hermès purse. Constance and her mink fled the bar reeling, trying to process it all; the pieces were clear, but none of it made sense to her. Over the next two weeks, she picked up the phone during the day or in the middle of the night to call Marilyn a dozen times, wanting to hear her voice, her acerbic remarks, and tell her everything was going to be okay, to reassure her, but each time fear stood in her way and she couldn't bring herself to dial the numbers. She didn't want to be, couldn't be, publicly associated with a *lefty* lesbian, she kept telling herself. There was no place for her despite her feelings.

It was a clear Tuesday morning and she arrived earlier than usual to prepare for an architects' meeting for the new Lavender Door Salon she was planning in Detroit. She always read the business section of *The New York Times* first and then read the first section as she sipped her tea. She liked and felt comforted by her morning routine, always the same. Today would be different. She picked up the *Times* and something searing caught her eye: NOTED SCREENWRITER DEAD DAY OF UN-AMERICAN HEARING. Her mind could not process what she was reading: "Marilyn Rollins, the distinguished Academy Award–nominated screenwriter of eighteen movies and five Broadway plays, born Miriam Goldstein from the Bronx, was found dead the day of her scheduled appearance in Washington before the House Un-American Activities Committee. She committed suicide by throwing herself in front of an oncoming subway train." The color drained from her face, and for the first time in years, Constance Gardiner wept.

Weeks later, she heard from the chorus boys who heard it from the gay coroner that when they found her on the tracks, she looked like an angel. She was wearing a lovely chiffon dress and was perfectly made up, with lipstick, eyeliner, and rouge. The perfect lady.

50

OUR LOVE

New York City | Palm Beach, 1948

The weather was as clear and brisk as her business decisions. Josephine was like a general approving a battle plan, firm and resolute. She was going to launch "Our Love by Princess Orlove" and Alexei was going to receive all the profits from the sales. She woke up one morning in her new mauve satin-sheathed bedroom and had had a dream where Alexei was spritzing the new fragrance on a white-veined marble statue of Aphrodite and vivid green dollar bills were falling from trees. That sign was enough for her. Since meeting him, she had always wanted him to become wealthy and secure in his own right, and since he wouldn't take any money from her directly, this appeared to be the perfect solution. Especially since it was *his family* name. He actually quite liked the concept when she initially floated the idea but was a bit hesitant at first at using his title for commercial purposes. He also felt it would open them up to criticism as a couple that she had married him for the title. Josephine's eyes instantly became grey and stormy, and she wagged her finger at him. "If I cared about what people thought about me, I'd still be in Melbourne working for my uncle, the bastard." She paused. "And I will make it very clear in the press that you, my dear husband, *you* own the brand, not me." And to cement the idea, Josephine cleverly invited an old friend to one of her Thursday evening salons at the apartment: Norina Matchabelli, the Georgian princess who, with her ex-husband, had founded the successful Prince Match-abelli perfume brand in the late 1920s. Alexei was convinced after meeting the elegant and regal princess and realizing that the commercial venture had only enhanced her life and reputation. He also knew that once she made up her mind, Josephine would not take no for an answer. She soon had Felix draft a legal document establishing that Alexei would own the brand and the trademark, and only in the event of his demise, and if they did not have children, would it revert to the Herz parent company. It would be his brand to design, market, and profit from and Herz would fund, manufacture, and distribute the line.

On the morning of their anniversary, Alexei woke up early and made Josephine breakfast in bed—pancakes in the shape of hearts—which he brought up on a silver tray after they had made passionate love. Josephine was giddy as she insisted on blindfolding him to give him her surprise gift.

"It's my present to you, my handsome prince," she said as the elevator man took them both down to the lobby and she led him out to the curb. She gingerly removed the blindfold and he literally fell to the sidewalk, speechless. She knew he would be reluctant to accept the Maserati A6 1500 Pininfarina she had shipped over from Europe and made it clear to him that "I can't take it back . . . there are no returns on this one . . . so enjoy." It sat parked in front of the building like a silver UFO with a huge red bow. He couldn't get over the triumph of form and design; it was like nothing he could ever have imagined owning. He accepted it graciously and then, since he was so overcome with emotion, he kissed and hugged her and presented her with her own gift, which he had hidden in his pocket. He beamed at his beautiful and successful wife as she teared up at the sight of the navy velvet jewel box. He had had his friend Fulco di Verdura fashion a special ring that featured his own design for the forthcoming perfume. The Duke of Verdura had successfully translated the rendering he created—of a crown from the Orlove family crest over a ruby heart—and the design would soon appear on all the perfume bottles and be an embossed feature on the thick cream paper box that housed it.

Our Love by Princess Orlove would start with a line of color cosmetics. Beautiful shades inspired by Russian and European royal portraits in the Met Gallery. "Czarina" would be the name of their leading seller, featuring a royal red taken from a portrait of Catherine the Great. Alexei enjoyed the design process the most and spent weeks at his drawing table perfecting the right bottle for their fragrance called "Princess Orlove." Josephine was stunned by his gift and how beautiful and commercial the perfume would be. She even knew deep down that Princess Orlove would be a far greater success than Parfum Empress Josephine. The actual fragrance—a mix of iris, vanilla, sandalwood, jasmine, and orange blossom—was also unique and modern. It had a clean, fresh finish and was so delicious it prompted someone to kiss and "taste" the person wearing it. It was exactly how Josephine felt about her handsome young husband.

They both worked feverishly over the next few months, and Our Love by Princess Orlove cosmetics was presented to the public on the Sunday before Christmas at the Herz Beauty flagship salon on Fifth Avenue. The Russian imperial–themed opening was a huge press event with a *Who's Who* guest list filled with celebrities and visiting socialites. The pièce de résistance occurred when Josephine and Alexei were dropped off in front of the red carpet by an imperial horse-drawn carriage. Prince Orlove sported his great-grandfather's medals on his notched grosgrain tuxedo lapel and Josephine was in a gold lace Empire-style gown and the former empress Josephine's old mine diamond tiara, which she had acquired in a feverish bidding war at auction after the first profits of Lashmatic had come rolling in. A thousand people gathered outside the salon to watch the procession and the celebrities and socialites on the red carpet. That month, *Town & Country* wrote, "Princess Orlove is the crowning achievement for Herz Beauty," and *The New York Times* wrote that "Princess Orlove herself, the cosmetics titan Josephine Herz, is the P. T. Barnum of the cosmetics business. Every launch has unique interest and commercial fanfare." The perfume was sold out within hours, and a waiting list was created for her most important vendors. The only thorn in Josephine's side was that she could accompany Alexei on only five of the ten-city PR tours. They had never been apart from the early days of their meeting, but she had three other important appearances scheduled by her advertising and public relations firm related to the launch of the newly developed waterproof Lashmatic mascara made from ingredients including beeswax. Before he left for the airport, they kissed and made passionate love and then parted for their individual and highly scheduled travel appointments.

Farther down south during Christmas vacation in Palm Beach, Constance was keeping tabs on the Princess Orlove launch over lunch in the loggia overlooking the pool.

"That woman would turn her dead mother into a perfume if she thought she could sell it. . . . I have it!" She paused dramatically to the group of socialites and old-money heirs who had come for an alfresco lunch. "The name of her next perfume launch is"—she hand-blocked the word—"Babushka!" The crowd roared.

Princess Paley spoke up. "Well, dahling, I have to disagree. Alexei, whom I know quite well, told me she gifted the perfume to him. So he owns it entirely," she said, defending her friend.

"I must agree." August Wheeler, the rubber-tire heir, inhaled his cigarette. "You know, broke princes still need to make a living apart from their . . . services," he said gleefully.

"Who even knows if it's a real title? From what I hear, if you own three sheep in Georgia, you're a prince."

Another socialite added, "Although he is quite attractive."

"Now, now, my dear friends. I am married to a White Russian," Princess Paley stated. "And Prince Orlove's grandmother was a cousin of the czar. It's not a phony title. And one cannot overlook the fact that Alexei Orlove is one of the handsomest men of his generation."

"Traitor!" Constance laughed. "You know I'm just having some fun at that woman's expense. She is quite clever; you know how *they* are." She suddenly caught herself, thinking her words a bit too tart. "Although you know it is quite terrible what happened during the war," she added to make herself appear more sympathetic. Public sentiment was now changing because of the horrors of the death camp reports that appeared in newspapers daily.

"Oh, look"—she changed the subject quickly—"the boys!" She was trying to play the part of the involved and doting mother and pointed out the group of boys coming in from an afternoon swim. She was hosting Van Jr. for a few days from boarding school with his friends and they were all tall, lean, and tan, all sporting the nonchalance and confidence of the rich and privileged. Since the divorce and Marilyn's death, Constance had mellowed slightly. She knew she was tightly wound and sensed she needed to embrace a more tolerant approach. She even tried a bit harder to be closer to Van Jr.; they both knew it was a bit forced, but he appreciated the effort. He was also grateful she now allowed him to bring friends to the Palm Beach mansion during Christmas and spring break without complaining too much about the disorder and the mess. Indeed, there was more of a sense of normalcy and less loneliness when she awoke to a group of youngsters having breakfast or lunch on the terrace. She sat and had coffee with the group but left promptly to have her hair done. She had accepted a dinner invitation from the Winston Milfords at their storied ocean-front mansion Villa Lysis for the Duke and Duchess of Windsor before they left for France. Although she always found the conversation as dull as the bland lemon sole and baked Alaska, she was honored to be invited, especially as a single woman. She knew it would be the same talk over and over with the duchess—all pugs, couture, and nonsense—and everyone was expected to hang on every word and make a fuss as if she possessed the wit of Oscar Wilde. However, such was the pull of the former king and the woman he abdicated for that it cemented her social status, and she reveled in the fact that *she* had been invited and not Lally and Van. She relished besting the Seward Oil heiress and the nondescript Wyke. She had something they never had: success and glamour! It was her own social vindication, as she knew the guest list would be published in the *Shiny Sheet*. The ever-dapper James would accompany her that evening and would pick her up, as he was staying at the newly opened Colony with Gregg in a separate single. There would be no homosexual uncle or his *friend* on the premises when Van Jr. was in residence for his holiday!

She had chosen her outfit for the dinner with great care: a one-shouldered white chiffon Mainbocher with a cinched waist. She always liked the combination of aquamarine and diamonds, as it set off her blue eyes and blond chignon to best advantage, and with her long white gloves she looked like a Grecian goddess come to life. Herve, her hairdresser, convinced her to be a bit daring and add a fresh gardenia in her hair. She waited in the grand coquina-stone entrance foyer until she heard the crunch of tires on gravel as James's driver pulled in, and then Gerta, her maid, handed her the mink stole with her usual German efficiency. She knew she looked fabulous and was happy to be among the chosen few who were now part of the Windsor set when they vacationed in Palm Beach. The fascist-friendly royal couple were a social triumph for their island hosts, who were expected to house, feed, and entertain them for the privilege of their company.

"Well . . ." James looked a bit torpid after five days of nonstop "bachelor" cocktail parties. He rolled his eyes at her. "You look very movie star–ish, my dear sister. I have some news for you, though. I feel terrible saying this, because I do feel a bit awful about it, although you might be doing the Irish jig."

"Out with it, dear brother." She slid next to him, searching her evening bag for a cigarette as the driver closed the car door.

"Well, it's all over the news. I don't suppose you've heard yet?"

"Heard what? Enough of this suspense."

"Her prince died." There, he had said it.

"Who died? Which prince are you talking about? This island is filled with them, real and fake."

"Orlove, the dreamy one. He was in Chicago for the launch of his perfume and he apparently died of a heart attack. It seems, from what I read, he had rheumatic fever as a child and he caught a strep or some such thing and then it turned into something more serious. And he just . . . well, *expired*."

"That can't be! We were just talking or joking about them this morning." She was visibly stunned. It didn't seem quite real and brought back thoughts of Marilyn.

"For shame, my dear sister. I hope you didn't wish him ill." He shook his head at her, knowing her sharp tongue.

"No, quite the opposite. I hope you don't think I'm happy about this."

"You're not?"

"I know what it's like to lose someone. . . ." She had been a bit more verbal with James than usual about Marilyn, since it was an open secret that they had been together.

"You mean someone you loved?" He surveyed a crack in the ice queen.

"You could say that, or quite liked. I can only imagine what she is going through."

"You know what is truly crazy?" James rolled down the back window and blew the ghostly grey smoke into the humid air.

"What's that?" she said, sitting straight forward in stony silence.

"The two of you always seem to do things in pairs."

51

FACE-OFF

New York City, 1950

It was Josephine's fiftieth birthday, and while she did not feel like celebrating this marker with a large party, or really celebrating at all, she decided to take Miles to Le Pavillon, Henri Soulé's acclaimed French restaurant on East Fifty-fifth Street. Miles had been in town on Christmas break from the University of Pennsylvania. At twenty, he had grown into a nice-looking, fair-haired young man, but he had a certain weakness of character and ambition that reminded Josephine of his father and which she had tried hard to accept. Still, she loved her son and was excited to dine with him and catch up as Henri himself led Josephine and Miles to one of the best up-front and center tables, a strategically located banquette that highlighted the evening's *Who's Who* list as everyone else, i.e., the masses, were shepherded to the bar or main dining room. Henri's seating philosophy was simple: the rich and famous were in first class, the general population in second, and the riffraff traveled steerage at the bar and Siberian hinterlands of the main dining room. Henri mentioned he was happy to see his "princess out again," as Josephine had become something of a shut-in after Alexei's death, going only to work and then home. There were no more festive Thursday evening salons or nights out on the town for dinner. The last two years had been something of a somber blur. It had all seemed so surreal, and she was still only just emerging from the fog. Loss wasn't something Josephine was good at, but Alexei's death had been so swift and so painful she felt as if a limb had been cut off, and she was now something of an emotional amputee. She often thought back to that day when Alexei had called her from his hotel room, chilled and coughing. Chicago had had a record low temperature, and he had worked so late into the evening meeting and accommodating the customers and the press. The launch at their North Michigan Avenue flagship salon had record amounts of people. He had gone outside in the cold in his tuxedo and medals, without his coat, to take a quick photo in front of the store for press purposes. The next day he had woken up with a sore throat and a cough, and Josephine had urged him to go to the doctor, which he had not done since he hadn't wanted to cancel his early-morning press meetings with the *Chicago Daily Tribune.* The Midwest had gone mad for the handsome young prince, and women turned out in droves to buy Princess Orlove, cleaning out the entire stock in a matter of hours. He was so proud and happy and excited at the prospect of a commercial success and meeting his actual customers. And then within the next two days he was diagnosed with strep after a visit to the emergency room. He called Josephine from his room and reassured her he was fine and told her he loved her. Within twenty-four hours, he was pronounced dead since the strep infection affected his heart, which was already weakened from his childhood malady. Josephine was in the office when she received the phone call. She had screamed, a single, anguished, piercing scream with the word *"No!"* Everyone who heard *knew.* Josephine wept uncontrollably and took to her bed for three days without being able to rise. She was so overcome with grief, she was barely able to stand at the funeral and fainted a number of times. There was so much crying and hand-wringing at the funeral at the Russian Orthodox church on Ninety-seventh Street that the papers reported there hadn't been this much hysteria since the death of the czar's family. And then it was all a monotonous and horrendous blur, with the hours and days and weeks going by, rote and grey. Continuous yet unfulfilling.

Josephine would later write in her memoir that her business literally saved her. And with Miles off at school, she was even more alone. To-night, she felt a tiny bit better sitting at the best table at the celebrated French restaurant in the city in black silk and diamonds, fussed over by the staff, who brought them each a glass of champagne before the menus. She was overcome that Miles had been so thoughtful as to buy her a diamond star pin from Tiffany's. "Because you always shine," he had written in neat script on the card. She was so touched and in a rare moment gave him a warm kiss. She reached out tenderly for his hand and looked into his beautiful blue eyes. How had he grown up so quickly? It seemed like only yesterday she had given birth to him in London. She surveyed him, trying to be objective. He was lovely, smart, handsome, and well mannered, and she did love him. Then she also saw the weakness, his lack of drive. He has a weak chin, like his father. The good-for-nothing. Yet, tonight she would try to minimize the negatives and accentuate the positives, as a woman did when making up her face. She would apply her own philosophy to her son. Across the room she nodded to a few captains of industry and society ladies, all of whom nodded back or spoke in hushed, reverent tones laced now with respect. And in the nether regions of Siberia in the main room and bar, tourists and the unknown whispered and pointed at the woman they had seen in magazine ads. "There's Josephine Herz, Princess Orlove, poor thing." They all nodded. Those in the know were also happy to see her out among the living.

Suddenly, heads turned and a tall blond woman in a chic navy, tailored Chanel suit entered the restaurant, blowing in on a gust of frozen air to fanfare among the staff, with a young man in his teens in tow. The hatcheck girl took her sable from her in a swift, singular movement that suggested she was an important regular. It took Josephine only seconds to realize the glamorous blonde was *her*. She hadn't so much aged as ossified into a more handsome version of herself. "Mrs. Gardiner-Wyke, so wonderful to see you. And who is this handsome young man?" They fussed and scraped as they brought them to a burgundy banquette directly opposite Josephine's table. Such perfect symmetry. Both front and center, seated in positions of power. How fitting, Josephine thought. She looked once briefly and noticed the reaction in *her* eyes, as well, when she saw her and *knew* she was in the room. The frozen look of disappointment and awkwardness and then the forced smile. Josephine knew that the blond boy was her son, her adopted son. She knew everything from CeeCee. They avoided eye contact, although each tensed at knowing the other was there. Sharing the same space, jealous at inhaling the same air. Being served by the same staff, wondering who had better service, the better table, the better soufflé. Whose was higher and laden with more *fromage*? Whose was more golden, more delicious? Then they noticed there were heads turning and subtle whispers, their feud having reached legendary status. Now that they were older, richer, their reputations secure, what would happen? Everything or nothing? The room let out a collective sigh after Constance and Van Jr. were seated. That was Henri's genius. He knew how to make everyone feel special in the same room, even bitter rivals. Yet those who were dining that night knew they were witnessing something special. The two richest, most famous businesswomen in the world, who couldn't, wouldn't, publicly acknowledge each other. As the evening progressed, patrons started to leave; some went over to one table and then the other to bid them good night, others offered a slight smile and wave. The main room and bar emptied after the chocolate mousse and the coffee and tea. Neither would be the first to leave or make a move. Suddenly, Miles reached over and whispered something to his mother after checking his gold Patek twice. He had a train to catch to Philadelphia. He had an early-morning exam. "Go, darling. I understand you have an exam,"

Josephine proclaimed for effect. She looked up and kissed him, thanking him for the star pin, which she had proudly affixed to her dress. He stood and kissed her and she tousled his silky hair.

"Happy birthday, Mother. I will see you next weekend." He blew her a kiss as he left the main dining room. She now sat alone as the maître d' brought over another complimentary glass of champagne. It had been a lovely evening despite *her* being in the room. Still, she was not giving in.

Suddenly, she noticed the young man across the room was also getting up. She felt a reprieve. He must have had a game, an exam, or a date. He gave his mother a somewhat frosty, perfunctory kiss on the cheek. She noticed he was also well mannered and looked the part of the perfect prep. And then after he departed, she saw her out of the corner of her eye in a blond haze. The maître d' brought her over a glass of champagne as well. "Compliments of Monsieur Soulé, madame," she overheard him say. They sat in the empty front room. Both withdrew their compacts: Josephine's was round, slim, and gold, and Constance's was square and platinum. They checked their makeup, first lipstick, then eye shadow, mascara, and rouge. Both were satisfied when they returned their artillery to their bags. They looked around at the details, at the gilded moldings and opulent flower arrangements being subtly refreshed. They were the only ones left now, after the attentions of the staff, the rich, the powerful, and the social. Both reached out to the glass of golden bubbly liquid before them. And as happened many times in their lives, each raised her glass at exactly the same time, and before taking a sip, each looked at the other, for the first time directly, squarely, in the eye. And then, with the most subtle and graceful gesture, each slightly raised her flute, Josephine's cabochon emerald and Constance's diamond ring glittering, and each . . . toasted the other.

EPILOGUE

Palm Beach, 1993

Palm Beach days can be lovely, languorous, yet also monotonous. Seeing perfection day after day can wear on one's nerves: the waving royal palms, bright, glaring sun against the white, yellow, or salmon stucco, and perfectly manicured hedgerows can prove downright depressing. Not to mention the slowest traffic lights and drivers on the planet. Can *anything* be more maddening than following an eighty-five-year-old coiffed blonde in a dinged lemon Corniche on South Ocean Boulevard going ten miles an hour? Such things can drive one to drink, but I try to look at the glass half-full, as it only enhances my martini schedule. Three o'clock is the new five o'clock. *Bien sûr.*

There are worse places, though. Winter banishment has one escaping icy, slushy February mornings in New York, as Charlene constantly points out in her singsong voice. I, of course, have been on the family's travel schedule for a few years now—New York, Southampton, Palm Beach, and in the summer . . . Cap d'Antibes. When all things are taken into consideration, it ain't too shabby, as we used to say in the bayou.

After Madame's unfortunate demise, I looked in the mirror and saw a drawn, weary, and empty face before me and right then and there decided on something I had never done before: to take a three-month vacation to Bali, Thailand, and Singapore. Accompanying me was a younger, sometime underwear model and trainer also named Bobby, whose body was a ten and IQ was a one. I must say that there is nothing more annoying than two "bachelors" with the same name traveling together. Bobby and Bobby. Or "the two Bobbies," as we were referred to by a catty few in my set. Is anything more horrendous? I ask you. I put up with it, of course, because of his obvious charms, until Bobby found a younger and richer partner in Phuket (at the pool, where else) and left yours truly high and dry. The king without the "I." I found myself listless, depressed, and bingeing on pad thai when I received a fax from Miles. It went something like this:

> Dear Bobby and Bobby,
> Greetings from Palm Beach. We all hope you are enjoying Thailand and having the vacation you needed and deserve. I have hesitated reaching out to you for some time, lest I disturb your idyll, but to quote Josephine, "A vacation is only WORKING (VORKING) in a nicer location."
> So in Mother's spirit and knowing how much you loved her, we are pleading with you to return stateside, to help us and the legal team prepare for the upcoming trial. Our high-priced lawyers do not think that Constance has a case, but I don't trust the wily old fox and don't know what she has up her ermine sleeve. If you would consider cutting your trip short, the board is prepared to triple your salary and I would, personally, as a token of my appreciation for your service and dedication to our family, gift you the van Dongen portrait of Josephine, which is being returned from the exhibit at the Jewish Museum. You always told me you loved it as it exemplified her unique profile, and I know she would have wanted you to have it. Not to mention,

helping us beat the evil Constance is something Josephine would have cared deeply about. But you know that better than anyone. Just say the word and there is a first-class ticket waiting for you.

Until then.

Yours truly,
Miles

Of course, my decision took less time than saying *"Thea hir shrab kar nwd?"* (How much for massage?) before I made my way to Thai Airways' first-class lounge and sped home to New York.

Strangely, despite all the drama and fuss, Constance's case never actually got to trial, as she herself expired from uterine cancer three months before the depositions. Her legal team all but admitted she had no case and was just doing it for show, her legacy, and, more important, spending her money to make everyone miserable. Her son, the dolt, Van Gardiner-Wyke Jr., was too busy chasing skirt in Saint-Tropez to care and the case was dropped before you could say "lawyers' fees." The legal system is clearly broken when crazy old dykes like Constance Gardiner can sue people just for sport. That said, before it fizzled out, I actually had a bit of a rollicking time. I had pressed Miles to let me fly to L.A. to visit with the now legendary CeeCee, who was living in a Pacific Palisades aerie with Layla, her daughter by Mickey, who was living close by. Her granddaughter Lonnie is now an up-and-coming model and actress.

CeeCee, who as she has aged resembled the actress Diahann Carroll, welcomed me into her sun-filled oasis and was more than happy to give us the gory details about her relationship with Constance.

"The woman was a mean wretch. She was still beautiful in her midthirties when she came after me. Today it would all be considered sexual harassment, but what was a poor, young mulatto girl like me to do back then? I just saw the attention as a way out of poverty and obscurity. I was also a bit of a wild thing and she couldn't get enough of my *cooch*." She laughed in a throaty way. "She had a custom-made dildo strap-on in pastel pink," she revealed without any embarrassment.

"I do know that she was working on a mascara product around the same time as Josephine," she offered.

"How did you know?" I pressed her.

"Because it was *my* idea. She stole it from me. That was Constance for you. And she actually thought it was hers or actually believed it was her idea. That said, those two old gals were always launching the same product. It's like two movies coming out at the same time in Hollywood. Now if you really want to talk about crazy, being with Mickey was like being with the Rat Pack. It was twenty-four hours of sex, martinis, and gambling. And all he would do was just sit back and rip off 'what the old broads were doing.' I would tell him what was in the pipeline when I could and he would just laugh and make it in Asia for half the price. It was all a rip-off shell game. Mickey is fun. And not many people knew for years that Layla was Mickey's. How things have changed. Now my granddaughter Lonnie is an 'It' girl. Black, white, and Jewish, and she's an actress and socialite! I just love it. Niles, her brother, is taking over the business. Queen CeeCee will never be as big as Herz Beauty, but we're a solid top ten, own our market, and are preparing to go public! Look, we all have to kiss ass and more to get to the top." She laughed huskily again. All in all, CeeCee had one thing Josephine and Constance never had—a fabulous sense of humor! As she walked me to my car she gave me a kiss and said, "I want you to be the first to know. After all these years, Mickey and I are getting married."

"Married?" I was a bit shocked but congratulated her. "Good luck!"

"I'll need it!" She laughed. I laughed. It was a wonderful present.

And it was all so juicy that it was worth the trip for that alone.

Once the case was dropped, Miles soon passed away from bladder cancer. Miles was always very nice, but to quote Josephine, he was "a bit of a nebbish." She couldn't abide weakness from anyone in any way, and their relationship was always strained, although he inherited.

The scene, of course, is classic Josephine and imprinted in my mind: her sitting on a Louis XIV settee in a ball gown, smoking her Larks and watching Lawrence Welk on the television.

"I just *luff* that Cissy and Bobby dance team." She blew perfect blue smoke rings in the air. "So much talent for such people. I always vanted to dance but had two left feet," she complained bitterly. And then she would become wistful, adjusting her diamond Riviera necklace. Was it my imagination or was she wearing her tiara? Perhaps.

"I'm a Jewish American princess. Me and Diane," she would exclaim of the Jewish, Belgian-born Diane von Fürstenberg. "Only she is prettier and younger and married a von Fürstenberg. Much higher-quality title than mine was, but my business does more turnover," she would say with a shrug. "Pffft. And Orlove was the love of my life." Her eyes would water.

"If only Miles found a profession like this Bobby and Cissy," she would mutter, eating Poppycock on the sofa from the tin and stroking her diamonds. "You laugh." She wagged a finger at me. "But I would much prefer he was a dancer on TV than a . . . loafer." She would sigh. "Poor Miles. He takes after his father, may he roast in hell. He was handsome, but you know . . . I should have known better. He had a veak chin. And I cannot abide a man with a veak chin," she said.

"Bobby De Vries"—she scrutinized me—"your chin is passable, but lucky for you, you have a strong jaw." She sighed. *"I vant you to know,"* she said forcefully, "I *never, ever* vould have hired you if you had a *veak chin!*" She banged the table.

Once Miles died, I thought about going into retirement. Soon after helping to plan and execute *his* funeral, also a Temple Emanu-El affair, I received a call from Jonny and Charlene, who wanted to know if I would consider staying on as a board member (the chill with him had thawed by this time), and Charlene also wanted me to become her personal assistant. Charlene, whom I have come to adore, in many ways is a Nevada-born version of Josephine, and her drive to succeed is admirable. I immediately jumped at the chance, as in this phase in her life she wants direction as opposed to giving me orders, so it's been quite satisfying. In the last four years I have helped mold and guide her and have used the substantial Herz fortune to help relaunch and, yes, *repackage* her. Yours truly has helped her with every aspect of her campaign, helping her identify and oversee the finest and chicest decorators as well as couturiers to tone down her gorgeous Las Vegas rump and advise her to not show as much cleavage, as it upsets the ladies who lunch. With the addition of Madame's fabulous jewel box, Charlene Blake-Herz has become the poster child for nouvelle society. Let's face it, it's hard to compete with the name and figure, not to mention the open checkbook, although there are still a few clubs in Palm Beach that cater only to white bread and not rye.

I myself have become, although I hate to admit it, the ultimate walker. I think I put my dear friend Jerome to shame, as no one cuts a better figure in a tuxedo, has better manners, or is known for being a more amusing dinner companion than yours truly. I sometimes even regale the ladies with stories of which Hollywood star I serviced or which (late) member of society enjoyed my lavish attentions between squash games, often inviting me to the steam. Hmm . . . that's entertainment. Or as Josephine would say, *"That's YENTA-tainment!"*

I am, however, my most lonely in PB. It's not that I don't have a young decorator friend or find it boring having dinner at Ta-boo, but I enjoy city life more. This year I did manage to help Charlene and Jonny pull off one final major coup, one that gave us all a great deal of satisfaction and one that we know Josephine is applauding wherever she is.

In one of my shrewdest moves, I managed to help Charlene and Jonny buy the former Constance Gardiner estate, one of the grand Mizner properties that through backdoor channels never came on the open market.

The deal was done through the discreet "bachelor" network. The house was purchased under a corporate name and no one was the wiser until the press broke the news that Mr. and Mrs. Jonny Blake-Herz, the grandson of Josephine Herz, archrival of Constance Gardiner, were now taking possession of the former beauty magnate/society matron's storied Palm Beach property. It has been, needless to say, a social triumph for the Herzes and not overlooked by social historians and preservationists as well. Especially now that the striped sunroom is decorated in Palm Beach pink-and-green Lashmatic colors with Lilly Pulitzer prints. The name of the estate was immediately changed from Constant Gardens to the chic and clever Malmaison. If one takes the time to do the research, Château de Malmaison was the home of the original empress Josephine de Beauharnais, and the rechristening has a certain wit, if I say so myself, since I named it. And that Lashmatic is still printing money, dispensing bills like an ATM, is a triumph in itself, as the proceeds pay for all the opulent upkeep. Of course, there was an uproar when a rumor surfaced that Jonny and Charlene were going to remove the statue of Constance's most prized racehorse, Constant Gardiner, and throw it into the trash heap. I, of course, put the rumor to rest and advised Jonny and Charlene to do something much more interesting. We placed the famous Jacques Lipchitz bronze bust of Josephine directly across from the horse sculpture in the topiary garden. Now when guests arrive and are given the tour, Jonny often remarks, "This garden is a testament to the two women who founded the beauty business: my grandmother Josephine, who was the brains behind the business, *and* the former owner of this house"—as he dramatically points to the horse sculpture—"who was a horse's ass." This always gets a laugh or evokes a nervous titter.

It was all *très amusant* and bucolic until last month, when we heard news that Van Gardiner-Wyke Jr., after living in France for twenty-five years, had moved back to the States with his new wife, the actress Nicole Moiret. Their housewarming party next Saturday night opens the social season, and people are frothing at the mouth for an invitation to their new manse, Gardiner's Bay. *La tout* Palm Beach has been invited. My own invitation arrived personally by their houseman. That said, there was no invitation for Jonny and Charlene. Now that the Gardiner-Wykes are back in town, I have a feeling it may not be as tranquil or monotonous in the Palm Beaches as I once thought. Things are about to get interesting again. . . .

ACKNOWLEDGMENTS

In the summer of 2015, I received a surprise call in my office from the incomparable Liz Smith, whom I did not know. She said she was a fan of a controversial column I was writing at the time for *The New York Observer* on the 1 percent and wanted to meet yours truly for a lunch. "Hurry up, though," she declared, "I'm ninety-two." My repast with Liz at Michael's was thrilling, especially when she declared, "You have the chops. I knew them all—Truman, Dominick, and Tom, and you are a natural observer." Liz offered me the best thing an aspiring writer could ever receive: a quote for my book and confidence. So, dear Liz. It was oh-so-brief but I did love you.

I also want to thank my agent, Laura Yorke, who has championed me at every turn and whom I adore, love, and respect. I am eternally grateful to the wonderful Elizabeth Beier, executive editor at St. Martin's Press. Thank you for your extraordinary eye and push. You exemplify the art of editing. My gratitude to Sona Vogel for truly monumental copy editing. Thank you to the legendary Sally Richardson, chairman of St. Martin's Press, for believing in me. I am so appreciative of my uber publicist and friend Dini Von Mueffling. Thank you for all your wonderful efforts.

I am so very lucky to have a cadre of the most influential and talented authors, directors, and producers who have hopefully helped this man become a novelist through their generosity, advice, and inspiration; Galt Niederhoffer, thank you endlessly for your invaluable guidance; Adriana Trigiani, I sit at your feet; Marisa Acocella Marchetto, I revel in your talents; Wendy Finerman, I am honored by your involvement. Wednesday Martin, Risa Mickenberg, Emanuele Delle Valle, the amazing Venus Williams, and my one-time boss James Patterson, you are all an inspiration to me. And to my business partner and friend the legendary Chris Blackwell, who inspires me regularly with his creativity.

I want to thank my dearest friends whose encouragement gave me strength to write this novel. My chosen Family: Mark Glimcher and Fairfax Dorn, Jay and Amy Kos, Jamie and David Mitchell, Jordan and Stephanie Schur, Patty and Danny Stegman. Thank you, Muffie Potter and Sherrell Aston, Bruce and Maura Brickman, Dustin Cohen, Kevin and Susie Davis, Shoshana and Kenny Dichter, Alexis and Erik Ekstein, Chip and Susie Fisher, Mark and Karen Hauser, Susan Krakower, Stephanie and Ron Kramer, Joseph Klinkov, David Lauren and Lauren Bush Lauren, Agatha and Steve Luczo, Jennifer Miller and Mark Ehret, Rabbi Adam and Sharon Mintz, Joyce and Michael Ostin, Mark E. Pollack, Meg Blakey and Glen Pagan, Robert and Serena Perlman, Ali and Jason Rosenfeld, Lizanne and Barry Rosenstein, Steven and Ilene Sands, Bippy and Jackie Siegal, Andy Spade, Tim Stephenson, Michelle and Howard Swarzman, Charlie and Lauran Walk, Lois Robbins and Andrew Zaro, and all who have been on this incredible journey with me. Thank you to David and Chip for allowing me to make mention of their legendary fathers: Jan Mitchell and Avery Fisher. To my sister, Susan Kirshenbaum Perry, and Rob Perry, Marcia Geier and Fred Geier. And to Aunts Paulette Kirshenbaum and Jackie Kalajian.

Thank you to my assistant, Carol O'Connell, who has been the world's best sounding board, and my partners at NSG/SWAT, Gerland van Ackere, Joseph Mazzaferro, and Woody Wright.

To my amazing children, Talia, Georgia, and Lucas, work hard and follow your dreams—and don't ever listen to negativity. And to my wife, best friend, lover, and muse, Dana, this book is dedicated to your incredible intelligence, humor, beauty, and strength. You have made me the best I can be and I love you for it.

Much of this novel was written in my favorite places: GoldenEye in Jamaica, sitting at Ian Fleming's desk to start the novel; the Beverly Hills Hotel Bungalows and Cabanas; The Quisisana and La Fontelina Beach Club in Capri; Hotel de Russie in Rome; Claridge's in London; the Hotel du Cap-Ferrat; the Edition Pool in Miami; Ashford Castle in Ireland; and Mozzarella & Vino, Nerai, Nicola's, Nobu, Candle 79, Cipriani, The Thirsty Scholar, and Via Quadronno in New York City. I draw inspiration from my "places," a good meal, and all of the wonderful people I have met along the way. Everything, I like to say, is "material."